HER MUSINGS WERE INTERRUPTED BY THE SOUND OF A MOTOR CAR APPROACHING. SHE TURNED TO LOOK AND SAW A LARGE RED MONSTER SWEEP PAST AT AN INCREDIBLE SPEED. IT WAS NOT GOING TOO FAST, THOUGH, FOR HER TO RECOGNIZE MARIGOLD SEATED BESIDE THE DRIVER.

She rubbed her eyes. It had been Marigold, she was sure. Her eyesight wasn't as bad as that. Despite the shawl draped around her head and the enveloping fur rug, she had seen enough to be certain it was her daughter. But she'd seen nothing of the driver. It must have been a man, but who?

Mary began to shake, and had to put the shopping basket down as she clutched both arms around her trembling body. Surely Marigold wasn't being trapped by the snares of riches, the prey of some heedless young man! Not her beloved eldest daughter! That would be more than she could bear.

ABOUT THE AUTHOR

Marina Oliver was born in Walsall near Birmingham and took her degree at Keele in Staffordshire. She began writing when her children were small and is the author of more than thirty historical novels, among them *Cavalier Courtship*, *Runaway Hill* and *Masquerade for the King*. Most of them were written during the years she lectured in further-education colleges and were an escape from her main subjects, economics and politics. Between 1991 and 1993 she was chairman of the Romantic Novelists' Association; currently she is chairman of the Oxford Writers' Group and lectures widely on writing. This is her first book to be published by Signet and is to be followed by a series of sagas, also set in the Midlands.

Marina Oliver now lives in the Chilterns with her husband.

MARINA OLIVER

THE COBWEB CAGE

PAN BOOKS

This edition published 2000 by Pan Books
an imprint of Macmillan Publishers Ltd
25 Eccleston Place, London SW1W 9NF
Basingstoke and Oxford
Associated companies throughout the world
www.macmillan.co.uk

Published by the Penguin Group
Penguin Books Ltd, 27 Wrights Lane, London W8 5TZ, England
Penguin Books USA Inc., 375 Hudson Street, New York, New York 10014, USA
Penguin Books Australia Ltd, Ringwood, Victoria, Australia
Penguin Books Canada Ltd, 10 Alcorn Avenue, Toronto, Ontario,
Canada M4V 3B2
Penguin Books (NZ) Ltd, 182–190 Wairau Road, Auckland 10, New Zealand

Penguin Books Ltd, Registered Offices: Harmondsworth, Middlesex, England

First published by Michael Joseph 1994
Published in Signet 1994
1 3 5 7 9 10 8 6 4 2

ISBN 0 330 39682 X

Printed and bound in Great Britain by
Mackays of Chatham PLC, Chatham, Kent

To my family, who have given me so much

Chapter One

MARIGOLD squatted on the edge of the fender, huddled as close as she dared to the banked-up fire. Despite the heat from the coals, which warmed her face and chest, and her thick flannel nightgown, she shivered uncontrollably. Twisting round to warm her back, she clutched her thin arms about her body in a vain attempt to dispel the bewildered emptiness within her.

When would Johnny come home? What would Pa say if he came home to find the table still littered with dirty plates, and no dinner cooked?

At this thought she shook still more. Pa loved them. He wasn't cruel, not like Mr Potter next door, who took off his belt to thrash Fred and Tom and little Betty for the slightest offence, and could be heard through the thin walls beating his wife regularly every Saturday night when he staggered home from the Cross Keys.

Pa only smacked them when they'd been very naughty. And he'd never smacked Mom. But it was naughty not to have dinner ready for him. Mom said that, so would he smack Mom? Slow tears began to slide down Marigold's plump, rosy cheeks.

Her tears, and thoughts of dinner, made Marigold sniff. She longed for the comforting smells of the stew her Mom normally kept simmering in the big black pot, but today the pot was empty.

She was cold, bewildered, and hungrier than she could ever remember. The chenille curtain was caught up on a nail instead of falling over the door, and a bitter cold draught whistled through from the scullery. She wanted Mom, but Mom was upstairs, and someone upstairs was groaning, occasionally crying out with pain.

'When can I have my breakfast?' she'd timidly asked Mrs Whitehouse on one of her sudden appearances hours ago.

'Don't myther me now, chick. I need this quick,' Mrs Whitehouse had replied fretfully, swinging the trivet out from above the fire. She lifted the huge kettle and poured boiling water into the old tin ewer. Then she refilled the kettle in the scullery and heaved it back on to the trivet.

'Goo an' find a noggin fer yersen, an' keep out me way,' she said over her shoulder, disappearing through the narrow doorway and clumping up the stairs.

Marigold shivered even more. The bread was in the dark, dismal pantry under the stairs, and Johnny had whispered to her one night in bed that wolves hid there in wait. She dared not venture into the pantry. She'd rather die from hunger than let wolves eat her.

She wasn't entirely sure what wolves looked like, except they were bigger and fiercer than old Mr Farraday's dog, Towser. Towser growled and snarled at everyone who walked past his house, and all but the bravest or most foolhardy children went the long way round rather than pass that gate. It had been left open once and Towser had escaped. He'd bitten Joe Tasker, the biggest man in the street, and Joe had been off work for a month, Pa said. If wolves were worse than Towser they must be dangerous, terrifying creatures.

Marigold sighed, and rubbed her eyes with the edge of her nightgown. She would just have to stay hungry until someone came to help her. Johnny might be home from school soon.

But he'd jeer to find her still in her nightie. Another tear slid down her cheek. It really wasn't her fault. They wouldn't let her get dressed. Mrs Whitehouse had shouted at her when, feeling guilty at her unwashed, uncombed state, her nightie unbuttoned, she'd tried to creep upstairs to fetch her clothes.

Bewildered, she thought back over the very peculiar day. What had she done to make everyone forget her? It had started when Mom, instead of dressing her as usual, crept back into bed after giving Johnny a piece of bread and dripping, packing up another for his dinner, and sending him off to school.

Half an hour later, as Marigold, puzzled and frightened, had been sitting quietly on the end of the big bed, Mom had gone stiff and cried out. 'Go and fetch Mrs Tasker!' she gasped.

'I haven't got my frock on,' Marigold said, shocked. You never went out into the yard in your nightie, not even to the lavatory.

'Put my shawl round you, but mind you don't trip. Hold it up.'

Mary Smith paused and closed her eyes, biting down on her lower lip to suppress the pain. After a minute the spasm passed and she smiled weakly at Marigold.

'Can you pull your boots on by yourself? They're in the scullery where Pa blacked them last night. Don't try to fasten them. And don't wait to put stockings on. Marigold, be a good girl and go quickly!'

Terrified by the groans her mother didn't seem able to suppress, Marigold fled. She forgot the shawl and discarded the boots when they proved too tight for her trembling hands. She ran barefoot through a thin sleety drizzle towards the end house of the yard, crying so much she couldn't speak coherently.

Mrs Tasker seemed to know what was wrong, however. Pausing only to throw a few words over her shoulder to someone in the house, she waddled as fast as her considerable bulk allowed along the path between the houses and gardens, and vanished up the narrow stairs.

Marigold had seen her no more, and didn't dare go upstairs to discover what was happening.

After a while Mrs Tasker called down to her. 'Run an' fetch Mrs Whitehouse, quick,' she ordered, and once again Marigold fled, too frightened by now to object to going down the narrow ginnel and across the street in her nightgown in the middle of the day. She was past caring whether people saw her and laughed.

Then there had been nothing but Mrs Whitehouse's forays downstairs. Nothing to hear from the bedroom apart from the occasional groan, and once a high, piercing scream. Too terrified to think clearly, Marigold shrank into herself, shivered, and gave the occasional hiccuping sob.

But hunger gradually overcame her other fears. There was bread in the pantry. Johnny had put it away while Mom smeared the dripping on his piece, and he hadn't pushed the door to. She could see the slight gap. She'd be able to open it without fetching a stool to reach the latch. If she left the door open surely she'd be safe. Wolves didn't like the light.

Marigold glanced anxiously out of the window. The short winter day was almost over and darkness would soon fall. If she wanted to eat she'd better brave the pantry now or daylight would have gone.

Slowly, fearfully, she rose from her cramped position and took a couple of steps across the room. Then two more. A short run and she was grasping the edge of the door, which hadn't been properly closed. Trembling, Marigold pulled it open further and peered inside.

There didn't seem to be any wolves, or none that she could see. The loaf was in the cracked old earthenware bread crock which had belonged to her granny. Marigold was reaching for it when she became aware of a far more enticing smell.

She licked her lips. On the slate shelf was the remains of a meat pasty. Now she remembered Mom saying last night she didn't feel hungry and would finish the pasty later, when the children were abed.

Tempted, Marigold stretched out her hand. A sound from above made her pause. The hesitation gave her time to think. The pasty was Mom's, she'd had her own share of half a one last night. It would be stealing to take this.

As hunger battled with conscience, and Marigold's hand reached slowly, inevitably, towards the pie, she heard Mrs Tasker's voice in the kitchen behind her. ''Er'll do now. But I asks yer, what an ockerd name!'

'Daft, innit. But childbirth meks some women befumbled.'

''Er wants the gels called after flowers! Says wi' a name like Smith they need summat diff'rent.'

Mrs Whitehouse sniffed. 'Allus did think too much on 'ersen. If 'er wants flowers why not summat dacent like Rose or Daisy or Lily then? Instead o' some 'ighfalutin' 'eathen name. Mark my words, 'er'll regret it!'

Marigold heard but understood nothing. She was petrified of being caught stealing from the pantry. There wasn't time to get out. What could she do? In desperation she tried to pull the door to. They might not notice it was open. She hovered, balanced precariously on the narrow step inside the door, clinging to the crossbar, all fear of wolves for the moment banished from her mind.

'Where's that dratted Marigold got to? Out in fode, playin', desay. Well, 'er'll cum back when 'er's clemmed. I've got my Joe's tea ter get, an' these 'ere sheets ter put in soak.'

Mrs Tasker heaved the bundle of sheets past the pantry door. Her superfluous fat brushed against it, and it swung to. As the latch clicked home, Marigold lost her perch and fell down the steep step into the black hole, landing with a thump on the sack of potatoes propped against the tub of salted beans.

She let out a shriek of alarm, but the door was made of thick planks and Mrs Whitehouse was laughing, a loud, raucous guffaw. No one heard the child sobbing convulsively at her sudden terrifying descent into this dark place she dreaded even in the brightest daylight.

For an unknown length of time Marigold lay where she'd fallen, quivering with anguish. Johnny had locked her in once when she'd plagued him to take her out to play with his friends, and she knew she couldn't hope to open the latch. It was high on the door, way beyond her small reach even without the high step, and that was too narrow to stand on when the door was fully closed.

Eventually she lay quiescent, almost asleep, but then she heard a low rumbling noise. Wolves! They were coming for her! It was like a dog's growl but many times worse. How big were wolves? Would they swallow her whole like the whale had swallowed Jonah? Or would they nibble her bit by bit, as Johnny said rats ate people?

It was too much. Marigold began to scream hysterically, beating her puny fists against the unyielding door until a blessed oblivion overtook her. She slid down on to the floor, her arm trailing over the side of the egg bucket, her hand in the opaque, sticky waterglass.

It was Johnny who found her when he arrived home from school. Without a thought about where his mother and sister were, or why the house was in darkness, he discarded his jacket and cap in the scullery. Then he lit a candle and, leaving it carefully on the chest nearby, plunged into the dark pantry in search of food. Bread and dripping hadn't been enough for dinner, and anyway Johnny was always hungry.

He yelled with fear when Marigold, disturbed from her stupor by the opening of the door and the gleam of candlelight, raised her wet sticky hand and clutched at his ankle. All he could see, as he explained repeatedly to his father later, was a ghostly shape rising from the floor and coming towards him.

When Marigold cried out to him and he realized his mistake, his fear was followed by anger at having been for a moment afraid. At five years and six months he was one of the biggest boys in his class at school. Because of that and his fiery temper he was rarely teased, and prided himself on his toughness. It was shaming to have been scared by Marigold in her nightie.

In the midst of the succeeding tumult, with Marigold sobbing her relief and Johnny venting his anger in loud scolding, they heard Mary's voice.

'Where's Mom?' Johnny demanded, his fury forgotten. 'Why were you locked in?'

'She's been in bed all day. I don't know why. Mrs Whitehouse was here. They shut the door and I couldn't get out,' Marigold gasped through her sobs, but Johnny didn't stop to hear more.

He caught up the candle and, holding it carefully, went upstairs as fast as he could. Marigold, terrified of being left in the dark again, followed.

Mary lay in the big bed in the front room, dark shadows under her eyes. An oil lamp had been placed on the washstand and cast a soft glow through the small room. Marigold saw that the bottom drawer of the big chest, the only other item of furniture in the room, was wide open, but she didn't stop to wonder why. Her sobs renewed and she flung herself on to the bed to feel her mother's arms close about her, warm and comforting.

Mary gradually persuaded her to tell what had happened while Johnny, more curious than his three-year-old sister, got bored and went to look in the drawer.

'A baby!' he exclaimed. 'Is it a boy? Can he play football?'

Mary shook her head and Marigold, calm now she was ensconced safely and warmly within her mother's arms, thought how pretty she was when she smiled.

'It's another little sister, Johnny. Hyacinth, she's called. Isn't that a pretty name?'

'Never heard it. There's no one called Hy– whatever, at school.'

'It's the name of a flower, like Marigold. A blue flower, it is sometimes, and blue's my favourite colour. I want all my little girls to be called after flowers.'

'Johnny isn't a flower. I'm called after Pa. Boys aren't called after flowers,' Johnny said, a tinge of anxiety in his voice.

Mary laughed. 'You're the eldest, it's only right you should be called after your father. Now be a good lad and get Marigold some tea. She's had nothing all day, poor mite. She can have that pasty, and can you cut some bread without cutting yourself?'

'Course I can.'

Proud of his responsibility Johnny clattered down the steep stairs. Marigold, fear and hunger forgotten, crept over to gaze with awe at the tiny red face of her new sister, crowned with red curly hair.

'She's pretty,' she breathed softly, her heart bursting with love for this tiny doll of a creature. 'Can I help look after her?'

'Of course you can, Marigold. But first go and get your clothes. And bring me the comb.'

It felt strange to be washing and dressing at the wrong end of the day, but Marigold didn't care. She had a new sister, another girl to play with, to look after and to love. When she went down into the kitchen to eat the pasty and the inexpertly hacked pieces of bread and dripping Johnny had prepared, she felt it had almost been worth while being locked in the pantry.

Mary lay back, smiling. Hyacinth was a lovely name; different, unusual. She'd seen it many years before when she'd been parlourmaid at Old Ridge Court, just outside Rugeley, and allowed to borrow books from Mr Nugent's library there.

John wasn't so sure. He'd had to stoke the almost dead fire and heat his own water, drag in the zinc bath which hung on the outside wall, and wash off the coal-dust before he could go to Mary. She had the highest standards in the street, and was very particular about never taking his pit clothes past the kitchen. When Johnny assured him she was well he didn't like to break her rule even to see his new daughter.

Normally Mary had his bath all ready for him. The baby hadn't been due for several more weeks, until the end of March. Then proper arrangements for his comfort would have been made. But he wasn't a harsh man and didn't resent this extra chore. Mary couldn't help it. Babies came when they would.

He admitted to himself – as he scrubbed the dirt off his face and dunked his head to wash the coal-dust out of his fair hair – that he'd have liked another son, a sturdy boy like young Johnny, though he wouldn't let Mary even suspect such a thing.

Yet his slight disappointment vanished when he finally went upstairs to find Mary sitting up in bed, the infant sucking greedily at her breast. She was so beautiful. How had he, plain John Smith, been lucky enough to find such a clever and pretty girl like Mary willing to marry him? She had vivid blue eyes, curly brown hair, and two neat dimples. Even after two children she'd regained her trim figure, and no doubt would after this baby too. She was brisk and competent about the house; quiet and submissive, although always cheerful; worked hard; and spent his money wisely.

It was her good management as well as his promotion to overman which had enabled them to move from the single room they'd rented at first into this through house. Here they had two good bedrooms, a front parlour and kitchen. They even had their own scullery attached to the house, instead of sharing a brewhouse across the yard. In the scullery was a tap, and they shared a lavatory in the yard with only three other families, luxury compared with his own boyhood. One day, he vowed as he looked down at his newest child, they'd have something better still.

'Isn't she pretty?' Mary asked, wanting reassurance, for the child was far smaller than either of the others had been.

'Not so pretty as her mom. Were you all right?'

'Yes, apart from her being early. Mrs Whitehouse came, and Mrs Tasker. They've taken the washing to do for me. They're good neighbours.'

'They might have spared a thought for Marigold.'

'It all happened so fast. I should have thought, asked, but somehow I expected they'd see to her. Is she all right?'

'Seems so. Had a fright but that's all. Told me she thought there were wolves in the pantry. How does she get such ideas?'

'Johnny has been trying to frighten her.'

'I'll frighten him! He's got to learn to look after his sisters. What do you want this one called?'

Mary smiled to herself. She knew full well John had been hoping for a boy, and had chosen Edward after his own father. 'I'd thought Hyacinth,' she said softly. There was no use prevaricating with her John. It would irritate him.

So did this suggestion.

'What sort of outlandish rubbish is that?' he exploded, so loudly that the baby, startled, lost Mary's nipple and let out a howl of fright and frustration.

Mary bent her head over the child, attempting to console it. She sighed. It had been nice to dream but obviously she wouldn't get her way.

'Why not Eliza after your mother?' he asked, ignoring the screaming baby. 'Or perhaps Victoria?'

'I'm not fond of Eliza, and there'll be a lot of girls named after the old Queen this year, now she's just died. Hush, now, lovey. They're old-fashioned names, and she's so bright looking.'

'Red faced, as well as red haired,' John said with a laugh, as the tiny scrap continued to bawl. 'If you really want another flower name, how about Poppy?'

At that moment a silence fell as the baby's mouth once more found the breast, and Mary smiled up at John. 'I like that,' she said slowly. 'Johnny's hair is brown like mine, Marigold's fair – she takes after you – but this one's going to be a redhead. Poppy? Look, John, she's waving her fist. Oh, yes, it must be Poppy.'

By the time Mary's third daughter was born, four years later, after she'd suffered two miscarriages, John was so relieved they'd both come safely through he lost all objections to floral names.

'Look at the way her little fingers cling on to mine,' he said proudly. 'They look so tiny, yet they're strong. Like ivy. Now that would be a good name: Ivy.'

Listlessly Mary agreed. It had been a difficult birth, more tiring than any of the others. Each one seemed to get worse, as if she had too little strength left to push the babies out into the world.

Perhaps that accounted for the dream. Normally she slept soundly but a few hours after Ivy's appearance she had woken, trembling, and had difficulty in suppressing her sobs. She mustn't wake John, he had to go to work in the morning. She turned over carefully, gasping as the blanket slipped and the freezing midwinter air hit her bare neck. She'd left her nightgown untied so as to feed the baby more easily during the night.

The baby. Suddenly she remembered and a surging anxiety swept over her. Careless now of waking John, she twisted in the bed and leant out to where the baby slept in the drawer, placed right beside the big bed. With the aid of the tiny nightlight left burning, she could see the infant swaddled in the big shawl her mother had knitted for Johnny. She was breathing, a little noisily, but she was alive. And cosy, her cheeks rosy and warm to Mary's gentle exploratory finger.

Sighing, Mary lay back in bed. She shivered and felt with her feet for the flannel-covered brick at the bottom of the bed, but it had lost all its heat and was no comfort.

She never had nightmares. She could barely recall the occasional dreams she'd had as a child. She smiled ruefully. Now she thought they might have been daydreams since they almost always contained some mysterious, handsome stranger who would whisk her away from a life of drudgery and cosset her for ever after. Not like this dream where she'd been fighting off some smothering monster. She shuddered, and to ward off the memory began to count her blessings as the Minister was endlessly advising.

John was a good husband. He'd been a handsome stranger once, so blond that in bright sunshine his hair looked white. Her life was not exactly drudgery, but it wasn't the fairy tale she'd envisaged. He worked hard, gave her almost all his wages, never beat her, and promised one day he'd finish with the pits.

'I'll find a job where you can be proud of me,' he'd said when they were first married.

'I'm proud of you now,' she reassured him, but he smiled and shook his head.

'A clean job, with no dirt and coal-dust getting everywhere, or filthy old clothes,' he went on dreamily.

She always smiled and agreed, but what else was there in Hednesford except the brick-and-tile works? They'd no influence to get him a job on the railway, even though her father had been a platelayer before he died, just after her fifteenth birthday. He could work in the brickyards or the Edge Tool Works at Bridgetown, but that was no better than the pit, and he'd have to start at the bottom again.

He'd risen to overman at the mine, after starting as an air-door boy, and had already been a skip loader when they'd met. He'd risen by his own ability, for he'd had very little schooling, preferring to be out in the fields earning coppers by scaring birds, or catching rabbits on Cannock Chase. Not like her, devouring every book she could get her hands on.

Although John could write a careful letter and tot up his money, he didn't know enough to be a clerk. He was clever, he could learn, but after a day underground he didn't have the energy for going to an evening institute, or walking to Rawnsley to use the new Colliery Workmen's Reading Room there.

The nightmare was kept at bay for some weeks and Mary almost forgot it. She was busy with the house and her four young children, and with the sewing she took in to earn a few extra shillings. She'd always been clever with her needle, and embroidered initials on all the table linen at Old Ridge Court when she'd worked there.

'You could earn a living with your needle,' Mrs Nugent declared, and had given Mary her other linen to do. Now she brought all new items for Mary to embroider at home. And as camisoles and drawers and petticoats became even more elaborately frilled and trimmed with lace and ribbons, she asked Mary to make them too.

Mary could have done far more. Mrs Nugent's friends clamoured for her services, but it was delicate work, needing clean hands and a room free of coal-dust. There wasn't time during the day. It was only after the children were abed and John's bath cleared away that she could sit at the big table, the lamp close by, and ply her needle. 'It's enough for now,' she explained to John. 'Perhaps when the children are all at school I could do some dressmaking.'

Ivy was three months old, and a few signs of spring were visible in the small back garden, when the nightmare recurred. After that it came every few days, and each time details became clearer, though they varied.

Sometimes she was in an orchard similar to the one at Old Ridge Court, or a wooded place like parts of the Chase she'd been to on the miners' annual outings. The trees were struggling for survival, almost hidden under the rampant, invasive growth of dark, impenetrable ivy. Occasionally, after rain or when a gleam of sunlight strayed beneath the branches, the leaves shone. But it was not a friendly glossiness like the rich deep red of the mahogany dining table Mrs Nugent was so proud of, which had to be polished each day until you could see your face in it. It was slimy, secretly triumphant, repelling.

At other times she was in a dark room, the windows only faintly discernible where the growth of ivy covered them, threatening, stretching out tendrils towards the cracks in the ancient glass. One day, Mary knew, the glass would break and the ivy would sweep into the room and smother her, imprisoning her in an embrace she could never escape.

Awake, sweating yet bitterly cold inside, Mary wondered if the name they'd chosen influenced this dream. But it was too late. Ivy had already been christened at St Peter's, and it couldn't be the child's fault. It was just a name. It didn't conjure up bright, cheerful pictures like Marigold and Poppy did, that was all, she told herself.

Then one day Mary saw a different ivy, a cultivated plant with lime-green, yellow and cream leaves, and the nightmare receded. She sowed marigold and poppy seeds in a small patch in the narrow garden, where she could see them from the scullery window. Behind them, against the fence, she planted variegated ivy, and chided herself for being too fanciful.

Every time she contemplated her daughters she tried to push away reflections on how appropriately they were named. All three plants were tenacious, thriving in the haze of coal-dust which pervaded the town. They were tough, dependable, resilient. They all withstood the buffets of the weather. The marigolds always seemed to be smiling cheerfully, while the poppies were flamboyantly glorious, their petals vulnerable to each breath of wind, but renewing their promise a thousandfold each year as their seeds scattered and flourished. And the ivy, though now it clung to the fence, would in time become stronger than its present supporter.

Marigold was tall, sturdy and strong. A happy child, always cheerful and placid unless strongly moved by some injustice, she longed to be like her mother. She helped willingly with tasks Johnny should by rights have done, like bringing in the coal or taking the swill to feed the pigs; even emptying the big copper in the scullery at the end of washday.

Poppy, also tall, was slender, quick tempered and excitable. She wanted desperately to be loved by everyone and to please them. Yet she could be cruel and vicious when thwarted. Once Mary had found her smashing her doll angrily against the bedroom wall because the doll's dress had caught on something and wouldn't come over its head. Her red hair was always in a tangle, and when she was angry her freckles seemed more prominent.

But Ivy was small and delicate, with big dark eyes and smooth dark hair which grew in a decided widow's peak, a pale complexion and rosebud mouth. She was neat, almost finicky in her habits, and clung to everyone. Perhaps it was because she was the youngest. Poppy was four years older and the others were at school. Ivy spent her days with Mary, preferring to follow her about than go and play with the other little ones in the yard or street. When her sisters were at home she trailed after them continuously, entwining herself remorselessly into their lives, demanding to be included in their games and pursuits.

'She's just shy, Mom, don't fret,' Marigold said when Mary voiced her concern. They were folding sheets ready for ironing, while Poppy took down the smaller things from the line stretched up the garden path.

'Look at her now, tagging after Poppy when she knows she can't reach the pegs. If Poppy doesn't lift her up to do some she sulks. And she wants to go everywhere with you. You'll not be wanting her along for ever.'

'She's no trouble, honest. She's small enough to be carried when she gets tired, and she's not very strong since she had scarlet fever. I think some of the others frighten her, especially that nasty little Janie Whitehouse.'

Mary tried to believe Marigold was right. As Ivy grew taller, too heavy even for Marigold to carry, she seemed more willing to stay indoors. She sought no company apart from that of her sisters. Mary began to worry how she would behave when she started at the school on Church Hill.

John whistled as he strode along towards the pithead. It was still pitch dark, just the gas lamps to guide him, but there was a steady sound of heavy boots and clogs as the men tramped towards the shafts ready for their descent into the deep underground maze of passages and caverns.

'That you, John?'

'Bert? Thought you were on night shift?'

'Changed wi' owd Danny. 'E's no family left, so Christmas don't mean much ter 'im now. Said 'e di'n't mind not 'aving a sleep.'

'How old is he?'

'Gettin' on fer eighty. Danged if I'd still want ter be pushin' skips at 'is age.'

'I suppose he's got nothing else to do. It's company, and he'd have to leave his house if he stopped. He's no children to take him in, either.'

'What us wants is dacent pensions when us gets ter seventy. Not the privilege of workin' under as long's us can.'

'It'll come. We get better wages here in Cannock pits than most colliers, Bert.'

'Aye, s'pose so. An' it's good clane 'ouse coal, an' plenty new shafts. Lots o' jobs.'

They walked along in silence for a while. John was recalling something he'd been told recently, about the ten-yard seams in the Dudley and Tipton mines, and why the Chase coalfield was made of thinner seams, deeper down.

'Have you heard of the Bentley Fault?' he asked suddenly.

'Summat that breaks up seams, ain't it?'

'Yes, between Wolverhampton and Walsall. That's what makes their seams thick, easier to get out.'

'I worked there once. Pulled it down, they did, an' left great big caverns. Not so safe, more ter 'old up, like.'

'But we don't have so much gas and fires like they had at Hamstead this year. Wasn't it two dozen men lost?'

'There could 'a' bin that many lost when Coppice at Brereton were flooded back in February. 'Twere a blessin' 'twere night shift, or more'n three'd 'a' gone.'

'Things are a sight better than even twenty years back. We've got cutting machines, the haulage is better, and the lifting.'

'An' could be better still. Comin' ter Union meetin' next week?'

John sighed. 'I might.'

'Well, see yer at the King's Arms, per'aps, ternight. I wants ter find out if Mr Coulthwaite's got another National winner over at Rawnsley, like that Eremon two year ago.'

The sky was lighter now, lit by the glow from the lamphouse. The headgear, sombre and skeletal, stood outlined against it. The cage was waiting, and men were standing round, some sullen and silent, still comatose from the Christmas revels, others cracking jokes. John got his lamp and joined them.

'Got yer pig salted?' one asked.

'Weeks ago. Got a couple of young piglets now. If you've built your sty in time, Barney, I'll sell you one!'

The others roared with laughter. Barney had been going to build himself a sty and raise his own pig for at least five years, but had got no further than marking out where it was to go.

They were still jeering at him when it was their turn to squash into the cage.

'Hey, you there, lad!' John suddenly shouted out urgently. 'Come into the middle.'

The boy he spoke to was small and skinny, with fair hair which would be black by the end of the shift. The lad gulped and nodded, but didn't move. Then he cried out in alarm as one of the men grabbed his arm and jerked him forward.

'It's all right, lad,' John said calmly. 'Thanks, Ted. It's your first day, isn't it?' he asked gently. 'You see, lad, you'd got your hand on the outside of the cage. It could have been crushed if the cage had swung against the wall of the shaft. We had a broken arm last week just because someone was careless.'

The lad looked across at the post he'd been hanging on to, and his face turned green. Just then the cage shifted, the winding gear creaked, and the cage plummeted downwards into the velvety black hole. There was no gleam of light. The only sounds were the clanking of chains and the whooshing of the air sweeping past them. Without warning the lad doubled up and spewed his breakfast over their feet.

With a jerk the cage stopped, and the men, laughing or cursing the unfortunate lad, got out. They lit their lamps, and the weak, flickering glow slowly disappeared as they set off in single file on the two-mile tramp down the roadway to the face where they were working.

'Sit down a minute,' John ordered, cutting off the lad's terrified apologies. 'Did you bring a flask?'

He nodded, blinking in the light from several lamps hung around the bottom of the shaft. Timidly he looked round at the bewildering structure of wooden props and beams, the black gleam of exposed coal, and the rails snaking off into the distance.

'Have a drink now, but not too much, mind. It's got to last all day and it'll get a sight hotter than this. And remember to keep the flask and your snap in your rabbit pocket, or the mice'll be after them. You're opening doors for the ponies?'

Again the lad nodded.

'Here's Mr Thomas, he'll tell you what to do. Cheer up, you'll get used to it.'

John went on towards his cabin, from where he supervised his section of the colliery. Four hours later he joined the coal-face workers as they stopped for ten minutes to eat their dinners, and then went back with them to the seam they were working.

In the faint illumination of the lamps he could see sweat pouring off their naked, dust-caked backs. The passageway was less than four feet high, and one collier was almost lying down as he hacked away at the coal with his pick.

Then there was a low rumble, a distant scream that echoed, endlessly reverberating through the passages, and the sound of running feet.

'Come quick! There's bin a fall!'

John was the first out of the passage, running along bent almost double. As he turned into a wider, taller tunnel, he could see silhouetted in the faint light of a single lamp on the far side an untidy tangle of broken props and a heap of coal. It splayed right across the floor, almost completely blocking the tunnel. The only gap, through which the feeble light shone, just piercing the cloud of dust, was where the roof had given way and released the coal.

'Jem Sykes, he'm trapped under it!' the man who had shouted to them gasped, and John nodded, swiftly assessing the situation.

'Get the rescue team, we'll need a stretcher. You two, start moving the lumps from the edges as carefully as you can, don't disturb the ones behind or underneath yet. Pass them along and pile them into a tub at the end of this tunnel. Don't let it come in for fear of vibrations bringing down more coal.'

Swiftly and silently the men formed a chain, and John supervised. When there was room and he was certain he would not dislodge further coal he eased himself gently over the heap of coal and found Jem, his legs trapped, groaning in agony.

'Get me out!' he pleaded. 'Fer Gawd's sake get me out! Me legs is crushed!'

'Easy does it, Jem, and we'll have you out in no time. I'll take off a few of the lumps from this side now. Don't move in case you upset any.'

He worked feverishly but with immense care for five minutes or more, lifting the coal away from Jem's body while on the far side of the fall the others made space for the rescue team to carry out the injured man. As Jem's legs were finally uncovered, and John could see the bloody, mangled mess, he heard another ominous rumble from just above his head.

'Stand back!' he hissed in a sharp whisper, fearful that a shout would precipitate another fall. As he heard the men moving backwards, he seized Jem under his armpits and dragged him along the suddenly hell-dark tunnel just as more coal fell in blinding, crackling, choking clouds of dust.

Several hours later John was carried home by two of his mates.

'It's not so bad, luv,' he gasped as they helped him up the stairs. Mary for once cared nothing for the coal-dust they carried with them, even when they trod it into her newly scrubbed quarry tiles and spread it all over the pegged rug beside the bed. They stripped John and put him between the sheets.

'What happened? What's wrong?'

'Just a fall o'rock, Missus,' Joe Tasker said soothingly. 'There's no bones broke, just a cut or two and a few bruises. 'E were out fer a couple o' minutes: lump o' coal must 'a' caught 'im. Could 'a' bin a lot wus.'

'It's them new seams. Thinner, yer see,' his companion explained. 'The owd uns are gettin' worked out, an' we 'as ter go deeper, so we 'it the rock faster. Yer man'll be fit again in a week. 'E saved Jem Sykes's life anyroad, draggin' 'im out way just in nick o' time. Though poor chap'll never walk no more. They've teken 'im ter Accident 'Ome, but yer man'd not let us tek 'im.'

''E don't trust that young matron,' Joe grinned. 'Too young, on'y bin there a year or so. Says 'e'll do better wi' you, an' I can't say I blame 'im! If my missus were such a dainty lass I'd feel same.'

John's injuries, however, were far more severe than they'd thought at first. He suffered terrible headaches, and the torn muscles stubbornly refused to heal. The bruises faded but the cuts suppurated, the flesh round about growing white and puffy. Mary tried all the remedies she knew, and when the ointments she bought had no effect she searched the lanes for old witch hazel leaves, since none of the other healing herbs she knew were in leaf or flower.

Eventually she had to call a doctor.

'You should have called me or one of the nurses from the Annie Ker place weeks ago, woman!' the elderly, weary Dr Mackenzie grumbled. It was always the same. He was called in only as a last resort, when it was usually too late for him to do anything but alleviate the pain.

'We haven't the money for doctors if we can do without!' Mary snapped, rubbing her eyes. She'd had no sleep for two nights, was worried sick, and had already pawned everything they could possibly do without.

'Doesn't John get compensation? The Act of '06 provided for that, I thought.'

'It's not enough,' Mary sighed.

The only other money coming into the house was the few shillings Johnny earned as a delivery boy, and the coppers Marigold was given when she did errands for neighbours after school. To pay for this visit she'd have to sit up all night again finishing some sewing for Mrs Nugent.

'You needn't pay me until your man's back in work,' Dr Mackenzie said mildly. He knew Mary from the days she'd worked at Old Ridge Court. 'He will be, I promise, but not for several weeks. Send one of your lasses round to the dispensary for some ointment, and make sure you stay in bed, John. Every time you get up will put you back a day. Remember that and you'll be at work again as soon as possible.'

When Marigold returned from fetching the ointment Mary had made up her mind.

'You're a good child, and sensible,' she explained. 'If we're going to be able to pay the rent I'll have to earn more money. I can get a job cooking or doing housework. Mrs Nugent will recommend me to one of her friends. But you'll have to look after the little ones and help even more in the house after school. Can you manage, do you think?'

'Yes, Mom, I'll do whatever you say. I'm eleven now, I can do lots of things.' Marigold swallowed back her tears. She hated seeing her Pa in bed, so still and pale, helpless and in pain. And she hated seeing Mom look ill with worry, her pretty face pinched and drawn. She'd do anything to help.

'I can get something ready for tea before I go out in the morning. You can give everybody some bread and cheese when you come home at dinnertime, make up the fire and see to your Pa before you go back to school, and then do some cleaning when you get home. Poppy must help you; even Ivy can do something.'

'Who'll look after Ivy?'

'I'll have to ask if I can take her with me. Perhaps they'll let her start school early, even though she's only just four. Or Mrs Tasker will look after her.'

'You can't even sing!' Johnny said scornfully.

'Yes, I can!' Poppy retorted, and began to warble a hymn somewhat uncertainly.

'Be quiet down here! Pa's trying to sleep!' Marigold came into the room carrying their father's empty dinner plate. 'Why are you singing "Away in a Manger", Poppy? It's long past Christmas.'

'She wants to join a choir,' Johnny replied, and began to sing, in a high, falsetto voice: '"Come all you colliers in this town that loves a bonny lass, That loves to drink good ale that's brown, that will sparkle in the glass –" Why can't you sing something jolly instead of hymns?'

Poppy was almost weeping with fury. 'They sing hymns!' she said angrily.

'Who do?'

'Chapel choir,' Johnny said disgustedly. 'We always go to church, not chapel.'

'Why on earth do you want to go to chapel?' Marigold asked, bewildered.

Poppy sniffed. 'They went to Alton Towers for their outing. They have better outings than anyone else,' she said resentfully. 'Why shouldn't I go? Why can't I go to chapel if I want to?'

'Because you don't understand anything about it, and you're too young to go on choir outings anyway,' Johnny said dismissively. 'I may be late for tea, Marigold. Will you feed the pigs tonight?'

She sighed. 'That's the third time this week. I don't know what you and your friends get up to.'

'I'm earning money, I've a right to do what I like,' Johnny retorted, and went swiftly out of the door. He hated getting into an argument with Marigold, because too often he had the impression she won, although he wasn't always sure why. It was just an uncomfortable feeling left behind that made him wish he could find better reasons for whatever it was he wanted.

'You'll be going on the Sunday School treat in a few months,' Marigold said to Poppy consolingly. 'You don't have to do anything special for that, but if you were in a choir you'd have to go to practices, and go to chapel three times every Sunday, I expect.'

Poppy looked thoughtful. 'Well, perhaps I'll join a bicycling club when I'm old enough.'

Marigold suppressed the retort that there would be no money for bicycles. Another tantrum had been averted, she must be satisfied with that. 'Come on, it's time we went back to school.'

It had been arranged that Mrs Tasker would look after Ivy while Marigold was at school. Mary's wages paid the rent and bought coal. For the time being the colliery owners permitted them to stay in the house, for John was getting better and would soon be back at work. Her money, supplemented by the food she was able to bring home with her, thrown out by her wealthy and profligate employers, meant she could just feed her family.

Marigold struggled to do all the jobs her mother had no time or energy for. Poppy ran errands for neighbours, and Ivy had her own tasks such as feeding the hens, collecting eggs, fetching in kindling and washing up the few dishes they'd not pawned.

'Proper little 'ome body, your Ivy,' Mrs Tasker commented one afternoon when she brought Ivy home, along with a bag of potatoes she'd bought from the shops. 'Mek some lucky feller a good wife one day. 'Elped me mek pastry terday, didn't yer, duckie?'

Ivy glanced up at her through long, dark lashes. She held out a small pie-dish covered with rather grey-looking pastry for Marigold to admire. 'It's for Pa's tea,' she said proudly. 'I made it all myself, didn't I?'

Marigold smiled at her. 'We'll cook it later, shall we? Thanks for bringing the potatoes, Mrs Tasker. It's good of you to do the shopping.'

'What's neighbours for if not ter 'elp? An' it's a long drag up 'ere from Market Street. How's yer pa doin'?'

'A bit better, I think. Dr Mackenzie says he'll be able to work again in a few weeks. But his leg will never be as strong again. And it's been much longer than we thought.'

''E deserves a medal for saving Jem Sykes's life. Joe said ter tell 'im there's still a job fer 'im, an' not ter fret.'

Marigold had never considered the possibility that her father's job might be at risk. She glanced worriedly at Mrs Tasker and then looked away, afraid of revealing she hadn't even wondered about it. She should have done, and she didn't want to appear thoughtless. And if he lost his job they'd lose the house too. Where could they go then?

'I'd best be off. Oh, 'ere's a bit o' baccy Joe sent. 'E know's yer pa likes a pipe.'

'Thanks.' Marigold was touched. Pa never complained because he wasn't able to afford tobacco now, but she knew he missed the comfort of his old clay pipe. Although it was empty he kept it beside the bed, and when he thought no one was around he sucked it quietly, drawing in what remnants of flavour lingered from the tobacco it had once held.

Apart from that his only occupation seemed to be whittling away with an ancient knife at pieces of wood, carving animals so lifelike Mary had once screamed at seeing a mouse apparently asleep on her pillow.

'When can we bake my pie?' Ivy demanded as soon as Mrs Tasker, growing ever more huge over the years, waddled away in her enormous felt hat with its vast crown and wide brim.

'It's too soon yet. And I need to rake the fire first, it's been damped down all day.'

'Pa can have it early. Why should he wait for Mom to come home?'

'Because he always does. He likes to think we're all eating together, even if he has to stay in bed. Now stop pestering me, Ivy,' she added impatiently as Ivy opened her mouth to argue. 'Let me do some potatoes and when they've been in the oven a while we can put your pie in. Take Mrs Tasker's tobacco up to him.'

'She calls it baccy.'

Marigold bit her lip to stop an angry rebuke. She knew that because her mother had been in service with the gentry and insisted her children spoke properly some of the neighbours thought they were snooty. How could she explain to Ivy?

'Never mind. Take it up to him.'

'I want to finish putting patterns on the pastry. Mrs Tasker showed me how to make patterns with a fork.'

It was easier not to insist, and Marigold hadn't yet found time to go and see her father since she came in from school. 'Put some paper on the table first then, and don't drop crumbs,' she ordered. She picked up the screw of paper which held the tobacco and went upstairs.

John was sitting up in bed whittling away at a small chunk of wood.

'What's that, Pa?'

He held it out to her. 'There, just finished. It's for you, but I'll paint it first with a bit of black paint. Then it'll be a lucky black cat.'

'Pa, it's lovely! Oh, please, can I have it now, like it is? It doesn't need paint. Look how its tail curls round, and I can see the whiskers! Pa, it's so real looking! Is it truly for me? Thank you. I'll put it on the mantelpiece in our bedroom.'

There were already a dozen small carvings displayed there, and Marigold spent several minutes rearranging them to give her 'lucky' cat pride of place. Then she fingered it admiringly, imagining it was purring as she stroked its back. She'd love to have a real kitten, but Pa made such lovely carvings they were almost as good. He'd often bought them small treats before he'd been ill, sweets and toys, and now they had much less money he tried to make it up to them with his carvings. She loved him so much.

'Marigold!'

The thin whining voice came through the bare boards of the floor and Marigold frowned. Drat Ivy, couldn't she wait just a few minutes? She hardly ever had time to sit and admire her carvings, and just for once she meant to enjoy looking at her new one.

'Be quiet! I'll be down in a minute!'

Sighing, she put the tiny cat back on the mantelpiece and went back downstairs. She pushed open the door into the kitchen, and for the moment couldn't see her sister. There was no protecting newspaper on the table and she assumed Ivy had abandoned the pie and found something else to do.

She came through the doorway and suddenly caught sight of Ivy, the pie in her hands, stretched out towards the open door of the oven.

'No! Ivy, you'll hurt yourself!' she exclaimed, and jumped down the last step into the kitchen.

Ivy, startled, lost her balance. There was a confused medley of sound; crockery breaking; fire irons clattering on to the hearth; stacked kindling skittering down. Above it all rose the piercing wail of a terrified child.

Chapter Two

MARIGOLD screamed and leapt towards her sister. She slipped on the poker and fell headlong, but ignored the pain in her knee as she scrambled up to snatch Ivy from where she lay screaming in the hearth.

'Mom! Pa! Oh, help! Ivy, it's all right, I've got you now,' she tried to comfort the little girl, sobbing herself with fear and shaking uncontrollably.

Ivy's screams continued, and Marigold, mesmerized, watched as the sleeve of Ivy's dress shrivelled and wrinkled across her shoulder. Unaware of the stench of burning wool, Marigold slowly pulled away the ruined material and saw long, angry weals forming across the top of Ivy's arm and round her shoulder, three parallel lines made by the bars of the grate.

Then, making Marigold jump nervously, a lock of Ivy's dark hair fell loose and rolled across her face, curling as it went and causing Ivy to bat at it with renewed screams of terror. Another weal became visible across Ivy's temple.

A pungent, sickly reek, the mingled smells of burning wool, hair and flesh, gradually penetrated Marigold's numbed senses, and as she understood, she gagged, horrified. No! It couldn't be Ivy's skin smelling like that! Not her little sister!

It seemed like hours to the petrified girl, but was less than a minute before her father stumbled into the room.

'Go and get me a bowl of cold water!' he yelled, and gently eased Ivy from Marigold's convulsive grasp.

She fled to do his bidding, and then, still sobbing, fetched the unguent Mary kept ready for soothing the frequent small scalds and burns they suffered. By the time Mary arrived home, Ivy, hiccuping in her sleep, was wrapped in a blanket and cradled on John's lap in the chair before the fire.

John grimly suppressed the pain in his leg, made worse by having to support his daughter, and the cold striking through the back of his thin nightshirt. He concentrated on willing away the agony inside his skull which threatened to blow him apart.

Poppy, told what had happened in whispers by her distraught sister, helped silently. Marigold, pale and trembling, crept round getting their dinner ready. If only she could live those few moments again, if only she hadn't spent so much time admiring the carving, ignoring Ivy, shouting at her even, being selfish, her little sister wouldn't have been so horribly, painfully burnt.

Johnny arrived home on Mary's heels, and stood in the doorway, mouth agape as he listened to John explaining what had happened. Ivy awoke, and began to scream again as the pain of her burns overwhelmed her, unresponsive even to Mary's gentle cuddling.

Marigold, accusing herself, apologizing, almost incoherent with fear and remorse, clutched her mother's skirt as she knelt beside Mary.

John eased himself to his feet trying to rid himself of the cramps and aches in his leg now Mary had taken Ivy from him. 'Where have you been, young Johnny?' he snapped, and Johnny blinked in astonishment. He'd never before heard that cold, venomous tone in his father's voice.

'I – I was with Ted and Arthur,' he stammered.

'Messing about when you should have been here! Why weren't you at home, helping Marigold? You finished work an hour ago. You're older than she is, and it's about time you began to think of someone else instead of yourself!'

'It's not my job to do housework!' Johnny retorted. 'That's for girls!'

'Marigold, fetch my belt from upstairs.'

He was cold, ice-cold, and implacable. Even dressed only in an almost threadbare, neatly darned nightshirt, he was more impressive and frightening than they'd ever imagined he could be. None of them had ever seen him like this.

'No, John, don't! It was an accident, it wasn't anyone's fault!' Mary whispered, but he didn't even hear.

'Marigold?'

Sobbing afresh, she fled. She daren't disobey him. As she came back and handed the thick leather belt to her father, she trembled violently. This was all her doing. Johnny was going to be thrashed because of her!

As John ordered Johnny to bend over the table and raised his arm, Marigold screamed. 'No, Pa! It was my fault! Hit me, not Johnny!'

The belt sang through the air and Johnny let out a howl of anguish, then another and another.

Mary struggled to her feet and clutched at John's arm, Ivy still wailing in her arms.

'John, stop! That's enough! John, your leg's bleeding, you've done more damage! Oh, please, don't make it all worse!'

'Get back, woman! Get out of the way! I'll beat some sense into the lad if he won't learn it any other way! I should have done it long ago!'

'I won't go, so there!'

'But you've got to go, Ivy, love,' Marigold said wearily, while Poppy flung Ivy's coat on one chair and herself into the other.

'I won't! Don't make me go, Marigold! *Please.*'

'She's a spoilt brat,' Poppy declared petulantly. 'Ever since you left school she's whined and fussed and been mardy as hell every day.'

Marigold frowned, pushed her thick fair plait out of the way, and squatted down to Ivy's level. 'Why don't you like school?' she asked patiently.

Ivy glanced through her long dark lashes, first at Poppy, who looked cross and fed up, then at Marigold, who always smiled at her and let her do what she wanted.

She bit her bottom lip between small white teeth and gave a heartrending sob. 'Janie,' she whispered, slipping her plump arms round Marigold's neck and hugging tightly.

'Janie Whitehouse? What's she been up to? What's she said?' Marigold demanded, her protective instincts rearing up at the sound of that name.

'She calls me names. I hate her!'

'But she's not in your class, she's older. And Poppy's always with you on the way to and from school. She wouldn't dare call names in front of Poppy.'

'She doesn't,' Poppy said shortly. 'And I stay with the brat till the bell's rung, and get there as soon as I can at hometime,' she added resentfully. 'She's mollycoddled and it's time she stood up for herself.'

It rankled that since Ivy had started school she hadn't been able to stay with her own friends, but had to take care of her little sister.

'In the playground,' Ivy sobbed. 'She calls me "scarface" and says I'll never get a sweetheart!'

'That's bad talk! You're too young to think about sweethearts,' Poppy said self-righteously.

Marigold didn't hear her. She'd caught her breath in dismay. This was something she'd been dreading for more than two years. Gently she pushed Ivy's dark hair aside to reveal the ugly, puckered flesh across her temple, the only scar visible as a result of that terrible day.

'Nobody can see a scar when your hair's hanging over it,' she said softly. 'Look,' she added, and picked Ivy up to carry her across to the small mirror beside the scullery door.

Ivy buried her head in Marigold's shoulder and sobbed convulsively. 'They can! Janie says they can!' she wailed. 'And everybody can see my arm and my shoulder, she says!'

'That's a lie, and you ought to know better than believe that little tyke,' Poppy said angrily.

'Hush, baby, no one can see your arm or your shoulder under your dress and your pinafore sleeves,' Marigold tried to console Ivy, who by now was heaving great tearing sobs.

'They can! They can!' Ivy screamed. 'Janie says they laugh at me behind my back.'

'That's rubbish, and if you don't come soon you'll be late,' Poppy warned, picking up Ivy's coat. 'I'm not going to wait for you and be late myself.'

'No, you go on. I'll bring her later when she's feeling more like it,' Marigold said, and Poppy, scenting an hour of liberty, scampered out of the door almost before she'd finished speaking.

Sitting in the big rocking chair beside the fire, Marigold fretted. Ivy was curled up on her lap, fast asleep after her tantrum, her thumb in her mouth.

She hadn't realized until recently how the scars from that dreadful day were still affecting Ivy. Marigold still smelt in nightmares the stench of burning wool; and worse, heard the screams of agony as the hot metal bars of the grate charred Ivy's tender flesh. The skin had healed rapidly – leaving scars, it was true, but by great good fortune in places where they didn't show. Yet what of a deeper effect on the little girl?

In some ways, Marigold thought guiltily, the rest of the family had been hurt just as much. Pa had wrenched open his own wound again and hadn't been able to return to work for another month. He still limped and couldn't go back to his old job underground. He'd had to accept a worse paid one at the pithead, and was often in too much pain from the dreadful headaches to go to work.

Johnny had been moody ever since, furious at his father for the unaccustomed beating – and above all for humiliating him in front of his sisters. Sometimes in recompense for his sulking he brought home small delicacies from the grocer who employed him. It made up a little for things they could no longer afford with Pa's lower wages. 'I get them cut-price,' he'd say brusquely. 'They'd be thrown out, like as not, if I didn't have them.' Most of the time, however, he bitterly resented being made to feel guilty and as often as he could slunk off to join his friends.

Marigold blamed herself entirely, despite her mother's attempts to convince her otherwise. She shouldn't have spent so long upstairs, and when she'd seen what Ivy was doing she shouldn't have shouted at her, startling her into toppling over.

'Better now?' she asked as Ivy stirred into wakefulness.

Ivy smiled brilliantly. 'I love you best of all, Marigold. Can I play with Goldie?'

'But you have to go to school, Ivy. You can't stay at home all day playing with your dolly.'

Ivy pouted. 'Janie will laugh at me, call me names,' she sniffed dolefully, tears threatening once more.

Marigold sighed. Already half the morning had gone and she was dreadfully behind with the work. If she had to spend time persuading Ivy to go to school and explaining to the teacher why she was late she'd never catch up.

'If I let you stay here today promise you'll go without a fuss tomorrow?' she said at last, pushing down the suspicion that by tomorrow Ivy would have forgotten her promise.

With barely a nod Ivy was already scrambling off her lap and running to the cupboard between the window and the chimney where her toys were kept on the bottom shelf. Goldie was her most precious possession, a beautiful china doll with delicate clothes Mary had fashioned out of scraps of silk and lace Mrs Nugent had given her. Ivy would play contentedly for hours, dressing and undressing Goldie, combing the real hair, and gently crooning some wordless tune.

When Poppy came home for dinner Marigold waylaid her in the yard. 'Don't set her off again,' she begged. 'I've let her stay at home today, and she's promised she'll not make a fuss tomorrow.'

For once Poppy didn't argue. She preferred the freedom to dawdle with her friends on the way home, giggling and teasing, eyeing the big boys from Standards Six and Seven, and shrieking with pretended fear when one of them left his friends to chase after them. And if anyone got into trouble it would be Marigold. She could hardly be blamed for her sister's actions. Mom had made it clear that even Poppy, though a mere three years younger, had to do what Marigold said while she and Pa were at work.

'That's good!' John said, surprised.

Ivy preened, scrambled on to his lap as he sat beside the bright, cheerful fire, and began to point out all the subtleties of the drawing he held in his hand.

'Miss Riley says I'm the best in the whole school at drawing and painting,' she boasted.

Marigold glanced at Mary and they exchanged relieved smiles.

'It was a blessing when Miss Riley came,' Mary said quietly, sorting out the embroidery threads for the traycloth she was doing for one of Mrs Nugent's friends.

'She never moans about going to school now,' Marigold replied softly. 'I thought we'd have the attendance officer round more than once, but I doubt even Mr Purslow could make her go if she didn't want to.'

'It was too much responsibility for you to cope with on your own, love.' Mary sighed. 'I should never have left you.'

'Now, you're not to go blaming yourself, Mom,' Marigold said quickly. 'You know it was the only way or we'd have been crowded into one of those back-to-back hovels near the pit, sharing a lavatory with a dozen other families and not even a tap in the house.'

'Maybe, but I'd set my heart on you going on to the higher standards at Chadsmoor. Why, you could have been a teacher yourself one day. You're bright enough.'

'It was my fault Ivy got burnt and Pa didn't get right, and I never wanted to be a teacher anyway,' Marigold protested swiftly.

'Of course it wasn't your fault, love. Accidents happen. And your Pa – Well, never mind.'

Marigold glanced across at her father, but he was still absorbed in Ivy's drawing.

'I didn't mind leaving school, honest. I wish I could have gone out to work instead of you having to, that's all.'

Mary shook her head. 'You know we agreed. You couldn't have earned much, especially part time. Children get paid so little, not nearly as much as I can earn, but you can do everything in the house for me. When Poppy's old enough to leave school she can stay at home while you get a job. What a thing it would be if you got a place in a shop – a nice ladies' outfitters perhaps?'

'I don't mind doing the house, really I don't.'

'You're a good lass but it's only fair you should get out and meet people, have a bit of money of your own, and find a lad.'

'Oh, Mom!' Marigold wriggled, embarrassed, and tried to change the subject. 'Why a ladies' outfitters? Don't they want girls who've been to the secondary school and speak nicely if they're going to be serving the gentry?'

'It's a clean, easy job, better than service. And you do speak properly, and you can sew. That would help a lot. You could start as an alteration hand and when you're a bit older serve in the shop. You might be able to get things cheap. You'd look lovely in some of those dresses. The long straight skirts would suit you, you're so tall and slim.'

Marigold smiled at her mother, but as she hemmed the edge of some napkins to go with the traycloth her thoughts whirled. She'd never really considered what she would be doing in a few years. It had been enough to get through one day at a time, doing all the scrubbing, polishing, washing, ironing and cooking for the family. If Poppy could take that over the world would open up for her. Perhaps she could leave Hednesford, maybe go on the train as far as Birmingham.

She was lost in thought, trying to recall everything she'd ever been told about Birmingham: the huge buildings and wide streets; the thousands of workshops producing everything anyone could ever want. For the first time Marigold began to contemplate a future away from the endless grind and dirt and smell of a pit community. Why, she might even travel to London one day and see the enormous palace where the new King George lived, and the cathedrals which were bigger still than the one at Lichfield. She'd seen that once when they'd all been taken to the town on a Sunday School outing.

She came to with a start as Johnny, always noisy, burst in through the door

'Wipe your feet and take off your jacket, it's wet,' Mary said automatically.

'Not much, it's been drizzling a bit, that's all,' Johnny replied, but he shrugged off his jacket and hung it and his cap to dry on a nail in the passageway between the kitchen and scullery. 'Here's some meat,' he added, coming back into the kitchen and dropping it on the table.

'Mind my sewing!' Mary exclaimed, and picked up the meat. 'But this is best roasting beef,' she added as the paper round the meat slipped.

'I know. Special treat,' Johnny said.

'But surely Mr Todd didn't give you this? It's usually the scrag end or bits left over,' Mary said, puzzled.

'I bought it. Tip from a customer. I told you old Toddy let me have it cheap,' Johnny explained, raking his hand through his hair, making it stick up more than it usually did.

'Don't speak like that of your employer, son,' John put in, but Mary ignored the lapse. Sometimes she thought Johnny was concerned only with his own comfort, then he'd do something generous like this. Often he brought home small packets of tea, a pat of butter, or a few biscuits. She didn't understand him.

'Johnny, that's kind, spending your money on us. Look, Ivy, some lovely beef. We'll have it for dinner on Sunday.'

'Johnny, look at my drawing,' Ivy commanded, ignoring the promised treat. Somehow she always seemed to get the things she liked best and didn't find it strange; indeed, had come to expect it. She thrust the drawing under Johnny's nose and he sat down at the table, staring at it.

'It's the Drill Hall in Victoria Street,' he said in surprise. 'Look, Pa, she's got the front of it just right. Are you sure you did this all on your own?' he asked Ivy suspiciously.

'Course I did,' Ivy said indignantly. 'Miss Riley showed me how, but I did every bit of it!'

'I wish she'd been there to teach me,' Johnny said wistfully. 'Pa, I heard Bill Jenkinson saying that his older brother – you know, Teddy who works on the maintenance at the pit – well, he's going to evening classes to learn drawing. Can I go too?'

'What good would drawing be to you, lad? It wouldn't help you get a proper job. You can draw any time without lessons.'

'Not that sort of drawing,' Johnny said quickly. 'Not like Ivy does. This is for drawing machinery, or – or buildings, things like that. Bill says Teddy's going to make things when he's got some letters after his name.'

'What sort of things?' Mary said. 'I've never heard of people being paid to draw, not unless they were teachers like Miss Riley, and she teaches everything else as well.'

'Just things. Machines, I think,' Johnny said vaguely.

'Well, it's no use dreaming, son, there's no money to spare for drawing classes. It's time you decided whether you're going down the pit or staying with Mr Todd. You've learnt to drive the cart and could take over from Sam Peters when he can't do it any more, and by the look of him that won't be too long.'

'Driving that old nag round and round the same streets is dead boring,' Johnny said sulkily. 'I'd earn more money down the pit.'

'Only at first,' Mary put in quickly. She dreaded the thought of her only son going down into the pit which had injured his father. 'You were lucky to get taken on by Mr Todd. It was only Mrs

Nugent putting in a word for you got you that job, but it could lead to better things. Mr Todd's got no one to take over the shop, only two daughters, and they can't run it on their own. He'll need someone to manage it for him in a few years.'

'He'll choose a smarmy type from behind the counter,' Johnny said dismissively. 'They're bound to think they'll have a chance if they make up to one of those pasty-faced girls.'

'That's no way to talk,' his father said reprovingly, but Johnny scarcely heeded him.

'I don't want to sit behind a smelly horse all my life, neither. Horses are finished. In a few years everybody'll be driving motor trucks.'

'Mr Nugent's got a motor car,' Poppy put in.

She'd been sitting in the corner, peeling potatoes for the next day's dinner, apparently lost in her dreams. Hopeless with her needle, always pricking her finger and spilling blood on to the linen, she couldn't help with Mary's sewing, but she quite cheerfully did as much as she could of the cooking.

'How do you know? Have you seen it? What sort?' Johnny demanded eagerly.

'He drove past school just as we were coming out today,' she said carelessly. 'Mom, is this enough?'

'Just a couple more, love, and then it's time Ivy was in bed. Come on, chick, I'll take up the hot bricks while you get washed.'

'What sort of motor car?' Johnny persisted.

'A black one, I think. I didn't look much. Nasty noisy thing, it scared the little ones.'

'A black one! That's not much help! Mom, ask Mrs Nugent what it is, please? I'd love to have a ride in it.'

'I will if I remember. But I won't ask for a ride. The cheek of it! Ivy, what did I say?'

Ivy made token grumbling noises but went out to the scullery without further chivvying. Mary took the bricks out of the oven and wrapped one in a thick piece of blanket. She handed it to Johnny.

'Might as well put it in your bed early,' she said, and he took it into the front parlour where he slept now the girls, who shared a big bed in the back bedroom, were getting older.

Marigold jumped up to take the other bricks upstairs. 'I'll do that, Mom, you look tired.'

'Thanks, you're a good lass. My back does ache a bit, but I want to finish this traycloth tonight.' She rubbed her eyes. 'I've got a lot to do. Mrs Nugent's bringing me some more work tomorrow and she wants it back soon. It's for a present.'

Sunday was the first hot day of spring, and after dinner the whole family walked up on to the Chase. Ivy insisted on taking her hoop to bowl, and Poppy had a skipping rope. Many other townsfolk were taking the air, and a pair of Mr Coulthwaite's racehorses were being exercised.

'Two Grand National winners in four years, he's had. That's a good record,' John said admiringly as the riders trotted past.

'Will you have a bet on the next one, Pa?' Johnny asked.

'I might be tempted,' John replied, and Mary laughed.

'You'll never waste your money on such folly,' she said with utter certainty. Not for her John the gambling at pitch and toss, or on the horses, which made so many of his workmates poorer than they might have been.

'It's the only way people like us can get rich,' Johnny said provocatively.

'Don't you think the Liberals will bring in the schemes they've promised, now they've shown the Lords who rules Parliament?' his father asked.

'Not them. Now Members of Parliament are to get paid we'll soon have a Labour Government. They'll make sure the working class gets more money.'

John smiled. Johnny was just beginning to take an interest in matters outside football and what he and his pals were doing in their free time, and he encouraged the lad to think things out for himself.

Marigold frowned. 'How can they give more money to people if they don't work for it?'

'Higher wages, pensions for everybody, money when you're ill – lots of ways.'

'Where'll they get it from?'

'Rich folk, of course.'

'I don't think that's right. It's like stealing, taking from one lot of people to give to others.'

Johnny frowned. 'No it isn't, it's just that the bosses won't keep so much, more will go to the workmen. They can afford it. Look at the big houses they live in.'

'People should work for their money,' she insisted.

'However hard we work we'll never get a house like – well, like Mrs Nugent's. Owning it instead of paying rent to the colliery bosses.'

'No, I suppose not,' Marigold conceded. 'But they got their houses from their fathers, and so on back for hundreds of years. We must all have started out equal one time.'

'We are all equal, and a Labour Government would make us equal again.'

'Women as well, Johnny?' Mary put in, amused at this serious discussion between her two eldest. 'Would you give women the vote like the suffragettes are demanding?'

'That's different,' Johnny declared. 'Women can't think like men, they can't be proper judges.'

'If you want to make a bet, Johnny, I'll bet you a shilling women will be in Parliament one day, and rule the country!' Marigold said heatedly.

Johnny scoffed, but fortunately for peace he spied some of his mates and went off to join them, while Poppy persuaded her mother and Marigold to turn the rope for her. By the time they strolled back down the hill to the town Marigold had forgotten all about Parliament and politics. They had nothing to do with her, after all.

A few weeks later Marigold returned home from shopping one morning to find Mary huddled in the big chair over the fire. 'Mom, what is it? Are you poorly?'

Mary looked up at her, struggling to suppress the worry she felt. Marigold already carried more of a burden than she ought. She could do without learning of this latest calamity for as long as possible. 'Just tired, I expect,' she said. 'Mr and Mrs Andrews have gone away for a few weeks to the south of France so there isn't much to do, just the children and the governess to cook for. I came home early. It won't matter, just the once.'

It would matter, she thought wearily to herself, when her pregnancy showed and she had to give up work. Each pregnancy had made her more and more exhausted, each birth had been more difficult than the last. She knew she ought not to have taken the slightest risk of ever having another child and John was as considerate as any good husband could be, not wanting to put her through such peril again. But he'd been so disheartened at not being able to do his old job, so full of self-condemnation as she and Marigold struggled to keep up the standards he'd originally acquired for them: the pleasant house in one of the better streets, with gas lighting downstairs and a tap in the scullery. Sometimes it was too hard not to take comfort from one another. She was to blame more than he was, and if she hadn't been frightened of the consequences she might even have gone to the same woman Mrs Whitehouse had tried to send her to when she'd been expecting Ivy.

'Ye're a daft bugger to let 'im put so many buns in it,' she'd said then. 'I've 'ad enough wi' our Art an' Janie. Catch me goin' through that agin! Mrs Simpkins down in Burntwood'll see ter yer, an' 'er don't charge much. Wouldn't get custom if 'er did!'

Mary had refused indignantly then, but she knew where old Mrs Simpkins lived and had heard whispers of other women who used the old crone's services. Yet despite her fears of what this new pregnancy would do to her, she was even more terrified of letting an old hag destroy a child she and her John had made with their love. Marigold needn't know yet, and with her job being less arduous for the moment she might get over the worst before the Andrewses returned and be able to keep her job for a few more precious weeks. In the meanwhile she would have to save every penny possible.

Busily contriving ways and means Mary pushed away the thoughts of her own danger. After all, her own mother had produced ten children and eight of them had survived. And both her older sisters had six children. She was being fanciful to imagine she was not so tough.

She couldn't contain her fears that night though, and wept bitterly when she told John the news. Afraid of waking the children she tried to stifle her sobs by pressing her face into his shoulder as he held her close.

'There, there, love, don't fret,' he tried to console her, at the same time berating himself bitterly for the lack of control which had put his beloved Mary into this plight.

'What can we do? When I have to give up work we won't have enough money.'

'We'll manage. Johnny will be earning more soon, and Marigold's almost fourteen. She can get a job. Between 'em they'll be bringing in almost as much as you do now. And my leg's getting better every day. I don't have to have so much time off now. I'll be getting more.'

Mary was in a strange way both comforted and dissatisfied by this answer. It was what she'd already worked out for herself, and she was thankful he didn't have any objections to it, but despite knowing deep down this was all they could do she'd hoped he might have something better to suggest.

'Don't let's tell anyone yet,' she whispered, suddenly calm, and John was thankful to feel her relax against him. Tired from a heavy day's work he soon fell asleep, not perceptive enough to realize that Mary's apparent acceptance was the coldness of despairing resignation rather than willing consent.

For a week more she struggled to preserve a façade of normality, sitting up long into the night trying to do as much embroidery as possible. Always at the back of her mind was the thought she might never be able to finish it. Every night fears about the fate of her babies if she herself died brought tears coursing down her cheeks.

It was late one evening and John had just cleared away his bath, a task he'd insisted on doing ever since he learnt of Mary's condition, when there was a sharp knock on the front door.

They were all seated round the kitchen table. Mary and Marigold were sewing; Poppy was eagerly reading an old cookery book Mrs Andrews had given Mary; John whittled away at a carving and watched Ivy drawing flowers, copying the patterns on Mary's embroidery, while Johnny drew elaborate sketches of improbable motor cars.

They looked at one another in surprise. No one ever came to the front door except Mrs Nugent or other ladies who had work for Mary, and they never came after dark. If a neighbour wanted something they came through the communal yard and knocked on the back door.

'I'll go,' John said after a moment, and took the oil lamp from the table, leaving them with just the flare of the single gas mantle and the glow of the fire.

They strained to hear voices but could distinguish only a vague murmur. Then John opened the door leading into the parlour, out of which the front door opened direct to the street, and called to Mary. 'It's Mrs Nugent, love. Wants a word with us.'

Mary rose to go out and put her hand to her back, feeling a sharp shooting pain. 'I wonder what she wants? More work, I hope, though it's odd of her to come at this time. Make a pot of tea, Marigold, and bring a slice of that fruit cake Johnny brought home yesterday. The good china cup, mind.'

'Yes, Mom.'

The kettle was always simmering on the hob, and it took only a couple of minutes to find the one tray they possessed and a cloth used only at Christmas. Marigold set out the teapot, some sugar Johnny had brought home last week, which they kept for Sundays, and the last of the milk, which had been intended for Ivy's breakfast. Then she found the china cup and saucer, so little chipped it was barely noticeable, which John had bought in the market only last June for Mary's birthday. Meanwhile Poppy carefully cut a slice of the cake and laid it on the matching plate.

'I wonder if she'll be wearing a hobble skirt?' Poppy asked eagerly. 'She's ever so fashionable, Mrs Nugent, and they look so elegant. Or perhaps she'll have a motoring coat. I saw a lovely one the other day, with a red-and-black-check lining.'

'Never mind that now. Open the door for me, Poppy, and I'll take it through,' Marigold said when she'd made sure everything was correct.

Eagerly, for she didn't often see Mrs Nugent, Poppy went towards the parlour door. She flung it open and squeezed herself against it to give Marigold room. Just at that moment Mary, who had been standing in the middle of the room, uttered a faint cry and slid senseless to the floor.

'It was a miracle the tray didn't follow her,' Mrs Nugent told her husband later. 'But Marigold seems a very sensible young girl. It was the other one who started to scream with hysterics.'

Marigold herself didn't know how she'd managed to replace the tray on the kitchen table before rushing back to her mother. By that time Mrs Nugent had taken charge, casting off her high-crowned straw hat and grey alpaca dust-coat. She directed John to carry Mary upstairs and sent Marigold ahead to turn down the bed. 'Stop that caterwauling, girl!' she ordered Poppy brusquely, 'and look after your little sister, don't let her come upstairs.' She looked at Johnny for a moment. 'You can bring up as many bricks as you have warming in the oven. Your mother looks as though she needs them.'

It was an hour before the terrified children, shooed out of the way and told to stay in the kitchen, saw their father again. Mrs Nugent appeared once and sent her uniformed chauffeur to fetch Dr Mackenzie. He came and went, shaking his head gloomily, and by the time her father and Mrs Nugent came downstairs Marigold was ready to scream with frustration and fear.

'Is she all right? Is Mom –' She couldn't complete the thought, let alone the words.

'She'll be all right now. It's time you girls were in bed. You can go in and kiss your mother goodnight if you promise not to talk to her or ask questions. Will you make sure they don't, Marigold? Johnny, go and wait in the parlour until I call you. I must talk to you later, but for the moment I have something to say to your father. You can see your mother in the morning.'

'I'm so sorry, Mr Smith. I had no idea Mary was expecting another child. Otherwise I wouldn't have spoken so abruptly about your son,' she said ruefully when Johnny, wary and reluctant, had gone into the front room and closed the door.

'We'd not intended it, ma'am, but you know how it is. I've been scared out of my wits worrying about her. She had a bad time with Ivy.'

'Well, that worry is one you can forget now. It's probably a blessing in disguise after all. But you heard Dr Mackenzie. Never again, or you'll almost certainly have a motherless family to cope with.'

'I heard, and there'll be no more risk, I promise. I love Mary, she's the best wife a man could have.'

'I knew she'd chosen well when you came courting her all those years ago at the Court. Though I was sorry to lose her, mind. She was one of the best maids we ever had. You say her present employers are away? Give me their direction and I'll make it right with them. She won't lose her job.'

'It's very good of you.'

'The least I can do. Now, about Johnny.'

John turned haggard eyes towards Mrs Nugent. She was a tall, slender woman with a sharp-featured face, but as he had reason to know her frowning expression hid a kind and compassionate heart. Her servants were the best treated in the whole of Staffordshire, and she worked tirelessly to raise money for miners' charities.

'I didn't properly take it in,' he confessed. 'You say Mr Todd suspects he's been stealing from customers?'

'For several months Mr Todd has had occasional complaints from customers that some little thing was missing. He thought it was carelessness by whoever packed the order. Has Johnny brought unusual things home?'

John sighed despondently. 'Yes, butter and tea and suchlike. Good cuts of meat, too. He said he'd paid for them with tips, got them cheap from Mr Todd. He's a liar too, and we've tried to bring them all up decent and honest. They've always been sent to Sunday School.'

'I know, and I confess it has me puzzled.'

'If he won't give you a straight answer I'll thrash him within an inch of his life.'

Mrs Nugent looked at him curiously. She wouldn't have expected Mary's husband to be a violent man, and his eyes were too gentle, even now when he was bitterly angry with his son, for her to take his threat seriously. 'I must talk to Johnny.'

Mrs Nugent looked at the boy carefully. He was tall, like John, but straighter. John's back had been bowed by years of crawling along pit passages sometimes barely high enough for a man to squeeze through. The boy's complexion was ruddy with the days he spent in the open, not pale and unhealthy like most of the men in Hednesford.

His eyes were shifty, though, sliding everywhere else in the room except at her face, as though afraid to look at her. She was quite sure he knew why she was there, and was guilty.

'Why did you steal from Mr Todd's customers?' she demanded.

'How's Mom? What's wrong with her?' He ignored her and faced his father across the table.

'Answer Mrs Nugent!' John glared at him.

'You're old enough to understand, Johnny,' Mrs Nugent said quietly. 'Your mother was carrying another child and the shock of what I told her caused her to faint, so she lost the baby.'

'Then that's my fault too,' he whispered, the words dragged painfully out of his mouth.

'Sit down, Johnny.' She marvelled that anyone could lose such a ruddy colour so suddenly and completely. 'It was inevitable, probably,' she explained gently. 'Your mother was ill and could have lost the baby at any time. Or if she'd had it she might have died herself. It could have been my fault for speaking too suddenly, or the fact that she hasn't been eating properly. I gather there is not always enough good, nourishing food?'

'That's why I did it!'

To her intense dismay the boy, for despite being as tall as a full-grown man he was still a boy, put his head on his arms and burst into noisy, racking sobs.

'Hush, Johnny, don't wake your sisters!' she urged, glancing up at the thin boards of the bedroom floor. 'That's better. Let's talk about it calmly. Is it true?'

He nodded, sniffing and wiping his sleeve across his face.

'I can understand you wanted to help out at home, but that's not the way, Johnny.'

'They all said it was my fault,' he managed to get out.

'What was?'

'Ivy, getting hurt. I wanted to make it up to her, bringing her little treats. I bought them to begin with, honest I did!'

'Why did it get to stealing?'

He cast a glance at his father, but John was looking down at his hands clasped together on the table.

'Everything went wrong,' he said in barely more than a whisper. 'Pa couldn't go back to work for ages, so Mom had to, and we had to pop – pawn almost everything we had, and the bits I brought home pleased Mom so much.'

'She wouldn't have wanted you to steal, though,' Mrs Nugent said gently.

'Mom wouldn't let me give her the tips, like I did my wages,' Johnny gabbled. 'She said I had to have a few coppers for myself so as I could go out with my mates, but I wanted to bring something nice home, and it was easy, so . . .'

'So you took more and it was too difficult to stop? Is that it?' Mrs Nugent finished for him.

He nodded miserably. 'What will Mr Todd do? Shall I be sent to gaol?'

'Do you promise me, on the Bible, never to steal again? Whatever the temptation?'

'Oh, yes. I didn't like doing it! I swear I didn't! It's not just getting caught,' he added with a pathetic attempt at recovering his dignity. 'I wanted to stop, deep down.'

'Then I think I can persuade Mr Todd not to take it any further. But you'll lose your job, Johnny. He can't be expected to keep you on.'

'Thanks, Mrs Nugent, thanks ever so!'

He burst into tears again, tears of relief and emotion released by the removal of what must have been a terrible burden of guilt on the shoulders of a normally honest, if rather immature lad. 'I'll pay him back some day, I really will!' he gasped through his sobs.

'There won't be any need for that, Johnny.'

'But I must! It'll be years, I expect, before I can earn enough to spare, but I'll go and ask for a job at the pit tomorrow and as soon as I can I'll start paying it back.'

Mrs Nugent changed the subject. 'Do you want to work at the pit?' she asked instead.

Johnny shrugged. 'What else is there? I don't know anybody at the works in Bridgetown to speak for me, and Mr Todd won't let any other shopkeeper take me on even if I wanted it.'

'You've been driving the delivery cart?'

He nodded, puzzled.

'Do you want another driving job? I might know of someone who wants a coachman.'

'Horses aren't what people'll want soon,' he replied, the first gleam of interest in something outside his own problems altering his face so that he almost smiled.

She looked at him intently. 'Do you mean we'll all have motor cars?'

'And trucks, for delivering stuff. Big ones, much bigger than even a dozen horses can pull!'

'Would you like to work with motor cars?'

The sheer bliss of such an incredible prospect took Johnny's breath away. He gaped at her, but his eyes, bright and eager, were answer enough.

'How can he do that? Begging your pardon, Mrs Nugent, but what do you mean? He can't drive a motor car,' John said.

'He could help make them. Would you like that, Johnny?'

Wordlessly he nodded.

Mrs Nugent laughed. 'Why are all men so fascinated by the internal combustion engine? My husband's the same. Then this is what we'll do. It will mean leaving Hednesford, Johnny. Do you mind that?'

'Mary won't like it,' John said doubtfully, but Johnny turned such a look of despair on him he knew he would manage to allay her fears somehow.

'John, however careful we are, if Johnny's still here the story's bound to get out. That would upset Mary far more. And it wouldn't be so far away he couldn't come back home occasionally. Besides, there are no such jobs here.'

'Then where – how can he do it?'

'They make motor cars in Coventry,' Johnny broke in eagerly. 'And Oxford, though that's further away.'

'I'll arrange it.' She turned to John, who was looking somewhat bemused. 'My brother is connected with Herbert Austin, who is making the contraptions at Longbridge, near Birmingham. He would be glad to take on an eager young fellow like Johnny. He'll arrange lodgings for him, and I can promise he'll earn enough in a short while to be able to send home something to help you here. Would you do that, Johnny?'

'I'll send every penny home – every one I don't need for paying my keep,' Johnny declared. 'Mrs Nugent, thank you, I don't know how to – or why you should help me!'

'I'm very fond of your mother, Johnny, and you've all had a lot of misfortune. Now I'd best go home or you'll never be able to sleep.'

'I won't anyway,' he said with a shy smile. Just like John in his youth, Mrs Nugent mused. It was no wonder Mary had fallen in love with such a handsome fellow.

'You needn't see Mr Todd again, but I'll come back the day after tomorrow, when I've heard from my brother, I want to see how your mother is, then we can make arrangements. It will be best if you go as soon as possible, by the end of the week.'

'I don't know how to thank you,' John said, his voice thick with emotion. 'I can see it was all my fault.'

'Nonsense! I've never known such a family for trying to take the blame for every misfortune!' she said briskly, standing and picking up her gloves. Johnny and his father hastened to stand up too, moving to open the door for her, but she hadn't finished. 'Mary says Marigold blames herself for Ivy's accident, now Johnny is trying to prove it was his fault, and both you and Mary want to claim culpability. We're none of us perfect, John, accidents happen, and we have to learn any lessons involved and then look forward. It's going to be of no use to Mary to have everyone wrapped up in their own misery. I'm sorry now I told her, but it wouldn't be any use trying to keep her in ignorance, so it's up to you both to put it all behind you and be cheerful for her sake. Do you promise?'

Standing side by side, with the same hair that obstinately refused to lie down flat, they were absurdly alike in many ways. They nodded in unison, and she smiled. Johnny wasn't by any means a hardened criminal, and they would be all right.

Chapter Three

HEARING the kitchen door open, Marigold looked up, sitting back on her heels and pushing a vagrant lock of hair behind her ear. 'Who –? Oh, what are you doing at home in the morning, Pa?' she asked anxiously. 'I thought your leg was better this week? Watch the floor, I've just scrubbed the tiles.'

John trod carefully across to a chair, tossing his cap on to the table. 'The strike,' he said wearily. 'It's on. Just when I thought things were getting easier, and perhaps your Mom could give up work. It's a strain for her, two miles there and back each day, and up these hills too.' He sighed. 'Now this, and no idea of how long it'll last. They're already talking of setting up soup kitchens to feed the little ones.'

Marigold got to her feet and sat opposite him. 'Soup kitchens? Who'll organize that?'

'All sorts of folk. Church and chapel groups, some of the gentry – they don't all despise us. Mrs Nugent will probably do something or send some money. No doubt the Salvation Army will help. I remember when General Booth came to Hednesford to lay the foundation stone of their barracks. I was lodging here, in my first job. I was fifteen at the time, 1885 it was. That was something to remember.'

'Is it him Booth Street's named after?'

'Yes, he was a great man, though I wonder sometimes if all this marching and singing hymns ever converted sinners!'

'Well, the Temperance Band won't stop people drinking, though their carol concerts in Chasetown High Street are popular enough every Christmas morning.'

'It's lively when they're about,' John agreed. 'Like the times the Territorial Army band plays.'

'Their tunes are more exciting,' Marigold said. 'It's all the excitement some of them'll ever get, playing marching tunes. Can't see them being sent to India, and the trouble in Africa's finished.'

John was silent for a while, and Marigold quietly finished scrubbing the tiled floor. She took off her sacking apron, got out her mixing bowl and flour, and began to mix bread dough. John watched, half asleep.

'I wonder if I could make bread?' he said suddenly, and Marigold looked at him in surprise.

'You?' she exclaimed. 'But baking's a woman's job.'

'Not where the bread's made for selling. I suddenly thought of that chap Foster, at Heath Hayes. He and his family run a shop, a bakery, and he bakes the bread as well as working at the pit.'

'So he's covered in white flour half the day, and coal-dust the rest?' Marigold asked. 'That could make it confusing for him!'

'I don't know how he's got the energy. But since I can't go to work I might as well do some digging. It's almost time to put the potatoes in.'

He went outside and Marigold, as she kneaded the dough, worried about this setback. She knew the colliers wanted better wages, and when she saw a newspaper they always seemed to be full of strikes by one or other group of workers. Yet she honestly couldn't see how it helped their families for men to stop work, sometimes for weeks on end. Even if they gained a shilling or so a week, how long would it take to earn the money lost while they'd been on strike?

This would mean less food, worse food, for all of them, and she began to plan yet more economical meals. Through all their troubles they'd managed to keep a pig and some hens, and there was still part of a side of bacon hanging from a hook in the scullery. The pullets were coming into lay, and though at the end of March there weren't many vegetables in the garden except cabbages, she could use bread as a basis for many filling dishes like bread pudding and savoury pudding. She had suet and many dried herbs, and there were still some onions left. Dried peas, lentils, cabbages, swedes and turnips could be made appetizing with shreds of bacon, or the occasional leftovers Mom brought home from the Andrewses'.

It was strange walking down into the town to do what little shopping was essential and see so many men loafing about the streets. Odd little huddles developed into impromptu meetings, and for the first day or so the beer houses did a roaring trade. Then it began to dawn on even the least perceptive that this wasn't just an extra holiday.

'Mrs Whitehouse says we ought to go up to the tip and get the best coal,' Poppy reported one evening.

'The place is crawling with folk picking over the rubbish,' John said. 'Carrying it home in buckets and baskets, even babies' prams. Perhaps I'd better go and get a permit tomorrow, or we'll miss our turn and all the stuff fit for burning'll be gone.'

'Do you need to?' Mary asked, worried. 'We haven't a cart or a pram, and you'd not carry much in a couple of buckets.'

'I'll help,' Marigold offered, but her father shook his head vehemently.

'I'll not have you crawling over a slag heap, luv. Anyway, it'll be something for me to do, I'll feel useful.'

The following day Poppy came home with even more exciting news.

'The colliers have been rioting at Littleton!' she announced. 'And they've brought the army to Cannock to stop them!'

It was true, they discovered. John, disbelieving the wilder rumours, came back with the news that five hundred men from the West Yorkshire Regiment had been billeted in the town. 'There doesn't seem to be any trouble, though,' he said. 'The Regimental band is playing on the bowling green every night.'

'Let's go and watch,' Ivy suggested, and Poppy bounced up and down in excitement.

'Yes, Mom, let's go! Pa, can we? Please?'

'It's two miles each way,' Mary warned, but the children promised they'd not complain, and John confessed he'd like the chance to see a real army band. So the following afternoon, which was Mary's day off, they went on the long walk to Cannock, taking with them some pies Marigold had baked and a bottle of nettle pop, one of Mary's favourite brews, to make an outing of it.

Mary put on her best white blouse and black serge skirt, with the straw hat Mrs Nugent had given her. She'd trimmed it with some blue ribbon, her favourite colour. John had on his Sunday bowler, and all the children seemed to be wearing their best pinafores.

A steady stream of people was going the same way, and Poppy soon found friends to walk with. Ivy clung to John's hand, shaking her head when Mary asked if she wanted to walk with her schoolfriends.

'They don't like me,' she declared petulantly. 'But I don't care, I don't like them either.'

In Cannock a large crowd congregated round the bowling green, and the band entertained them with a medley of both military and other music. Everyone, even a group of colliers from Littleton, where the trouble had erupted, was good humoured, and when the band played popular tunes the voices roared out in unison.

Poppy gazed awestruck at the soldiers, and later that night in bed, when Ivy was safely asleep, whispered to Marigold that she meant to marry a soldier. 'Their uniforms are so smart!' she breathed softly.

'You shouldn't be thinking of boys,' Marigold chided.

'Why not? We'll all get married one day, and I mean to marry someone smart like that nice dark man on the outside playing the drum. Did you see what a big chest he had? Fancy being married to someone like that!'

'He wouldn't wear his uniform all the time,' Marigold said warningly.

Poppy giggled. I should hope not.'

'I meant he might not be so smart without it, in other, ordinary clothes, so do stop sniggering like that! You'll wake Ivy, and then she'll cry and disturb Mom.'

Poppy suppressed her giggles, and asked in a whisper, 'Wouldn't you like to marry a soldier, Marigold?'

'No.'

'Then who would you like to marry?'

'How can I tell when I haven't met anyone? I'm not sure I want to marry anyway.'

'I shall, but he'll have to be rich. With enough money to have at least a dozen servants, so I never have to do anything I don't want to.'

'Where are you going to find someone like that in Hednesford?'

'There's other places than Hednesford,' Poppy said softly, and to Marigold's relief, for talking of boyfriends and marriage always made her feel slightly uncomfortable and awkward, her sister turned over, gave a deep sigh, and lost herself in her dreams.

'Poppy, go and pull some rhubarb. I can stew it to go with what's left of the tapioca pudding.'

'Ugh, it's too hot for tapioca. And anyway I'm writing to Johnny,' Poppy objected. It was a year later and still nothing had happened.

'You can finish that and take it to post after tea. It'll still get there in the morning. I need the table anyway. Mom and Pa'll be home from work soon, and I've still got to heat the water for his bath, and try and finish the ironing,' Marigold said briskly, hiding her impatience with difficulty.

Poppy looked mutinous, but she got up from the table and went into the garden, where a root of rhubarb flourished in the corner behind the hen-run. She sat and trimmed the sticks with no more complaint than several heaving sighs, and even helped Marigold lift the heavy kettles on to the hob, ready for John's bath.

'It's time Ivy did some of this,' she muttered as she put the knives and forks on the table. 'I was doing far more than she does when I was seven.'

'She's delicate,' Marigold automatically defended her youngest sister.

'When it suits her,' Poppy snapped. 'She's never too ill to go on Sunday School treats, or to do her everlasting drawing. Just when there's something to do she doesn't like.'

Marigold refused to be drawn into the argument Poppy was obviously hoping for. Every few weeks she would have this sort of mood, and niggle away until someone else lost their temper, after which she was back to her normal self. And that wasn't exactly peace and light, Marigold smiled to herself. Poppy lived up to her red hair, and was continually letting fly with her sharp tongue. But her rages and tempers were normally over and forgotten almost as soon as they started. Only these fits of petty fussing disturbed the pattern.

She began to think about Poppy's remarks. Ivy did seem to suffer a lot of colds, and was forever complaining of toothache or earache. She was thin and pale, but privately Marigold thought that was because she never played outside with the other children. Always she had a pencil in her hand, and the whole family scrounged any scraps of paper they could to provide her with material for her drawing.

If there was no paper she would take a piece of chalk or coal and scribble over the bricks of the outside walls. She had stopped doing it on the whitewash of the passage and the lavatory when Mary, for the only time in Ivy's life, had slapped her hands enough to hurt.

She didn't pretend, though, Marigold reassured herself. When she was ill she really did look poorly. Like today, when she'd been complaining of a sore throat. 'I wonder if she'll feel well enough to come downstairs for tea?' she said now, but at the sceptical look on Poppy's face decided she'd better not send her upstairs to Ivy.

Ivy was sitting up in the middle of the big bed, drawing on the back of the last letter Johnny had sent from Longbridge. She did feel flushed, Marigold thought as she put her hand on Ivy's forehead. 'Feeling any better?' she asked.

'Yes. I've nearly finished this drawing of Johnny,' she said, holding it out for inspection.

'That's really good.'

Marigold couldn't draw a recognizable picture of anything, but she was aware Ivy had a startling talent for one so young. The drawing of Johnny was a bit lopsided, and his head was too big, but in some strange way Ivy had reproduced the features and the untidy hair so typical of her brother accurately enough for someone who knew him well to see the resemblance.

'Do you want to come down for tea?'

Ivy nodded, and Marigold helped her pull on her clothes and plaited her hair for her. She left Ivy buttoning her boots while she went down to heave the bath from the hook outside and start filling it with the hot water.

'I've cleared the table and done the rhubarb,' Poppy said sulkily. 'What else?'

'Be a love and scrub the potatoes.'

With a huge sigh Poppy went out to the scullery. Marigold spread the sheets over the table, then went to lift one of the irons she'd put to heat on the hob.

'I want the table, I want to draw!' Ivy said from behind her, pausing on the last step before coming into the kitchen.

'Not yet. Look, go into the front room. You can draw in there, so long as it's just with a pencil, until I've finished the ironing. Only a few minutes, while Dad has his bath and I finish these sheets.'

An hour later tea was over; cold meat Mary had brought home from the Andrewses', pickle and potatoes, then the rhubarb and tapioca. Poppy and Marigold cleared away and washed up, while Mary got out her sewing and John slumped in the fireside chair, Ivy perched on his knees.

'Phew, it's hot today!' Marigold said as she came in and sat down to her own sewing.

'They do say it's the hottest day ever recorded,' John glanced across at them.

'Even hotter slaving over cooking,' Mary agreed. 'Poppy, what are you doing in there?'

'Looking for my letter to Johnny, I hadn't finished it,' Poppy's voice was muffled. There was a brief silence, then she let out an enraged yell. 'Ivy! Where's that little devil? Mom, Pa, look, she scrawled all over my letter!' She was almost crying as she emerged from the front room, the sheet of paper held out before her.

Ivy cowered into her father's arms, but Poppy, angry as she was, knew better than to approach her little sister.

'Ivy, that was naughty!' Mary sighed.

'I didn't know what it was! I can't read yet!' Ivy whined plaintively.

'It was my only piece of nice paper, and it was important! Now I can't send it!' Poppy complained.

'I've got a postcard you can have,' Marigold said swiftly. 'It's in the drawer.'

'I want a letter, not a postcard anyone can read, even if it does only cost a halfpenny.'

'Ask next time you find some paper, don't just take it,' John ordered, and Ivy, chastened, nodded before scrambling off his lap and crossing to where Poppy stood in the doorway.

'I'm sorry, Poppy,' she whispered, her big eyes filling with tears. 'I won't do it again.'

Poppy bit back the retort that Ivy always forgot promises when it was convenient for her, and took the paper Marigold produced.

'What's so secret and important?' John asked. 'Your Mom's going to write to Johnny in a day or so, you can send it then.'

'But I wanted to send it today. It's not a secret really, I just wanted to ask Johnny if there were any jobs for me.'

They all looked at her in blank astonishment.

'A job? In Longbridge?' Mary demanded.

'What sort of job?' asked Marigold.

'You can't possibly leave home, you're far too young,' John said loudly, drowning the others.

'Why can't I? I'll be getting my leaving certificate soon, and Johnny's gone. He left home. There are lots of jobs in Longbridge or Birmingham I could do.'

'Be quiet, girl! You're not going!' John thundered.

'You're far too young, Poppy, you couldn't live in lodgings like Johnny does, so it would be impossible unless you went into service,' Mary said more quietly. 'And I don't like the thought of you going to someone we don't know, so far away. Besides –'

Poppy interrupted, one of her swift rages consuming her and making her blind to the fierce look in her father's eyes. 'Service! I'm not going into service, to be a skivvy! I'm going to work in a factory where I can earn more money, like Johnny does –'

'That's enough! I've told you to be quiet! You're not going. You're staying here when you leave school to help your mom.'

Poppy swallowed, but persisted. 'But Marigold helps Mom. It doesn't need both of us, so why can't I –'

Mary sighed, and as John was about to speak again put out her hand to catch his. 'John, let me.'

He looked at her, then shrugged.

'Poppy, it was only arranged yesterday and there hasn't been a chance to tell you all yet. Mrs Nugent came last night to collect some sewing, and she's offered Marigold a job.'

'Me?' Marigold gasped.

'Yes, love. With her daughter. Pa and I've talked it over and decided you shall have the chance. You've been such a good lass all this time, never complaining.'

'But what about the house? Will you stop working for Mrs Andrews?'

'No, we can't afford that. The strike put us back just when things were looking better, though it's easier now Johnny's sending so much money home. He's a good lad.'

'I'd send a lot home too,' Polly put in, seeing a chance to retrieve the situation.

'I need you at home to take Marigold's place and look after Ivy.'

'But Mom! It's not fair! Why shouldn't I get a job? Marigold likes doing the house and things, and I wouldn't, I'd hate it!'

Mary shook her head. 'When Pa says you're too young he means you'll not be allowed to do a job, not full time. Apart from our not letting you go all that way, you couldn't earn enough in a few hours to pay for lodgings. Now be quiet, it's all decided and that's that!'

After a few moments of stunned disappointment Poppy spoke in a small voice. 'How old do I have to be?'

'Fourteen before you can work full time. Two and a half more years.'

'Do you promise I can go out and get a job then?'

'If it's possible, love. I can't promise when I don't know what's going to happen, can I? But if it's possible you can.'

'That'll be 1915,' Poppy whispered, 'ages away,' and with a gulping sob she turned and rushed up the stairs.

'Mom,' Marigold said quietly, and Mary turned back to her, sighing.

'I'm sorry, love, to tell you like that.'

'What sort of job? Does Mrs Nugent's daughter want a kitchen-maid, or a housemaid perhaps?'

'Better than that, Marigold. It seems her daughter's carrying another child. She's got two already, and wants a sensible girl to help the nanny, partly nursery-maid, partly under-nanny, and sometimes parlourmaid when they have visitors. She thought of you, love, and I was so proud when she asked me.'

'Her daughter doesn't know me!'

'Mrs Nugent recommended you. She said what a sensible, polite girl you are.'

'But can you manage without me?'

'Would you like to go? You've worked so hard since you were a little one, and never had the chance to get out of the house, it would be such an opportunity for you. I remember Miss Alice – Mrs Roberts now. She's a real nice lady. Wouldn't that be something?'

'What do you say, pet?' John asked gently. 'It's in Oxford, Mrs Roberts's husband is a Professor at the university there. It's a long way off, but you could come home by train sometimes. We could still see you.'

'Oxford! That's miles, even further than Birmingham!' Marigold exclaimed, overwhelmed.

'You wouldn't be frightened, that far away, alone?' Mary asked quickly. She hadn't wanted to send her beloved daughter so far, but it was a much better job than she could hope for in Hednesford. The money would be useful, and Marigold would have more chances to improve herself in a big city.

'No–o' Marigold hesitated.

'We'd never make you go.'

'I'd be all right. But what about Poppy? She doesn't like doing the house, only cooking. Would Mrs Roberts take her?'

'Poppy's too young, as I said, and Mrs Nugent didn't offer her the job. Besides, it's time you had a chance to do something else. Now. Mrs Nugent's coming tomorrow, so shall I say you'll go as soon as her daughter wants you?'

Marigold paused, propping a corner of the heavy tray on the newel post and easing her back. She'd never have believed how tiring it was carrying heavy metal trays up two flights of stairs.

'I thought I was used to lifting heavy buckets of water here at home,' she'd said on her first free weekend as she and Mary walked home from St Peter's.

'It isn't too much for you, is it?' Mary asked anxiously.

Marigold laughed. 'No, Mom, of course not. It's just different. At least I don't have to carry up coal, Ethel does that, and all the housework, and though she's smaller than me she's as strong as a horse. I'm not used to all those stairs.'

There were ten at home, narrow and steep, and they only used the bedrooms for sleeping and when someone was ill. Even then they rarely had fires in the tiny grates so it wasn't a constant climb up and down, fetching and carrying, all day long. At Gordon Villa there were sixteen steps in the first flight, then another ten to the half landing and four more to the top floor. But she was getting used to them, she told herself firmly. She didn't notice the ache in the back of her legs until quite a way through the day now. And after the inevitable first week or so of severe homesickness she had settled in. Everything – apart from the stairs – was unbelievable bliss.

'Fifteen pounds a year and one Saturday and Sunday a month free, Marigold,' Mrs Nugent had explained when she told Marigold about the work she would be expected to do for Mrs Roberts. 'You'll be able to come home by train. And you can have Wednesday afternoons too, from three o'clock, after the children have had their dinner. You will help Miss Baker with the children and be under her direction. Do you understand?'

'Yes, Mrs Nugent, ma'am,' Marigold said, her voice hoarse with nervousness.

'I have some suitable dresses I can give you, and caps and aprons, so there is no need for you to make any, Mary,' Mrs Nugent said briskly. 'I'll send them to Oxford to be ready for Marigold.'

It was only when she'd seen these that Marigold appreciated what a strain it would have been if her mother had been obliged to buy the material for so many garments as well as underwear.

'Three of everything, you'll need,' Mary said briskly, 'and the best quality I can afford.'

'Mom, it's threepence three farthings a yard,' Marigold gasped.

They were in Mr Holland's draper's shop in Market Street, and Mary didn't reply. She was busy working out how many yards she would need for vests, camisoles, drawers, bust bodices and petticoats, as well as nightgowns.

'And six pairs of black cotton stockings. You can buy woollen ones with your first quarter's wages,' she added to Marigold as the assistant turned from the counter to reach for the box on a high shelf behind her.

They had so much to do Marigold didn't have time to think until she was on the train. It seemed an endless journey, for Marigold had never before been further than Lichfield. Pa had taken her to Birmingham on one train, and they'd walked across the city from New Street to Snow Hill Station where he'd seen her safely on the train for Oxford. She had been too bemused to take in much of Birmingham, for the buildings were immense and the main streets so wide. But John made sure she'd know her way back for her free weekends.

At Oxford she was limp with relief when an elderly coachman appeared and said he'd come to meet her. As they drove along the Woodstock Road Marigold gazed about her in awe. She'd never seen such big houses, so many close together. Gordon Villa was larger than most, set back in its own big garden. It had stables and a coach-house behind, with rooms above where Jim Dangerfield, the coachman, and his wife, who was Mrs Roberts's cook, lived.

Inside the house Mrs Roberts welcomed her warmly. She was a small, slightly faded woman, pale faced and thin, but her smile was kind.

'I know you'll be a good worker, Marigold, if my mother says so. I hope you'll be happy with us.'

Marigold was shown to the room next to the night nursery by the other maid, Ethel, who shared it with her. There were two narrow iron bedsteads, a marble washstand, and a small mahogany chest of drawers the girls were to share. There was no wardrobe, but the alcove beside the fire had been curtained off and the dresses Mrs Nugent had given her already hung there.

There were three heavy cotton dresses, in dark green rather than the more usual black. For winter there were two more made of wool, and on the chest was a pile of aprons and pretty frilled mob caps. The dresses were rather loose and shorter than Marigold thought seemly, but she could alter them to fit and was grateful to have them. She now had more dresses than she'd ever had before.

The work, though strange at first, was neither difficult nor harder than she'd been used to. She soon grew to love the children, Master Peter and Miss Eleanor, and when she wasn't fetching food or hot water for them, cleaning the nurseries or washing and ironing their clothes, she sat in the day nursery happily mending their clothes or sewing new ones. It was a palace, beautifully furnished and decorated, and she always enjoyed being there.

'I've never seen such pretty wallpaper,' she said to Miss Baker one evening after the children were in bed. 'We had some in the parlour at home, but it was dark brown and red. This is lovely, with the flowers, and all different colours.'

Although Miss Baker was not exactly old, she was several years older than Mary. Her conversation was sometimes about her much younger brother and sister, but mainly about the children she had nursed and their parents. After a few weeks Marigold sometimes felt Miss Baker knew more about these children than she did about her own family.

'It's too cold to play outside, Ivy!' Poppy's voice was tense with exasperation. The strain of keeping a hold on her temper got worse, yet she dare not give way to her feelings of fury and frustration.

'The sun's shining, and it's only October, and Mom didn't say I wasn't to play outside,' Ivy retorted, fastening the buttons on the thick coat Mary had made for her last birthday from her own old one.

'There's all the ironing to do, as well as potatoes to peel and Pa's bathwater to get ready,' Poppy told her sharply. 'You're old enough to help with some of it.'

'But I don't like ironing, I might burn myself again,' Ivy said with a sniff, smoothing down her gleaming black hair so that it hid the scar on her temple. She wound the thick scarf which had been Mary's birthday present to Poppy round her neck.

'You could do the potatoes.'

'My hands get chapped, and I'm not big enough to lift the kettles, so there's nothing I can do. Besides, Lizzie's waiting for me.'

'That's my scarf, you're not to take that,' Poppy said conceding partial defeat.

'But I lost mine the other day, and you know Mom said I mustn't catch another cold. Please, Poppy, I'll be ever so careful, I won't lose it. Please?'

'Oh, get out, but mind you're back by teatime.'

Ivy, a beaming smile on her face, danced across the kitchen and bestowed a wet, smacking kiss on Poppy's cheek. 'You are nice, Poppy. Lizzie's brother says you're the prettiest girl in the street, even if you have got carroty hair and freckles,' she threw back over her shoulder as she ran out of the door, forgetting as usual to pull it to behind her.

Poppy's face flamed, and she held her hands up to cool her cheeks as she went to close the door. Lizzie Bannister had two brothers, twelve-year-old Billy and fifteen-year-old Sam, but she didn't think Billy, who had been in her class at school, would have said that. He'd never paid a moment's attention to her.

The smell of scorching sheets sent her racing back to the ironing. To her relief the burn was slight, and on the edge of the sheet where it would not matter. But the image of Sam Bannister's tall, rather gangling figure, and his thin wrists sticking out of sleeves which always seemed too short for him, remained with her long after the rest of the family came home.

'Am I pretty?' she demanded of Marigold the following Sunday, when they were in the scullery washing up after dinner.

Marigold laughed. 'Are you getting vain, Poppy?'

Poppy scowled. 'How can anyone know if they're pretty or not unless someone says?'

'Well, you're thinner than I am, and I suppose you might grow up to be tall and willowy, and if you like red hair . . . oh, all right, Poppy, you are pretty. But who's been saying you are?'

'Ivy.'

'Ivy?' Marigold almost dropped a plate in surprise. 'Why should Ivy say you're pretty? Does she want to draw a picture of you?'

Poppy shook her head. 'Well, it wasn't really Ivy,' she confessed. 'She told me, you see. She said Lizzie Bannister's brother said so.'

'Is she friends with Lizzie?'

'She's always out playing with her instead of helping me,' Poppy said resentfully.

'I don't know Lizzie very well, but Sam was in my class. Is it Sam thinks you're pretty?'

'I don't know,' Poppy said sharply. 'Marigold, I don't like Lizzie, she always seems so sly when she comes to call Ivy out to play. They've all got narrow, slitty eyes. I don't care what Sam says. And Billy was a dunce, always at the bottom of the class.'

'Who else does she play with?'

'A whole lot of them from round the corner. They don't often play in our yard, so I'm not sure.'

'She's changed, then. When I was at home she'd never go out. I thought her cheeks were rosier.'

'But she shouldn't leave all the work to me.'

'She's only little.'

Poppy snorted. 'I did far more when I was her age. It's not fair.'

Marigold sighed. Poppy always felt the world was against her, and railed impotently against cruel fate. 'Nothing's fair, Poppy. Have you talked to Mom?'

'She says the same as you. Ivy's the youngest, and delicate. And Pa always takes her part. She's a spoilt little brat!'

'I suppose we should be glad she's made some friends.'

Poppy subsided. There was nothing Marigold could do, coming home just for one night. She'd had her say and, as so often with Poppy, once she'd got a grievance off her chest she cheered up.

At first, though she'd been disappointed over the collapse of her plan to go to Birmingham, she had secretly enjoyed being in charge of the house. She imagined it was hers, and that instead of her parents and Ivy she had a tall, handsome husband for whom she laboured to make the house attractive. Of course her husband would not work at the pit, and the house would be far larger than it really was. She still had dreams of marrying a soldier, but he'd have to be an officer, not just a private.

By the use of a little ingenuity, and a slight rearrangement of the chairs, she could pretend the front parlour was really several rooms. In her few free moments she strolled negligently between the drawing room by the window, to the morning room just inside the door. A smoking room, study, billiard room and library, the preserves of her shadowy husband, took up very little space since she rarely went there except to tell him dinner was ready. The dining room, housekeeper's room, servants' hall and kitchens occupied the kitchen, while the scullery housed everything else, changing every time Marigold came home and she gleaned more information about life as lived by the gentry.

Marigold may have wondered at the avidity with which Poppy demanded exact details of the arrangements of the rooms at Gordon Villa but she knew nothing of Poppy's secret dreams.

As time passed and the novelty of being in charge vanished, Poppy again grew discontented. She hadn't realized how much there was to do, and Ivy did little to help except when her parents were at home.

Poppy missed school, something she'd never thought she would. It had been her ambition to leave as soon as possible, and for that she'd worked hard to pass her leaving certificate. But then she'd anticipated having a job as her friends did, never expecting to become the drudge she now regarded herself.

She had a little pocket money but it wasn't enough to pay for the clothes she wanted, and without them she felt ashamed before her erstwhile friends. She wanted brightly coloured clothes instead of the drab grey ones Mom insisted on, saying they didn't show the dirt.

'I can't go out with them in this shabby old thing,' she'd complained to Marigold one Sunday. 'I'd love a button-through skirt and a bolero coatee in pale green like that one I saw in *The Lady* magazine Mrs Andrews gave Mom.'

'Things will get better soon,' Marigold consoled her. 'Without Johnny and me they don't need so much money.'

'It was difficult during the pit strike, and Mom had to pay for all your underclothes. They still owe money.'

'I'll be able to pay Mom back some more when I get my next quarter's wages, and Pa is much better now.'

'He still gets his headaches though, and then he can't go to work,' Poppy put in. 'He just lies in bed all day, not speaking to anyone, even Mom.'

'Mom didn't say! Is he bad, Poppy?'

'I don't know. Mom says he'll get better soon.'

Marigold thrust this new anxiety from her mind. Mom would tell her if Pa really was worse. It was probably just Poppy feeling hard done by. 'Johnny still sends quite a bit home. Perhaps Mom can afford to stop work in a few months, then you could go and get a job. What would you like to do? Work in a shop?'

The trouble was, Poppy didn't know. She enjoyed cooking but

hated the thought of domestic service. It didn't seem to her much better to slave away for long hours in a shop, being polite to overbearing customers. Nebulous dreams of glamour and comfort such as she'd never known hovered at the edge of her consciousness, but she knew better than to breathe a word of this to Marigold, who'd have told her sharply not to be a fool.

'When I get the chance'll be the time to think of that.'

Marigold had little time for brooding over her sisters. It was almost Christmas and Mrs Roberts was planning several dinner parties for her husband's colleagues during the university vacation. She would be expected to help in the dining room, and was nervous of not knowing what to do.

'Don't worry,' Jim Dangerfield said comfortably. 'If I can pretend to be a butler you can act parlourmaid.'

In the nursery there was an air of excitement. Marigold was busy sewing new velvet dresses for little Eleanor, one in red and one in green.

'I had lots of presents last Christmas,' Eleanor said importantly to her brother. 'You were too little, but I 'spect you'll be able to see the Christmas tree this year.'

'Saw it.'

'No you didn't, you were too little. It had candles on it.'

'Want Cissmas tree,' Peter insisted, and his face puckered threateningly. Marigold hastened to distract him.

'Shall we get ready? It's time for our walk. Let's go down and feed the ducks on the river.'

He brightened instantly. He adored all animals, and to reach the ducks they had to pass a field where some ponies always stood looking over the gate.

Marigold, used only to the plodding carthorses pulling the delivery carts in Hednesford, and the racehorses from Mr Coulthwaite's training stables at Rawnsley, which they had sometimes seen exercising on Hednesford Hills, had found herself, surprisingly, unafraid of the ponies. She enjoyed stroking their rough coats, and the feel of their lips, soft and questing, against her hand as she fed them.

'When can I ride?' Peter demanded as they stroked the ponies.

'I don't know. When your father says you may, I suppose,' Marigold replied.

'I want to ride too!' Eleanor began to jump up and down. Marigold snatched her away from the ponies which had started back in alarm.

'You'll have to learn not to frighten them first,' she said sternly, and Eleanor began to howl.

'I want my papa! He'd let me ride! Where's my papa? I want to go home! I hate you, and I hate ponies!'

Luckily Eleanor's tantrums were speedily over, and by the time Marigold had walked the children to the river and back the little girl had forgotten the incident, and was eagerly planning which of her new dresses she wanted to wear on Christmas Day.

Before then, however, Marigold had to face the first dinner party at Gordon Villa. It was customary for Professor Roberts to invite some of his final-year students at the end of each term, and there were to be five of them at the first such party, along with five young daughters of neighbours and fellow academics.

Mrs Roberts gave her instructions on how to lay the table during the morning. Marigold and Ethel spread the newly washed and ironed damask cloth on the long mahogany table, and set out the cutlery and glasses. Marigold had never seen such a quantity of silverware and crystal, and wondered how anyone could ever afford so much.

'Lucky the Professor's got his own fortune,' Jim explained when she said it to him. 'He'd not be able to live in this style if all he had was his university salary. Now, this is how you serve the vegetables. Show me.'

Though she was nervous, all went well until she was handing round a second helping of roast beef. As she offered the platter to one of the young men the girl beside him turned sharply and her shoulder caught the platter. Marigold gasped and clutched it in desperation, but if the young man had not reacted extremely fast the meat would have landed in his lap.

He seized the other side of the platter, and as Marigold fought to hold it steady his hand closed over hers.

'Oh, I'm sorry!' she gasped. She closed her eyes briefly in relief, then cast an anxious glance towards Mrs Roberts.

'No harm done,' the young man said quietly. 'No one's noticed, they're all talking too much.'

It wasn't quite true. The young man opposite, tall and thin with narrow blue eyes and a languid air, was watching with a faint smile on his lips. Marigold looked away, again discomfited.

Her hand was suddenly released, and Marigold stepped back, weak with a sudden trembling that attacked her legs. Jim, who had seen the incident, came across and took the platter from her. 'Go and see if there's more gravy,' he said quietly and, as she escaped, bent to proffer the meat once more. Marigold, her face already flushed at the near accident, blushed even more when she realized she had been about to deprive her saviour of his second helping, and turned to flee.

Later she handed round cups of tea in the drawing room. Her rescuer gave her a fleeting smile and winked at her before turning to the girl beside him to reply to some question.

Marigold watched him unobtrusively. He was tall, with dark brown hair which flopped in unruly locks over his forehead. His eyes, so dark as to appear black, were deep set in a bronzed face, which was unusual in the students she had seen about the town. Normally they looked pale. His mouth was wide and seemed always to be smiling in amusement or approval. He had strong bones, and long, tapering fingers. As she recalled the feel of those fingers over hers, Marigold reddened and turned hurriedly away. When it was time for her to leave the drawing room she escaped gladly. She was uncomfortable in the presence of such lively young men and beautiful girls.

She had her supper in the kitchen with Ethel and the Dangerfields. Normally she and Miss Baker ate upstairs, with the children or, in the evenings, together, but with this evening's duties it seemed silly to carry a tray up to the empty nursery. Miss Baker had eaten long ago and would be engrossed in the book she was reading.

Afterwards, Jim's words of praise for her help ringing pleasantly in her ears, she left the kitchen to go to bed.

'Put this jug of water in the master's study on your way up,' Mrs Dangerfield asked as she said goodnight. 'He always feels thirsty after a party.'

Marigold took the jug, found the study glowing with a bright fire, and by its light set the jug of water on a small table near the window. She turned to go, and found her way blocked.

'Aha, the pretty little maid!' a rather slurred male voice said. 'How about a kiss for me?'

He was standing in the doorway and she could not get past. She shook her head, wordlessly. From his rather tall, slender silhouette she thought he was the man who had watched her near disaster in the dining room.

'Please let me pass, sir,' she said quietly.

'Not without a forfeit. Come, what harm will a kiss do? It's Christmas, time of goodwill to all. Show your goodwill to me.'

'I'd rather you showed yours to me by allowing me to pass,' Marigold retorted, suddenly bold, angry at being placed in such a ludicrous situation.

'Spirited! I like that!'

He moved forward and Marigold, suddenly afraid, stepped hurriedly backwards. It was a mistake, for as he came further into the room he pushed the door to behind him.

'No!' Marigold raised her voice, and to her immense relief the door opened again. The newcomer felt for the switch and snapped on the electric light. Once more Marigold was looking into the eyes of her former rescuer.

'Edwin, it's time to go. Your uncle is saying farewell to the others.'

The other man looked round and gave a rueful grin. 'You always were a damned spoilsport, Richard. I suppose you're preparing the way for yourself. Some people have more luck than they deserve. Come on, then.'

Without a word he turned and pushed past the other. Marigold waited until they were inside the drawing room and then ran hastily up the stairs. The encounter had shaken her, and all night she dreamed of a tall dark man with smiling eyes who seemed fated to save her from embarrassment.

During the next few days she had little enough time to think about it, for Miss Baker succumbed to a heavy cold and had to remain in her bed. With the extra work that gave her it was an effort, once the children were in bed, to drag out her sewing and finish the dress she was making for Ivy. But it was finished two days before Christmas, and when Miss Baker, recovered, sent her off for a rest on Christmas Eve, she was able to finish the other dress she had made for Poppy with some material Mrs Roberts had given her. Both would be ready to take home on her first weekend off after Christmas.

'Two more guests for Christmas,' Mrs Dangerfield announced the following morning. 'It usually happens. Professor Roberts discovers some of his students haven't been able to go home, and asks them here for a few days. At least it's not that sneaky nephew of his, that Edwin Silverman. Him I can't abide.'

'Nephew? You mean the man who was here the other night?'

'Yes, that's him. One of the guests he's asked was here too, but I forget his name, or why he's not going home. The master said something about America, but I don't think he's American. The other's German, I'm sure of that.'

Knowing by now how easily Mrs Dangerfield became muddled with names, Marigold decided to wait and see. She fervently hoped Cook was right about Edwin, who must have been the man who tried to kiss her. And however firmly she tried to push away the thought, a portion of her mind kept wondering whether the expected guest could possibly be the other man, Richard.

Chapter Four

JOHNNY sighed contentedly. 'No one cooks like you do, Mom.'

Mary smiled at him. 'You look well fed.'

He had grown several inches in height and filled out a great deal during the time he'd been away. Instead of the lanky boy who'd left Hednesford in disgrace, her son was a burly man, bigger than his father but not, she decided, quite as handsome. He was full of confidence, too, though rather bashful about his new trilby and spotted four-in-hand tie.

'Mr Barlow, my foreman, gives me all the tricky jobs,' he'd explained during Christmas dinner. 'And I've got two lads under me, learning. When Mr Fortescue moves out to the new place he's promised to put me in charge of one of the shops, and next year he'll send me to night school.'

'What do you want with more book learning?' John asked.

'Shops? Are you selling cars?' Ivy interrupted.

'It's a workshop, silly, not a shop like Mr Todd's,' Poppy informed her with a superior air. Ivy got away with too much, and it wasn't often she had a chance to put her down and show Mom and Pa what a pain she was.

'It's not book learning. At least, I s'pose there will be books, but it's drawing mostly, so's I'll be able to design the engines, fit all the bits together properly, take up less space, things like that.'

'Remember when you wanted to go to night school to learn drawing here?' Mary asked with a reminiscent smile.

Things were getting better, despite John's headaches which sometimes made it impossible for him to go to work. Johnny was earning almost as much as John did, and still only seventeen. Marigold was doing well, from what Mrs Nugent told her, and perhaps when Poppy was old enough to go out to work full time she'd be able to give up her own job and stay at home.

The thought of Marigold made her sigh. It was the first Christmas they hadn't all been together. But at least Johnny had been able to stay two nights, and didn't have to get the train back till after tea on Boxing Day.

'It was good of you to bring the goose,' she said now. 'We've never had one at home. It leaves the cold beef for tea, with my chutney.'

Johnny groaned, then laughed. 'I doubt I'll be able to eat another thing till New Year.'

'Tell me about your landlady. Does she feed you well?'

'Mrs Kelly? She's fine, plenty of food, but not so good as yours.'

'You're fishing for compliments, Mary,' John said with a chuckle. 'My mom was the same when I first came to Hednesford and moved into digs. And remember how you always spent the whole day cooking before she came to see us? Scared she'd think you weren't feeding me proper.'

'It was different, her living Brockton way and only coming here occasionally,' Mary defended herself. 'Not like most folks, having their families round the corner.'

'Is your landlady Irish?' Poppy put in.

'No, her husband was, or at least his pa was. He came over here when he was a nipper, sixty or seventy years back.'

'They're not Romans, are they?' John said suddenly.

'No, chapel folk. You needn't worry, Pa, I'm not being turned into a Papist.'

'Have you got a girl, Johnny?' Ivy considered she'd been left out of the conversation long enough.

'That's enough, Ivy. You can come and help me wash up. Poppy, you put the leftover potatoes away in the pantry. Stir yourselves, now.'

Mary had seen the dull flush creeping up Johnny's neck at Ivy's question, and acted instinctively to give him an excuse not to answer. Afterwards, when he'd gone back to Longbridge and the girls were in bed, she sat with her sewing beside the fire and wondered whether she'd done so to protect him or herself most. The thought of her firstborn, her only son, with a girl was curiously painful. She chided herself. It was only natural, and as he lived away from home she ought to be glad he had someone. But he was still so young. And she didn't know the girl, as she would have done if it had been someone local.

She rubbed her eyes. They were often sore now when she was doing fine sewing and had to squint to see properly. Not knowing the girl was the main reason for her concern. A strong, handsome lad earning good money would be a good catch.

'I hope Johnny doesn't want to get wed too soon,' she said suddenly, and John, who had been dozing in the other chair, his pipe gone out, yawned and looked across at her.

'Lad's got more sense than to wed until he finds someone as good as his mom. It'll be Poppy wanting to get spliced first, mark my words.'

'Poppy? But she's not twelve for another month!'

'And going to be the beauty of the family, when she takes that sulky look off her face.'

'Is she? With her freckles? I'd have thought Marigold was prettier.'

'And has a sweeter nature, but Poppy's face is rounder, softer. And I'll bet she's going to be plumper too, when she's a bit older. Haven't you noticed some of the lads hanging round lately, on the watch for her when she goes to the shops? That Sam Bannister and some of his crowd?'

'Sam Bannister? He's years older than Poppy!'

'Only a couple. And he's got a good job, working for the apothecary.'

'What should I do?' Mary asked worriedly.

'Nothing. She'll come to no harm, and a bit of admiration might make her feel better. It's hard on her, being tied to the house. If only –'

Swiftly Mary put down her sewing and crossed to him. She stood behind his chair and cradled his head against her breasts. 'Stop it, John. Stop blaming yourself. It was an accident, no one could help it. And I'd rather have you safe at the pithead than down there in those tunnels, liable to be crushed by falls of rock, any day.'

'Not much longer, eh? As soon as Poppy's fourteen she can get a job and you can give up yours.'

'Perhaps. But it's work tomorrow for both of us, so go on up while I bank up the fire.'

Mary let him hope. She'd done the calculations endlessly, but she knew they couldn't manage, and stay in this good house, without her wages. It was pointless saying so, however.

As she bustled round tidying up the kitchen, heaping slack on the fire and pulling the pegged rug back so that a stray spark shouldn't set it alight, she began to worry about Poppy. She made sure the doors were locked and bolted, lit her candle, and turned down the gas light. Sometimes Poppy was reckless, rebellious, but surely she wouldn't –

Mary suppressed the thought, it was too horrible. They'd brought the children up properly, she and John, sending them to Sunday School, making them read the Bible. That hadn't saved Johnny from becoming a thief, a small inner voice reminded her.

But he'd repented, he'd changed, he was a son to be truly proud of, doing well in a good job with real prospects. It had just been the circumstances; his guilt over Ivy's accident that had led him astray. He'd made a mistake, that was all.

A girl need only make one mistake and her life was ruined. She'd have to talk to Poppy soon, warn her. All her pleasure in Christmas and seeing Johnny was spoilt, and Mary tossed restlessly all night.

Mrs Dangerfield breathed a sigh of satisfaction when the servants sat down to their own dinner on Christmas Day. Jim and Ethel had waited on the family, so Marigold had not yet seen the visitors. While Miss Baker took the children for a walk after their family dinner, Marigold ate in the kitchen.

She looked and wondered at the lavish display. There was enough food here to feed her family for a week, and a greater variety than she had ever before seen.

Afterwards, feeling in need of exercise to keep herself awake, Marigold decided to walk towards the Cherwell, hoping to meet the children as they returned.

Richard Endersby, also needing exercise, had left the house an hour earlier. The winter dusk was falling as he strolled back towards the house. He caught sight of Marigold first and slipped swiftly behind a convenient tree. He needed a few moments to analyse the strange emotions which assailed him.

With her bright golden hair for once unbound and spread in rippling waves over her shoulders, her cheeks flushed with the cold, and her blue eyes shining, she seemed to grow with a vitality and strength he instinctively recognized and was drawn to. Yet she was enticingly different from the girl who had made such an impression on him at the dinner party. He was still bewildered at the surge of fury he had felt when he discovered Edwin with her that night.

It was the loose hair, he thought in some confusion, which changed her completely from a demure maiden into an enchanting girl. He longed to feel the silken locks brush his hands, his cheeks, his bare shoulders and chest.

At the dinner party he'd felt a spark of interest, known a faint urge to discover what she was like beneath her neat, starched uniform. Then the way she'd bitten her lip and the vulnerable look in her wide eyes as the meat dish had almost been knocked from her grasp had caused a wave of protectiveness to sweep over him. Now both urges, to know and defend her, intensified. He had no understanding of why he was so moved – only that it was a significant moment in his life.

As Marigold approached Richard stepped out on to the path. 'Good afternoon.'

She swung round and looked up into dark, smiling eyes. His sudden appearance sent a series of shivering shocks through her body. Her mouth dry, her breath caught somewhere behind her ribs, her hands suddenly clammy, she stood transfixed, a golden butterfly impaled on a silver pin.

'I was hoping to meet the children. Have you seen them?' she asked breathlessly.

'No, but I heard Miss Baker say she was taking them the other way this afternoon. I believe she thought it was too damp by the river. It's getting dark, you shouldn't go down there alone. May I walk back with you?'

She found she couldn't speak as they turned and slowly retraced their steps.

'I know you're called Marigold. Very appropriate with your glorious hair,' he said softly. 'I'm Richard Endersby. Professor Roberts is my tutor. He asked me to stay for Christmas because my parents are in America for a couple of months. Was that fate?'

Bemused, Marigold shook her head. 'I don't know what you mean,' she confessed.

Richard laughed. 'Never mind. Explanations are always tedious. You work for Mrs Roberts? With her children? Surely you're too young to be a nanny?'

'I'm helping Miss Baker, a sort of under-nanny,' Marigold said.

'Do you enjoy it? My brother's just a few years younger than I am, and I can remember only a dragon of a nanny before we had a governess. I don't think I've met one before.'

'I doubt if there are many at your college!'

He grinned. 'Unfortunately, if they're all as pretty as you. Does your family live in Oxford?'

'I live in Hednesford. It's a small town in Staffordshire.'

'I know it! I live in North Staffordshire near Stoke-on-Trent, and my father keeps some horses at Rawnsley.'

'With Mr Coulthwaite?'

'Yes. How did you come to have a job so far away?'

'Mom used to work for Mrs Nugent, she's Mrs Roberts's mother, and she spoke for me when Mrs Roberts wanted a maid,' Marigold explained breathlessly. 'It's better than anything I ever dreamed of doing!'

'I wouldn't have thought young Eleanor and Peter were easy to manage.'

'They're children! She can be a little devil at times – Oh, I shouldn't have said that!'

'Don't worry, I won't peach. Have you younger brothers and sisters?'

Gradually Marigold relaxed, and began to talk eagerly of her family.

It was dark, and they had strolled almost into the centre of Oxford before she recalled the time. Then she came back to earth. 'They'll be looking for me!' she said, dismayed.

'Why?'

The simple question make her pause. Then she flushed, slowly but completely, as she thought of the comments Ethel would make if she knew she'd been walking all this time with one of the gentry, a guest at the house.

'Marigold, you're not doing anything wrong,' he reassured her gently. 'We're both on our own, away from our families at Christmas. Can't we talk to each other for a while?'

She bit her lip. How could she explain?

'Come on then, we'll go back.'

As they turned into the gate she smiled quickly, and with a swift shy farewell vanished round the corner of the house towards the kitchen door.

Richard, suddenly deserted, found he did not wish to rejoin his hosts just yet. It was an icy, starlit night, bright enough to see the garden. He decided to walk some more. He was bemused, and at an unaccustomed loss.

He recalled once more his first glimpse of Marigold when she had been serving dinner. Her classical beauty, the pale clear skin, bright eyes, and upright slender young figure, had struck him as unusual for a servant. Her low voice, which was musical and had very little accent, despite her nervousness at the near accident, had enhanced his interest. Surely she came from a better class than most servants. And then, after he'd rescued her from Edwin's attentions, he'd been unable to forget her shy smile.

Again, as he strolled around the lawn, he was shaken by the urge to sweep her up and carry her away from harm. He smiled as the odd thought came to him. He'd never before felt the slightest need to protect any woman. Rather he had schemed to detach himself from overbearing, persistent females who tried to order his life. That was precisely what had brought him to Gordon Villa now, visiting his tutor's family.

It was a strange sequence of chance events, going back almost a year. As a student of foreign languages, he'd elected to spend a year at German universities. After a term at Munich he'd moved to Bonn, and from there obeyed a summons in February to visit his mother at Baden Baden.

That had been a mistake. Slender, arrogantly beautiful, from one of the old New England families, Sophia Endersby was totally assured and accustomed to dominating her husband and sons. She took kindly neither to illness nor to opposition. 'I can't abide people who are always ailing,' she said over lunch. 'That's why I came here, to put myself right as quickly as possible. Fortunately another week should be enough and then I can go home.'

'I'm pleased to see you almost back to normal,' Richard commented. 'I'd have come sooner if I'd known you were here.'

'I didn't want to worry you. But now you are here you can accompany me to a small soirée tonight. I've met a most delightful family, from Boston. My sister's mother-in-law was some sort of cousin, and the Kentons are related to the Winthrops in some way. Very eligible.'

'Mother, I'm sorry, but I must catch the train back this afternoon. I have an important lecture first thing tomorrow.'

'Richard! How inconsiderate! I depended on you to escort me. I can manage without your father – he seems to imagine the business will collapse if he spends a few weeks away from it – but it would be nice to have an escort for once! It was hardly worth your coming if you meant to rush off again immediately.'

'I'm sorry. If I'd known earlier you were here I could have managed a few days last week, but tonight is impossible.'

'Why couldn't you have gone to somewhere more acceptable, like Heidelberg?' Sophia asked fretfully. 'Bonn is unheard of, so what good will it do you?'

'They have teachers I want to study with.'

'It's very perverse of you. I know everyone goes to Oxford, but you don't have to take it seriously! You already speak the language like a native. If you must come to some Godforsaken country like Germany you might go to the best places instead of jumped up workmen's institutes!'

He forbore pointing out the credentials of his chosen universities, instead asking her how she occupied her time away from home.

'It's abominably tedious, made bearable only by interesting company. Luckily there are several American families, good families, here. Like the Kentons. Their girl is so charming, I'd hoped you could meet her. A lot of money, I believe. Never mind, they're touring Europe and have promised to spend a few days with us at The Place as soon as your term ends, before they sail to New York.'

It was the threat of being thrust into the company of an eligible American heiress, however charming, that made Richard accept Edwin Silverman's invitation to visit his home in July. Edwin had also been at Bonn, although they had not previously met in Oxford.

'It's undiluted feminine company, I'm afraid,' Edwin warned him when issuing the invitation. 'I'm blessed with four younger sisters, though none of them are out yet.'

Richard harboured a faint suspicion Edwin might want him to squire one of these sisters, but on discovering the eldest was barely sixteen he'd jumped at the opportunity of evading the Kentons's visit to The Place.

His mother was not pleased, but could do nothing about it. Richard had begun to feel it was time he showed some independence. For too long, perhaps, he and his brother Henry had gone along with the opinionated Sophia, as their father did, on unimportant matters. It was easier than sustaining the barrage of argument she employed if anyone contradicted her. But he knew that if he was to live his own life he needed to make a stand.

In fact Sophia accepted his absence with astonishing calm. It wasn't until September he understood why. Then she tried to insist he absented himself from Oxford for three months in order to accompany her and his father on a visit to America.

'Your father means to export there, and is going largely on business. It would be very useful for you to be with him.'

It had been a battle royal, with Sophia inadvertently disclosing they had been invited to stay with the Kentons at Christmas.

'I am not taking time away from Oxford.'

'But you did to go to Germany!'

Knowing it was pointless to argue, Richard allowed the storm to rage round him. To all pleas and threats he maintained a straight refusal. Eventually Sophia acknowledged that her elder son had inherited some of her own spirit and determination. After she gave in the atmosphere at home during the final week of his summer vacation had been surprisingly pleasant and uncontroversial. He had wondered what else she was planning, but back at Oxford soon shrugged off his concerns. She could not force him to marry her heiress, after all.

He'd intended to spend Christmas with an older cousin, Archie Cranworth, and his wife Lexie, in Birmingham. Then in November Lexie lost the child she was expecting, and was very ill. Archie took her off to the south of France for a few weeks, leaving Richard to face a lonely Christmas. Professor Roberts had rescued him.

'Come to us. I'm inviting a chap from Berlin, too. Actually he's an army officer, bit older than you, but a nice chap. You'll be company for one another, have something in common.'

And so he was at Gordon Villa, unable to keep his thoughts from a young, a very young, girl. Eligible American heiresses, buxom German Fraüleins, the girls he met at Oxford garden parties, and the shadier women who occupied other milieux: none made him feel as Marigold, so young and innocent, a mere servant, did. None inspired him with this urgent need to shield them from all unpleasantness and danger. He found it totally incomprehensible.

'What'll your mom say?'

'She's at work, and Poppy's gone shopping. She's always hours at the market,' Ivy said impatiently. 'Come on, Lizzie, it's too dark and cold to play in your shed.'

Lizzie looked cautiously about her as she sidled up the yard and through the back door. Billy, equally anxious not to be seen, crowded behind her.

'We'll go in the parlour,' Ivy announced importantly, and led the way through the kitchen. She stood on a chair to light the gas mantle.

'I'm goin' ter be the patient this time!' Lizzie claimed eagerly.

'No, Lizzie, that's not fair, you were the patient last time.'

'Wasn't!'

'You were! And it's my house!'

'Shurrup, our Lizzie! It's Ivy's turn.'

Lizzie scowled, but knew better than to argue with Billy. He was a lot bigger than she was and had no qualms about taking advantage of his superior strength. With a smile she meant to appear kindly and condescending, but which to Lizzie looked remarkably like a smirk, Ivy went across to the horsehair sofa and lay down on it.

Billy carefully deposited his cap on the old but gleaming oak dresser, which had belonged to John's mother, and went to stand beside her.

'I've broken my leg, doctor,' she said, putting as much anguish into her voice as possible.

'Yer did that last time,' Lizzie pointed out, disgruntled. 'Yer oughter choose summat diff'rent.'

'We've done everything else, and it's *my* leg!' Ivy replied indignantly.

'Why not break yer arm?'

''Er did that weeks ago, that time yer wasn't playin',' Billy said. 'And then yer wouldn't let me roll yer sleeve up.'

'No one's going to see my scars! Not even Sam!' Ivy said fiercely. 'Not even if he's almost a proper doctor!'

''E's just old man Potter's assistant. A chemist's not a proper doctor!' Billy said scornfully.

'Well, he knows all about poisons!' Ivy retorted. 'He said he's an apot– something. That's nearly a doctor. As good as. Now I've broken my leg.'

'Let me look at it. Nurse, 'elp the patient wi' 'er boots, an' take 'er stockin's off.'

Ivy pulled up her skirt and Lizzie, too angry to be careful, pushed aside the petticoat and dragged off Ivy's boots.

'Ouch! You didn't undo all the buttons!'

'Lizzie, play proper or go 'ome!' Billy ordered and Lizzie, inwardly fuming, hid her resentment and stood beside Billy as he prodded Ivy's leg, asking in gruff tones where it hurt.

'No. Not there. Higher up. Ouch! Oh, doctor, that's it! It hurts! Help me! Please help me! Make it better!'

'Oh, shut up,' Lizzie muttered.

'You made a lot more noise when you broke your ankle!' the patient said indignantly, suddenly sitting up and glaring at the nurse.

'Let's get on wi' it. Shall I bandage it? What shall I use?'

'Yer needs a splint,' Lizzie said with an air of triumph.

'A what?' Billy was bewildered.

'I know!' Ivy forgot her broken leg and pushed him away in order to scramble off the sofa.

'Oi! What yer doin'?'

'The poker!' Ivy brandished it gleefully. 'You have to tie that to my leg to hold the bones straight. That's what you mean, isn't it, Lizzie?'

'Sam di'n't say. It looks a bit long.'

'It'll do. Now bandage it to my leg. Use my stockings.'

Five minutes later Ivy was hobbling about the parlour, one leg shackled to the poker, demonstrating how much better she was.

'See, it works. Oh, doctor, you've saved my life! Thank you, doctor. What does it cost?'

'An 'undred pounds,' Billy said eagerly.

Ivy pretended to count out a hundred gold sovereigns, and hobbled about a bit more. The others grew bored. All the action was over.

'It's time ter take yer splint off,' Billy said, but without much hope. He knew from past experience that when Ivy was the patient in these games she prolonged the glory of being the centre of attention as long as possible.

'No, it isn't. You have to teach me to walk properly again. You've both got to help me.'

The three of them, locked together as they supported an increasingly uncooperative Ivy, staggered about the room, gradually succumbing to giggles.

'Now the poker – I mean splint – 'as ter come off!' Billy shouted, and made a sudden dive for Ivy's leg. The bandage had slipped, and it needed only a swift wrench before he had the poker in his hand.

Ivy shrieked in pretend fury and tried to grab it from him, but he was far taller than she and easily held it out of her reach.

Lizzie clung to his coat, urging Ivy to climb up on a chair and get it.

'Can't catch me!' he taunted.

'I will! I will!' Ivy screamed and as Billy, hampered by Lizzie's full weight swinging on his coat, staggered backwards, she scrambled on to the chair behind him.

'Go on, Ivy, get it!' Lizzie yelled.

'I can't reach! Pull him nearer, Lizzie, he's too far away!'

Lizzie was panting with the effort, Billy was laughing in triumph, but by standing on the very edge of the chair Ivy managed to get hold of his arm. She tugged and Billy lost his footing. As he tried to regain his balance Ivy seized the poker and with a yell of triumph waved it over her head.

'We've won!' she crowed.

'Two to one's not fair,' Billy complained, taking a step towards Ivy.

She swung the poker back out of reach, and they all froze in horror as the window behind her shattered into hundreds of fragments.

It was two days after Christmas. Marigold was still in a daze of wonder. How could she, plain Marigold Smith, have talked and even laughed with a rich young man who belonged to the same class as her employers?

'What do people learn at Oxford colleges?' she'd asked Mrs Dangerfield the previous day.

'Goodness knows, I don't,' she replied.

'Are they learning to be doctors, or lawyers, or what?'

'I don't think they're learning a job.' The cook considered it with a look of surprise on her face. 'Come ter think of it, most of 'em don't need to work, especially this young Mr Endersby. Have you seen his big motor car?'

'Motor car? No, I haven't. I didn't know Rich– Mr Endersby had one.'

'Keeps it in someone's old coach-house, no doubt.'

'But if they don't need jobs, why are they going on with schooling? Why do they need any more?'

'I suppose he's learning French and German. That's what the Master teaches. He's been at a German college for a year, I think.'

How long would he stay at Gordon Villa? Would they talk together before he left? Would she see him at all?

It was late morning. Marigold took the children down to the Cherwell for their daily walk. As she came through the gates she heard Richard's voice and almost turned tail and fled.

'Marigold! Wait for me!'

Marigold gulped, and let go of Peter's hand nervously as she tucked a stray curl under her bonnet.

The little boy darted ahead of her towards the path leading past the field. 'Want stroke pony! Lift me up!' he was soon commanding as Richard and Marigold reached the gate together.

'Master Peter! Where are your manners?' Marigold demanded, scandalized, but Richard laughed and lifted the child so that he could pat the pony's neck.

'Hello,' he said casually over his shoulder, giving Marigold a brief smile before turning back to answer Peter's imperious, if slightly incoherent questions.

'Come on, Peter, I want to go and walk by the river,' Eleanor said impatiently. 'Pat the other one and come on. He'll be getting jealous,' she added self-righteously.

Richard grinned down at her. 'Do you want to stroke the pony too?' he asked, holding out a hand. She shook her head, and in a sudden gush of shyness buried her face in Marigold's skirts.

Richard set Peter down. 'Can you ride a pony yet?'

'Yes.'

'Ooh, Peter, you're telling fibs! You don't! He can't,' Eleanor emerged to explain to an amused Richard. 'Not until he's a good boy, Mama says.'

'Can! Am good boy!'

'Not if you cry and shout like that,' Marigold intervened. 'Come on now, we'll go down to walk by the river.'

Marigold was breathing rapidly. The sight of Richard, so handsome and still so friendly, had shaken her out of the golden haze she'd inhabited for the past day and a half.

Would she ever see him after this Christmas? There was no reason to suppose he would visit the house again. And suddenly she knew how badly she wanted to see him, not just once or twice, but every day of her life. To realize the impossibility of this was a physical pain that invaded every inch of her body. Because she was unsophisticated, even immature in the sense that she did not gossip about boyfriends with Ethel, and through being kept at home had missed sharing confidences with her former schoolfriends, Marigold was bewildered. Why did it matter so much? Why should she need to see him, with a longing that created this overwhelming agony deep within her?

She wrapped her shawl about her and walked slowly towards the river. Eleanor and Peter scampered ahead and were soon involved in a game of hide and seek. A rabbit scuttled across the path in front of her, and a bird, squawking in fright, flapped through the branches of an ancient oak. Marigold pulled her shawl even closer, hugging herself to keep out the cold.

'May I accompany you for a while?'

Once more, within seconds, the easy camaraderie surrounded them as if by magic. Marigold's fluttering heart expanded, became a glow of warmth that suffused and enfolded her. She forgot he was one of the gentry, forgot she was unused to talking with young men, and chattered away in answer to his questions.

They talked about Oxford, and Marigold's work at Gordon Villa. She discovered that he was indeed studying languages.

'My father owns a pottery manufactory,' he explained, 'and I will be helping him sell the china overseas. That's one reason he's in America now, to arrange for exporting there.'

'One reason?'

'Yes. My mother is American and is visiting her family. It's the first time she's been back for ten years. That's why they're staying over Christmas.'

'Where is your brother?'

'He's with them. He doesn't come up to Oxford until next year.'

'What sort of china? Tea services and things?'

'We do make them and all sorts of tableware, but we also make ornaments.'

'Mom buys cups sometimes from the market. Mrs Andrews often gives her old plates which are chipped, but Mom says the cups usually get broken and there's always plates and saucers left over. I wonder if she's ever bought one of yours?'

'There are hundreds of firms, making all sorts of different things. She may have done.'

'I'll ask her when I go home. Mrs Roberts has given me two extra days' holiday at New Year.'

By the time she returned he might be gone.

Then the children, tired and by now fretful and hungry, came rushing up, she gave him a stricken look.

'I must take them back home. Goodbye.'

*

'Johnny! Johnny Smith! Where are ye, lad?'

Johnny, who had been lying underneath the bonnet of a car, emerged and stood up as his foreman entered the workshop. He wiped his greasy hands on a piece of rag. Here I am, Mr Barlow.'

'Good lad. Here, look at this.' He thrust a sheet of paper under Johnny's nose, pointing eagerly at a diagram. 'Would it work, d'you think? If we bent the steering arm like this, there'd be less pressure here, so it'd be less likely to break. Mr Fortescue wants us to try it if we think it'll work.'

'Shall I make one and try it on this motor here?' Johnny asked, already working out lengths and angles in his head.

'Aye. Do that now, and if you can get it fixed by morning we'll take it out and try it. I can give you another lesson. Way you're shapin', you'll soon be able to drive by yourself. Then you can impress young Lucy Kelly!'

'When am I ever going to afford a motor?' Johnny asked with a grin. 'Mr Fortescue may want me to be able to deliver his motors to customers, but I don't think he'd be very pleased if I took girls along with me!'

'Who knows?' Mr Barlow had a faraway look in his eye. 'I've been readin' about Mr Henry Ford. It takes so much less time to build one of his motors they say quite ordinary chaps'll soon be able to buy 'em.'

'He just puts them together, doesn't he? Like that place up in Manchester. And the chap in Oxford, Morris. People will always prefer quality, knowing it's been properly built, every little piece made to fit.'

'But this new method, all the motors are the same. All the pieces slot into any of them. It makes sense in a way.'

'Saves time, perhaps, but who wants to have the same motor as every other fellow?'

'Better that than no motor at all.'

'I'll believe it when I see it, that I could ever buy one! Might as well dream of owning an aeroplane and flying across to France like that chap Blériot.'

'Don't scoff, lad. The world's changing fast these days. I wouldn't be surprised to see lots more aeroplanes soon. And air-ships.'

Johnny laughed. 'You wouldn't catch me risking my neck in one. I'll stick to motor cars!'

Mr Barlow was barely listening. 'They've built the first ocean-goin' motor ship in Copenhagen, and finished the *Jutlandia* on the Clyde. They'll all improve, you'll see. Modern science can do anything!'

'It can't stop the *Titanic* hitting icebergs, or get Captain Scott back from the Antarctic. Beats me why people want to go into cold, snowy places anyway. It's cold enough at home for me.'

'We'll do better one day. All these inventions and making things better's just a matter o' putting money into finding different ways of making 'em.'

Johnny shrugged. 'Not from me. Why, Mom's always complaining about prices going up, money doesn't stretch so far. Where's all this money coming from? It must be the same for everyone. And if I didn't have good rises I'd not even be able to send her the same as I used to.'

'You're a good lad. If you were mine I'd be proud of you. It was a good day's work when Mr Fortescue's sister sent you to him.'

Johnny turned away, flushing. Even now he couldn't bear to think of what he'd done, the thief he'd been. He knew deep down that if he hadn't been caught then he could have gone on to greater crime. It became easier. You gained in confidence through not being caught, and your conscience got weaker. 'I'd best get on with this if we're going to try it out tomorrow,' he muttered, and walked away.

That evening, when he and Lucy were walking back from the Bible class they attended at the chapel, enjoying the balmy sunshine, he told her about the thefts.

'Johnny you didn't!' she said, scandalized. 'I'd never have thought it of you.'

'It's true,' he said miserably, 'and if you never want to speak to me again, I'll understand. I don't feel as though I could ever be forgiven.'

'When a sinner truly repents, then God will forgive,' she replied primly.

'But will you forgive me?'

'You didn't steal from me.'

She would say no more, and they walked home in silence until they were at the gate opening into the tiny front garden.

'Will you tell your mom?' he asked anxiously, knowing that if she did he would be forced to find other lodgings.

Lucy looked at him consideringly. 'Have you truly repented?'

'Oh, yes. I didn't enjoy doing it, but Ivy liked the things I bought, and I felt guilty about her scars.'

'Then if God can forgive you so must I. I won't tell Mom unless you do something else bad.'

That night Johnny's thoughts were so full of Lucy he found it difficult to go to sleep. He thought about her black, glossy hair, so wild it never stayed confined however many pins she stuck in it, and her blue eyes, the deepest blue he'd ever seen. Her complexion was pale, with that peculiar translucence he had come to expect of Irish girls – though Lucy would not have appreciated this, for she shrugged off any reference to what she called pagan ancestry. Altogether Lucy Kelly was the prettiest girl he'd ever seen, but he hadn't quite plucked up courage to tell her.

At least she now knew the worst of him, and it hadn't made her turn from him in disgust. Perhaps, when he could drive one of Mr Fortescue's motors, he'd ask if he might take Lucy out in it for a short ride. No one else she knew would ever be able to do that.

It was with glorious dreams such as these that he curbed his impatience. Lucy was only sixteen, and though he was positive she was the girl he wanted to wed, he knew they would have to wait a long time before they could afford a home of their own. For one thing he had to send most of his money home, to make up for his wickedness in the past. But when his younger sister was old enough to go out to work things might be different, and he could begin to save. Then, if Lucy would wait for him, he could look forward to a future brighter than any he might have the right to expect.

Marigold set off early the day before New Year's Eve. It would be the first time she'd slept more than a night at home since going to Oxford, and she wanted to make the most of it. Mom would be working, but she could help Poppy prepare a meal. Cook had given her a huge piece of ham to take home: it would be a feast for them all. What a pity Johnny wouldn't be there too.

As well as the ham, she carried the new dresses for Ivy and Poppy. The only fly in the ointment was that she wouldn't see Richard for four whole days. She anticipated with trembling delight each morning when he joined her as she walked by the river with the children.

That would end soon. He would return to his college, and she knew he would forget her.

She trudged towards the Woodstock Road. It was far too early for most people, still dark with only a faint dawn light to allow her to pick her way.

She didn't often venture into the town. It was so big and strange, with the huge ancient college buildings, which at first she'd found rather forbidding. People were always so busy, preoccupied with their own concerns. They didn't stop to chat like they did at home, or wave cheery greetings as they passed.

Then she heard a distant chug-chug sound. A motor car! Perhaps it was one of those Mr Morris was making. She turned and stared at the monster, red, huge and gleaming, as it bore down on her. She still found motor cars a novelty. They rarely saw any in Hednesford, and although there were quite a few in Oxford she was still fascinated by them.

The driver was muffled up in a huge fur coat, a hat pulled down over his eyes, and goggles. Marigold was watching the machine, though, worried that the slushy mud in the road might be splashed all over her clothes. When the driver slowed down her only thought was thankfulness that he didn't mean to shower her with dirt.

'Marigold!'

She jumped. It couldn't be! She was dreaming. She'd been thinking so much of Richard she was hearing his voice everywhere. Then she looked up at the man in the motor car. He was tearing off his goggles, and it was indeed Richard.

'I've decided to go to Rawnsley. Would you like to ride with me?' he asked, clambering out of the motor.

'Me? But I've never ridden in a motor car! I never imagined I would,' she added longingly.

It would be so exciting. Marigold was discovering that the world was very different from that she'd known at home, and was eager to sample all she could. She knew it would be frowned on, travelling in such a vehicle alone with a young man. None of the young ladies, daughters of the professors, would be allowed to do so. But she wasn't a young lady, and it would save her half the fare home. She'd be able to give Mom a little bit more, as well as the presents she'd spent too lavishly on.

'Then you'll come with me now.'

Before Marigold could reply he had picked her up and swung her into the motor car. Then he produced a thick fur rug and tucked it in around her. Astonished that this could be happening to her, that a man had held her closely, that ordinary Marigold Smith should actually ride in a horseless carriage – or any carriage at all, for that matter – she was unable to speak until he'd climbed in beside her and they were bowling along the road to the north.

'Do you go home every weekend you have off?' He had to shout over the noise of the engine.

'No,' Marigold managed, taking a deep breath to steady her nerves at the sensation of speed and power, and the many other inexplicable emotions which overwhelmed her. 'It's too far, and anyway it's too expensive,' she explained. 'Mom needs as much money as I can give her. After Pa was injured he was ill for a long time, and we owed money. Then there was the strike and now he doesn't earn as much,' she added.

He was silent and she glanced up at him, wondering if he were offended. But his goggles hid his face and although he turned towards her and she thought he smiled, she couldn't be certain.

As he drove without speaking Marigold had time to grow accustomed to the speed and noise of their progress. She didn't cling quite so tightly to the seat, and when a gusty breeze seized her hair and dragged it loose from the confining pins she laughed and revelled in the freedom of it streaming in the wind.

Birds skittered away at their approach, squawking in fright. A rabbit, busy nibbling the sparse grass on the verge, sat up on its hindquarters and watched, its huge soft eyes enigmatic. She looked across the expanse of rolling hills all around them. High and bleak in the grip of winter cold, they stretched for miles.

As they approached Birmingham and could see the vast array of buildings, Richard pulled the car on to a patch of turf and stopped the engine. In the sudden silence they heard a blackbird trilling away, oblivious to all.

'I have a cousin living in Edgbaston.'

'Oh. Do you want to go and see him?' Marigold asked in a small voice. She was terrified at the thought of meeting anyone she knew, for how could she explain why she was riding in a motor car? But to meet any of Richard's family would be worse. They were gentry. Although she was learning fast how wealthy people behaved, she knew she would be tongue-tied and embarrassed in their company.

'Not this time. We don't actually go through Edgbaston, it's more to the west, but I think you'll enjoy seeing the city as we go through.'

'I've seen it from the train,' she told him, not wishing to appear totally untravelled.

'The main roads are something else, they are so wide and spacious. But before we do let's eat. I persuaded Mrs Dangerfield to pack me a hamper. It's windy here, so let's walk a short way and find a more sheltered spot,' Richard suggested. 'December isn't the best time to have a picnic.'

Before she could disentangle herself from the enveloping rug he came round to her side of the motor car and opened the door. With impatient hands he dragged the rug away and threw it on to his seat, then grasped Marigold round the waist and lifted her from the vehicle.

For a fragile yet endless moment she was suspended there, her eyes level with his, her lips a few inches from his own. Then it was over. He set her on the ground, picked up the hamper, and took her hand in his. 'Over here. There's a clump of trees which will keep out the wind.'

He ran along a path across a field, pulling her after him, and they were both laughing and breathless when he halted by the trees.

He took a rug from the hamper and spread it out, then unpacked the food: pies and cold meat, with fruit and cakes to follow. There was a bottle of wine, even glasses to drink from.

The excitement of the drive and the cold wind had made Marigold hungry, and the food was soon demolished. She sipped one glass of wine cautiously, but hastily refused when Richard went to refill the glass. He forced the cork back and began to repack the hamper.

'Do you know Mr Coulthwaite?'

'Oh, no! He's too grand for us, but everyone's heard of him. He trained two Grand National winners!'

They walked back to the car and he spoke slowly as they went. 'I'm planning to stay somewhere nearby and visit my father's horses.'

'Is he – Are your father's horses going to run in the National?'

'One day, perhaps, but there's nothing of that class yet. I come to see how they are doing occasionally, and take one or two of them out.'

'Then you'll be –' Marigold stopped, aghast at what she'd been about to say. It wasn't for her, an insignificant nursery-maid, to presume. However friendly he'd been, Richard was one of the gentry, and she couldn't hope he'd want to see her again once he was back at his college. It would be unforgivably presumptuous of her even to hint at it. Her heart sank at the very idea.

'I could come back to Oxford the same day as you. We could drive back together, if you'd like to.' He stowed the hamper and turned to face her.

'Yes, I suppose so,' she whispered, her heart pounding in her chest in a strange, almost terrifying manner.

He pulled her round to face him and with a firm but gentle finger under her chin forced her to turn her face up to his.

'Why?' she asked baldly. 'Why should you want to help me?' It was all she could think of saying. It wasn't happening. It couldn't be true. The gentry didn't behave like this.

'Because I like you. I want to know you better. Because I want us to be friends,' Richard said quietly.

'It's not fitting,' she murmured distractedly. 'Not you and me.'

His gentle touch was creating a fluttering, tingling warmth that radiated from the spot where his flesh met hers. It spread up to her face, and she knew her cheeks were flushed. Her whole body felt hot as the blood pulsed through her veins, carrying his touch so that she was enfolded within it. Suddenly their companionable walks at Oxford seemed full of a significance they hadn't had at the time.

'We are friends, aren't we?' he asked now.

'But I'm just a servant, it wasn't – I didn't – 'she stammered.

'You're Marigold, a sweet, lovely girl I want to know better. What does it matter what you do to earn a living? Why should that come between us if we enjoy one another's company?'

'People will talk,' she managed.

'About us? Making vicious, ugly suggestions? Does it matter when we know they're wrong and untrue?'

'It would matter to me if I were turned off without a character,' she said a little more strongly. Why couldn't he see? People from his background didn't make friends with servants. 'Mrs Roberts wouldn't understand, she'd think you'd – well, taken advantage, and I'd been dishonest.'

'I can't bear never to see you again. If it's just what other people say we needn't tell them, though I'd be proud for them to know we were friends. No more, I promise. Just friends. Until you want more.'

She shook her head. It wasn't possible. She'd never heard of a servant being friends with a young man from an Oxford college, a rich young man with a motor car. 'It would be wrong to meet secretly,' she insisted.

'Would your father object? Is it fear of him that stops you?'

Marigold gave a slight laugh. 'He'd think you were a Fabian!'

'I'm not that. How could I be when my father employs so many men, and our money comes from manufacturing? And when the Government takes so much away from us in Income Tax? But you're trembling. We'd better go on.'

He didn't speak again until she was tucked up with the rug, and he had climbed in beside her.

'When's your afternoon off? Will you meet me then? Surely you'd not deny me that?'

It was tempting. The very idea of an occasional stolen hour with him was unbearably sweet. But she knew it was wrong. Everyone would condemn her. If Mrs Roberts discovered it she would lose her job. However kind and enlightened an employer she was, this would be too much for her to accept. And if Pa knew he might whip her. Mom would be disappointed, ashamed of her, and she wouldn't do anything to hurt her beloved mother. There could be nothing for her apart from shame and disgrace. And a few precious, delightful hours when she could talk to Richard in a way she'd never before talked to anyone.

As if he could read her mind Richard took her cold hand in his. 'Marigold, I promise no harm will come to you. I won't even kiss you if you are frightened of me, though I long for it more than anything else. I just can't bear to say goodbye, never to meet you again.'

And neither could she. The very thought of not seeing him again was a piercing agony she'd never before experienced. It was far worse than the terror she'd known when she'd seen Ivy falling towards the fire, or when Pa had been carried home from the colliery, so badly hurt.

She turned and smiled at him, her eyes shy but trusting, and Richard was desperately hard put to keep his promise, and not sweep her into his arms and cover her dear face with kisses.

Chapter Five

MARIGOLD insisted that Richard didn't take her right into the town. They came down the long hill from Heath Hayes, and before they reached the first house he stopped the motor car. 'I'll see you just here in four days, early in the morning. I'll wait for you by the gate to that field,' he promised.

She jumped down, and stood waving as he drove away. Then she walked down to the town centre with a light, springing step, and climbed Church Hill towards home. She still couldn't believe that she had ridden in a motor car, and that Richard wanted to go on seeing her. It simply wasn't credible, and yet she could still hear his deep voice, with the slight tremor in it as he countered her objections.

It wouldn't last. He would grow tired of her. He would meet some other girl, someone from his own world, who would be a more suitable . . . A more suitable what? Her thoughts halted.

There could be no future, their worlds were too far apart. He might say he just wanted friendship, but she had heard Ethel and the parlourmaid from next door confiding in one another, giggling about the young men they were walking out with. She wasn't entirely clear what they found so titillating. Marigold was unusually ignorant of the dangers and delights of sex, she only knew that in some strange and frightening way girls could be ruined if they became too familiar with men who said they wanted to be friends. Girls were shunned if they bore bastards, but Marigold had only the haziest notion of what they had to do in order to get into such a predicament.

She couldn't ask Mom. Nor could she tell them at home about the motor car, she realized with a sudden pang. It wasn't as if she wanted to brag about having ridden in one, but she had never before kept secrets from Mom or Poppy.

It was with a mixture of emotions, wonder that Richard liked her, and sadness that she would have to keep this incredible joy from her family, that she turned into her street.

She walked up the ginnel to approach the house from the back, as they always did, and didn't see the broken window, boarded up with roughly nailed planks. She knew, however, that something was seriously wrong immediately she walked into the kitchen.

Poppy was rolling out pastry, thumping the wooden rolling pin so fiercely against the table that Marigold winced. Ivy sat with her back turned, shoulders hunched, her knees either side of a bucket as she peeled potatoes.

'Marigold!' Ivy shrieked with joy and dropped the potato and the knife into the bucket, splattering the clean tiles with drops of dirty water as she flung herself on her sister.

Marigold returned the hug, then gently set Ivy aside and went to kiss Poppy, who had ignored her entrance. 'What is it, Poppy?' she asked fearfully. 'Is it Pa? Or Mom?'

Poppy pursed her lips, and glared across the kitchen to where Ivy stood. Her blue eyes were unnaturally bright. 'No, they're well. It's that little liar!'

'Ivy? What's she done?'

'I didn't!' Ivy shouted. 'I wasn't in the house, whatever she says! I don't know how it happened! I was just coming in from the lavatory when I heard the smash!'

'What smash? What are you talking about?'

'Look in the parlour,' Poppy said, picking up the pastry and thumping it down again so hard that she knocked the bowl of flour off the table. 'Damn you, Ivy! Now look what's happened! Just look at that mess!'

She collapsed into angry tears, and Marigold stared at her, aghast. This was clearly far worse than the normal squabbling her sisters habitually indulged in. Out of habit she took charge.

'Poppy, sit down a minute until you've calmed down. Ivy, be a love and sweep up this flour. Luckily there isn't much and it's a tin bowl.'

Firmly she took the rolling pin from Poppy's convulsive grasp, and put it on the table. Then she went towards the parlour and saw immediately the broken panes of glass, boarded over so that almost no daylight seeped into the room.

Sighing, she took off her coat and hung it up on a nail in the passage. 'Tell me,' she said gently, sitting opposite Poppy, who by now was weeping uncontrollably.

Gradually she disentangled the story, with Poppy and Ivy competing to tell their separate and contradictory versions.

Poppy, returning home from the shops, had heard the breaking glass from round the corner. When she'd turned into the street there was no one about, but as she came through the ginnel she'd been almost knocked over by Billy Bannister, running along without caring whom he bumped into.

'Then Lizzie came after him, screaming at him to wait. When she saw me she burst into tears.'

'Lizzie's a cry-baby,' Ivy said scornfully. 'And she doesn't like the dark. It's dark in the ginnel.'

'Shut up, Ivy! They'd been with her, Marigold, playing in the parlour, and they'd broken the window! I know they had!'

'We didn't! I don't know why they were here, I tell you. Perhaps they came to fetch me to play, but I was in the lavatory, and the first I knew was when Carrots came screaming out of the kitchen yelling at me.'

'Don't call me that, you little devil! You were in there, in the parlour. The cushions had been moved, and there was a lump of mud on the floor, and I cleaned the floor only that morning.'

'There wasn't any mud! It's you telling fibs. It was all clean when Mom came home.'

'Because you'd cleaned it up, you sneaky little rat!'

Ivy began to cry, and held out her arms to Marigold. 'It's horrid now you've gone,' she sniffed. 'Poppy's always getting at me, saying I did things when I didn't. I don't know who broke the silly window, but it must have been someone from outside, someone who ran away.'

'Where was the glass?' Marigold asked.

'Mostly outside,' Poppy insisted, but Ivy vehemently shook her head.

'It wasn't! It was inside, and you must have thrown some of it out so's you could make it look like my fault! You're mean to me, you hate me!'

'The curtain was all torn, a great big hole. That wasn't done by the glass catching in it. And there wasn't a brick or anything inside!'

There was no way of proving anything. Both could have been telling the truth. The glass could have fallen either way. It had to be some lad who had broken the window, then run away, or Ivy was lying. Marigold couldn't believe this of her baby sister, and she was rather shocked Poppy found it so easy to think the child was capable of telling untruths.

She supposed Ivy could have been frightened to admit it if she had broken a window, but if it had been an accident neither Mom nor Pa would have been too stern. They never were, especially with Ivy. Still, Ivy shouldn't have been in the parlour on her own. Unless she'd been making Christmas presents, and hiding them away when she thought Poppy was due to return home. They'd all done that.

But Ivy wouldn't persist in telling lies. And she wouldn't have taken Lizzie and Billy into the parlour. They were never allowed to play in there.

Marigold sighed. She had to believe Ivy.

'Go on with the potatoes now,' she said gently. 'Poppy, let me have your apron and I'll finish the pastry. What's it for?'

Poppy sniffed. 'Pies, to use up the meat.'

'We had ever so much meat at Christmas,' Ivy began to explain, her fury forgotten.

Gradually, under Marigold's calming presence, they set to again, and by the time John and Mary came home dinner was almost on the table.

No more was said about the broken window, and Marigold gave out the presents she had brought and received her own. On the surface it was a happy family evening, with her describing the festivities at Oxford, and them telling her all their news, and lamenting that she and Johnny had not been able to come home at the same time.

Later on in bed Marigold was unable to sleep. Fearful of

disturbing her sisters sleeping beside her in the big bed she rigidly controlled the impulse to toss and turn.

Her mind was a jumble of tangled thoughts. Always near the surface were those of Richard, a mixture of delight and fear. But her worries about Ivy intruded, and whether she told lies, as Poppy maintained. Poppy had always been in an odd way resentful of Ivy, yet Marigold had never before seen the vicious looks Poppy had been directing towards her younger sister today.

Perhaps being away from home made you see things more clearly, she mused. Perhaps it made obvious that which would be ignored when you lived with them all the time – like the cramped room and the smells she had never consciously noticed before.

After the spacious rooms at Gordon Villa, where even her bedroom was larger than the one she now slept in, and the day nursery could have accommodated the entire house, her home suddenly appeared tiny and horridly overcrowded. It had never before seemed so. Indeed she had thought it luxurious when she knew how many children had been crammed into the tiny back-to-back houses in the town.

Worse than that, however, were the odours. At Gordon Villa, which was at the edge of the town, everything smelt fresh. The linen and the clothes were kept with fragrant lavender sachets, and the beeswax Mrs Roberts insisted on using for all the furniture was redolent of some tangy spice. Bowls of pot pourri lay all over the house, and even in winter bowls of flowers and greenery scented the rooms. A bathroom had been installed for the use of the family, and water closets, even one near the kitchen for the servants.

Marigold had wrinkled up her nose as she came through the back yard. It was not only the pervasive, throat-catching smell from the spoil heaps, which always hung about the town, but the stench of pigsties and chicken-runs too close together in a small space. Somehow, on the farms they sometimes walked past near Oxford, animals didn't smell so strong, even though there were more of them! And even more offensive was the reek from the lavatories. The houses were never free of it, even immediately after the night-soil men had done their necessary but revolting work.

Inside the house it was worse. Wet steamy washing days had left the scullery with an ingrained aura of damp. Damp penetrated into the kitchen, seeping out from behind the wooden dado and up from the quarry tiles laid straight on the earth. Mingled with cooking odours, oil lamps and stale food, it was repulsive and degrading. Marigold wondered how she had endured it before, how her family could live there and not appear to notice.

They had no choice, she realized. She was only aware of it because she compared it with the luxury of Gordon Villa. Most people in the colliery towns lived in even worse conditions. It was to prevent their slide from comparative ease into an even more disgusting slum that Mom worked so hard.

Marigold vowed with a fierce determination that one day, however she achieved it, she would take her family away from here. She would give them something better, something clean and wholesome, where they didn't have to catch the cockroaches that crawled out from the cracks in the wall, and endure stinking chamberpots under the bed all night.

She'd find a better life for them, somehow.

Richard also lay sleepless in his bed at the George in Lichfield. The more he discovered about this girl, the more puzzled he became. She was painfully shy, which perhaps explained his desire to protect her. Underneath, though, he detected a core of inner strength which was more attractive than her surface beauty.

His mother entertained lavishly and since he was eighteen had ensured he met dozens of girls. He enjoyed female company but never felt deprived at the thought of any of these damsels departing from his life. He admitted ruefully to a secret apprehension that all they wanted from him was marriage and a wealthy future.

In Oxford he'd met different types. There were the daughters of his professors, some as empty-headed and frivolous as his mother's protégées, some determinedly blue-stockinged. About the town he and his fellow undergraduates were shamelessly ogled by girls eager to meet young men with money. And then there was Flo.

At the thought of her he squirmed in embarrassment.

'I'm visiting a friend in Jericho, why don't you come too?' Edwin had said one dismal October day, two months ago.

'Jericho? But that's no more than a slum. How can you have a friend there?'

Edwin laughed. 'There are many sorts of friends. Remember Berthe in Bonn?'

Richard understood, and felt his pulses quicken. For three months he had visited Berthe in her small apartment near the university. She had inducted him into a world of erotic sensual pleasures and voluptuous delights, and all with a delectable air of gratitude, concealing the fact they both knew that she had been subtly instructing him in ways of gratifying a woman as well as himself.

'Bessie and her sister are not whores,' Edwin reassured him. 'They just like a good time. Why not come?'

Richard succumbed. When Edwin and Bessie, with no excuse or apology, vanished up the stairs of the tiny, cramped house which was nevertheless surprisingly well appointed, Flo giggled. Loosening the neck of her blouse, she moved across the room to sit on Richard's knees, nestling close to him.

'There do be another bed in the back room,' she suggested, winding one arm about his neck, and guiding his hand on to her ample, uncorseted rump.

She was drenched in some cheap violet scent, and her unrestrained breasts were pressing against his chest, inches from his fascinated gaze. He was at the same time repelled but aroused. When she stood and tugged at his hand he went with her up the narrow stairs.

As Flo rapidly discarded the few clothes she wore, Richard tried to shut out the uninhibited sounds coming from the other bedroom. He recalled Berthe's more subtle approach, and wished he was back in her bed. And then, under Flo's skilled administrations, he forgot everything but the immediate release of tension.

That, he soon knew, was all it meant. Afterwards he wondered at his actions. Flo had none of the flattering tricks employed by Berthe. She was eager for his embraces, but more concerned for her own animal appetites to be satisfied than caring about his. And she was even more eager to accept the presents he gave her.

He vowed never to return, but the lure was insidious. He missed Berthe, and had found in Flo a very inadequate substitute. How could women be so different? Yet as he tossed and turned in bed he knew with utter certainty he never wanted to see either of them again.

His mother, perhaps deliberately, had never employed pretty maidservants. Through a sense of propriety Richard had never been tempted to seduce any of the maids in houses where he stayed, although he knew Edwin and his other friends had no such qualms and regarded them as fair game.

Where did Marigold fit in? She wasn't from his world, she was a servant. Yet unlike some of the maids she did not offer herself. From her shrinking behaviour when he touched her he guessed she was totally inexperienced with men.

Did he want her in his bed? He lay there, imagining her slim body beside him, and knew an intense longing. He did want her, more than he'd ever wanted Berthe, and infinitely more than he'd wanted Flo. It would be the most exhilarating thing in the world to hold her in his arms, to instruct her in the ways of love. With a deep sigh he turned over and began to make plans.

She had two full days at home, and spent the first, New Year's Eve, preparing a feast for the family. Mary had decided they were now all old enough to stay up and celebrate the changing of the year, and Ivy danced about in excitement at the thought of wearing her new dress.

'It'll be 1913, and soon I'll be eight! Marigold, when I'm old enough, can I come and stay with you in Oxford?'

'Yes, if I'm still there and Mrs Roberts allows it,' Marigold promished rashly. She was so happy knowing Richard wanted to see her again, and being at home with her beloved family, she'd have promised anything.

'Marigold may have another job by then,' Mary warned, smiling across Ivy's head at her older daughter.

Marigold looked so different! She'd only been home twice before during her six months at Oxford, but even since the last time she seemed to have matured. Instead of the childish plait she now put up her hair in a neat chignon. Her face was slightly thinner, but her beauty was increased by this, and she was developing curves, so it wasn't hunger. Mary smiled to herself. Of course she would be well fed in such a good household, but she couldn't help worrying.

They had their main meal late that evening, and the girls chattered so much that John's unusual silence was not remarked, even by Mary.

The first hint Marigold had that he had changed came just after they'd been outside listening to the church bells ringing in the New Year.

'Ivy, off to bed now, or you'll never get up in the morning,' Mary said. 'You too, Poppy. We'd all better go.'

'Not yet! Please, Mom, not for a bit!' Ivy wheedled.

Mary laughed. 'Yes! I know it's a special day, or night rather, but you can't stay up all night.'

'I will when I'm grown up. I'll stay up every night and sleep during the day!' Ivy declared, dancing round the table which was still littered with the remnants of their meal.

'Ivy, love, don't be naughty. I've got to clear all this up, and I'm too tired to argue, even if you're still full of life.'

'Do as your mom says. At once!'

Marigold jumped. She'd never before heard her father speak like that, except when he'd thrashed Johnny.

'John –' Mary began in a hesitant tone, and cringed when he turned towards her, his fist clenched.

'You spoil the little brat! Ivy, go to bed!'

Ivy was already at the door to the stairs. 'I'm going, Pa, I'm going,' she almost whimpered, and without bothering to visit the scullery and wash she sidled past the door and could be heard running up the stairs.

There was a silence in the kitchen. Poppy picked up some of the leftover food and took it to the pantry. Mary, with a sigh hastily suppressed, took some plates out to the scullery. John, his eyes blank, dragged his hand across his forehead, rubbed his eyes, and without a word went outside.

Marigold helped wash up, and then, before she could find any words to say to her mother, Mary, with a muttered 'Goodnight, love, happy New Year!', went swiftly up the stairs.

Some time later, when she was lying sleepless in the big bed with her sisters, Marigold heard her father return. He moved about downstairs, and she could hear him stoking the fire, putting on slack to keep it in till the morning, pushing home the bolts on the door, and finally climbing slowly up to bed.

She strained to hear, feeling guilty at eavesdropping, but oddly afraid. There were no sounds from the front bedroom, however, apart from one thump as John let his boot fall, and a creak as he got into bed. At last, exhausted, Marigold fell into a restless sleep.

The next morning she was the first up. Was Pa going to work? As she was wondering whether to tap on his door and remind him of the time Mary came wearily down the stairs.

'Isn't Pa well? Is it one of his headaches?' Marigold asked.

Mary shook her head, and brushed away a tear. 'I don't know what it is. He's had several days like this the last few months. He says he doesn't have a headache, but he can't get out of bed. Or if he does, he just sits huddled over the fire and does nothing all day.'

'Last night, he –' She stopped. How could she criticize her father?

Mary nodded, understanding. 'He isn't like that usually,' she said reassuringly. 'You'd know if you were here. It seems to happen just before he gets these moods when he can't force himself to go to work.'

'Is it all right at work? He's not worried, frightened of losing his job?'

'No, it's not that. Most of the time he's just the same as usual.'

Marigold took a deep breath. 'I thought he was going to hit someone last night,' she said bleakly. 'Has he ever hit you?'

There, she'd said it, openly expressed the fear that had haunted her last night.

Mary stared at her in astonishment. 'Marigold, how could you ever even think that of your pa? He's a good man, one of the best, and he's never laid a finger on me in anger. He's smacked you all at times, when you were little, but not hard. Most folk think he's too soft. He only ever thrashed Johnny that once, and regretted that. The others know he wouldn't hit them, or me.'

'I'm sorry, Mom. I was afraid, last night, for you.'

Slowly Mary nodded. 'I know. I'm afraid too, but not of being hit. I don't understand why he gets these moods, but it isn't very often, and it's not going to spoil your last day with us. I thought we'd all take a walk up on the Chase, as I've got a day off too. Best to leave the house quiet for Pa, too. He sleeps most of the time when he's feeling like this.'

And no doubt gets mad when he's kept awake, Marigold thought dismally. How could her kind pa have changed so? She had to take what comfort she could from her mother's assurances that the occasions were few. A quiet word some time later with Poppy helped, for Poppy confirmed the inexplicable attacks came infrequently, and were soon over.

'And he's ever so sorry afterwards, says he doesn't know what comes over him.'

She wished she was nearer to home and could see them more often. But then she would not have the opportunity of seeing Richard. If, indeed, he wished to see her when he was immersed in his studies again. The inward battle of her love for her family and impatience to be with Richard kept her awake the following night too, and she could barely drag herself out of bed when morning came.

At least Pa seemed his normal self when he left early for work. He kissed her, bidding her a cheerful goodbye as though nothing had happened, although she noticed he didn't meet her gaze. She could go back to Oxford slightly less worried than she'd been the previous day.

Marigold set off soon after Mary had gone to work, to meet Richard. She was early but he was already waiting.

'I thought I'd missed you,' he exclaimed, leaning over to open the door for her. 'I've been counting the mine chimneys. There are so many,' he said as he started the motor car.

'More than you imagine,' Marigold said with a slight laugh.

'What do you mean? What's amusing?'

'There are so many mine shafts, no one knows where they all are, so we have to watch our steps. Quite a few people have been lost through falling down them.'

'Shafts? Not just subsidence?'

'Oh, there's plenty of that too. But there are hundreds of old shafts dug in parts of the Chase when people were trying to find the coal. They just got left if nothing was found, and a few big colliery owners developed the pits underground from the main shafts, and didn't use these. Aren't there collieries near Stoke? Don't you have the same problems?'

'Not where I live. But what about the horses? Are Mr Coulthwaite's horses likely to vanish down a mine shaft?'

'I don't think there are any up on the hills where they exercise. Were your horses doing well?'

'My father's horses. Yes. There's one which might be good enough for the Grand National in a year or two. If it's entered I shall take you to the races to see it. You'll bring me luck.'

Marigold laughed. 'I thought it was in the north? How could I?'

He smiled, and shook his head.

Mary came out of Foster's Bakery with the fine soft rolls Mrs Andrews liked, and continued on her way to work. It had been like old times having Marigold at home again. She wished John had not had one of his turns while the child was home, though. The inexplicable explosion of rage, which as far as she could see was not caused by his headaches, had upset Marigold.

Despite all her worries she smiled. Her eldest daughter now had a much better life than she could have expected at home, worn down by the drudgery of keeping house for them all. Hard though it was to lose them, she hoped Poppy and Ivy might one day have similar good fortune.

She savoured the happier recollections of these few days, dwelling on the small changes she had noticed in Marigold. Her speech was even better than Mary had always insisted on, more confident in an odd way. She held herself straight still, but this upright stance now had a tinge of pride rather than mere habit.

She apparently was happy, enjoyed looking after the children, liked the other servants and Mrs Roberts. She was learning more than just being a nursery-maid, too, it seemed. If Mrs Roberts used her to help at table she might one day be able to get a job as parlourmaid.

The only aspect of her new life she had been reticent about was her new friends. She talked of the other servants, and had obviously met a couple of other maids from nearby houses, but she'd said she didn't like going into the centre of Oxford by herself; it was too big, and she hadn't once mentioned going in with anyone else.

This had disappointed Poppy, who had demanded descriptions of the university colleges. Mary had been dimly aware Marigold was uncomfortable talking about them, and only now had leisure to wonder why.

Her musings were interrupted by the sound of a motor car approaching. She turned to look, intrigued by these odd new conveyances Johnny seemed to know everything about, and saw a large red monster swoop past at an incredible speed.

It was not going too fast, though, for her to recognize Marigold seated beside the driver.

After the first shock Mary began to run after the vehicle, but within yards realized the futility of this. She stopped, breathless, and leaned against a wall as she tried to regain her breath and order her whirling thoughts.

She rubbed her eyes. It had been Marigold, she was sure. Her eyesight wasn't as bad as that. Despite the shawl draped about her head and the enveloping fur rug she had seen enough to be certain it was her daughter. But she'd seen nothing of the driver.

It must have been a man, but who? If it had been Professor Roberts why hadn't Marigold mentioned him? It was unlikely they could have met by chance, for Marigold would only have crossed this road in the middle of the town, on her way to the station. She must have arranged to meet him. But who was he, and why hadn't she said anything?

Marigold was never secretive, like Ivy. She'd always told Mary everything. Mary began to shake, and had to put the shopping basket down as she clutched both arms round her trembling body. Surely Marigold wasn't being trapped by the snare of riches, the prey of some heedless young man! Not her beloved eldest daughter! That would be more than she could bear.

As she grew calmer and slowly resumed her walk to the Andrewses' house, Mary realized that in his present state she dared not say anything to John. Poppy was too young and too jealous of Marigold to be a confidante. She would have to keep the knowledge to herself until she had a chance to talk to Marigold. It was not the sort of thing you could write in a letter. Fervently she prayed that by the time Marigold came home again it would not be too late.

Richard suggested they might picnic on the side of the river in Stratford-upon-Avon, and they spent an hour beforehand wandering about the town while Richard enthused about Shakespeare and compared him with the foreign writers he'd studied. Marigold, having read only the literature her teachers had considered suitable at school, usually improving moral tales by minor Victorian authors, was enchanted, longing to have the time to delve into this very different world of books and drama.

Back at the motor car again, they opened the refilled hamper, but Marigold scarcely heeded the food or her surroundings. She was absorbed in their talk. Richard told her more about his life at college, and the pottery on which his father's fortune was based. Many of his anecdotes were amusing, and he had an endearing way of telling stories against himself, with a wry humour she found odd but attractive.

He encouraged her to talk too, and had great difficulty in hiding his amazement and anger at the details she unconsciously revealed about her life and home.

He had been brought up in a wealthy home. He'd seen the houses in the slums of the Pottery towns, and the mining villages nearby, but had never known in such graphic detail exactly what conditions people had to endure. That Marigold accepted them as normal, and even considered her own home to be vastly superior to those of many people she knew, shocked him more than anything else.

Again that impulse, which made him want to sweep her up in his arms there and then, almost overwhelmed him. If only he could carry her off with him, and surround her with every luxury he could afford. He tried to laugh at himself. He was no King Cophetua. He was not accustomed to making grand gestures. And at the back of his mind, to his secret shame, was the niggling certainty that his parents, particularly his mother, would consider him a fit candidate for Bedlam if he told them he was besotted with a nursemaid whose father was a collier.

By the time Richard had driven Marigold back to Oxford she had agreed to meet him the following Wednesday in the Cornmarket.

'You do want to meet me again, don't you?' he demanded when she hesitated.

'Yes,' she admitted, 'but it's wrong to meet in secret, and I don't want people to gossip about us.'

'We could walk by the river when you take out the children, but then we'd be more likely to be seen, and the little ones surely would mention it,' he pointed out.

'But I'm just a servant! People like you don't talk to servants, only to give orders,' she tried to explain. 'It's not as though we had anything in common. What would we find to talk about?'

'I don't regard you as a servant, Marigold, and we've talked for hours today and when I drove you home.'

'I can hardly believe it. It's like a dream. And I don't think I should have let you drive me home. If anyone saw me they'd think the worst.'

'Do you care what people say? When you know it isn't true?'

'What I know to be true wouldn't matter a scrap where my reputation is concerned,' she pointed out. 'It may be all right for you to say it's unimportant, you have money and your own business to work in. I wouldn't be able to get another job if Mrs Roberts dismissed me without a character. How would I live, let alone send money home?'

Richard swept his hand across the frown on his face. 'It makes things difficult, I do see that,' he confessed. He hadn't appreciated how confined girls such as Marigold were. In his own class girls were always chaperoned, and trollops like Flo obviously did not need to be. He'd never before considered the situation of virtuous working girls in between the extremes he knew.

'I'm sorry,' Marigold whispered.

'If we can't meet openly without ruining you, we must find somewhere private, where no one will see us. I have the motor car, we could go for drives.'

'It's wrong. Anyway, we might still be seen.'

'Not if we take care to meet well away from the town. I can't think where now, since it might mean you have to take a horse bus to some village. Meet me for a moment next week in the Cornmarket and by then I'll have made some plans.'

'It's too public!'

'I know, but just for a few minutes. By then I'll have thought of somewhere else we can meet, where no one will see us.'

She was reluctant, but the thought of never seeing him was worse than the threat of ruin. She couldn't bear to lose him, and although she knew it was wrong she agreed. If they took care, no one would become suspicious.

'Half past three then. An apparently accidental meeting in the street, when it would be perfectly natural for me to speak to you, would do no harm. It's a busy street, and perfectly respectable,' he reassured her.

The only other disagreement came when she insisted on being set down before they reached the gates of Gordon Villa.

'It's almost dark. No one will see us,' he protested.

'Someone always sees.'

'Then I'll say I saw you near the station, recognized you, and offered you a ride,' he said, unwilling to let her go for the sake of a few more minutes.

'No. Please!'

'Are you so afraid of gossip?' he asked bluntly.

'Yes! I've explained that I daren't risk losing my job, I need the money to give to Mom.'

She couldn't tell him, for she was ashamed that she could put her own feelings above the needs of her family, that what would hurt even more deeply would be if others began gossiping about her, sullying this precious new experience in her life with their speculations and innuendoes.

As she went into the house she hugged to herself the bliss of her memories, still feeling his hand in hers, his arm about her waist. She barely responded to Cook's greeting as she passed through the kitchen and went straight upstairs.

Ethel was preening before the small mirror in their bedroom, pinning up her hair in a new way, coiling it low at the back of her head. 'Like this fashion?' she asked. 'Had a good time?'

Marigold nodded and smiled. She'd no intention of telling Ethel just how good a time it had been for her. Apart from her father's odd behaviour, 1913 promised to be a New Year full of unexpected delights, undreamed-of promises, and an ecstasy she had only just begun to comprehend.

Richard was utterly special. Their friendship was something magical to be cherished in a cocoon of precious secrecy known only to the two of them, hidden from the prying eyes of others.

Richard sighed as Edwin entered his rooms. He was deep in a

difficult book and resented the interruption. 'What is it?' he asked abruptly.

'You've been like an unsociable bear with the proverbial sore head since Christmas,' Edwin replied, throwing off his heavy overcoat and sprawling into an ancient but comfortable armchair.

'I'm working.'

'Too hard to visit Flo? She's been asking me for weeks past where you are.'

'I told you, I don't want to see her again.'

'Taken to religion? You're uncommonly prudish of a sudden. Not got the clap, I trust?'

'Of course not! I'm just tired of rapacious harpies like Flo. She's never satisfied. It's not even an honest trade, sex for money. She has to try and pretend it's different in order to prise more expensive presents from me.'

Unlike Marigold, who'd asked him for nothing, who was gentle and uncomplicatedly friendly, and whose face he couldn't dismiss from his dreams.

'She wants to see you. I'm going to see Bessie this afternoon if you need company.'

'She'll have to want.'

'I think you'd better come. Her brother's threatening to make a fuss with the Dean if you don't.'

'What!' Richard leapt to his feet and stood over Edwin, his expression both shocked and angry.

'Don't kill the messenger, old man. He was threatening to come yesterday but gave you a day's grace when I said I'd tell you today. I promised you'd be there.'

'What the devil for? How can he make trouble for me? Those girls are nothing but whores, whatever they pretend.'

'Even whores make mistakes, and Flo's mistake is growing bigger daily.'

'I don't believe it!'

He had to accept, when he saw Flo later that day, that she was pregnant. He utterly refused, however, to accept sole responsibility.

'You can't persuade me I'm the only man your sister's been to bed with,' he told the burly man who stood threateningly by. 'I've seen other men coming from the house, and sometimes when I've called she's not been dressed, in the middle of the afternoon.'

'But 'ow can you prove the brat's not yours? It's not as though she be expectin' you to marry 'er,' the man said in a wheedling tone, and Richard shuddered at the very thought. 'She just needs a bit of 'elp.' His tone changed to one of menace. 'An' I'm going to mek sure she gets 'er due! You'd not like the Dean an' your pore fam'ly to know, now, would you?'

'I'll think about it,' Richard stalled.

'Do that, an' I'll expect you to be 'ere again tomorrow.'

'The day after,' he insisted, and retreated after this minor victory, his dignity severely dented.

'What the devil ought I to do?' he demanded of his cousin Archie.

Archie Cranworth was smaller and slighter than Richard, ten years older, a former soldier. He had spent a good deal of his time abroad, but a year ago had been seriously wounded in India, and returned to England for good. Now he was connected with the university in Birmingham, although he had his own money.

A hurried exchange of telegrams had sent Richard to Birmingham the following morning. Archie met him at the station and they were sitting in a discreet corner of the waiting room.

'You'll have to pay her off, you young fool. Serve you right for mixing with a girl who isn't a simple whore. Give her enough to keep her for a year, and forget about it.'

'I'd never feel safe if she stayed in Oxford. They'd be threatening me and demanding more the whole time I'm there.'

'Then send her to me. I'll pay her the money on condition she doesn't see you again.'

'Thanks, Archie. I'll let you have whatever you think is enough. But can you persuade her?'

'Don't worry. I'll find a room somewhere in Birmingham for her, and keep my eye on her to make sure she stays there, at least until you've gone down from Oxford. You can be sure that before the brat's a month old she'll be back at her trade.'

'The child? What will become of it?'

'You said you couldn't be sure it was yours?'

'No. I know she went with other men.'

'Then the chances are it isn't, but you're the richest one for plucking. Forget it,' Archie advised.

'But if it is, brought up by such a woman? What would become of it?'

'If you prefer I'll insist she sends it to an orphanage. I know of a good one in north Birmingham, where the kid will have a better chance than with her.'

'That would be best. I wouldn't like to condemn any child to her care.'

'Many are worse off.'

'I know, but this one could be mine.'

Partially satisfied, Richard returned to Oxford where he made arrangements for Flo to go to Archie for the money, and tried to forget the whole sordid business.

Chapter Six

POPPY picked up the last of the eggs and turned to go back into the house. It was really Ivy's job to collect them, but as usual Ivy was out with her friends.

A year, even a few months ago Poppy would have railed bitterly against the injustice, but she had given up. Besides, it was a chance to get out of the hot, stuffy house and breathe some fresh air – or as fresh as it could be with the pigsty a few yards away.

'Ivy just smiles sweetly, hangs her head pretending she's sorry, and promises not to forget tomorrow,' she complained to Marigold when her sister came home again in the middle of February.

'And then forgets?'

'Not always. That's how sly she is. She does it for a day or so, just so much that when I tell Mom she's off again, she can say she's been doing it, and Mom just tells her to be good next time.'

'What's she doing? Playing with Lizzie and her friends?'

'Sometimes. But she's taken to roaming up on the Chase collecting flowers to draw, she says.'

'And does she?' Marigold asked.

'She brings plenty home. Leaves and roots and all sorts of nasty things. She does draw lots,' Poppy added slowly.

Later on, when Ivy came home and tea was cleared away, Marigold asked to see her drawings.

She was startled not only at their accurate detail, but at the beauty Ivy managed to capture in the simple sketches. She didn't know what it was, except for a sense of grace in the pictures of dainty flowers or waving grasses. Each precisely delicate petal, shaped and shaded, seemed alive, ready to float off the page if a mere breath of wind caught it.

'Johnny showed them to his teacher at the evening institute he goes to in Birmingham,' Ivy said proudly. 'He said I should go to art college.'

'Art college? But where could you do that?'

'There's lots, in Lichfield, or Birmingham. I could go to a big college in London and learn all sorts of things, painting as well as drawing.'

'We could never afford it, luv,' John said wearily. 'You know I'd love to give you the chance, but it's just not possible for the likes of us.' He was sitting as usual in the chair beside the fire, carving his little animals. That must be where Ivy got her talent, Marigold thought, both proud and regretful. If only Pa had had a better start in life, he might have become famous. His carvings were so very lifelike.

Pa was beginning to look old, Marigold realized with a pang. His fair hair was receding fast, and turning almost imperceptibly grey. This time he had not shown the sudden anger which had terrified her so at New Year, and Mom, in the few snatched words they'd managed alone, said he was better. Marigold couldn't see it. He was not much more than forty, but had worked so hard, and suffered a great deal of pain and worry and disappointment. There were deep grooves on his forehead, and his mouth was drawn, his cheeks sunken.

She glanced at Mary, sitting by the window to take advantage of the daylight as she did her endless embroidery. She too looked old, her once dark hair much greyer than Pa's, her face lined. Her trim figure had thickened, and although she laced herself into tight corsets she no longer had the slim waist and straight back of her youth.

It made Marigold unbearably sad to see her parents growing old. They were still determinedly cheerful in front of their children, but the early sense of optimism that life would one day have more to offer than endless toil and mean living conditions seemed to have gone.

Ivy was full of questions about Marigold's job. 'What do you have to do when you help at table? Do you have to wash up the silver? What patterns are on the china?'

After much more of this Mary looked up and spoke firmly. 'Ivy, it's time for bed. Church in the morning, and there's a lot to do before we go.'

Ivy pouted, but said no more and went into the scullery to wash. Poppy went soon afterwards, and then, to Marigold's surprise, Mary asked John if he'd take a jug and get a quart of cider from Thomas Bailey's beerhouse on Church Hill.

'I thought it would be a change from my parsnip wine, a special treat for Marigold,' she explained, and with an indulgent smile John heaved himself to his feet.

'I'll go, Mom,' Marigold said quickly.

'Sit still, love, you've had a long journey, and have to go back tomorrow,' John said.

'Did you come by train?' Mary asked the moment the door closed.

Marigold cast her a swift glance. Did she suspect? Mom so often seemed to know things long before you thought anyone else could. 'Yes,' she replied slowly. Richard had wanted to bring her but she'd insisted that this time she went by train. It was too risky, and their weekly drives into the country round Oxford, though making her tremulously happy, also filled her with dread of discovery.

'Not in the big red motor car?'

Marigold sighed. It was, she realized, relief. Now she could talk to Mom, and perhaps begin to understand the odd feelings which even the thought of Richard sent coursing through her blood.

'How did you know?'

'I saw you driving away in it last time, up the hill to Heath Hayes. Who is it, love, and why didn't you say? How did you come to be riding like the gentry in a big motor car?'

'He's one of Professor Roberts's students,' she said quietly. 'He lives near Newcastle-under-Lyme, and his father keeps some horses with Mr Coulthwaite. He spent Christmas with the Robertses, because his family are in America. Last time he was coming the same way to visit Mr Coulthwaite and offered to bring me.'

'You shouldn't have let him, love! What would people say? You know what some of these young men want!'

'Richard's not like that!' Marigold defended him.

'It's Richard, is it? Have you seen him again? Since he took you back to Oxford?'

'Yes. A few times. Mom, it's not what you think! We like to talk. That's all, I swear it is.'

'It may be all now, but rich young men don't make friends with maidservants, Marigold. They just don't. It's my duty to warn you, pet. I had one or two young men who wanted to make friends with me when I worked for Mrs Nugent, but all they really want, and no doubt this Richard's the same, is to use you for their sport. And then you'd be ruined and they couldn't care less. It's not right! You'd best wait for a decent working lad who'll want to marry you before persuading you into his bed.'

Marigold still had little inkling of what that involved, or why girls like Ethel set so much store by it. Richard had not kissed her, although sometimes when he lifted her down from the motor car she thought he wanted to. She loved the strength of him as he held her in his arms. But she was still unawakened.

A vague assumption there was something more she'd not yet experienced hovered at the back of her mind. Never, though, could she associate the crude descriptions of Ethel and her cronies with the magic of what she felt for Richard.

They came from totally different worlds, yet her feelings for Richard, and his for her – for she had an inner certainty they were the same – were special, reverent, and gentle. She dared not call it love, for how could a man like him love a servant? But it had nothing whatsoever to do with the warnings her mother hinted at.

'Does Pa know?' she asked.

'No, and I won't want to worry him if you stop seeing this man and promise not to do anything wrong.'

To Marigold's intense relief, for she knew she could not bear to give up seeing Richard, her father could be heard walking up the yard.

She nodded, thinking guiltily that her Mom might believe it to be the promise she'd demanded. She had never before deceived her parents, and had no wish to now, but her father's return had saved her from uttering a promise she knew she couldn't keep.

There was no more opportunity for private talk. When she went to catch the train the following afternoon it was as if Marigold had escaped, and she was ashamed to realize that that was how she now thought of leaving her home. What had happened to her? Had knowing Richard, which should have been all joy, turned her into an ungrateful daughter who didn't want her family?

'Richard, you really have become most exasperating! Surely you don't have to spend all your time this vacation studying your wretched books?'

'I do, Mother. Next term I sit my final examinations. I must do a lot before I go to Archie's. I've promised to visit him for a couple of days on my way back to Oxford. I can't afford the time to pay calls on the entire neighbourhood.'

'Don't exaggerate. I propose visiting Lady Thornton, that's all.'

'And yesterday it was Mrs Blake, and tomorrow it will no doubt be some other mother with an eligible daughter or two!' Henry, Richard's younger brother, chimed in mischievously, with a wry glance at Richard. 'Why are you so anxious to get him married off, Mother? He doesn't need to marry a fortune, he's got his own money and part of the business.'

Sophia gave him a look which would have annihilated anyone less irrepressible than Henry, Richard thought, hiding a grin.

'It has nothing to do with money, Henry. You are not now a man of the world just because you've travelled a little. I want both you boys to meet suitable young ladies, girls who can be moulded into conformable wives. Heaven knows what sort of dreadful, opinionated blue-stockings Richard is meeting at Oxford, and now you want to go there too. I lose sleep worrying one of you might come home saying you wish to marry one of these frightful suffragettes.'

'I promise I won't marry either a blue-stocking or a suffragette, Mother. In fact I have no desire to marry for years yet, and it would hardly be fair if I did meet some eligible young lady to expect her to wait for ten years or more, would it? Now please excuse me, I really do have work to do.'

'And that silenced dear Mama for at least a minute,' Henry told him later that day. 'Oxford is doing you good, old fellow. In the past you'd have agreed to go with her just for the sake of peace.'

Richard supposed he would. Until recently he had avoided open conflict with his overbearing mother, but he had discovered unexpected pleasure in his academic work, and when the demands of study clashed with her unreasonable plans, made without consultation, he summoned the strength both to refuse her and withstand the subsequent storms.

'Maybe I've grown up at last,' he said now. 'At least you've defied her since you were in the cradle, so you'll not face the same problems.'

'Only when it suits me,' Henry pointed out. 'Most of the time it's simpler just to agree, like Papa does, and hope she doesn't find out I'm not doing what she said.'

'Which she rarely seems to do. You almost always get away with it.'

'Our dear mama, Richard, is so supremely confident she never dreams anyone could disobey her!'

Richard laughed. 'Did she try to throw any American heiresses at you?'

'The ones old enough to marry had no interest in me, I'm too young, so even though she tried it was in the knowledge she had no hope of succeeding. I think it was that failure which makes her even more determined to tackle you as soon as practicable. But don't you know any women at Oxford? Surely they can't all be ugly even if they do have brains?

'There are lots of pretty girls, but you'll have to wait till you get there and find out for yourself!'

Marigold had been given an extra couple of days at home after Easter. The new baby had arrived, and Mrs Roberts planned to spend several weeks with her mother at Old Ridge Court.

'As it's so near your home, and my mother has plenty of maids to help, as well as Baby's new nurse, you could go and visit your mother. Once we've all settled in Miss Baker wants to visit her sister, so you can take charge of the children while she's away, and see your own family when she's back. It all fits in very conveniently.'

Richard immediately suggested meeting her in Hednesford. 'We won't have seen one another for several weeks,' he urged on their last afternoon together before Marigold left Oxford.

'I have to go home during the vacation, but I mean to be in Birmingham for a week. Is there any way you could have time off and come to spend a few days there with me?'

'I couldn't!' Marigold was shocked and at the same time disappointed. Was he, after all, just like the young men her mother had warned her about?

'Then at least we can meet when I am on my way to Birmingham. Marigold, it gets harder to let you go every time. It's not enough, seeing you just for a couple of hours once a week.'

He was sitting with his arm stretched along the back of the seat, and as he spoke he dropped his hand to clasp her shoulder. He turned her to him and slowly drew her into his arms.

Although he often lifted her in and out of the car, he had never kissed her. Now Marigold knew with a tremor of wonder that he was about to do so.

She sighed deeply, and smiled trustingly up at him. Keeping one arm about her shoulders, he traced the delicate lines of her face with his fingers, looking all the time into her eyes.

'You are so incredibly lovely,' he murmured, his mouth slowly approaching hers. She could see the fine hairs of his lashes, long for a man, and smell on his skin the clean, expensive soap he used. His breath fanned her cheeks, and then, as she moved slightly and instinctively raised her face towards his, he pulled her hard against him. His lips, firm and demanding, confidently claimed hers.

For Marigold every other sight and sound and feeling vanished. She could hear nothing except the beating of his heart against hers, and feel nothing except the strength of his body and the warmth of his lips.

At last he released her, and with a sigh of pure contentment she laid her head against his chest.

'My beautiful Marigold! I want you with me all the time, every day of my life!'

The sheer impracticability of that brought her down to earth. It was an impossible fantasy. And if dreams were allowed to become too strong it could prove astonishingly painful when they dissolved, as they invariably must, into reality. She raised herself from where she had leant against his chest.

'It's time to go back. Miss Baker wants to go out tonight, and I said I'd be back early.'

'But you'll meet me while you're at home?'

'I'll try.'

'Where is Old Ridge Court?'

'Near Rugeley. Why?'

'How will you get home?'

'I could go by train, but as it's only four miles, I shall probably walk.'

'I could drive you home from there. What day will you be going? I can arrange to go to Birmingham the same day.'

They planned where to meet, and despite her fears that something would prevent it Richard was there waiting for her.

He leapt out and kissed her eagerly, then lifted her up into the motor car and swung the starting handle. Soon they were bowling along, and came over the brow of the hill, looking down across Hednesford.

'Please stop, I really ought to get down here, Richard,' she said urgently.

As she sat with her back resting against the trunk of a silver birch, sorting out the flowers she'd gathered, Ivy heard the chug-chug of an engine. For a moment, so absorbed was she in her task, she thought it was the steam plough Johnny had taken her to see at Pye Green earlier in the spring. Then she realized it was a motor car approaching the bend in the road just below where she sat on Rawnsley Hills.

There was a small patch of level ground, covered with close-cropped turf, just after the bend. Ivy watched as the motor slowed and came to a stop. The two people in it were talking so intently they had no idea she watched them.

Then as the man moved slightly and his companion was revealed Ivy caught her breath in surprise. She narrowed her eyes. Yes, it was Marigold. The sly creature, driving in a motor car with a man, and none of them at home had the slightest idea of it!

After a moment's thought she dragged a rather crumpled sheet of paper and a stick of charcoal out of her pocket. Using a flat stone as support, she quickly sketched the man's profile. He had a high forehead, a strong nose, and a determined chin. She considered the drawing carefully, her head on one side. It was good, despite the unevenness of the stone. She made one or two slight changes, drawing his brows a little straighter, sketching in a flopping lank of hair, adjusting the angle of his jaw and making his lips fuller, and was satisfied. Anyone could recognize him.

As they continued to sit there, Ivy began to sketch the car. They didn't see many in Hednesford, and it was something new. She enjoyed the challenge of using unfamiliar objects as models, and getting every last detail accurate.

But before she could complete it the man got out, walked round the motor car and lifted Marigold down. As he held her she stretched up and kissed him, then they walked away together, hand in hand.

Ivy pushed herself back against the silver birch, knowing that if she kept still they would be unlikely to see her in the dappled shade. But they did not look her way, and soon vanished along a track winding amongst the trees, which eventually led down into the town.

Ivy pondered, then smiled slowly to herself. Hastily she gathered up the flowers, bundled them into a shopping basket she'd brought with her, and scrambled down the hill towards the motor car.

An hour later Richard returned alone to find her absorbed in doing another more detailed drawing of his motor car. 'Hello, there. What's that?'

She smiled shyly up at him. 'I was drawing,' she told him, holding out the sheet of paper.

'This is incredible!'

He studied the page, crowded with several drawings of his motor car from different angles. In between she had crammed more detailed sketches of certain parts, and he marvelled at the sure touch she exhibited.

'I wanted to do it for Marigold,' she said, and watched intently as the shock registered on his face.

'Marigold?'

'My sister. I saw her with you earlier, and I thought she'd like a picture of your motor car. My name's Ivy.'

'You're Marigold's sister?'

'I drew you, too,' she said hesitantly, taking the paper from him and turning it over. 'Before you and Marigold went for a walk. I was sitting up there.' She gestured vaguely behind her. 'Look, don't you think it's like you?'

'Yes. Yes, it is, very good.'

'I wish I had the money for some good paper, then I could do proper drawings. I'm sure Marigold would like one of you in your motor car. I didn't draw her in it, I can do that any time, I've often done pictures of her.'

He looked at her suspiciously. Was this innocent-looking child, with her smooth dark hair and pert lips, no more than seven or eight years old, trying to blackmail him? Surely not!

'Sometimes Mrs Nugent buys my drawings. Do you work for her too? This isn't her motor car, it's a black one, so you can't be her chauffeur.'

'No, I don't work for her. But I – met your sister at Old Ridge Court, and when I saw her today I offered her a lift. It's a long way for her to walk.'

'Would you like a drawing of your motor car?'

'Would you sell me that one?'

'If you want.'

'It's good. Yes, I would like it. How much does Mrs Nugent pay?'

'A guinea,' Ivy said quickly.

'A guinea!' This was outrageous, and by now Richard's suspicions were hardening. But it was becoming clear that if he did not silence this child, she could make trouble for Marigold. Mrs Roberts would be horrified if she found out about their friendship. He dared not risk the chance that Marigold might lose her job.

'I'll buy it for half a crown,' he offered.

Ivy shook her head. 'Mrs Nugent will give me a guinea. 'Specially if I make it tidy, and put Marigold in it, like she was.'

'A guinea then.' He dug his hand into his pocket, frustrated and angry. He'd like to tell the obnoxious little brat to do her worst, but he wanted to spare Marigold. If he had the drawing Ivy could not cause trouble.

'Here's a sovereign and two sixpences.'

'Thank you. Here's the drawing. I'll be able to buy some really nice paper now. I must be going home for my dinner. Goodbye.'

He watched as she picked up the old basket and walked sedately away. She didn't turn round, and he marvelled at her self-possession. How could Marigold, who was so sensitive, so kind and thoughtful, have a sister who could so effectively blackmail strangers?

He was in no doubt about her intentions. She had known precisely what she was doing. Give me money or I'll cause trouble for my sister!

Swiftly he climbed into the motor car and drove away. Should he warn Marigold about Ivy or trust the child would now be satisfied? It would be several weeks before they could meet again, and he dared not write to her. There was nothing he could do.

To Marigold's delight she found Johnny at home.

'Johnny! I didn't know you were coming today,' she said happily.

'Came by train,' he said with a grin. 'You've grown up a lot, Sis.'

'And how are you getting on, son?' his father asked.

'I've got more lads under me, in the new works,' he said proudly. 'And I drive the motors to the customers,' he added.

'You can drive a motor car?' Poppy asked eagerly. 'Oh, will you take me out in one? Please, Johnny! It's what I want most in all the world!'

Marigold felt a stab of guilt. Richard would be delighted to give her sisters rides in his car. But she daren't tell them about him. It was bad enough that Mom thought she was not seeing him any longer. Perhaps Poppy would never achieve her ambition.

'I realized I hadn't been home since before Ivy's birthday, and might not see you again till after yours, Marigold, so I brought presents for you all,' Johnny announced. 'Where's Ivy?'

'She went to meet Marigold, but must have gone the wrong way. I expect she's gone off in one of her dreams, looking for flowers,' Mary said.

'Still likes flowers, does she? Good, I've brought her a book on plants. It isn't a new one, I found it at a sale, but it's got every single plant ever known in it, I should think. She can have it later.'

As well as a shawl and a parasol for Marigold, he'd brought Poppy a cookery book, Mary a shawl, and for his father there was some tobacco and an intricately carved pipe.

When Ivy returned, just as Mary was serving the chicken she'd roasted on a spit over the range, she was carrying a huge bunch of flowers, but she dropped them immediately and insisted on showing Marigold and Johnny her latest drawing. 'Look, it's Pa.'

After dinner, as the others exclaimed over what was a very lifelike portrait of John bent over his carving, Ivy was poring over the book Johnny gave her.

'Mom, this book says what plants poison us!' she said excitedly. 'And which ones are good for curing illnesses! And how to make ointments and medicines!'

'I didn't bring it to make you into a doctor,' Johnny said with a laugh. 'I thought you'd like it to copy the pictures, and find out what all these flowers you bring home are.'

Ivy nodded, and smiled shyly up at him. 'I will. It's the best present I've ever had,' she reassured him.

The next week after dinner Ivy slipped away. Sunday afternoon was the best time to find Sam Bannister alone. The Potters always went to visit their daughter in Heath Hayes on Sundays, and Sam was alone in the room where he slept behind the chemist's shop.

When he came to the back door he was rubbing his eyes. 'What d'yer wanna wake me up fer?' he grumbled.

Ivy pushed past him. 'Why are you asleep in the middle of the day? I've got sixpence for that ointment you told me about.'

His eyes lost all trace of sleepiness and grew sharp with suspicion. 'Where'd yer get such a lot o' money from?' he demanded. 'A tanner? You? Show me, then.'

'Not unless you promise I can have some. You said you'd give me some for sixpence.'

'Oh, all right. But I gotta put it on.'

'No! I don't let anyone see my scars!'

'Aw, give over, Ivy! Nobody cares abaht yer flippin' scars but yerself! Yer'd let a doctor see 'em. It's on'y so's it gets put on right. See, it don't work if it's done wrong. Yer wouldn't want ter waste a tanner, now, would yer?'

Suddenly Ivy made up her mind. 'I'll let you put it on if you'll show me how to distil things. My book says lots of things have to be distilled, but it doesn't say how to do it.'

'Why should I show yer? I 'ad ter work 'ere for years before I were shown 'ow ter do it.'

She sighed. 'How much do you want?'

Sam guffawed. 'What d'yer think I am? Proper daft? Yer still 'aven't shown me yer tanner. If yer's got that, which I doubt. I don't believe yer's got more!'

Ivy was about to reveal the untold wealth she had acquired from Marigold's fancy friend a week ago, when she paused. Sam had an unusually crafty look in his eyes.

'I have got it, so there,' she retorted. 'But if you don't believe me . . .'

'I was goin' ter suggest summat else.'

'What?'

He gulped. 'This is a deadly secret. Yer gotta promise never ter tell anyone! Never, or the devil'll come an' get yer! It's magic, yer see.'

'Oh, do get on with it, Sam! We're wasting time, and the Potters could be back any minute.'

'Nah, they won't be back till it's dark. I'll give yer the ointment ter cure yer scars fer sixpence, right? An' I'll show yer 'ow ter distil things. But I want yer ter try another ointment fer me – be a sorta experiment.'

'I don't understand. Another ointment for my scars? Why should you give me that and show me how to distil stuff?'

'Well, it's a sorta new ointment I've invented. Not fer scars. If it works I'll mek a fortune!'

'But what is it?' She was growing impatient.

'It's fer mekin' bosoms grow bigger!'

Ivy stared at him in astonishment. He was red in the face and seemed to be finding it difficult to breathe.

'That's daft!' she declared dismissively. 'Bosoms grow when you get older.'

'No it ain't daft! I've bin readin' some old newspapers, an' there's lots of advertisements fer things like that. Some women'll pay pounds fer it!'

'But what do you want me to do? I haven't started growing a bosom yet. Poppy has.'

'Thass the point. It'd be no good tryin' it out on someone 'oo was already growin' a bosom, 'cause yer'd never know if it was the ointment causin' it ter grow. If yer started growin' one it'd prove it.'

'What would I have to do?'

'I'd 'ave ter do it, like the ointment fer yer scars. It'd need ter be done ev'ry week. Tell yer what, yer 'elps me do this experiment, an' I'll give yer the scar ointment in exchange.'

'And show me how to distil things?'

'Yer'll do it?'

'If you show me how to distil things. Show me first, I mean. And other weeks you can show me how to make pills and ointments.'

The bargain satisfactorily concluded Sam led her through into the small room between the shop and his own room at the back. Quickly he showed her the apparatus.

'Yer 'as ter boil up the stuff in this, which is called the still, then the steam goes through 'ere, an' as it cools the water wi' the oils in it drops inter this bottle. After a bit the oils float on top, an' that's it.'

Ivy was appalled. 'I can't do this at home. And I couldn't buy a still like this. How much does one cost?'

'Pounds an' pounds. But sometimes I could do it fer yer,' he suggested, slyly generous.

Reluctantly Ivy agreed. 'But I'd want to come and watch,' she stipulated.

Sam didn't argue. 'I s'pose yer'll 'av ter, if yer don't trust me,' he said huffily. 'Now come and let's do the ointment.'

Ivy followed him into the shop, which always fascinated her with the hundreds of different packages and little boxes neatly arranged on shelves that lined three walls. In front of the window, in which the gloriously coloured bottles were displayed, was a locked glass case holding a selection of more expensive soaps and perfumes. Another locked case in a corner held poisons.

Sam took down a small jar from a shelf near the window.

'Is that it? I could have bought it from Mr Potter,' she said in disappointment.

'Yes, but it'd cost yer two and elevenpence farthin', an' I'm givin' it yer cost price. We won't use all of it now, anyroad.'

Ivy began to roll up her sleeve. Sam shook his head.

'No, I can't do it like that. Yer'll 'av ter come back in my room, where yer can lay down. Like on a doctor's couch,' he explained.

It took him a considerable time, and many reminders that he'd already performed his side of the bargain in showing Ivy how things were distilled, before he persuaded her to remove her blouse and unbutton her liberty bodice.

'It's on'y like when yer play 'ospitals wi' our Lizzie and Billy,' he reminded her.

'I don't have to take my clothes off then,' she said petulantly.

'Yer pushed yer skirt an' drawers down when yer said yer 'ad yer appendix out,' he reminded her.

'Then why can't I just push my blouse up?'

''Cause then I can't get at yer arm prop'ly.'

At last she was sitting on the side of the bed, naked from the waist up. She watched with critical eyes as he sat beside her and smoothed the first ointment into the scars left from the time she'd fallen against the hot bars of the fire.

First he held back her smooth black hair and rubbed the ointment into the scar on her forehead. It smelled of a herb she didn't recognize, and something astringent which made her want to cough. Then he held her arm with one hand, turning it this way and that so as to reach the full length of the criss-crossed scars on her upper arm, shoulder and neck. Ivy rarely looked at them, normally shuddering away from the red, puckered flesh, but now she subjected them to a close scrutiny. She would need to know whether they were getting better.

'Now the other. Stay there, it's in one o' the drawers,' Sam ordered.

He was soon back with the other ointment, which was creamier, white and with only a faint perfume. Lavender, Ivy thought.

'Lay yersen down, I can't do it wi' yer sitting up,' he ordered.

Ivy sighed, but complied. She was eager to be done with it and go home, where she had several new flowers to identify from her book.

Sam knelt beside the bed. Slowly he spread the ointment on his hands, then began to smooth it gently over her flat chest. Ivy wriggled. It tickled. And his fingers were rough. Then she was distracted by the look on Sam's face, and frowned, puzzled. He was flushed, and began to breathe heavily. After a while he began to tremble, and then suddenly he turned away and leant across the bed, rocking backwards and forwards.

She sat up in alarm. 'Sam, are you ill? What's wrong?'

'It's nothin', just a cramp,' he said hoarsely, and turned away from her to push the lid back on the jar. 'I'll 'ave ter do it every week, mind. Get dressed now, but come back next Sunday afternoon, same time.'

Mrs Roberts didn't return to Oxford until the beginning of June. On the first Wednesday afterwards Marigold took a bus for Woodstock, where she hoped to meet Richard.

'I shall know from Professor Roberts when you get home, so as long as I'm not actually sitting an examination I'll be meeting you as usual,' he'd said before they parted outside Hednesford.

She got down from the bus in the pretty market square, and walked towards the entrance to the park of Blenheim Palace.

'We can meet inside, no one will mind. In fact we go skating on the lake sometimes, so I know it well,' Richard said.

It was the first time Marigold had been there, and she was rather hesitant about crossing the high-walled courtyard outside the gatehouse until she saw Richard's car parked in one corner.

He must be inside. She stepped hesitantly through the archway, and saw him immediately, strolling along the edge of the lake to the right, an enormous palace visible on the far side.

'Darling Marigold, it's been so long!'

It seemed so natural to kiss, and Marigold held up her face expectantly.

'Let's go this way.'

Richard, his arm about her waist, guided her alongside the wall which surrounded the entire park and the lake, away from the huge palace which was bigger even than the Oxford colleges.

They soon reached a secluded spot on the shores of the lake, in the shelter of trees heavy with summer foliage.

'I brought a rug for us to sit on,' Richard said, pointing to a tartan rug he had already laid on the ground. 'And I'm cooling a bottle of champagne in the lake. To celebrate our reunion.'

'Mom makes elderflower champagne,' Marigold said. 'Is it like that?'

'It's bubbly. I came early so that it would be cool. It should be ready now. Let's try some.'

It was, Marigold decided, not quite as nice as the elderflower champagne, which tasted more like lemonade, and after one glass she laughingly refused more. 'No, really, I don't think I like it. The bubbles get up my nose and make me want to sneeze. Why do people like it so much?' she asked, puzzled.

'An acquired taste, I suppose. Tell me what you've been doing. It's seemed so long since I saw you.'

She talked mainly about the large country house where she had stayed with Mrs Roberts, even more imposing than Gordon Villa, but as she spoke she realized with some surprise that she hadn't been nearly so overawed as she would have expected. She seemed to be getting accustomed to living in rich, even opulent surroundings.

Richard told her about his examinations, which were now almost over, and his father's business, which he expected to work in after the summer.

'He wants to export more to America. He thinks the situation in Europe is getting more dangerous.'

'Dangerous? How?'

'The French and the Germans are squabbling in North Africa, the Balkans are in turmoil yet again, the Turks and the Italians are fighting. It just seems that nothing is the same as it was. Father believes we shall do better in America, and he intends to set up a shop there.'

'Will you have to go too?' Marigold turned to him, suddenly realizing that this enchanted time in Oxford was about to end.

'No, I don't think so.'

'You'll still be so far away,' she whispered. 'I don't think I can bear it.'

'We'll see one another again, I promise.'

She didn't know how this could possibly be, but when he bent to kiss her Marigold turned her lips towards his, seeking comfort. This was no gentle kiss such as she'd been used to, a tender exploration of mouth and lips and tongue, soft flesh meeting and mingling and giving exquisite pleasure. This was fierce, demanding, a craving to reach one another's very souls, to crush and be crushed. Marigold was overwhelmed by a need she'd never known before.

Richard had intended no more for the moment than a gentle

comfort, but the passion he recognized in her could not be assuaged by a light touch. As she strained against him, her hands clutching his hair, her lips opening in a wordless plea, his resolve to keep a fierce rein on his own desires faltered.

She was so young, so inexperienced, nothing like Flo. He'd been aware from the moment he knew he wanted her that he'd have to proceed very slowly. It was a new experience. To his surprise he realized he was now treating her as he would a girl of his own class, with its very different code dictating the speed and extent of his courtship.

But her grief, changing so suddenly into this raging passion, inflamed him beyond caution. He removed the pins from her hair until it fell in a golden shower to float round her shoulders. The silken feel of it on his hands was a shivering ecstasy, and he wound it sensuously round his fingers, lost in the delight of it.

Gradually his hands came free of her hair. Marigold sighed as they slid down from her shoulders, moulding her slender body in the thin print dress she wore.

She pressed even closer to him, murmuring his name as he began to kiss her cheeks, her chin, and then her neck. She arched away from him, unconsciously willing him to explore further, and shuddered in astonished delight when his hand folded over her breast.

'My love, my dearest love!' he whispered. 'Marigold, I can't bear to let you go! Love me, let me love you properly!'

His hands strayed past her waist, and as he lay down and pulled her close to him she could feel the heat of his desire. Somewhere, in the deepest recesses of her mind, she knew she had discovered what it was that tempted girls into this sort of behaviour. The sensations were so delicious, making her want to forget everything else but the need to be close to him, to lose herself in the ecstasy of desire, to savour fully what she knew instinctively would be even more rapturous bliss.

But when he began to undo the buttons at the front of her dress it broke the spell. Marigold's eyes opened wide with shock, and she gasped as if just awakening from a dream. 'Richard, no!' she protested.

'It's all right, my darling. I won't hurt you, I just can't bear the thought of being away from you soon, perhaps for a long time. Darling, you want me as much as I want you. We love one another, and I need you so much!' he whispered. 'I can't let you go. When I leave Oxford come back with me. I can easily rent a cottage for you somewhere near my home. Of course, that's what we'll do! I can see you almost every day, and you wouldn't have to work any more!'

She shuddered, and moved suddenly away from him. When he reached out a hand to stop her she shook her head, pushing his hand away before beginning to do up her dress.

'What is it?' he asked, worried.

'I'm not that sort of girl,' she said quietly, struggling to prevent the sobs from breaking loose.

She wanted him to continue, she knew. How she wanted it! But it was wrong. They were two people whose lives had crossed, but who could never mean anything more to one another. She knew she loved him, but her mother's warnings echoed in her head. He would forget her. Soon he would be away from Oxford, and unless she did the unthinkable and went with him he would forget her.

'There's nothing wrong, my darling. It's natural, when two people love like we do, to want to kiss, and touch each other, make love together. We can have our own home.'

'You can't love me, not honestly,' she suddenly cried out, struggling to her feet. 'What would happen to me when you wanted to marry some suitable, well-bred girl? Would I have to find another man to keep me?' She backed away as he reached out to her. 'No! Stay there! I couldn't get a decent job. You don't understand, you're rich, from a rich family. I'm just a miner's daughter, a servant myself, and I might have known no good would come of it. We can't just be friends, and I won't be your whore!'

Chapter Seven

NINETEEN FOURTEEN was one of the finest summers of recent years, but Marigold moved through her duties oblivious to the halcyon days. It was a year since she and Richard had quarrelled, but she was still numb with misery.

Garden parties became the normal way of spending the afternoons, especially when the long vacation began. While the young people played tennis or croquet, and punted on the river, Marigold often had to serve tea to the guests on Gordon Villa's spacious lawn.

One day the Professor invited several colleagues and a couple of retired army officers to tea. Marigold was helping to pass sandwiches.

Two elderly men were sitting on wooden benches, conversing in the tones of the very deaf. As Marigold went towards them she could hear their voices plainly.

'Those damned Serbs are at it again.'

'What's that? Serbs?'

'Don't think the damned Balkans'll ever get sorted out. They're like Ireland, always a problem. Some fanatic shot an Austrian Archduke. Place called Sarajevo, or something like that. Ever heard of it?'

'Always get those places confused. Spent most of my time working on Chinese history.'

'Central Europe's one petty squabble after another. It's a wonder there's any royalty left, so many of 'em get shot at by some disaffected plotter.'

Marigold moved away to fetch more of the dainty sandwiches, but that night she mentioned what she had overheard to Miss Baker, whose brother, she had discovered, was an army officer.

'Are there lots of killings?' she asked. 'Is it worse than Ireland? It seems so dreadful to kill kings and queens.'

'We did it once,' Miss Baker reminded her.

'But that was hundreds of years ago! Surely we've become more civilized?'

'That's your answer. The Central European countries are very backward in many ways.'

By the end of July the situation had become grave. Every time there were guests Marigold heard talk of the happenings in Europe instead of university affairs and the perennial Irish question.

'It looks like war,' Miss Baker said one morning as they were taking the children into Oxford to order new shoes for them.

'War?' Marigold was shaken out of her lethargy. 'I heard Germany and Russia were threatening one another, but I don't understand why. What has it all to do with an assassination in the Balkans?'

'Austria is threatening the Serbs, after the Austrian Archduke Franz Ferdinand was killed. Germany supports Austria, Russia supports Serbia.'

'But will that involve us? None of our Empire is threatened, is it? Like it was in South Africa? Though I never did know the causes of that,' Marigold said ruefully. 'At school the only history we were taught was the dates of kings and queens and battles hundreds of years ago – nothing about recent times.'

'It may involve us if Germany threatens France. They're old enemies, remember.'

'That's terrible, but surely we wouldn't be in danger? If Germany is fighting Russia as well they wouldn't have enough strength to attack us.'

Miss Baker sighed. 'That depends. And it's not so simple. I heard the Professor say he suspects Germany will attempt a sudden strike to defeat France and make them helpless before turning on Russia. The best way into France is through Belgium, but Belgian neutrality is guaranteed by Britain, amongst others.'

'So if Germany attacks Belgium to get to France, we'll have to go and defend Belgium? Why do we have to fight other countries' wars?'

'It wouldn't stop there. Would you prefer a country like Germany to rule everyone else?'

'So what will happen?'

'I imagine if the diplomats can't find a solution, our armies will be going to France soon. It's not unexpected by everyone. We've been building the navy up for years, keeping ahead of Germany.'

'If war comes, many of the Professor's students will want to go, I'm sure of it.'

Johnny held Lucy's hand as they walked along the canal towpath. 'I have to go,' he said, the words forced out of him.

She could barely restrain her tears. 'I know, and really I'm proud of you for doing your duty, but – I shall miss you so much! I love you, Johnny.'

'Lucy, I love you too, I always have!'

'Johnny, you know there's no one else for me,' Lucy said firmly. 'We'll be married, before you enlist.'

He could hardly believe his ears.

'I'm only just nineteen, Lucy. Much too young, people would say, to get married, even though I'm earning good money.'

Lucy took a deep breath. The fire and spirit of her Irish ancestors seemed to flow into her. 'You may be killed,' she stated bluntly. 'That's what happens to soldiers. I'd never forgive myself if you were and we hadn't belonged to one another because of some silly notion that we were too young. I always meant to marry you.' She suppressed her tears with difficulty. 'And if you died I'd want to have your child. Something of you, to remember you.'

'Is there time? Before I go?' he asked.

'I can be ready quickly. I don't need a new dress, my best one will do. Let's go and see if we can get a special licence. I've read about them, but I don't know how to start! Then we could have a week or two longer.'

'But your mother?'

'Leave her to me. She won't be surprised. And she likes you, Johnny, don't worry. She knows you're a good, God-fearing man.'

'A house! I can't find you a house or even rooms in the time. And how can I support you?'

'Why would I want a house? There'd be no sense in leaving Mom and having extra expense just to to live on my own.'

'But, I – Lucy, I like your mom, it's not that, but I'd want us to have our own home.'

'And so I mean to, later, but it doesn't make sense now. We couldn't afford more than a couple of rooms, so we'll save the money and stay with Mom. I can go on working. There'll be lots of jobs for women if all the young men enlist. Why all these objections? Are you having second thoughts? Am I rushing you?' she teased.

His response left her breathless and in no doubt of his need of her. Some while later they strolled home busy making plans, the first of which was to take Lucy to Hednesford to meet his family and gain their blessing and permission.

Poppy was oblivious of the looming clouds. She had worked in the house during this summer like a zombie, ignoring Ivy's absences, doing her sister's work as well as her own without complaint. Every morning, when Ivy had gone to school, she had taken a small sheet of paper out of her pocket and crossed off another day. Only another six months and two weeks and three days before she was fourteen, old enough to get a job, old enough to escape from this claustrophobic drudgery which she hated with a fierce but unexpressed loathing.

She had no friends. How could she when she never had time to go out with them?

'Of course there's time,' Mary told her one evening when Poppy had refused to walk with them up on Hednesford Hills. 'You work much harder than you need, love, and I'm so thankful I can rely on you. But you can leave the ironing till tomorrow.'

'It'll be too hot to do it during the day. I'd rather do it now, while I can leave the door open and the air's a bit cooler.'

'It's a lovely evening, and lots of your old schoolfriends'll be going. Folk always walk up there when it's fine.'

'No one wants me,' Poppy said sullenly. 'It'll be different when I've got a job, a proper job, and can buy some nice clothes.'

'Well you can soon, when your birthday comes. Maybe I can stop working for Mrs Andrews then. If I can do more sewing at home, we'll manage fine. Sure you won't come?'

Poppy shook her head and defiantly plonked the irons on the fire to heat.

'There's a lot to do if Johnny's coming home on Sunday, like his postcard said.'

Mary sighed and left her to do it. She was worried, but had no idea how to treat Poppy in order to make her happier.

Poppy was oblivious to her mother's concern: she was counting the days till she could go out to work. And, she vowed to herself, it would not be in Hednesford or anywhere nearby. Nor would it be in service like Marigold. Beyond that she hadn't thought, but when Johnny came home on Sunday she'd ask him to let her know about jobs in Birmingham. Soon she'd be old enough, soon she could go to a big city and get away from the grime and grind of life in a colliery town.

Richard filled his glass and pushed the port along the table.

Henry swallowed hastily and refilled his own glass before pushing it on. 'I intend to apply for a commission, too, Father,' he said firmly. His voice was steady although his hands shook slightly as he tossed off the contents of the glass.

Mr Endersby sighed. 'I might have expected it. All the young fools will want to be involved. But it'll be over by Christmas, Henry. Wouldn't it be better to get on with Oxford? What's the use of joining at all?'

'Do you really believe it'll be over so soon?' Richard asked quietly. 'Is that why you're diverting most of your exports to America?'

His father glared at him. 'Whenever it's over, the Germans won't be buying expensive china for a while. Are you planning to join up too and desert the firm?'

'You're still hale and hearty, Father, well able to look after the firm without me,' Richard said. He bit back the retort that his father was so determined to remain in charge that for the past year he had never even considered Richard's suggestions. There was pain behind the old man's bluster, and he didn't wish to add to it. But he also planned to enlist in the war which had been declared a few days before.

'That's no answer. You're rushing to the colours too, leaving your poor mother to weep for both her boys.'

'Joining the army does not mean we inevitably get killed,' Richard said evenly. 'Many mothers will weep in the next few months, but if we don't stop the Germans soon thousands more will mourn for their loved ones. I can fly an aeroplane, and modern war will depend on modern inventions. I shall join the army as a pilot.'

He had anticipated the explosion of rage, but it still made him wince. At least it had turned his father's wrath away from Henry, and the regrettable fact that the younger son had drunk considerably more wine and port than normal.

'I mean to spend a couple of weeks visiting friends, saying farewell,' Richard said calmly when his father subsided. 'I will come here to spend a final few days with you and Mother and then go to enlist. Now ought we not join Mother in the drawing room?'

It was Wednesday, and rather than stay in the house where all the talk was of war, Marigold decided to go and sit beside the Cherwell. She knew of a quiet backwater where she could be sure of being alone, hidden by the drooping branches of the willow trees.

Would Richard be in the army by now? She walked along the river path, bunching her hands into fists, unaware of the pain as her nails bit into the palms. Had she been a fool to refuse the love he offered? Even if he didn't love her in the way she thought of love, it would have been better than the sheer misery which had clutched at her since that dreadful day in Blenheim Park when she had rejected him and run away.

She'd destroyed his letters, too. She hadn't dared open any of them, and after a month or so they had ceased. She'd been able to tell Mom truthfully that she no longer saw the rich young man with the car, and she knew Mary had breathed a sigh of relief.

But how she wished she'd been less firm! Even now he might be in the army, in danger, and she'd never know. She'd never know if he lived or died.

At the thought she uttered a heartrending sob, and pushed through the curtain of willow to throw herself down on the grass beneath.

'Marigold, my love, what's the matter?'

Marigold froze. She must be dreaming! It wasn't Richard's voice. Nor was it his hand on her shoulder . . .

But when he lifted her up and cradled her in his arms she knew it was no dream, and clutched him feverishly as she sobbed out her misery and fears.

'How did you find me?' she asked when she was calmer.

'I came to meet you. I hoped Wednesday was still your day off and waited, then followed you here. I didn't want to speak to you where we might be seen. I didn't know if you were still angry with me.'

'Oh, Richard, I was a fool! I've been so afraid I'd never see you again.'

'Why didn't you answer my letters? You did get them, didn't you?'

She nodded. 'I didn't dare read them,' she said quietly. 'I knew if you wanted me I'd come to you. I had to try and forget you, because it's wrong.'

'Then you do love me. It's not wrong to love.'

'It is when there's no future. You're different from us, Richard. You may think you love me but you'd no more introduce me to your parents than I would you to mine.'

He was silent, uncomfortably aware of the truth in what she said.

She was speaking again, and for a moment he did not realize she was referring to their parents.

'They'd all be scandalized. They'd think me no better than some of those poor girls who live in St Ebbe's or Jericho, trying to earn a living by selling their bodies because there's nothing else for them to do.'

'I know you're not like that. But I love you so much. You love me too?'

Shyly she nodded, and for a while was lost in the storm of sweet kisses he gave and demanded. At last, reluctant yet breathless, she drew away.

'You're not going into the army, are you?' she asked hesitantly.

'I must, my love. We can't let the Germans get away with what they're doing.'

'No!'

'Darling, I must. This year, partly to try and forget you, I've been learning to fly an aeroplane. They'll need pilots in this war, men like me.'

She began to shiver uncontrollably, and he wrapped his jacket round her and tried to soothe her.

Marigold was still trembling, but gradually her eyelids drooped, her breathing deepened, and she was still, exhausted by the stress of emotion.

Richard surveyed her with wry amusement. He'd tried to forget her, especially when his letters went unanswered. He'd expected she'd be no more of a memory than Berthe, if a sweeter one, but it hadn't happened like that. Marigold had burrowed her way into his heart and refused to be dislodged or forgotten, however hard he tried.

How often during the past lonely months had he dreamed of her in his arms? But she looked a child still, in her plain cotton dress fastened high under her chin, her golden hair in tumbled disarray, her cheeks flushed and her adorable mouth so soft and tempting. How could he abuse her trust? He didn't want to, but she was so desirable!

A few minutes later she opened her eyes to find her head nestled against his shoulder, and her arm across his chest. Her eyes filled first with alarm, and then confusion as recollection of recent events returned.

'I – I'm sorry!' she gasped, and tried to slide away from him.

'Don't move. You look so comfortable.'

She gulped, took a deep breath, smiled at him and nodded, and all his resolve instantly dissipated. He kissed away the tears, and when she trustingly turned her face towards him, lifting up her mouth to his, he surrendered to desire and kissed her long and deep.

Marigold clung to him, returning his fervour with a passion matching his own. 'Richard, I love you!' she murmured, and suddenly shy at her declaration, buried her face in his shoulder.

He laughed softly. 'I love you too. I didn't know how much until I saw you again. I don't know how I've survived all this time without you.'

Her ardour surprised him, but he realized she had missed him as much as he had her, and the knowledge made him wonderfully content. As their caresses grew more daring he marvelled at the firmness and perfection of her body.

Marigold was lost to every consideration but the sheer bliss of being held in his arms again, of knowing he was back and she was still his beloved. Instinctively she responded to his ardour with freedom and joy.

She had little to guide her. The crude insinuations of her fellow servants were nothing to do with this fever, this torrent of bliss which flooded her entire being. When finally he joined with her, she was engulfed by an ecstasy she had never dreamed of, and responded fiercely, triumphantly, aware only in some distant corner of her mind that now he was truly hers, and always would be.

'So we're getting married in Longbridge next Sunday, by special licence. It's all fixed,' Johnny said breathlessly.

They had scarcely entered the house and Lucy been introduced before he'd begun his explanations. Marigold, who had been on the same train but had not seen them as she walked slowly, dreamily, from the station, to enter the house a few minutes later, hadn't even taken off her hat.

'I hope you approve,' Lucy said quietly, looking from John to Mary with such unconscious appeal in her eyes that Mary stifled the protest she'd been about to utter.

She was a pretty girl, Mary admitted, with her vivid blue eyes, turned-up nose, and mop of black curly hair. So far as one could tell after five minutes' acquaintance she was nicely spoken and well mannered.

Before she could speak Ivy interrupted. 'Johnny! Oh, Lucy, this is exciting. Can I be a bridesmaid? Please?'

Lucy smiled at her, but shook her head. 'Ivy, I'd love to ask you if it were possible, but there isn't time. There isn't a moment to make a dress for me, let alone for bridesmaids.'

'I wouldn't want a very pretty dress, with lots of frills,' Ivy said hurriedly.

'Lucy won't be having a new dress at all,' Johnny intervened.

After a moment Ivy turned away, and quietly went to clamber up on to Marigold's lap, where she buried her head in her sister's shoulder. 'It's because of my scars,' she whispered, her breath catching in a sob.

'Nonsense, Ivy, that's got nothing to do with it,' Marigold tried to console her.

'Will you let me be bridesmaid when you get married?' Ivy asked.

Marigold did not reply apart from hugging Ivy close. She would never marry. Richard wouldn't marry a servant. And she couldn't endure being married to anyone else, sharing with another the intimacies she had a few days ago with Richard. The very thought made her shudder with distaste.

Mary was speaking to Lucy, and Marigold thrust aside her own thoughts.

'You're very young, both of you,' Mary said, suppressing a sigh. It had come far earlier than she'd thought, losing Johnny. If only he'd been honest, not stolen things, not had to be sent away. Then she chided herself for selfishness. He was happy, doing a job he loved and getting on well.

'We know our own minds,' Johnny replied.

'But if – if you were killed, lad, and Lucy was left with a child, it'd be hard for her,' John said gruffly.

Lucy turned to him, taking Johnny's hand in hers. 'We all know Johnny risks his life, and I'm proud he's willing to, even though I'd rather the need wasn't there. If he gave me a child I'd be just as proud, and there would still be something of Johnny left if he didn't come back. Would you deny us the chance of that happiness? And in case you're wondering, I'm not already with child, Johnny and I haven't done wrong. But if you refuse permission for us to wed I'll do my best to get pregnant, whatever my religion says, and whether his child be a bastard or not!'

Well spoken, Lucy, Marigold thought in admiration. She could never have faced Richard's parents so proudly. Then a thought hit her like a blow in the stomach and she paled, thankful she was already sitting down.

She had never considered the possibility of becoming pregnant. On both Thursday and Friday she'd managed to escape for a couple of hours and meet Richard in their private haven beneath the willows. She had willingly and joyfully given herself to him without considering possible consequences.

But her case was different. However much he loved her, or said he did – and she certainly believed him – he could never marry her. If he weren't enlisting he might once more offer to set her up in a cottage near his home, as he'd done when they quarrelled, but did she now want that? She couldn't be his kept woman, for she would be for ever cut off from her beloved family. Yet she couldn't endure to lose him. It was an insoluble problem. She forced her attention back to the present.

'It's earlier than I'd have wished to see Johnny wed,' her father was saying, 'but times are different now, and I like your spirit, young Lucy, so you'll have my blessing.'

Lucy gave an unladylike whoop of delight and crossed over to John's chair to kiss him, while Johnny turned to hug his mother. For a while all was confusion, and Mary hastily wiped away a tear. To disguise her emotion she began bustling about with preparations for dinner.

It was to be a simple wedding, Lucy declared as they sat round the big table, eating stewed rabbit, with potatoes and fresh peas out of the garden, followed by sippet pudding. Mary had opened a bottle of her new elderflower champagne, and Marigold thought fleetingly of the real champagne she had once drunk with Richard.

'You can get a train on Saturday to Birmingham, then change and get one to Longbridge. It goes from New Street. Or if you prefer you could get a tram to Selly Oak and then one of the new petrol buses towards Rubery. I've written down directions here for both ways, and where you're to get off,' Johnny said importantly. 'Lucy's mother will make up beds for the night. Will you be able to come from Oxford, Marigold? I'm going to pay for the tickets,' Johnny said.

'I'm sure Mrs Roberts would give me time off,' she said quickly. She couldn't refuse to attend her brother's wedding. It might be the last time she'd see Johnny before he enlisted in the army. It could be the last time ever.

'Mom will get a meal for us, but I suppose you'll have to be back for work on Monday?' Lucy asked, and Mary nodded.

'Yes, love, we'll have to come back Sunday night. Will you and Johnny be going away?'

'Just for a few days,' Johnny said. 'Neither of us've ever seen the sea, so we thought we'd go to Blackpool.'

'Where's Blackpool?' Ivy demanded, having recovered her spirits.

'The nearest I shall ever get to Ireland,' Lucy said with a laugh. 'I've an aunt there who runs a boarding house, she'll put us up, and we can wave across the Irish Sea and watch the boats.'

The rest of the day passed with lots to discuss. No one noticed when Ivy slipped away as usual and knocked on the back door of Mr Potter's house.

'Ain't Poppy 'ere?' Sam said, disgruntled.

'I've told you, she won't come, Ivy replied. 'I tried to get her to walk with us on the Chase, so's you could ask her yourself, but she always makes some excuse about too much work.'

'If yer 'elped 'er more she'd 'ave time,' he grumbled.

Ivy shrugged and pushed past him. She knew he'd never dare ask Poppy to come here, and she had no intention of disclosing her own activities to her older sister. Neither Poppy nor anyone else was going to share in what she'd discovered for herself.

'I can't come next week,' she announced as she stripped off her blouse.

'Can't come? But yer 'as ter, I 'ave ter put on the ointment ev'ry week,' Sam protested.

'It doesn't seem to be doing much good,' Ivy commented, squinting down at her still flat chest.

Sam was already breathing hard. 'P'raps I should put more on,' he said, approaching the bed. 'Lay down.'

'The other first, for my scars,' Ivy said firmly, and held out her arm. Sighing, Sam complied, and when he would have stopped after a cursory application Ivy protested vigorously. 'They're not getting any better either. Rub in more of that, slower,' she ordered.

Sam continued rubbing in the ointment, and to his surprise found that if he did it slowly, deliberately following the lines of the scars, it gave him almost as much satisfaction as did smoothing the other ointment over Ivy's board-flat chest. But it wasn't enough.

'I think I know what's wrong,' he said when Ivy was prepared to move on.

'What?'

'It's not enough to rub just yer chest. When bosoms grow bottoms do as well. P'raps I should be rubbin' it in on yer aase, too.'

Ivy knew by now that when his face grew red, and his eyes held that peculiar glitter, the inexplicable excitement had taken over and she could increase her own demands. 'I don't see why,' she stalled.

'Well, bosoms and bottoms is all ter do wi' growin' babies, ain't they?' he demanded. 'Stands ter reason.'

A sudden vision of Lucy's trim figure, her rounded bosom and curvaceous hips, came into Ivy's mind. They'd been talking of babies before dinner. Perhaps he was right.

'I'm not taking my skirt off,' she declared.

Sam sensed victory and his breathing grew heavier. 'Yer needn't, I can feel well enough what I'm doin' if yer just pulls yer drawers down,' he reassured her quickly.

'Sixpence, then.'

'Yer what?'

'Sixpence. Each time. Each time I let you put on the ointment, you'll give me sixpence.'

'But thass a lot! An' I'm doin' it fer you,' he added swiftly.

'No, you're not. I'm an experiment, like you said, for that ointment. I don't believe it's ever going to work,' she added, and reached over for her blouse.

'Oh, all right,' Sam complied. 'Let's get on wi' it.'

'Pay me first then. For all I know you haven't got sixpence.'

The following Saturday Marigold caught the train to Birmingham and walked across the centre of the city to meet the rest of the family before they caught the tram. This was a new experience for them all, and they liked it better than the petrol bus.

'It's smelly,' Ivy complained. 'I want to go back by train.'

Johnny and Lucy were married in a simple but moving ceremony at Lucy's chapel.

Afterwards they all crowded into the Kelly house, a rather larger one than their own, with bay windows and an attic storey above the three bedrooms, the smallest of which was as large as Poppy's at home. Every room was full of people. Lucy's mother had, it seemed, a large number of relatives and neighbours who all had to be invited to her daughter's wedding.

Poppy was even more convinced her future lay here in this thriving city, and went off once more into a dream of the house she would have at some nebulous time in the future. She no longer dreamed of a mansion. A modest house like this was, she finally admitted to herself, actually attainable. A spark of interest in life revived within her as she began to plot ways and means.

The wedding had been at midday, and Johnny and Lucy, flushed with happiness, left at four o'clock for their journey to Blackpool.

Lucy hugged Marigold after she had changed into her travelling costume, a dark green skirt and coat with a pale green blouse plus a cheeky straw boater with flying green ribbons.

'I'm so sorry we don't know one another better, it's all been such a rush. But afterwards, when' – her lip trembled, and she took a deep breath – 'when Johnny has enlisted, I'll come to Hednesford regularly, perhaps you'll be on the same train and we could travel together and talk.'

'I'd like that,' Marigold managed to say.

Would she be able to confide in Lucy as she couldn't in Poppy? When she too was left alone, her beloved Richard facing danger and possible death, could she share some of the agony with her new sister-in-law?

At least Lucy would understand her love, and would not condemn her.

Poppy heard the whimpering as she went to pick rhubarb. When she followed the noise she discovered a tiny, sharp-nosed puppy cowering against the wall of the hen-run. Despite the heat of the day he was shivering violently.

'You poor little mite!' Poppy exclaimed, forgetting her own misery.

She abandoned the rhubarb and picked up the tiny scrap. He was so thin she could feel his bones clearly. She carried him into the kitchen, found some rags, and wrapped him up in them. Then, hot as she was, she sat beside the fire with the puppy in her lap, stroking him and crooning until the shaking stopped, and a small wet tongue emerged, hesitantly licking her hand.

'Let's get you some milk,' she said gently, and carried the puppy in the crook of her arm while she fetched a saucer and filled it with milk. 'There, how's that?'

The puppy was starved. He guzzled the milk, clambering almost into the saucer in his eagerness to get at it. Then he licked up from the tiles the milk that in his uncoordinated enthusiasm he had splashed over the edge of the saucer, gave a huge sigh, curled up on the rags Poppy had put down, and went fast asleep.

By the time Mary arrived back from work he had made himself thoroughly at home, and Poppy for once was looking so cheerful Mary hadn't the heart to say she couldn't keep the animal.

'It's very small, yet old enough to lap milk and eat solid food,' she said to John in bed later. 'It won't grow very big. It can't be one of those big breeds like Mr Hodson's bloodhounds at Abnalls.'

'I should hope not! More a mixture of a dozen breeds,' John grinned at her. He had also been touched by the puppy, and immediately began to carve a piece of wood with Scrap, as Poppy called it, as an undisciplined model.

'It's my dog,' Poppy said fiercely the next day when Ivy came in from school and wanted to take Scrap out on a lead. 'He's too small to go out yet.'

Ivy shrugged. 'Don't ask me to take him out for you when you can't be bothered, then,' she retorted, and went off on her own.

Poppy didn't care. Life was so much better now she had Scrap to talk to all day, as he scampered about round her heels, playing with an old ball she'd found. He flourished with her attention, filled out, and became her devoted shadow. Mary breathed a sigh of relief to see the girl happy, and blessed the day Scrap, by whatever means – for they never discovered his origins – had arrived in the garden.

On the next Wednesday afternoon Richard came once more to Oxford. Careless of being seen now they wandered together round his old haunts in the city.

'I'm terrified of the thought of you up in an aeroplane,' Marigold confessed. 'They look so flimsy, far less well made than the motor car.'

'They have to be light or they wouldn't lift off the ground,' he explained. 'But they're quite safe, really they are.'

'What use will they be? They can't carry passengers or supplies.'

'Not yet, but perhaps one day they will. We have fewer than

two hundred, but they'll be used to fly over enemy troops and see what's going on. Far better than a lookout climbing a tall tree and trying to make out what's happening several miles away. With the information we can collect it will be so much simpler to make plans, and hopefully carry them out successfully. Whatever Haig says about their uselessness, I can't see his precious cavalry being of much better value.'

'It still sounds horribly dangerous.'

'War is,' he said quietly. 'Both horrible and dangerous. But perhaps they are right who say it will all be over before Christmas,' he added in a determinedly cheerful tone. 'I may not have finished my training before then.'

Restless and sad, both of them trying to conceal it from the other, they walked on. Everywhere posters exhorted men to join the army. Schools and other buildings had been requisitioned to accommodate the reservists. Already the war was affecting the lives of everyone, not just the families of soldiers.

They watched a troop of soldiers marching to the station from nearby barracks, and Marigold felt a stirring of reluctant pride. They looked so brave, so cheerful, so determined. Surely these experienced men, who had fought all over the world, in India and South Africa, could defeat any German army?

Then she saw a straggle of women, babies clutched in their arms, older children clinging to their skirts, running to snatch a last despairing glimpse of their loved ones, and she turned away, fighting her anguish. Tomorrow Richard would be marching away from her.

Silently Richard took her arm and they turned towards Gordon Villa. He must leave, and she must return to her work, hide the agony she was feeling, suppress all hints that she too had a loved one at the wars. And she would not know where Richard was, what danger he was in, even if he were dead.

Her heart rejected that, vehemently.

Of course she would know, she would always know in some inexplicable way whether he lived or died. It was incomprehensible otherwise. Why had they loved, what purpose did their love serve, if space and time could rob them of the closeness they had?

They didn't make love that day. It seemed somehow sacrilege to take pleasure in their bodies, when Richard's might soon be riddled with German bullets, his life draining from him.

Instead they walked slowly back along the Woodstock Road, recalling the day they'd first met. 'I knew you were special the moment I set eyes on you at that dinner party,' Richard said softly. 'I was making plans to get to know you better before we'd even spoken.'

Marigold sighed. 'I never believed it would be possible that you would love me,' she said. 'I hadn't even thought of love.'

'You were so young. You still are, my darling. Don't ever regret the love we've shared.'

Chapter Eight

THE next few days were, for Marigold, a numb void. Richard had gone home, and from there he would vanish.

He'd talked about a flying school on Salisbury Plain, but she barely knew where that was, and could not visualize it at all. It had never mattered when she could not picture him in his Oxford college or his home in North Staffordshire. Somehow they were enduring, he would always return to them. Salisbury Plain was a vast expanse in which he would be lost, disappearing into the sky, departing as did the migrating birds, becoming fainter like the morning star.

And if he survived that he would have to face the uncertainties of France.

The only certainty Marigold could comprehend was that she might never see Richard again.

As the first numbness wore off, agonizing shards of pain pierced her consciousness, sometimes immobilizing her with their ferocity. She marvelled she had become receptive to such anguish. Nothing had prepared her for the intensity of feeling assailing her.

Vainly searching for an explanation by recalling past griefs, she remembered when she had been told of the deaths of her pa's parents. Mom's father had died long before she was born, and her mother soon afterwards: she'd never known them. But her father's mother had only died just before Poppy's birth, and for many years she had the muddled impression that her grandmother's soul had passed into the body of her sister. Death had no meaning for her then.

Childish hurts, cuts and bruises, had been soon forgotten.

Terrifying experiences such as when she had been shut into the dark pantry were more enduring, but the worst agony she had so far suffered was seeing Ivy's pain when she was burnt, and the consequent remorse when she had blamed herself for her sister's disfigurement.

Now she had to endure loss, the dread that Richard would be injured or killed. She must face life with the probability she would never again see his beloved face, hold him in her arms, hear his voice murmur his love for her.

There was no one she could confide in.

'You look pale,' Miss Baker said a few days after Richard's departure.

'I – must be getting a cold,' Marigold lied.

For the first time a twinge of anxiety about her behaviour struck Marigold. The first untruth could lead to others. If her parents discovered what had happened her father would never forgive her, and though her mother might continue to love her, the love would be tempered by deep disappointment. By her reckless passion for Richard she could forfeit the good opinion of her family, and this further grief weighed heavily on her.

Not that it would have altered her behaviour, she concluded. Nothing could come between her and her love for Richard.

'Your brother will probably be used as a driver or a mechanic, so is unlikely to be in the front line,' Miss Baker said in an attempt to cheer Marigold, thinking perhaps it was fear for her brother that made her look so wan.

'I hadn't thought of that.'

'This is to be a modern war, my brother says. All the new developments we've seen in the past few decades will be employed – motor cars, aeroplanes.'

'They're appealing for so many men.'

'Most of the Regulars will be in France within weeks. Many have already gone. Mrs Roberts lent me two letters from her nephew, knowing I would be interested. You recall Edwin Silverman?'

'Yes.' How could she forget him, when in a way he had been the means of bringing her and Richard together?

'You may read them after the children are abed. In his opinion, and he is a Regular officer, the line they have to defend is just too thinly stretched. When we have more men there we can hold the Germans back easily. The letters are not private, Mrs Roberts said, and it may reassure you about your brother when he has to go.'

Marigold picked up the first letter, which had clearly spent a considerable time in someone's pocket. On the outside was a streak of dirt, and it looked as though it had been in contact with water. She unfolded it and began to read.

> My dear Aunt,
>
> I was sorry not to have been able to call and say my farewells in person, but as you may imagine the past few weeks have been exceedingly busy. I trust you and my uncle are both well. Pray give him my regards.
>
> Well, we are here at last, after the politicians have been scurrying fruitlessly about their embassies. I'm just thankful not to have been left behind in England trying to knock the Johnny Raws into shape. I pity the fellows who have that task. I hear most of their time is occupied exchanging hats and boots and so on for ones which fit more precisely! How men can be so concerned with irrelevancies at a time like this, when our country faces the biggest threat for hundreds of years, defeats me.
>
> We spent a couple of nights in tents outside Newhaven, then crossed over in a rather unpleasantly crowded boat. Not at all like civilized trips to the south of France!
>
> The French seem delighted to see us. They know we'll be saving their bacon for them. But they provide us with gifts of fruit and wine and cigarettes; poor quality, I fear, but better than many of our new recruits will ever have seen. There was a huge crowd lining the roads as we marched inland the first day, but we had problems that night.
>
> We halted to bivouac in a barn, but the farmer was most inhospitable. He complained bitterly that we would ruin the hay for his horses. Fortunate still to have horses; no doubt if they can carry a man they'll soon be requisitioned for the Cavalry or for transporting supplies.
>
> Since intelligence is as yet sparse, and we have little idea of the whereabouts of the German armies, we posted double

sentries. One of them woke us all up when he challenged the farmer's son, returning from some assignation with a local trollop no doubt, and the fool ran off screaming as though banshees were after him. If that's the quality of the French men, we will have problems stiffening their resolve.

The women are another matter. On the second day we were passing through a small town early in the morning, and the enticing smell of new-baked bread assailed our nostrils. In the market square was a small shop, the window full of fresh loaves. The men had broken their fast some hours earlier, at dawn, and were hungry, so the order to fall out was given. You would have thought the baker would be anxious to feed his deliverers, and left to himself he might, but a very harridan of a woman, weighing twenty stones, I vow, came and stood in the doorway, filling it completely, and screamed abuse at us. It appeared she wanted us to pay for the bread, and was prepared to resist to her last breath.

There were two ways of stopping the infernal noise – paying her or bayoneting her. The latter would not have unblocked the doorway, so we submitted to our admiration of her valour and paid what she demanded. Afterwards I learnt she had asked for double the normal price of a loaf.

We arrived at our position on the third day here, and the men were instantly set to digging trenches. The Germans are not far away to the north-east, it is reported, and we shall no doubt be seeing some action soon. The French seem very disorganized, it is as well for them we have joined in.

We can hear sporadic gunfire on our right, but for days now we have done nothing but dig trenches. The men are complaining bitterly. I will finish now, as I must take my turn in supervising this tedious activity. I never expected, when I signed on, to find myself a sort of head gardener in the wilds of Flanders!

My regards to you all. I hope to be able to send this soon, but so far the postal services have been somewhat erratic. No doubt matters will improve once we have settled in and begun to enjoy proper organization.

Marigold turned to the second letter. This was fresher, and showed no signs of a protracted sojourn in someone's pocket, but it was less neat, obviously written more hastily.

My dear Aunt,

What a lot has taken place in just two days! We are somewhere north of Amiens, a bleak plain with few pleasant features. There has been a continual bombardment, and in some places the lines have given way slightly. This appears to be a normal adjustment as the various regiments take their places. A few of the chaps have been killed or injured, but none of my special friends, thank God.

The French seem to know very little about the management of war, and the Belgians even less! Instead of keeping out of the way, thousands of women and children, and some cowardly men, are leaving their villages to the mercy of the ravening hordes and fleeing south. They are a confounded nuisance, clogging up the roads and making the supply lines less efficient. Even worse, they are spreading stories of millions of Germans on their trail, and I fear some of the ignorant men are prone to believe them. It does not make for good discipline.

However, we discount any real threat. We need more men to secure the defences more thoroughly, but only because the French are over-concerned with attacking the Germans on their eastern borders. They are blind to everything but the opportunity, as they see it, of recovering Alsace and Lorraine, when their real concern should be to prevent the march southwards from Belgium. I have no doubt that as soon as more of our recruits can be sent out to join us, and however ill-prepared they are, we can lead them in an assault which will push the Huns back into their own territory, and destroy once and for all the Kaiser's overweening ambition.

I must finish: the men are digging trenches during all the hours of daylight and beyond, so we have to take long spells of duty keeping them hard at it.

Marigold sat back, feeling for the first time a spark of interest in what was going on across the Channel. Until now her only concern had been what would happen to Richard. Reading these letters made her see that if she knew something about the background, and how matters were progressing, she would have a better chance of understanding what he was doing.

She ran swiftly down to the kitchen but Jim Dangerfield was on duty in the dining room, and she had to wait until he had finished before she could ask him if she might read his copies of *The Times*.

Since the middle of July he had carefully hoarded every reference to the possibility of war, once the Professor had finished with the paper and he had been able to carry it away from the library.

He was compiling a scrapbook, or rather, she thought with a shiver of apprehension, a series of them. The first was already full with reports of the diplomatic activities during July, and once war had been declared he had started another, which was rapidly filling up.

'May I read them?' Marigold asked breathlessly when he finally appeared.

'You haven't shown the slightest interest before,' he replied suspiciously. 'What's happened to change your mind?'

'I didn't think it was important earlier, and – my brother has enlisted, or is about to,' she replied.

With an indulgent smile, for no one else had taken any notice of his labours, he offered her the first book. 'Read this first, then you can have the next,' he suggested.

Marigold carried it away, and spent long hours poring over every account. The following day she borrowed the second book, and learned about the movements of the various armies, and the British Expeditionary Force, of which Edwin Silverman was a member.

It was difficult to understand at first, but gradually she began to recognize the names of commanders and locations, and piece together a picture of what had happened. It kept her from madness, she thought afterwards. Having something to do gave her a purpose, and made her feel closer to Richard. He was by now, she assumed, on Salisbury Plain, though she had as yet heard nothing from him. At some time he would be going to France, and at least she had an idea of the sort of conditions he would face, the type of country he would be flying over.

Until the end of August she was convinced it would all be over swiftly. Maybe Richard would not even have to go to France. It could all finish before he'd completed his training.

Then came the 'Amiens Dispatch' on the last Sunday of August.

*

'Marigold! Look at this report in *The Times*!'

Jim Dangerfield, his normally calm demeanour having deserted him, caught at Marigold's arm as she was carrying the children's meal tray upstairs.

'Careful! Please!'

'My dear! Oh, you saved it, thank goodness. What could I have been thinking of? But just look at what the special correspondent says!'

'Has the Professor seen it?' she asked practically.

'Not yet. He won't be here for half an hour or so. And it is on the front page. If we were very careful we could read it without unfolding it before I put it in the dining room.'

Marigold had seen the headlines and was not concerned whether she had to wreck the paper in order to read it.

Instead of the usual page of advertisements the news item was starkly displayed: 'LOSSES OF THE BRITISH ARMY. FIGHT AGAINST SEVERE ODDS.'

'May I read it too? When I've taken up this tray?'

'Of course.'

Marigold sped upstairs. Minutes later she was back in the kitchen, where Jim had spread the newspaper carefully out on top of a clean white linen cloth.

Together they pored over the details.

'Then all they've been saying is a lie,' Jim groaned. 'Look at this! "Since Monday morning last the German advance has been one of almost incredible rapidity." How far have they penetrated? The troops are retreating.'

'Look at this! "The German commanders in the north advance their men as if they had an inexhaustible supply." '

'And further down, "Last week, so great was their superiority in numbers that they could no more be stopped than the waves of the sea", and here, "To sum up, the first great German effort has succeeded." How far can they have got?'

'This is dreadful. Look, it says we must send more men, many of them. "We want reinforcements and we want them now." But thousands have already enlisted.'

They looked bleakly at one another, and Marigold thought of her vain hopes. It did not appear likely, if this were true, that the war would be over by Christmas. Richard would have to go to France. She might never see him again.

'Why can't I go and live with Lucy while you're in the army?' Ivy demanded.

Johnny sighed. It must have been the tenth time she'd asked the question since he'd come home to make his farewells.

'Lucy is living with her mom,' he explained patiently. 'When it's all over you can come and stay with us, when we have our own home, I promise.'

'But that might be years. Why can't I go now? She wouldn't let me be a bridesmaid,' she reminded him petulantly. 'She doesn't love me!'

'Of course it won't be years, girl! And stop pestering poor Johnny, for heaven's sake!' John spoke sharply. He hated the very thought of his only son risking his life on foreign soil, and Ivy's persistence aggravated this feeling.

Ivy stared at her father in surprise. He'd not had one of his rages for some time. She was used to Poppy's bad temper, and Mom was sometimes tired and might speak crossly, but unless he was ill Pa always had time to listen to her, time to spend with her, admiring her drawings or helping her make brews and concoctions from the flowers and herbs she collected.

'I'm sorry,' she whispered contritely, and went to kiss him.

'We're all nervy,' he replied. 'Come and sit on your pa's lap and be a good girl. Maybe we could all go and see Lucy one Sunday. Would she like that, young Johnny?'

'Yes, she told me to say you'd be welcome any time. Not to stay, Ivy, because when I'm gone they'll have to let my room again, or they won't have enough to live on,' he warned, and was obscurely unsatisfied when Ivy smiled at him and nodded, her head on one side.

He glanced over at Poppy. She was getting thin and he wondered guiltily if she was having enough to eat. There was no shortage of food in the house, and it was better food than many people ate, but he'd noticed at dinner she left most of it on her plate.

She seemed taut, her nerves ready to snap at any moment. He wasn't normally a very perceptive lad, but marriage had matured him rapidly, and he was more aware of the feelings of others since he and Lucy had achieved such a brief, if tenuous happiness. And yet when she cuddled her puppy, Scrap, she looked contented, completely different from the sullen, apathetic girl who didn't appear to care for anyone or anything.

'I'm going to see Tammy,' he said a few moments later.

'Tammy' was the name they always gave to the pig. John swore by the Tamworth Reds, and always had one in the sty at the end of the garden, fattening ready to kill before Christmas.

Johnny was leaning over the wall, tickling the bright red fuzz of bristles on Tammy's back, when Poppy came and leant beside him.

'When I'm fourteen, would Lucy help me find a job in Birmingham?' she asked abruptly.

'Do you still want to go there? I remember the letter you wrote me years ago.'

'I can't stand Hednesford much longer!' she groaned. 'Johnny, you escaped. You don't know how awful it is, with Ivy mythering me all day, and never being able to go out, no friends to go with, and Marigold away, no one even to talk to except my darling Scrap. Without him I think I'd die!'

By now she was sobbing and hiccuping, and Johnny awkwardly patted her on the back, muttering consoling words.

'Will she? It's my turn, not Ivy's!' Poppy gulped, when she was more in control.

'I'm sure she will,' Johnny reassured her. He didn't know what else to say. 'You write to her. She'd like to have letters from you, I know. She'll feel more part of the family then. Cheer up, now, and dry your eyes. It'd worry Mom to see you've been crying.'

Poppy regained control, and nodded. She gave him a rather watery smile, blew her nose hard, and when they went back into the house made an excuse to busy herself for a while in the scullery.

Marigold was so intent reading the news of the war, the initial battles and severe losses, and watching eagerly, hoping every day to receive one of Richard's hurried letters, that it was the middle of October before she gave a thought to herself.

When it occurred to her that her monthly bleeding was long

overdue, she was at first disbelieving. It took several days of nausea in the mornings before she admitted to herself that she might be pregnant.

She relapsed into the numb resignation she had endured before her interest in the newspapers had revived her. For a week she didn't even try to think about the future. What was the point? What could she do?

Then a few days passed when she quivered in panic, starting at every noise, and unable to think straight.

Of one thing she was utterly determined. She would never regret loving Richard. Afterwards came a stubborn, perverse pride. She would be glad to bear his child, proud of the evidence of his love for her.

Eventually she began to wonder how she could manage. Without help she would be doomed to a life of poverty and degradation, shunned by all decent people, never able to find another good job.

Would Richard discard her now she was pregnant? Yet how could she worry him? Her parents would be utterly furious and ashamed, but they'd hardly turn her out of the house. Would they? But she'd be a tremendous drain on them, for she'd have to leave Oxford soon, when her body thickened and her situation became obvious.

She recalled Lucy's quiet determination to accept the consequences if she and Johnny had not been able to marry. What Lucy could do, so could she. She would not permit this momentous change in her life to defeat her.

Suddenly she was seized with a fierce resolve that she would instead force life to give her things never before dreamed of. It wasn't a calamity. This child had been conceived of what, on her part at least, was an overwhelming, tremendous love. It would never suffer. She would work, she would plan and contrive, and make for Richard's child a far better life than she had yet known.

She would not tell Richard, though. She thought about this for a long time. It was unfair for him not to know, but he was about to go to France, to risk his life. He should not have further problems to face, more worries to distract him.

He might even reject her, deny he was the child's father. He could not be forced to marry her, as would have happened if she'd become pregnant by a neighbour's son.

She shuddered at the very idea. No one else would ever mean anything to her, and even the thought of making love to another man was so repugnant she hastily thrust the possibility out of her mind.

He would not be able to marry her even if he wanted to. It was enough that for a time he had loved her. To want more would have been greedy. She'd known he would one day lose interest in her, marry a girl from his own world, perhaps forget all about her. The parting had come early, that was all. First the war, tearing them from each other's arms, then this untimely appearance of the fruit of their love.

Marigold began to make plans. There was little enough time, and she needed to know what she meant to do before she had to admit to her condition.

Mr Dangerfield was still avidly collecting news of the fighting. 'From what we hear all of France might be overrun soon,' he said one Saturday morning when Marigold was in the kitchen. 'There's been fierce fighting, but thousands of men have enlisted and will soon be following the Territorials. I hear they're providing camps for the soldiers on Cannock Chase, near where you live.'

'Yes, Pa wrote they've already started making roads and marking out sites. Lord Lichfield is offering land at Brocton, he said. A lot of workmen are lodging in Rugeley and Hednesford. And there's a tremendous amount of work to be done.'

'I suppose there simply isn't room to accommodate them all in the barracks that exist, even though most of the Regulars have already gone overseas.'

'Let the girl go, Jim,' Mrs Dangerfield put in. 'It's her day off, and I'm sure she wants to go out.'

Marigold was listless and afraid, but she needed to escape from the house and her duties when she could, to have time to think. Usually she went down to the river, to their trysting spot, where she could imagine Richard was with her.

She'd been there for only a minute when he parted the curtain of slender branches and held out his arms. Hardly believing he was real she almost fell against him.

'My darling, beautiful Marigold, how I've missed you!' he murmured.

'How are you? When do you leave for France? Oh, Richard!' she cried, clinging urgently to him.

'I'm well, and I go in two weeks. That's why I'm here. Time is so short.'

'Two weeks?'

'Yes. We have a lot to do. Marigold, I never realized how much I would miss you. Oh, this isn't how I'd planned it these last few weeks! I'm sorry. I meant to bring it up gradually, but it isn't possible! There's so little time!'

'You can't announce bad news gradually,' she said in a low voice.

'Bad news? Is that how you regard a proposal?'

'A what?' She couldn't have heard correctly.

'I'm still not doing it right. I'm trying, my darling, to ask you to marry me. At first I didn't think it would be fair to tie you down. You are still so young, and I am likely to be killed. Then I realized that even if I were, I would be able to provide for you and leave you safely. It simply didn't cross my mind before. You will have me, won't you?' he added slowly.

'How – how did you know? No one else knows!' she said, her voice rising in a mixture of astonishment and panic.

'Know what? Marigold, what is it? I thought – well, that you loved me. Don't you want to marry me? What is it I should know?'

It was a dream, she told herself. And it didn't matter what you said in dreams. They weren't real. 'I don't want you to feel sorry for me,' she tried to explain.

'Feel sorry for you? Why should I? Marigold, sweetheart, I don't understand.'

She took a deep breath. 'We're not from the same class, Richard. People would be shocked.'

'We are not different, Marigold, because I was born into a wealthy family and you were not. And as for other people, it's not their lives, they have no right to criticize.'

'That's the way the world is,' she said sadly. 'I don't mean just your family and friends, they'd be horrified enough to discover you were considering marrying a servant, but my family would be shocked too. They'd all think I'd trapped you. It wouldn't work.'

'You're not a servant! That's just the job you do. It doesn't make you worse than anyone else. And I don't see where any sort of trapping enters into it, unless you call your beauty and sweetness a trap! But you'll have another job, as my wife, and one day, please God, if I survive, as the mother of my children.'

'Then you don't know?' she asked, puzzled. The whole situation had, it seemed, made her incapable of thinking.

'Marigold, I swear I'll shake you if you don't explain yourself,' he said, laughing at her bemused look. 'What is it I should know?'

'I'm going to have a baby,' she said baldly.

Afterwards she was to marvel that he didn't for a second doubt the child was his. His eyes lit up, and after a few seconds of stunned immobility he gathered her gently into his arms, covering her face with feather-light kisses, murmuring incoherent endearments.

They argued for an hour or more, Marigold protesting the unsuitability of herself as wife of a rich man, the scandal a marriage would cause, and the opposition of his parents. All her objections he swept aside with the retort that it was for them alone to choose.

'My parents will accept you when they know how sweet you are and how much I love you,' he stated confidently. 'I want to marry you immediately, and I have a special licence with me. I am well over age, but we need your father's consent. Let's stop wasting precious time and go and ask him!'

Marigold felt battered, drained of everything. She could no longer fight. Her worries over Richard's imminent departure, about her pregnancy, and her new determination to make a better life for her baby had exhausted her, and now she was prepared to let him assume responsibility.

He swept her back to Gordon Villa, sent her upstairs to pack her few possessions while he spoke to Professor Roberts, and then whisked her out to his motor car which he'd parked round the corner before he followed her to their favourite spot.

Then he drove straight into Hednesford, and they talked very little. She directed him to her street, and didn't even notice the following of excited children they collected, until they surrounded the motor car like a flock of eager starlings the moment it stopped outside her home.

Richard viewed the children indulgently. He beckoned to an

older, tough-looking boy. 'A shilling if you make sure no one climbs into it,' he suggested, and was reassured by the immediate response of the lad, who squared his shoulders and bunched his fists, and was marching up and down in martial fashion before they had reached the front door.

Marigold came to earth with a bump. What was she doing knocking on her own front door? But how could she take Richard along the ginnel and through the communal back yard? Into the kitchen, with everyone unprepared? It was all too complicated.

When Mary opened the door, she exclaimed in alarm at the sight of Marigold and a strange man, a motor car behind them. 'Marigold! Are you ill? What is it?'

'May we come in, Mrs Smith?' Richard asked smoothly, aware of several interested neighbours standing on their doorsteps.

Flustered, Mary apologized and stepped back. Then she narrowed her eyes and peered shortsightedly at the motor car. Surely it was the one she'd seen Marigold in before!

'Come in. Will you wait here while I fetch my husband?' she suggested, pointing distractedly at the horsehair sofa.

'Perhaps that would be best,' Richard agreed, and held Marigold's hand firmly in his when she tried to move aside.

When he had grasped the situation John sat down opposite Richard, regarding his visitor angrily. 'You have ruined my girl, and now you come and calmly expect me to give you my blessing! How do you have the nerve!'

'He is trying to make it right with her,' Mary put in timidly.

'Quiet, woman! I'm ashamed that my daughter, who's been brought up clean and God-fearing, should become a whore! That's the truth of it, and I wonder why such a posh gent wants to marry her when he can get her into his bed for nothing!'

She had expected abuse and recriminations to be heaped on her own head, but this attack on Richard could not be allowed to pass. 'Pa, that's not fair –'

Richard intervened. 'Mr Smith, I can understand your anger. What you must understand is that I love Marigold. I want to marry her whether or not she's carrying my child. We need your consent, but if you will not give it you'll be the one responsible for her bearing a bastard. If there were time, and this abominable war didn't mean I have to go abroad before the end of the month, I'd say be damned to you, we'll marry when Marigold is twenty-one and doesn't need your permission. But I could soon be killed. I can provide for Marigold and my child. I'll do that in any event, whatever you say, but if she's my wife she's better protected. Surely you prefer that for her rather than what you see as a disgrace?'

'I'll not have her wed here in Hednesford, for all to sneer at,' he said more mildly, and Richard breathed a silent sigh of relief.

'That I understand. I've made arrangements for us to be married tomorrow morning in Birmingham. If you wish to come you will be very welcome.'

'I won't condone it by being there,' John snapped.

'I hope you'll change your mind. But a letter from you will suffice.'

Grumbling, John wrote as Richard dictated, and then looked across at Marigold.

'Where are you staying tonight? Do you expect to stay here, or will you go to your seducer?'

'She will stay with my cousins in Birmingham,' Richard said swiftly. 'I do hope you'll forgive us and come tomorrow. I'm taking Marigold to my parents' home afterwards.'

Marigold held out her hand to her mother, and Mary, ignoring John's muttered protest, went to her and hugged her close.

'I'm sorry, love,' she murmured. 'Pa's had a hard life, and tried so much to do well for us. He'll come round.'

'I know. I'm sorry, but I love Richard so much!' Marigold sobbed, and clung to her.

'Then go with him and be happy. He's a good man.'

'Marigold's marrying a man who owns a motor car?' Poppy was incredulous.

'She's leaving me?' Ivy was distraught.

'She's doing nothing of the sort!' Poppy snapped. 'Marigold left home ages ago, it'll be no different.'

'Yes, it will! She won't want to belong to us any more,' Ivy wailed.

Poppy resolutely ignored her, bending over Scrap and combing the short brown and white hairs. Her hands were shaking, but the regular stroking movements helped to calm her.

Mary was sitting with her usual sewing in her lap, but her hands were clasped together, and her thoughts far away. John sat by the fireside, frowning and sucking hard on his pipe. For once he was not busy with his carving. Ivy took a deep breath.

'Can I be a bridesmaid?' she demanded. 'Marigold always promised I could be a bridesmaid when she got married. She loves me more than Johnny does.'

'No one's going to be a bridesmaid,' John said curtly. 'She's being wed tomorrow, he – is going overseas. Now it's time you were both in bed. Go up, now, no arguments!'

Realizing that although he was not shouting as he often did when in this mood, her father was not to be crossed, Poppy tugged Ivy out into the scullery. 'Shut up!' she ordered in a fierce whisper. 'Get washed and don't say another word! Can't you see he's mad about something?'

It was more than she could bear, having to control Ivy's impetuous outbursts when she wanted to lie on the floor and scream with frustration and jealousy herself. Marigold! Her older sister who'd never looked at boys, never wanted to walk with them on the Chase in the evenings, never confided any dreams of love and marriage to her, was marrying a rich man!

It was unfair! It was *wrong*. She didn't want it with the intensity Poppy felt when she dreamed about escaping from her dreary existence. Marigold was happy being nursemaid to Mrs Roberts's brats. She'd be happy living in this sort of house, cooking and cleaning all day long for someone like their pa. It was Poppy who needed, who was destined to get away.

In the depths of her mind Poppy was dimly aware that the chances of two of them achieving such unlikely marriages were remote. While Ivy lay at her side bemoaning the fact that she could not be a bridesmaid and flaunt herself in her finery before her schoolfriends, Poppy silently cried herself to sleep, eaten up with jealous fury.

Marigold and Richard were welcomed warmly by the Cranworths. Obviously fairly well off, if not in Professor Roberts's league, they owned a large new villa near the Hagley Road, quite near Birmingham town centre, in an area of large elegant houses which had been built on the former Calthorpe estate. During the previous century many wealthy industrialists had moved to this area, still largely rural.

Marigold noticed that Archie, Richard's distant cousin, still limped from the wound sustained in India. He had a long, lean face on which lines of pain were etched deeply, and looked much older than his thirty-two years.

Alexandra was a few years younger, petite, lively and pretty, with wide-set grey eyes that sparkled with irrepressible fun. Her fair hair was puffed out wide over her ears and coiled into a neat bun low down on her neck. She wore a very elegant day dress in silver-grey crêpe de Chine, with a cross-over bodice, tight sleeves and hobble skirt.

'I'm so pleased to meet Richard's darling Marigold at last,' she greeted them. 'He's talked about you so much!'

'He's mentioned me before?' Marigold was astonished.

'Endlessly. We thought he would go into a decline when you quarrelled. He came here, you know, when you didn't reply to his letters. Now I can quite see why he fell in love with you. You're beautiful. Come upstairs with me, and take off your hat. You must call me Lexie, Alexandra's such a mouthful.'

'Thank you. It's so kind of you to have us,' Marigold said shyly, overwhelmed by her friendliness, and warmed by the knowledge that Richard had confided in these cousins.

'I'm delighted. I'm bored with doing the polite round in Edgbaston. Now, don't be shy. You and Richard are to have the best guest room.'

Marigold looked at her, startled yet again. 'Don't you disapprove?'

'Of what? That you love one another? My dear, half the bedrooms at country house parties are occupied by people who have no right to be in them, or are with other people's wives! The only rules are that they must not be caught, and if they are that it doesn't cause a scandal. It's hypocrisy! You and Richard are honest about your love, and anyway will be married tomorrow. And you don't want to waste the rest of the time you have together,' she added seriously. 'I know what it's like. I hated it whenever Archie was away, while we were in India.'

That night Richard was gentle and especially tender in his loving. Marigold clung to him, unaware just how much she'd missed his kisses, his closeness. It had seemed a dreadful deprivation, being separated, but until she experienced the joy of reunion she hadn't fully comprehended the depth of her need for him – and the bliss of waking up in his arms.

In the morning Lexie helped her dress in one of her own gowns. 'No arguments, it's my wedding present to you.'

Marigold hadn't even stopped to consider what she could wear for her wedding, and she blushed at the thought she might have been forced to appear in her only dress, the faded blue cotton print she'd had for the past two years.

Lexie's dress was a slender-skirted, sophisticated gown of delicate apple-green tussore, with darker green edgings, and a matching wide-brimmed hat trimmed with dark green tulle and osprey feathers. The morning was chilly and Lexie produced a long ermine stole and muff which she insisted on Marigold borrowing.

When they were ready the Cranworths accompanied them to the nearby church. There were only a few curious bystanders outside to see them all arrive together. But as they stepped out of the Cranworths's motor another, sporty model arrived with a flourish and Henry leapt out.

He looked very dashing in his soldier's uniform, and so very like Richard that Marigold guessed his identity immediately.

'Richard, you old dog! I only heard yesterday! Wouldn't have missed your wedding for anything! And this is my sister-to-be?'

'Henry! I'm so glad to see you, but how did you know? Marigold, darling, this is my brother.'

Gallantly Henry bent to kiss her hand, and she blushed furiously as his candid eyes appraised her.

'Don't blame you, old boy. Wish I'd seen her first! I've joined the Prince of Wales's, and we're at the barracks over at Whittington, Lichfield way. Archie telephoned me late last night, after you'd gone to bed. Had the devil of a job to get here in time. But you mustn't be late. We can talk afterwards.'

He waved airily as he went into the church. He was so like

Richard, Marigold thought, but not quite so tall, nor quite so dark, and certainly not nearly so handsome!

They followed him and Richard led her up the aisle to where the rector awaited them. Marigold wondered if it was all a dream. There had been no time to arrange for flowers, or music, but Marigold didn't notice.

Then she stopped suddenly. There was a woman dressed in a black skirt and white blouse, with a familiar, brightly coloured shawl round her shoulders, kneeling in the front pew. Marigold broke away from Richard and in a moment was clasped in Mary's arms.

'There, there, child. I couldn't bear you to be married without being with you. But don't tell your father or anyone. They think I'm at work.'

Forcing back her tears, Marigold kissed her mother. Thank you, Mom. I'm so glad you're here.'

'I appreciate it too, Mrs Smith,' Richard said quietly, and then, as the rector gave a suggestive cough, drew Marigold away.

The ceremony was short, simple, austere. Afterwards Lexie tried to persuade Mary to go back to the house with them, but she smilingly refused.

'I have to get the train to Hednesford and I daren't be late. But thank you, I'm so thankful Marigold has such good friends.'

Marigold kissed her goodbye, promising to write in a day or so, then went to the wedding breakfast the Cranworths had hastily organized. Marigold was oblivious to what she ate or drank, and almost as little aware of the activities of the photographer who had been summoned to take pictures.

'We must leave now,' Richard said regretfully. 'It's a long drive home.'

By this time it was raining and he had to drive slowly. Marigold huddled under the hood of the motor car, wrapped in a fur coat of Russian sable he had given her as a wedding present, and further rugs Lexie had tucked round her before they set off.

'I'm terrified,' she confessed as they passed through Cannock and left familiar country behind.

'There's no need to be. Father can be rather gruff and autocratic at times. He hated the idea of Henry and me enlisting but he came round in the end. And Mother is preoccupied with village affairs. Being an American, she's in love with the idea of being the squire's wife and organizing the peasantry. Not that Father is the squire,' he added, seeing Marigold's apprehensive look. 'There are several other larger houses nearby, but Mother is the one who is most involved. No doubt she's already organizing the women into knitting socks for the troops, and collecting food parcels to send. She'll love having you to take care of.'

Then he had to concentrate on driving, for the rain had become a downpour, and the roads were slippery with mud. Marigold hardly noticed Stafford, or the villages they passed through. She was cold despite her furs, and sleepy. By the time they came to Newcastle and began to climb the hills beyond she was half asleep, waking only when Richard swung in through a pair of gates and along a short, laurel-bordered drive.

'We're home,' he announced proudly, and she looked up through the early dusky, wet gloom, to see a simply enormous house looming in front of her.

'This is your home?' she gasped. 'It's far bigger even than Old Ridge Court!'

'And I bet it's draughtier!' he said with a laugh as he came round the motor car and disentangled her from the rugs. 'Welcome home, Mrs Endersby,' he whispered as he lifted her down.

She didn't reply. Behind him, silently, the great oak door had swung open. A butler, stately and impressive, stood impassively at the top of a short flight of steps.

'Mr Richard,' the apparition intoned. 'We were not expecting you back so soon.'

'Marigold, this is Kemp. He's been with us since I was a little boy. Kemp, this is my wife.'

The butler inclined his head slightly, and Marigold was shaken with a fit of nervous giggles she had difficulty in suppressing. She wondered if, in the privacy of his pantry, he ever unbent.

'Welcome, miss,' he said woodenly, and stood aside.

'Come, darling, we'll go and see the parents. Are they in the drawing room, Kemp?'

'The green drawing room, Master Richard, since no company was expected.'

Richard nodded to him and put his arm round Marigold, leading her through a vast square hall. A flight of wide shallow stairs disappeared off one side, and opposite she could see through an archway into a seemingly endless corridor with windows all along one wall.

Richard led her forward along it, and opened the first door. Marigold gasped at the magnificent room they entered, bigger and more richly furnished than any she'd seen before.

The brightness of the electric lighting dazzled her. Portraits hung on every wall, surrounded by red flocked wallpaper, rich and glowing in the light from several crystal chandeliers. Below the portraits were cabinets displaying a bewildering array of china ornaments. A huge Turkey carpet covered the floor, and what seemed like dozens of damask-covered chairs and sofas and footstools, each with attendant pie-crust tables, filled the room.

'We only use this when we have a large party,' Richard said, taking her hand and leading her to a set of double doors. Beyond was another room, almost as grand, but the pictures here were landscapes, the wallpaper was gold, and there were vast numbers of small gilt chairs arranged round a dais on which stood not only a grand piano but also several music stands.

'Mother is very musical, we often have performances in here,' Richard explained. 'The parents are in the next room.'

When he opened the doors into a much smaller room, plainly furnished with oak tables and chairs, a William Morris wallpaper on the walls, Marigold sighed with relief. Although large by normal standards it was a far cosier room. This was a room she could like.

To her dismay, however, there was no one present, and Richard walked across to the further pair of doors.

'I thought they'd be here,' she said faintly.

'Here? Oh, this is the ante-room. We sometimes have breakfast here in the winter, it's got a very good fireplace.'

Before she could respond he'd opened the door and ushered her into yet another vast room. This must be the green drawing room. She had a confused impression of green wallpaper, plain but overpowering, and more portraits, before her gaze became riveted on one of the most beautiful women she'd ever seen, sitting in a chair beside a roaring log fire.

'Richard! Darling, why didn't you tell us you'd be home?'

Marigold had forgotten she was American. As Richard crossed the room to drop a kiss on her cheek Marigold studied her.

She was tall and slender. Her dark hair was piled high on her head, against the fashion, but it suited her wide cheekbones. Marigold could see where Richard got his dark good looks. Her complexion was flawless, although as she drew closer Marigold could see a web of fine lines round her mouth and eyes. Her evening gown was of silk, a deep ruby, hobble-skirted but with floating, diaphanous panels and trimmed with a profusion of cream lace, the finest Marigold had ever seen.

'Mother! Is Father not down yet?'

'He'll be along in a minute. Introduce your friend to me.'

Richard came back and put his arm round Marigold. 'Mother, I know this is sudden. Blame the war. I'd hoped to introduce Marigold to you soon, but as I'm going away – well, there wasn't time. Mother, this is my wife. We were married this morning.'

'Married? Richard!'

She seemed incapable of further speech, just stared from her son to the girl beside him. Then she made an effort to pull herself together.

'I don't understand. My dear, I apologize. I am so startled my wits have deserted me. Come and sit down. How did Richard meet you? Who are you?'

'I met Marigold when I spent Christmas at Oxford, with Professor and Mrs Roberts.'

'Ah, yes. Then you are a relative of theirs?'

Marigold shook her head, incapable of speech.

'A visitor. Don't be shy of me, my dear. Where is your home?'

'In Hednesford,' Marigold managed to find her voice.

'Hednesford? Isn't that a mining village? Near Rugeley somewhere? Is your father a colliery owner?'

'He works in a colliery,' Marigold told her. 'I am – was – Mrs Roberts's maid.'

'A maid? A servant?'

Mrs Endersby stood up suddenly, looming over Marigold. Suddenly she swung round on Richard.

'Have you gone mad?' she demanded harshly. 'Are you utterly

crazy, throwing yourself away on some trollop from the kitchens? Or worse? I don't believe it! This is some trick, some stupid masquerade! Tell me it's not true!'

Richard stood up to face her, his face white with anger. 'It is perfectly true, Mother, and you are behaving disgracefully! I will ask you to treat my wife with the respect she deserves. What she did to earn a living and what her father is are quite irrelevant. What she is herself is what matters, and she is the one woman in the world for me, the girl I love, my *wife*!'

'No, Richard.' His mother was calm now, and she stood facing him, dark eyes implacable, her chin thrust forward aggressively. 'You may believe you are married to this – wench! You may have gone through some form of ceremony, but I doubt very much it is legal. I will not accept it is, ever! And I will see your father is not foolish enough to be bamboozled into accepting it either. There are ways, there must be, of annulling this foolishness. You'll be grateful to me one day. Marrying a servant! How can you demean us, your family, and yourself so?'

Richard stared at her for a long, silent moment. 'Is that your last word?' he asked calmly.

'Until you have come to your senses, yes.'

She turned away and went to tug a bell rope beside the fireplace. Kemp appeared with suspicious promptness.

'Mr Richard and this person are not staying, Kemp,' she said haughtily. 'Show them out, if you please.'

Chapter Nine

'IT ISN'T private, and Johnny would want you to read it.'

Mary smiled at Lucy. She was very fortunate in her daughter-in-law. Ever since Lucy and Johnny had returned from their honeymoon at Blackpool and Johnny had enlisted, Lucy visited them in Hednesford regularly every two weeks. She was just like another daughter, and becoming as dearly loved.

Mary suppressed a sigh. It was almost a fortnight since she had been to Marigold's wedding, and she had heard nothing from her daughter. John had spent four whole days in bed, saying nothing at all, staring into space. He was still silent and remote, and she knew he was suffering, but he refused utterly to talk about it and forbade everyone else to mention her name.

'Does he say when he'll be going to France?' she asked now.

'In a week or so, he thinks. He'll be driving some of the officers about, he says, so he's not likely to be too near the fighting.'

'Thank God for that.'

'Here, read it.'

Mary took the letter, and despite her intention she could not help her eyes lingering on the words of love and longing Johnny wrote to Lucy.

She was still feeling confused. She was thankful Johnny had found such a good girl, but they were both so very young. Not only had she lost her son to another woman, she might lose him completely to the Germans. The news from France was far from encouraging.

The troops had retreated, there had been many deaths, and Mary was beginning to wonder whether the generals knew what they were doing. The war would certainly not be over by Christmas, as many had predicted. And the longer it went on the more chance there was that Johnny would be killed.

She tried not to think about it and concentrated on the letter.

> There were long queues waiting outside the building. Everyone was very jolly, anxious to get at the 'Germs'. By the time we'd waited hours to be sworn in and more hours for medical inspections we weren't so eager, I can tell you. I was passed fit, given a warrant for the train and some food for the journey, and we set off.
>
> It was all very rough and ready when we got to camp. There were a few huts, but they were for the officers. We had to sleep in tents, with just a blanket apiece and no pillow. The next day we were given some uniform, but there wasn't enough to go round, so some of us are wearing our own coats.
>
> My boots aren't a bad fit, though. That's lucky for me. I don't know what agony some of the fellows are going through, for we seem to have done nothing but march up and down having orders shouted at us. If you can knit me some good strong socks and send them that would be better than anything else.
>
> The food isn't very good. Half the time it's still cold, the other half it's burnt. I suppose having to feed thousands more men than they're used to must be a problem. I keep thinking of your cooking, Lucy, and those pies you made while we were at your aunt's. I wish I could taste one now.
>
> I also keep thinking of how happy we were then, and I pray all the time that I'll be home with you again soon, my dearest one. Take care of yourself. You are more precious to me than anything else, and I feel proud to be able to sign off,
>
> Your loving husband,
>
> Johnny

'I may be able to see him for a few days before he goes, God willing,' Lucy said as Mary folded up the letter, already creased with much handling, and gave it back to her. 'We'll come over to see you if we can.'

'Yes, bring him over. Do you think he'd like me to knit him some socks?' she asked diffidently. Lucy might want to keep that sort of loving gesture to herself, Mary thought with a pang. She might resent it, consider it interfering, or a slur on her own competence.

But Lucy was above such pettiness. For her Johnny's comfort was the prime concern. 'That would be a relief,' she confessed. 'I don't knit very well, and if he relies on me he won't get any winter socks till next summer.'

'The children at school are knitting for the troops, even Ivy.' Mary smiled.

'Is she still drawing? That picture she sent me of the wedding was really good. You'd think a grown-up had done it.'

'She's drawing all the time, except when she's playing chemists. You know this passion she has for collecting plants and making her potions, as she calls them? Well, she offered her teacher some ointments to make wounds get better quickly!'

Lucy laughed. 'It's a good job we don't believe in witches these days, or she'd have people wondering. It's a strange thing, it's not as if she's interested in cooking, like Poppy, and wanted to use the plants for that.'

'She isn't very pleased, because with so many men lodging in the towns nearby and working on the camps on the Chase, her pa's told her she mayn't wander off up there like she used to.'

'There were some men loafing about near the station. I wondered what they were doing.'

'Looking for trouble. There've been quite a few fights. Nothing for them to do but drink. The Chase will soon be one big camp for soldiers.'

They chatted for a while longer, and then Lucy had to leave to catch her train. Mary kissed her, and told herself to be sensible when she found her thoughts dwelling once more on Marigold, wishing it was her own daughter she held in her arms. Marigold had a wealthy young man to care for her. But she might have written to say she was well.

Marigold poured another cup of coffee for Richard, and smiled across the table at him. 'So many letters,' she teased. 'I thought you didn't want anyone to know where we were?'

'Not the first few days. I wanted you all to myself,' he replied. 'But we have to be practical. I have to make arrangements for you.'

'I wish we never had to leave here,' she sighed. 'Even when it rains it's beautiful, with the mists swirling across the hills. And the heather is still so bright, even at this time of year.'

'It isn't so beautiful when it's really stormy, or when the roads are blocked with snow,' he replied. 'Although we're only a few miles from Leek people get cut off quite often in winter.'

When they had been so unceremoniously rejected by his mother, Richard, white faced, had marched back through the sumptuous rooms of his home, thrown their luggage into the motor car, and driven off at a furious pace.

Marigold had been silent, fighting back her tears. It was all her fault! She ought never to have married him. She'd known it would cause trouble. First her father and now his mother had rejected them.

When they'd driven down into Newcastle-under-Lyme, Richard had booked a room at an hotel, and made a tremendous effort to behave normally. Marigold did not attempt to talk apart from polite comments about the hotel and the food until they had eaten and retired to their room.

'I'm sorry,' she said then.

'Sorry? What for, sweetheart?'

'Your mother. I didn't want to cause you to quarrel.'

'If my high-and-mighty mother is too grand to see that she has a beautiful, sweet angel for a daughter, that is her loss. I am not proposing to plead with her or my father to be treated with common courtesy. When they can be polite to you, and accept you properly as my wife, I will see them again. Darling, you mean far more to me than the whole of the rest of my family. I could leave them, never see them again, without more than a slight pang, but I will never, ever, give you up. I love you too much.'

He refused to speak of it again, but that night he loved her with an intensity Marigold recognized as an inner need for comfort. She felt so much older as she held him close, and afterwards when he rested his head on her breast she stroked his hair and crooned to him as she would have to a hurt child.

The following day they drove up into the hills and moorlands of the utmost northerly tip of Staffordshire, and found a charming little inn, secluded in its own valley, where they had been the only guests.

For a week they made love, walked on the hills, braving the wind and the rain, ate the delicious country food, talked endlessly of anything except their families, and made love again. Marigold thought nothing about the past or the future, she was too absorbed in soaking up every experience of the present.

Now she realized Richard had, with loving care, been making plans.

'What are we to do?' she asked trustingly.

He frowned, and spoke brusquely. 'You cannot live with my parents, and yours have no room for you, even if they forgave you once I go back. It isn't fitting for you to live on your own, and I don't think you would like having just an unfamiliar maid for company.'

Marigold shuddered. It would be enormously embarrassing, apart from other considerations, to be thrust suddenly into the position of employer, when a few days ago she had been a maid herself.

'I feel so guilty at letting Mrs Roberts down.'

'Don't worry, the Professor was sympathetic, said he understood my need of you was greater than theirs!'

'Richard!' Marigold blushed deliciously.

'He wished us well, said you would make an excellent wife, and hoped we might one day go and stay with them.'

Marigold stared at him in amazement. 'Why didn't you tell me before?' she demanded.

'Don't you believe me?' His eyes gleamed with amusement. 'But that doesn't provide you with a home while I'm away.'

'Did you expect your mother to reject me?' she asked softly. 'You were prepared to defy her?'

'I thought there was a good likelihood of it, but hoped that if we took her by surprise she would be too startled to do anything until she'd had a chance to get to know you, when of course she would have begun to love you.' He smiled ruefully. 'I didn't know my mother very well after all. I thought Americans treated everyone as equals, for it is said to be the land of opportunity, where a man's background is unimportant and it's what he is and does that matters. I tend to forget she comes from the old Boston aristocracy. They are more determined to behave as if they were royalty than any British dukes and princes!'

'So what have you planned for me?' She had to stop this self-torture which was causing him such agony.

'I've been in touch with Archie and he and Lexie write that they would be delighted for you to stay with them. You can have your own rooms if you wish, it's a big enough house. Lexie in particular hopes very much you will agree.'

'With the Cranworths? In Edgbaston? Oh, how good of them!'

'Would you like that?'

'Do they really mean it?' Marigold was dubious. It was such a generous offer, and Lexie seemed impulsive. She might regret it.

'Yes. I think she is lonely. And she did say she liked you enormously, you felt like a sister to her.'

Marigold longed to go, and soon Richard had persuaded her the offer was genuine.

'I'll arrange with Mr Thane, my lawyer, to pay a proportion of the household expenses, and he will make you a monthly allowance. The rest of my income apart from my own expenses will also be available for you, so if you need it you can apply to him for whatever you wish.'

Marigold had not even thought about money. She realized how naïve and heedless she had been, leaving it all to him. 'Your income? Does your father pay you a salary? Will he continue to do so?'

'I am a junior partner, I have income from the profits of the firm. My father cannot touch that. And I've made a will leaving everything I have to you.'

These prosaic words made her realize with a sudden stab of fear that he faced death. She had known it in the depths of her subconscious, but pushed the knowledge away from her.

Now it was she who needed comfort.

'There, my love, don't cry, I'll come back to you, I promise I will,' he murmured. 'Nothing can separate us for long. Even death wouldn't destroy our love. We'll still be together, it'll just be a parting. Now dry your eyes,' he went on after the storm of weeping had subsided. 'You need to be strong to look after our son. Shall we drive to Birmingham today and settle in for a day or so before I have to leave, or stay here?'

Marigold looked out on the moors, bleak suddenly as the low

clouds rolled down into the valley. It was no longer a haven. She could not forget again.

'Let's go,' she said quietly.

Lexie welcomed them warmly, apologizing for Archie who had gone to London. 'Something to do with the War Office. He hopes to be back before you leave, Richard.'

'You are both exceedingly good.'

Lexie grinned wickedly. 'I never was especially fond of your mother, Richard. She's behaving in her usual high-handed way, and she'll be the only loser. Marigold is a gem, and you would have been an unutterable fool if you'd let her go.'

'I know.'

'Don't worry, I'm sure your father will make her see sense. I know he likes a quiet life, but he has his own ways of getting what he wants.'

Marigold was at first scandalized, then amused, when Lexie, with a naughty gleam in her eye, led them into the large bedroom overlooking the pleasant garden at the back of the house which she had prepared for them.

'I've had it fitted out as a sitting room,' she said innocently. 'I don't imagine you'll want to be in the drawing room all the time. So stuffy, you can't relax. No one will disturb you here. I've given orders it's only to be cleaned when you're out of the house.'

'You are a wicked angel,' Richard told her. 'I'm eternally in your debt.'

Over the last few days they had together, Richard showed Marigold the city which he knew well from frequent visits to the Cranworths. Like Hednesford, which had been a tiny village until the discovery of coal and the expansion of the collieries half a century before, Birmingham had grown enormously in the previous hundred years or so, built on the vast industries and innumerable workshops which had developed there.

Marigold was fascinated by the majestic buildings of New Street, and the wide new Corporation Street.

'They hoped to recreate the Paris boulevards,' Richard told her.

They went into the older part of the city, to the ancient High

Street and the still thriving market in the Bull Ring, and drove into the rapidly expanding suburbs where seemingly endless rows of little houses spread in all directions. In Edgbaston and the surrounding areas there were hundreds of large new villas like that of the Cranworths.

'I can't believe there are so many people rich enough to afford these,' Marigold exclaimed.

'Apart from the manufacturers there are the bankers and the shopkeepers, the professional men who supply their needs and grow rich themselves by doing so,' Richard explained. He had rarely before given it a thought, and seeing life through Marigold's eyes made him appreciate the vast gulf between his world and the mean one she had been born into.

They drove out into the countryside, to Kenilworth and Warwick, where Marigold gazed in awe at the castles.

'It's like a fairy story,' she gasped. 'I never thought real buildings could be like that, I thought the artists had made them up to put into books. I could look at them for ever, imagining everyone who's ever lived there!'

'We'll come back another day. Now shall we go and have tea somewhere?'

Richard had also bought Marigold some new clothes. Under Lexie's expert guidance, they had plundered all the best establishments. As well as ready-made clothes, they were fortunate to find a dressmaker who had some clothes that fitted Marigold, which had been ordered by the wealthy but capricious young wife of a leading jewellery merchant who had then changed her mind.

'I can do the finishing touches within a day,' the dressmaker declared, thankful that the garments would not be left on her hands. 'Which would you like first?'

'The evening dress, and, let's see, this blue walking dress. Then the dust-coat for driving,' Richard decided. 'We'll dine at the Grand tomorrow night,' he said as they left the shop. 'You can wear the evening gown. Now for some shoes and gloves and a cloak.'

Marigold suddenly realized that when he took her to public places he wanted her to fit in. That was why he needed to buy her proper clothes. She had to become accustomed to the fact that she was now married to a rich man. He would have been ashamed to be seen with her in her old clothes, especially where he might meet friends, and the only good dress she had was Lexie's, the one she'd been married in.

Richard seemed to delight in heaping gifts on her. For the first time in her life she wore silk stockings and underclothes, brightly coloured gowns instead of utilitarian dark ones, and sprayed herself lavishly with French perfume instead of one of Ivy's flower-water brews.

He also bought her jewels, fine gold chains, a string of pearls, a sapphire necklace to match her eyes, and a brooch of garnets.

'One day, my darling, when we've time to look properly, I'll give you better jewels than these,' he promised.

On their last evening they ate dinner at the Grand, a luxurious hotel completed thirty or so years earlier. Marigold had never before been in such a luxurious public place. She had also never before been treated with such deference by waiters and flunkies.

It was the gown, the lovely soft rose-pink silk, with full skirts and deeper pink flounces. She was embarrassed to be showing so much *décolletage*, but other women in the room were – many of them were showing much more – so she squared her shoulders, smiled confidently, and held her head high.

'My precious one, you look like a duchess,' Richard declared, and Marigold dissolved into helpless giggles.

'If they only knew,' she murmured, watching the waiter bow almost double as he presented her with the menu.

That night their lovemaking was more intense than usual, and Richard carried her to heights of ecstasy she'd never dreamed possible. When she thought they were both exhausted and replete, the slightest touch would set her afire again, tingling with the need to meet his every demand with joy and delicious abandon. She wanted to imprint every inch of him on her memory, to savour every last moment, for the following afternoon Richard had to return to his unit.

My beloved Marigold,

Your last letter finally caught up with me. We have been moving about such a lot, flying over different parts of the front.

It was good of you to send the hamper. Thank you also for the books. There are often days when we cannot fly, and time would hang heavily without them to read. The potted meat and sardines were much appreciated, and we are keeping the Christmas pudding for the day itself, when you may be sure I shall be thinking of you.

Not that I don't think of you and long for you all the time, my darling, but it will be particularly sad not to be together on our first Christmas. And to celebrate the anniversary of our first meeting. Two years. Sometimes I feel I have known you for ever. Certainly I have always known you were there waiting for me. But let us hope that next Christmas we can be together, with our child, and for always after that.

Many thanks also for the coffee and chocolate you added. It is amazing how, when one cannot obtain something, one develops an insatiable craving for it. Harrods made a good selection with their hamper, and apart from the food the matches and soap are invaluable, neither being easy to obtain here. And when one does find some matches they are probably unusable because of the damp!

I am so pleased you are happy with the Cranworths. They have been very good friends to us. You don't say whether you have heard from your mother? I am surprised, if she receives your letters, that she does not reply. She was brave enough to defy your father and come to our wedding.

The situation here seems to have settled into a stalemate, with troops of both sides preparing defensive positions, and settling in for the winter into their 'dug-outs', deep trenches which from all I hear are filled either with mud or water. The poor devils have to endure those conditions, in the freezing cold, for days on end. Flying, and driving the generals about, are far preferable occupations, so you can be thankful your brother and I are not down in those awful holes.

In fact we move about quite a lot, and sometimes our quarters are large hotels, or even private châteaux. Quite luxurious compared with the poor devils in the trenches.

I had a letter from Henry a week ago. He has just been posted to France. He implies, although from my own knowledge of Father I think it is more hope than true belief, that Father was displeased Mother threw us out without referring to him. Perhaps I should have been less impetuous and demanded to see him first, but I cannot help feeling it is all for the best. You are happier with Lexie than you would have been with the old folk, as Mother is so uncompromising.

It will soon be Christmas. The country here is far from festive. Many of the people have left and gone further into France. I can see on my reconnaissance flights that the nearby villages on the far side have been devastated. They are deserted, often razed to the ground, with just a ruined church tower and a few stone walls as reminders of what they once were, thriving communities. Many of their people came across the border, fleeing from the Germans during the first weeks of the war. God knows what has happened to them. Many must have died by the wayside.

All the barns and farm buildings are occupied by the troops, or their horses. This kind of war, with constant bombardment over a vast area, is not the sort of warfare the cavalry know how to deal with. It seems strange that we are fighting with men on horseback, as has been done for thousands of years, as well as the latest weapon, my flying machines.

They are not much use for fighting, though. We cannot get near enough to enemy planes. Pistols are not very effective at such long range, nor when you are flying in one direction and aiming in another, trying not to hit the wings or propellers.

There is much debate about our carrying machine-guns. It must come, if we can solve the problem of how to aim them. We already carry grenades to toss out at suitable targets, and firebombs, and darts, but none of them are very efficient. Neither is the rifle our observers carry.

One of our squadron actually chased a German pilot to the ground, forcing him down and landing himself. He cornered the poor fellow in a barn and brought him back in triumph.

Soon we may have faster planes, able to fly above seventy miles an hour. Though this varies with the wind, much faster going out, sometimes desperately slow coming back with the wind against us, as it invariably is. We call it the 'uphill run home'.

It's neither foggy nor raining at the moment, so we can fly today, and I must finish. I'm flying a Henry Farman at present, but hope to get my hands on a BE8 soon. They are much superior.

I am writing to you so much, can you please send me some

more writing paper when next you send a parcel? That is something else unobtainable here.

You are always in my thoughts, beloved. I need you, and praise God for giving you to me. Take excellent care of yourself and our baby. Perhaps I may be able to have some leave before you are confined. God bless you both,

Your devoted
Richard

Dear Mother,

As it is almost Christmas won't you forgive me, at least enough to write and tell me all is well with you?

I have sent letters every week, but received no word from you. I realize you were ashamed of me, but I am sorry only for hurting you, not ever for loving Richard, as we had so little time together before he had to go to this dreadful war.

How is Pa? I hope his headaches are getting better. Please beg him to forgive me. I love you both too, and hate not hearing from you.

Give my love to Poppy and Ivy, and Lucy if you see her. I would like to write to Johnny, but have no address, and just pray he is not amongst the casualties.

Will you let me send you something for Christmas? Richard is so generous I have far more money than I need and would like to give you all something.

I am always,
Your loving daughter,
Marigold Endersby

'Where's that dratted Ivy? Lizzie, have you seen her? She's never here when there's a job to do. She should have been home from school an hour ago, and I've all this shopping to carry back. I told her to meet me here and help me.'

'I thought 'er was ill,' Lizzie replied, turning away from the brightly lit shop window. 'Ain't that a smashin' 'at? Wish I could 'ave it.'

'What do you mean, ill? Where is she?'

''Er weren't at school terday.'

'She didn't say anything this morning. Do you think she could have fainted or something on the way? Where is she?'

'I'll goo an' ask our Sam.'

'Sam? Why should he know anything about where she is?' Poppy demanded, even more bewildered, but Lizzie had darted across the road and into Mr Potter's shop.

Before she could move on Sam appeared in the doorway, shrugging on his coat and pulling his cap firmly down on his head. 'Poppy? Lizzie says your Ivy might be ill. I 'aven't seen 'er. 'Er didn't come in fer any medicines.'

'Why on earth should she? She hasn't got any money to pay for medicines.'

Sam gave her a strange look and was about to speak, but Poppy rushed on.

'Where can she be? She's so late, and it's dark, and – Do you think it could be any of those men working on the camps? Could she have been up on the Chase picking those wretched plants of hers?'

''Ere, let me carry some o' yer bags. I shouldn't worry, there's nowt ter pick this time o' year.'

Poppy allowed him to take some of the shopping, and hurried on in front of him, almost running up the steep hill. 'I'll have to go and tell Mom. Oh, but it's nearly time for her to come home. I might miss her, I know she was going to get some more things on the way home.'

She fretted as they went, and didn't notice when Sam followed her into the kitchen and put the shopping down on the table. She bent to pat Scrap, who bounced eagerly towards her, his tail wagging furiously.

'Where's yer matches? I'll light the gas,' Sam offered. In the glow from the fire he turned on the gas taps and put a match to the mantle. It plopped noisily and then glowed steadily. 'I don't s'pose 'er'll 'ave come ter any 'arm,' he said awkwardly, and as Poppy stood there, indecisively staring about her, he stepped across and tried to take her in his arms.

'Sam! Get off! What do you think you're doing?' she asked, startled. She backed away from him, an odd feeling in the pit of her stomach.

'I were just tryin' ter 'elp, gi' a bit o' comfort, like,' he muttered, turning a bright red. 'I likes yer, Poppy. Yer real pretty, an' I likes red 'air. Won't yer walk out wi' me on Sunday after church? We could go an' see 'ow much o' the camp they've done.'

Poppy turned away, embarrassed. It was the first time a boy had asked her to walk out with him, and though she knew her parents wouldn't allow it, she felt flattered. But she didn't like Sam. She didn't want to walk out with him.

A wave of jealous fury swept suddenly and unexpectedly over her. She wanted a handsome, rich young man like Richard, not a clumsy oaf like Sam. She wanted someone to take her away from Hednesford, to give her the sort of life Marigold was now no doubt enjoying. Why didn't Marigold write to them? Was she too grand now she was married and had money and a motor car?

'Will yer, Poppy?'

She was recalled to the present as Sam came up behind her and put his arms round her, pulling her close against him. Suddenly she felt hot and uncomfortable, and his hands were sweaty as they grasped her own.

'Don't!' she gasped, but somehow he had twisted her round and she was clamped to him, face to face, and he was breathing down on her.

'Gi' us a kiss, Poppy! There's no 'arm in a little kiss!'

As well as stale body odour, Sam stank of nameless potions from the chemist's shop, which had been absorbed into his coat for many months past. Poppy struggled furiously but he was too big and strong for her.

'I wouldn't ever walk out with you, Sam Bannister!' she gasped, and as he bent his lips to hers she bit hard, and kicked out as he stepped back, yelping in pain and fury and disappointed masculine pride.

Flustered, Poppy looked round for a weapon, and bent swiftly to grab the poker. Scrap tried a tentative growl, and finding it came out from his throat satisfactorily, repeated it with growing confidence as he approached Sam, stiff legged and bristling.

'Get out, and don't ever come back, or I'll tell Mr Potter!' Poppy threatened, sobbing now with shock and disgust.

Sam edged round the table, his eyes on the poker. 'All right, yer spiteful little cat! See if I'll carry yer shoppin' 'ome fer yer again!'

He went, aiming a kick at Scrap and slamming the door behind him. Poppy flopped on to the chair by the fire and hugged Scrap to her. Tears threatened, but she blinked them back. She thought once more of Ivy, and began to shake. What should she do? Where was the child?

At last she heard footsteps in the yard. For a moment she thought Sam was coming back, and she picked up the poker again, then she realized they were much lighter steps. Ivy was home. Why was she so late?

Marigold slipped out of the house by herself. She wanted to get a very special Christmas present for Lexie. She took a cab to the bank in Colmore Row, where Richard had opened an account for her. Afterwards she went to one of the shops in the Great Western Arcade, where she'd seen a pretty fob watch a few days earlier.

She left the shop, the watch safely tucked away in her purse, and walked back towards St Philip's Churchyard. She was by the Blue Coat Schools when she heard someone calling her name. Startled, she looked up, and saw Ivy running towards her.

'Marigold, wait! Please wait for me!'

'Ivy! What are you doing here? Is Mom with you?' Marigold demanded, hugging Ivy fiercely to her. 'Oh, how I've missed you all!'

'I came on my own,' Ivy confessed. 'On the train. I saved up the pennies I earned running errands, until I had enough to pay for my ticket. I've wanted to see you for so long. I love you so much, Marigold. Pa won't let us even say your name!'

'Did you get my letters?' Marigold asked.

'I've only seen one.'

'Well? What did they say? Why didn't someone answer it?'

'Pa – said he wouldn't read it,' Ivy hung her head. 'At least, I heard him shouting one night after we'd gone to bed, and that's what I think it was about. He spent days in bed afterwards, like he does after he's been angry.'

'I sent them to Mom!' Marigold said. 'Does she refuse to read them too?' She experienced a pang of mingled anger against her father, and distress that both he and her mother seemed to have rejected her.

'I found a bit of it, in the fire. The next morning. Most of it was too burnt to read, but this bit had floated out and was hidden under the tongs. I don't know if they read it. It had your address on, that's how I knew where you were.'

'Well, you came. Look, let's walk through to New Street, there's a refreshment room where we can have a cup of tea and some cake. Would you like that?'

Ivy nodded eagerly, then paused. 'Are you rich enough to afford that, Marigold? As well as not having to go out to work?'

Marigold nodded, a lump in her throat. She thought briefly of how much Richard gave her each month, a vast sum which would have kept her whole family in comparative luxury. Most of it was still unspent, for her needs were few and she was not accustomed to buying anything but bare essentials.

'How is Mom managing, now both Johnny's and my money have stopped?' she asked.

Ivy shrugged. 'It's not so bad, I think. Poppy will get a job soon, and Mom says if she can afford it I can stay on at school as long as I like. I wish we lived here in Birmingham. There's a special art school here. I could go to that.'

'Do you still draw a lot?'

'I brought these for you,' Ivy said with a smile, and drew a roll of paper, carefully protected with a piece of cloth, from her deep pinafore pocket.

Marigold spread out the drawings and felt tears pricking her eyes. They were so lifelike! Then she looked more closely. Her family even in this short time looked different. Her father, instead of whittling away at his animal carvings, which was how Ivy usually drew him, was staring into the fire. He seemed in some peculiar way sad and old. She couldn't see how Ivy had managed to convey this, but it was there.

Her mother also looked old, far more so than when they had met at her wedding, and as she bent over some embroidery she screwed up her eyes so that she looked about to weep. Marigold could not bear to dwell on this thought, and passed on hastily to the next drawing.

Poppy stared out at her, looking cross and resentful, just as she did when things went wrong, and Marigold felt a wave of pity for her. There was a lost, forlorn look in her eyes even though her mouth was twisted in anger. Although she hadn't felt the same urge to escape, she knew how her younger sister fretted, and how hopeless she thought her chances were of getting away to a better life.

Johnny was handsome and brave in his army uniform, but there was a remoteness about the eyes which made him look afraid. And Lucy, clinging to his arm, looked smug and possessive.

'These are wonderful, Ivy. Are they really for me to keep?'

'If you want.'

'I do. They're better than photographs. But there isn't one of you. Can you draw yourself?'

'There isn't a proper mirror,' Ivy said, grinning at her. 'I have to draw what I see, and there would be cracks across my face and spots where it's all flyblown. You wouldn't like that!'

Marigold laughed, but there was pain in her laughter. 'Come home with me, and after we've had dinner you can try using one of our mirrors. Will you have time to get home if you do that?'

Ivy nodded. 'Yes. I can be home before Mom gets back from work. Oh, Marigold, I didn't like coming without telling anyone, but I couldn't, or they'd have stopped me. Pa would be so cross if he found out.'

Marigold had been wondering whether she could use this opportunity to send some money home for her parents, but at these words she realized how impossible it would be to involve Ivy. She must find some other way of helping them. Perhaps, after a while, when the hurt they felt had dimmed, she would just go home. They could hardly turn her out of the house if she just went to visit one Sunday.

'Come on then,' she said briskly. 'I'll buy you some paper and charcoal on the way home. Perhaps you'll do one of Mrs Cranworth for me, if there's time?'

'Who's Mrs Cranworth?'

'My friend. I'm living with her while – while Richard's away.'

Lexie was delighted to meet Ivy, praising her daring in coming to visit Marigold. Ivy did a rapid sketch of the two of them, and shyly presented it to Lexie for her approval.

Lexie looked at it in astonishment. 'This is incredible! If I hadn't seen you do it, I wouldn't have believed it possible. How old are you?'

'Nearly ten. But I've always been able to draw.'

'You really should have special lessons. You're so talented. Do you like drawing people best, or do you do other things?'

'I do anything,' Ivy told her. 'I think I like doing small things best, plants and flowers. If you look really closely they're so different, all of them. If we could afford some paints I'd like to learn to do watercolours too.'

'I'll make it possible, somehow,' Marigold promised, and smiled at Lexie over Ivy's shoulder as the child embraced her warmly.

After they'd eaten, and Ivy had exclaimed in wonder at the snowy tablecloth and napkins, the silver and the delicate flower-decorated china, she settled down in front of a mirror Lexie arranged for her and drew a picture of herself.

'This isn't right,' she said after several efforts. 'It doesn't seem to come out the same.'

'Let me see.' Lexie picked up the paper, considered the drawing, and then looked at Ivy. 'Oh, it's because you're looking in the mirror, and your hair really goes the other way,' she said after a moment. 'See, if I push your hair over this way instead it looks the same.'

'No! Don't touch me! Leave my hair alone!' Ivy almost screamed, and then collapsed into floods of tears and threw herself into Marigold's arms.

Lexie had seen the still livid scar on Ivy's temple, and the one on her neck. She bit her lip, looking at Marigold. 'I'm sorry,' she breathed. 'I didn't know. How on earth? What happened?'

'I'll explain later. She hates people to see them. Ivy, darling, hush. Don't cry. Lexie didn't hurt you. Say you're sorry for making such a fuss. Come, Ivy, you're behaving badly and Mrs Cranworth won't ask you here again.'

Ivy sniffed, but fought to control her tears. 'I'm sorry,' she muttered, 'I'm sorry, Mrs Cranworth. I forgot you didn't know.'

'I'm sorry, too, Ivy, I wouldn't have upset you deliberately.'

Soon afterwards Ivy had to go. Marigold took her in a cab to New Street Station, and promised she would try and visit them in Hednesford after Christmas.

'You won't tell them I came, will you?'

'No, it shall be our secret. But I'm so glad you did, Ivy. And thank you for the lovely drawings. Look, I can't send them any presents, or they'll know you were here, but take this sovereign, and buy yourself some sweets occasionally. Not too many, or they'll be suspicious. Give Poppy some too. Give Mom a special kiss for me, will you?'

Ivy promised, and Marigold stood waving to her as the train pulled out of the station. Then she walked home to recount to Lexie the story of that horrific day when Ivy had been burnt.

My darling Lucy,

Thank you for your last letter and the muffler you sent me; also the food. It made Christmas away from you better when I knew you'd touched the wool which is now round my neck. Very cosy, too. And do we need it! I've never known cold quite as awful as here in Flanders!

Both armies have got stuck in. And I mean stuck, in trenches full of mud. How the poor devils manage to keep cheerful is beyond me, I doubt if I could. In some places the trenches are only fifty or sixty yards apart, Germans facing us and sending over shells all the time, to which of course we reply with our own.

As there's almost no movement on the Front, I've had little driving to do, so I spent a few weeks riding about on motor cycles, taking dispatches to the various commanders. This was quite exciting as well as dirty, but it isn't really dangerous, so you are not to worry your pretty little head about me.

Usually I get covered in mud because the roads – or tracks, rather, there are very few proper roads – are so muddy it sprays up all over me. Last week I got plastered with mud when a German shell landed in a pond right next to me. Luckily for me it didn't go off. It's the nearest I've been to any real action, though you can hear the guns all the time, and occasionally bullets fly past if I'm near the lines.

Do you remember Reg Browning? He used to work with me, and he joined up at the same time. It's very sad, but two days ago he caught it. He was just going into a trench to take over from the chaps there, when a shell burst and buried everyone in the mud as the walls of the trench collapsed.

They said when they pulled him out there wasn't a mark on him. He wasn't killed by a bullet, just by drowning in the mud. What a dreadful way to go. Better thanbeing maimed, though

Some of the men have lost one or even both legs. One I heard of had both legs shot off, and he pulled himself a hundred yards before they got to him. I hope he survives. Though what sort of life he'll have, even with artificial legs, I don't know. Would it be better to go quickly than to face that sort of life afterwards?

Several times I've stopped when there's been time and helped dig graves. There are so many to bury, some of them younger than me. But they have to be buried before the bodies putrefy, poor souls. I'm just thankful it's not hot weather. I can imagine the flies and the stench there'd be then. It's horrible enough, and I keep thinking of their loved ones, perhaps thinking they're still alive. And it's so difficult to keep track. Often we don't know who they are, so we can't tell their families. And I heard of one lot digging graves who dug up some bodies which had been buried just a week or so earlier. How horrible for them.

But I'm being morbid. It's missing you so much, my darling wife. Wife! It seems so long ago since I held you in my arms in Blackpool. Sometimes I think it was a dream.

On Christmas Day it was all rather strange. It was so quiet! It was misty first thing, and none of the guns were firing. Lots of the fellows had put little Christmas trees above the trenches, and suddenly, at several places nearby, they began calling across to Fritz. Or he started it, I don't know the truth of it.

I saw it myself, or I wouldn't have believed it. The men began to walk over the area in between the two lines of trenches, swapping cigarettes, and beer, and chocolate. Then some mad Scots got up a game of football, and though the ground was frozen hard they played against the Germans for an hour or so. There wasn't a referee, but they all played honestly, and the cheering from both sides was tremendous.

Then on Boxing Day, when it was snowing but still oddly quiet, I managed to have a hot bath! Imagine that. It seems weeks since I was warm, and clean, and both at the same time. The last few baths I've had I had to get in after several other fellows. This time I was the first, and they had to drag me out, it was so comfortable.

Well, Lucy darling, it's now 1915. I wonder if we shall be together next Christmas Day? Surely this horror can't go on for much longer? Take great care of yourself, give my love to your mom, and when you go to Hednesford again tell them all I love them. I will answer Mom's letter soon, but today I wanted to write a really long one to you. I have to be cheerful when I write to Mom, or she worries, and it's such a relief to put down some of my real feelings to you, for I know you understand.

God bless,
From your ever-loving husband,
Johnny

Marigold stepped off the train and looked about her. It was unusually busy for a Sunday afternoon.

She walked slowly along Market Street. Having been away from Hednesford for four months she saw it with new eyes. How shabby and dirty it all was, she realized. Not like the huge, newly rebuilt city she now knew so well, with its bustling market, proud buildings, grand houses and wealthy people.

She hadn't written again after seeing Ivy. If Pa burnt her letters there didn't seem much point, so she hadn't told them she meant to visit them.

She carried two large parcels. She'd pondered on what to bring, discarding the idea of money for she was afraid her father might refuse to take it. But it was almost Poppy's birthday. Surely he'd allow her to have a present?

Lexie had suggested food, some good beef and dried fruits. She'd added tobacco for Pa, and lengths of dress material in soft, warm wool for Mom and the girls.

As Marigold drew nearer home her pace slowed. Then she heard footsteps behind her and glanced round.

'Cor, look at 'er! What's a toff like 'er doin' in ower street?'

Marigold's smile froze on her face. They were girls from Ivy's class at school. She'd known them since they were born, and they didn't know her!

She quickened her pace. Was she so different? Yes. Her clothes were good, fashionable even, for Lexie insisted she dress well to be a credit to Richard: she had on a tweed skirt and jacket, trimmed with musquash, and a high fur toque. She had suede shoes with gloves and handbag to match. Gloves and handbags were unknown luxuries before she married Richard. Did new clothes make her unrecognizable though?

She reached the entry between the houses and started along it. She had almost reached the end when someone turned into it. There wasn't room to pass. The other woman, vast and ponderous, stepped back.

'After you, miss. Were yer lookin' fer someone?'

'Mrs Tasker! Don't you know me?'

'Why, it's Marigold Smith! Oh, lass, it's good ter see yer! Yer mom'll be that chuffed. 'Er's fretted not 'earin' from yer. Yer's come up in the world, now, though, ain't yer? Got a real nob to marry yer! I allus knew yer was a smart lass.'

'I did write,' Marigold defended herself. 'It's lovely to see you. How is everyone?'

They chatted about her family and the other neighbours, then Mrs Tasker shooed her away. 'Go an' see yer mom, I mustn't keep yer 'ere. Don't suppose yer've got much time ter spare, wi' yer fine 'usband ter look after now. No doubt 'e keeps yer busy!' With a deep laugh she winked at Marigold, and stomped off down the ginnel.

So the neighbours didn't know Richard was in the army. She shrugged. Why should she care? Why should she be hurt if Mom never told anyone about receiving her letters?

She went slowly through the yard, turned up beside the scullery, and raised her hand to knock on the back door.

Then she paused. It was her home. Why should she knock as if she was a stranger? Even neighbours often walked in without knocking.

'Mom? Hello, it's me,' she called as she went in, and Mary appeared swiftly from the kitchen, to cry out in joy and sweep Marigold, parcels and all, into a warm embrace.

My sweet love,

I think of you constantly, especially as your time gets near. I was so glad to hear your parents seem to have become reconciled. I knew they would in time; they are good, generous people. But it is odd they haven't received the letters you sent, and did not even appear to recall the one Ivy saw. By the way, do send whatever money you wish to help them.

The stalemate here continues. Near the Front it is desolate, and I can see it is similar on the German side when I make my sorties. But there are more reserves coming now, and things will soon improve, no doubt.

We had Easter services yesterday in a field, a very strange but oddly uplifting experience. To hear several hundred men roaring out the hymns, when usually many of them are very reluctant attenders at church parade, was heartening. The Bishop spoke very movingly, remembering those who have been killed, and using the occasion, naturally, to speak of life after death.

I am making my flights further across the lines now. Life seems to be going on more or less as usual further away, especially as the fighting is all in one place. Some people who fled have apparently returned to their homes, especially farmers who must be worried about the crops.

When I am home, after this horrible war, I must take you up in an aeroplane. It's fantastic to see such a wide panorama below, people moving about like tiny dolls amongst dolls' houses. I feel like Gulliver must have done when he came to Lilliput. I am glad you enjoyed the book, it was always one of my favourites.

If this stalemate continues there is a possibility of leave. Wouldn't it be wonderful if I could be at home for the birth of our son? I am convinced it will be a boy, but you know I would be equally pleased to have a replica of my adored Marigold.

I am sure Lexie is looking after you and making all the necessary arrangements. If your mother wished to come and stay with you in Birmingham, Lexie would be delighted. Ask for anything you wish, my dearest. Your comfort and happiness are my chief consideration. But how I long to hold you in my arms again. It's been the happiest time of my life since you married me. I cannot imagine ever being as happy again as when we were together, and yet when I come back, and we have our own home, and perhaps other children, life will be even more wonderful. I do not know how, just that it will be so. To have you ordering my house for me, sitting at my table, cherishing our children, but most of all lying in my arms, is all I desire.

Farewell, beloved. I will write again in a few days.

Your devoted
Richard

May 3, 1915.

To Mrs Richard Endersby

Dear Madam,

It is with great regret that I have to inform you that Lieutenant Richard Endersby's aeroplane was shot down yesterday morning while he was on a reconnaissance mission over enemy-occupied territory. No other aeroplane was near enough at the time to see exactly what happened, but the plane landed amongst some trees and was set alight. In such circumstances it is unfortunately unlikely that he or his observer could have escaped alive.

He has been reported officially missing, presumed dead. If we receive any further information you will, of course, be told at once.

He was a fine officer and a skilled pilot, much liked by all the men. He served his country well and we can all be proud of the example he set.

With my deepest sympathy, I remain,

Yours sincerely,

D.A. Somers, (Colonel)

Chapter Ten

'CAN you see anything?'

Richard had to shout over the noise of the engine, and Frank Parsons, his observer, shook his head.

'How can you spot gas cylinders from this height?' he grumbled.

His words were cut off by the ping of a bullet on the struts of the plane, and Richard veered sideways.

'Archie's busy. I'll turn eastwards, see if we can spot any troop movements.'

He flew on below the low cloud, dodging 'Archie', the German anti-aircraft guns, as best he could as he circled round behind the German lines facing Ypres.

Nothing exceptional seemed to be happening. There were no extra troop concentrations, nothing to verify the reports they had been receiving of a German offensive. And as Frank said, how could you spot gas canisters from more than two thousand feet?

'Watch it, Fritz coming up!' Frank suddenly shouted, and Richard glanced over his shoulder to see a German Albatros approaching.

He began to climb, circling round so as to be above and behind the Albatros, but the German had the same idea. For ten minutes or more they both tried to gain the advantage.

Richard had a slight edge in speed, and far more cunning. He soon demonstrated his superiority, and manoeuvred into position so that Frank could aim his rifle at the Germans.

'Now we've got 'em!' Frank exulted, and fired.

They were barely thirty feet apart. Richard, glancing across, saw a stain of red spreading over the chin of the German observer, and an expression of horrified dismay on the pilot's face.

'That'll teach 'em to chuck filthy choking gas at us!' Frank crowed with satisfaction. 'Can you get me close again so that I can get the other bastard?'

Richard slowed his speed slightly, but the Albatros pilot suddenly dived and set off northwards, Richard in hot pursuit.

Twice more they caught the Albatros, but Frank's aim was less sure, and as they circled again to recover lost height Richard saw two more German planes converging on them.

'Damn, we'll have to leave it,' he muttered.

They were by now well into German-held territory, but in the excitement of the chase both Richard and Frank had lost track of their position.

He turned towards the south-west, but found his way blocked by yet another Albatros. Their former quarry, aware of rescue at hand, turned back to rejoin the fight. Richard concentrated grimly as a macabre game of tag began.

Twist and turn, climb and dive as he would, Richard was unable to evade his pursuers. One would harry him until he contrived, by greater speed or skill, to get away, only to be attacked by another waiting, circling enemy. Their clear intention was to prevent him making for the safety of the Allied lines, if they could not shoot him down.

Frank managed to damage their first adversary again, hitting the fuel tank so that the pilot had to make for a safe landing. A few minutes later he shot the pilot of a second plane and it went spinning downwards out of control.

'We'll do it yet! After the next one,' he cried out, but Richard shook his head.

'We're almost out of fuel. I've got to head for home. Just wish I knew where home was.'

Frank glanced round, then pointed. 'Isn't that Lille, straight ahead? If we turn westwards we'll be heading for Ypres.'

'Let's hope we make it.'

They might have done if one of the German shots hadn't punctured their fuel tank. The bullet lodged in the hole, but there was still a slight seepage. Richard soon became aware of the fuel level dropping faster than it should have, and he did his best to take advantage of every favourable current of air.

They were still a dozen miles short of the trenches when Frank, staring ahead, exclaimed in dismay. 'Hell, Richard, they seem to have used the gas. See that greenish cloud straight ahead, right above Ypres? We can't land there now.'

'We won't make it anyway. I'm going to have to come down.'

He looked swiftly about him. There was a flat-looking field, well away from all houses but surrounded by a belt of trees, to his right, and he turned towards it. It looked isolated, and if they were lucky they would be able to set fire to their plane before the Germans discovered them.

They were a few hundred yards away, approaching the trees, when the bullet slipped loose, and the remaining fuel gushed out of the tank. The engine coughed and spluttered, and though Richard fought to hold it, he was unable to prevent the plane from starting to spin.

Two twists was all there was time for, then the fragile vessel crashed into the top branches, and as Richard was flung out his last conscious recollection was of crashing, splintering twigs and branches, and his last emotion a piercing loss as he knew he might never again see Marigold.

Lexie came into the morning room eagerly. It was a beautiful spring day, and she had plans to take Marigold on the train to see her mother. It might well be the last time Marigold could make the trip before her baby arrived.

She'd heard Marigold come down ten minutes ago, but had been delayed by her parlourmaid, Janie, who'd waylaid her in the hall to complain about the housemaid's failings as regarded dusting the dining room properly.

Their feud was an ancient one; their grievances imaginary. They were both excellent workers and Lexie had long ago discovered that all she had to do to resolve their differences was to listen with as much patience as she could, murmur appropriate but meaningless words of sympathy, and she would hear no more.

'Yes, Janie, I understand. I will see to it. I am sure Emmie will do it better in future. Mrs Endersby is already down, I think?'

'Yes, ma'am, some time ago. I took in the post.'

'Good, then perhaps you can get some fresh tea? I think I'd prefer it to coffee this morning.'

Janie departed, the ribbons of her cap floating out behind her, and Lexie went to join her guest.

Marigold had become more of a sister to her than a guest, she reflected. It was a joy to have her in the house, particularly now that Archie had to be in London so often. Unfit to fight, he was working in the War Office, and without Marigold she would have been very lonely.

'What a lovely day!' she exclaimed as she opened the door, and then saw Marigold. The girl had slid into a heap on the floor, her chair overturned, a sheet of paper clutched in her hand.

Lexie ran across to her and bent to feel her pulse. 'Marigold, oh my dear, what is it?'

The pulse beat erratically, but Marigold was deathly pale, and she made no response to Lexie's frantic questions.

Lexie hurried to tug on the bell, then, impatient, went to the door and called frantically for help. Janie came in, followed by Emmie, and, somewhat further in the rear and puffing slightly, Mrs Tompkins, the cook.

'Why, Mrs Cranworth, whatever's the matter?' the latter gasped.

'Mrs Endersby's fainted, I think. Emmie, run for the doctor as fast as you can, and Janie, help me lift her on to a sofa. Mrs Tompkins, ought I to give her sal volatile or anything, in her condition? I don't know anything about childbirth!' Lexie asked as she rushed back into the room and, with Janie's help, carefully lifted Marigold on to the sofa.

'Is the babby comin'?' Mrs Tompkins asked calmly.

'I don't know! It's too early.'

'Looks to me like she's just fainted. Keep her warm, and wait till the doctor comes.'

'Is that best? Janie, get some blankets, and should we have hot-water bottles?'

'I'll see to them,' Mrs Tompkins offered, and departed.

For the first time Lexie noticed the paper Marigold was clutching, and gently removed it. By the time Janie ran back with an armful of blankets she had read the letter.

Marigold recovered from her swoon, but for some days did nothing but stare in front of her, not speaking, heedless of Lexie's pleas.

Mary came, and John, but Marigold lay in bed, supine, apparently not aware they were in the room.

'It's the shock. You must give her time,' Dr Leigh said.

'But the child!' Mary worried. 'What if she goes into labour?'

'It's three days now since it happened, and if she'd been going to lose the child there'd have been some sign. All seems well, and by the time the child arrives let's hope she will have recovered.'

But when Marigold went into labour a week later, she had still given no indication that she recognized anyone. She permitted Mary and Lexie to feed her, wash her and comb her hair, but uttered no word.

Lexie insisted that she be dressed, at least in a dressing gown, and taken down into the garden. 'It can't be good for her to lie in bed all day,' she said worriedly to Mary.

Marigold sat when she was told, walked when Lexie commanded her, silent and unresisting. Mary slept in her room, and talked and crooned to her as she had when Marigold was a baby, but elicited no response.

They all began to fear she was losing her mind.

The first change happened when Marigold, obediently sitting up in bed while Mary fed her toast dipped in tea, winced and put her hand to her back. It happened again some while later and Mary went quietly from the room.

'I think labour is starting,' she told Lexie. 'Can you send for Dr Leigh?'

It was a long and difficult labour, but to Mary's intense relief it seemed to jerk Marigold back from the brink of insanity.

The pain banished the blankness from Marigold's eyes. When the doctor patiently questioned her she nodded in reply. The first sound she uttered since reading the letter announcing Richard's death was a groan as his son thrust his way into the world.

Ivy skipped along, holding her father's hand. It was two whole weeks since her nephew Dick had been born, and she had begged to go and visit him and Marigold.

'Not yet,' Mary said. 'Marigold is still not well.' She was almost back to normal, though, Mary thought with relief, remembering that marvellous moment.

When she had turned towards Marigold after seeing the healthy baby boy the midwife had just delivered, she had seen her daughter's expression, anguish and anticipation combined, and known the worst was over.

'You have a lovely son, my dear,' she'd said, and Marigold had smiled, though her eyes were full of tears.

'Give him to me, please.'

Marigold's voice was hoarse, hesitant, but her words were clear. The midwife hid her impatience. It was not good practice to encourage this sort of sentimentality before mother and infant had been properly cleaned up and the bedroom tidied, but Dr Leigh had been adamant.

'Mrs Endersby's mental state is delicate,' he told her. 'Whatever nonsense it may appear to you, she must be humoured.'

So Marigold sat up and held her child. Her sight blurred as she saw the dark hair, the eyes which were Richard's eyes, and the expression which was exactly his.

For two weeks she had wanted to die. She had not cared what was done to her, all she wanted was to join Richard, to be with him in death. Now she was shaken out of that apathy of despair. Here, utterly dependent on her, was another Richard. Her beloved lived on in his son.

She glanced up and saw Mary looking anxiously at her. She smiled, and it was as if a pale moon had turned suddenly into a blazing sun.

'Thanks, Mom,' she whispered, and immediately turned her attention back to the baby.

He was looking about him, snuffling a little, and blinking as a shaft of bright sunshine fell across his face. Marigold turned him slightly, to escape it, and he reached for her breast.

With fumbling fingers she undid the tapes at the neck of her nightgown and pulled it down, letting the baby nuzzle her. She watched him, entranced, and some of the pain she felt at Richard's death was transmuted into a fierce, protective love for this child.

The midwife stepped forward, about to speak. She was willing to indulge her patient so far, in accordance with Dr Leigh's commands, but enough was enough. New mothers did not behave as if she weren't there. Only the lowest classes, who knew no better, went straight ahead and fed their infants in such an abandoned manner. It was perfectly clear the patient wasn't about to descend into a bout of madness, so the proper childbed procedures would be performed.

Mary divined her intention and seized her arm. 'No! I must talk to you for a minute. Outside, if you please.'

Before the woman could say more than a couple of words, Mary, the gentlest of souls, had physically dragged her out of the bedroom and shut the door.

'You will not disturb them!' she said fiercely. 'My daughter has suffered the most dreadful shock and loss, and now she is recovering. You will not take her baby away from her!

'For goodness' sake, Mrs Smith, what are you suggesting? I have to wash the child, tidy the mother, make all presentable.'

'Dr Leigh ordered she was to be allowed to do what she wanted.'

'That's all very well, but he's a man and only a doctor. I have delivered hundreds of babies and know what is best for both them and their mothers. Now pray take your hand off me. I mean to institute some order and sensible management into the nursery.'

'We'll ask Dr Leigh's opinion. Until he comes, you will not go back into that room. Come with me, please.' Almost dragging the protesting woman with her, Mary marched firmly downstairs to where Lexie waited in the drawing room. 'She has a son, a healthy little boy, and she seems well again.'

'Thank God! But shouldn't someone be with her?' Lexie asked, puzzled, looking at the midwife.

'That's what I say, ma'am, but Mrs Smith sees fit to dispute my professional expertise.'

Mary explained. 'So you see, Lexie, I don't want anything to disturb her, perhaps upset her balance again. I've seen lots of babies born, and none of them have been hurt by a little bit of love. I expect the same goes for their mothers. Will you send for Dr Leigh, and I'll go back and do what else is necessary when Marigold's ready.'

'Of course.'

'And what am I to do?' the midwife demanded aggressively.

Lexie glanced from her red face to Mary's determined one. 'I think you have done a good job delivering the baby,' she said quietly. 'You have our thanks. If you will come with me I will see that you are paid, and then I think you had better go. Mrs Smith can look after her daughter and grandson.'

Mary recalled this battle now as she walked along to the station. Lexie had invited them all to Sunday lunch, and they could see Marigold and her son.

She'd remained a week with them, but Marigold showed no signs of reverting to the shocked state she'd been in before little Dick was born. She'd even been able to talk quite calmly about Richard, so Mary had returned to Hednesford and her own family.

Poppy, having overcome her aversion to working in a shop – for no alternative had offered and it was better than staying at home – was by now working full time in the draper's, as the male assistants had all joined up. She had done her best to keep the house in order while Mary was in Birmingham, but Mary suspected Ivy had been of little help, and the place had practically needed another spring clean when she'd got home.

Mary considered Ivy, skipping along in front of her and Poppy. She was such a single-minded child. When she was drawing or painting nothing else mattered. She didn't even hear anyone speaking to her. It was the same with her plants. If she heard of some new plant she would walk miles to find it, totally forgetting John's strictures about not going on to the Chase while the soldiers were nearby.

At the moment Ivy was thinking neither of drawing nor plants. She would see Marigold again, and Marigold would come home with her baby, and once more be part of the family.

She'd hated it at home since Marigold had been away. She knew her parents loved her, but they were out at work so much, and somehow she always seemed to do something, or be accused of doing something, which made them get cross with her.

Poppy was almost always bad tempered. She fussed and shouted and gave Ivy orders, bossing her about. And she let her horrid little dog tear up Ivy's drawings.

Ivy frowned. She hadn't dropped the last drawing on the floor, she took too much care of them. So Scrap must have scrambled up on to the chair and snatched it off the table. 'So I won't do another! It was of the beastly dog, and I was going to take it to show Marigold, but I don't care if she doesn't ever see him,' she had shouted before slamming out of the house and going to call Lizzie out to play.

Marigold loved her and knew how she felt. She knew how hard it was for Ivy to go out and meet strangers. She knew how most of the other girls at school mocked her, called her 'scarface', and wouldn't play with her. Lizzie was her only friend.

If it hadn't been for the scars she'd have been the most popular girl in the class. They'd all have loved her and wanted to be her best friend. Instead she had to put up with Lizzie and her stupid brothers.

Her lips curled. Sam was ridiculous, getting so excited about putting on the creams. It was clear to Ivy that her scars were never going to heal, but her bosoms were beginning to swell, very slightly. She was only ten and a half, and they might have done anyway, but Sam was totally convinced his cream had been responsible. Ivy wasn't sure, but at least he was still willing to go on paying her. They'd had another argument the previous Sunday.

'Yer gotta keep doin' it,' he had insisted.

'It's not working fast enough,' Ivy had demurred.

Sam had been preparing for this. 'It needs more puttin' on, not just once a week,' he told her.

'Well, that's daft, Mr Potter's here all the rest of the time.'

'We don't 'ave ter be 'ere, now it's light evenin's. We could goo up on ter Chase.'

'Sixpence every time,' Ivy stipulated.

Sam argued, but she was adamant. He sighed. He was finding it a strain providing sixpence a week, but he'd been exploring other possibilities which, although less attractive in one way, had compensations.

'What yer needs is more rubbin' in. Massage, it's called. But it's 'ard work on me fingers. Awl right fer yer, yer just 'as ter lay there. Billy'd pay yer ter let 'im 'elp.'

'Billy?' she exclaimed in surprise.

Sam was red in the face. 'Well, yer can see 'ow it meks me pant,' he said. 'I need 'elp, an' yer'd get more money.'

'Sixpence each time as well?'

'Thruppence.'

'No. Sixpence.'

'Tell yer what, me friend Eddie, 'e'd pay thruppence too.'

Ivy had said she'd think it over. By now, with the money Richard had given her long ago, and the guinea from when she'd visited Marigold in Birmingham, she had quite a store of coins in the old tobacco tin she kept hidden under her knickers in the chest she shared with Poppy. But it wasn't enough.

She was determined to collect enough money to go to London. Once there, if she could show her drawings to the teachers, she knew she'd be welcomed at the best art college there was. And someone would pay for her to be taught and provide her with somewhere to live. But she needed several pounds, before she was fourteen and had to leave school, or her chance would be gone.

She could double the amount she got from Sam for no effort. It wasn't very much, but a shilling a week for the next four years or so would help a lot.

It had crossed her mind to ask Marigold to help her, but for the moment she preferred to keep her plans secret. She was afraid they would scoff at her, say she was dreaming foolishly. And just in case Marigold wouldn't help she had to be prepared.

She pushed aside these thoughts as they boarded the train to Birmingham. Life would be like it had been before, with Marigold at home all day, for she couldn't go out to work with a small baby. Besides, she had enough money not to need to work. Ivy would have her to herself again.

Briefly she thought about Dick. But he was a baby, he would lie in his cradle, and Marigold would only have to see to him occasionally. And Richard, who had stolen Marigold away from them, was dead; no longer a rival.

Ivy hugged these thoughts to herself as the train chugged towards Birmingham, ignoring the conversation of the others, which was all about Johnny's last letter and the boring, tedious war.

Mary sighed. 'How long will it go on? Johnny says they've been fighting nonstop for a month, and getting nowhere. And they're using dreadful gas, that chokes men to death.'

'We'll not think about it. I'm looking forward to seeing my grandson.'

'Mother, isn't it time to forgive Richard? His son is not in any way to blame.'

Sophia Endersby brushed the skirt of her pale pink satin gown, and held out her wineglass towards Henry. 'I have asked you not to mention that name in this house,' she said coldly.

'Richard is probably dead! And you sit there, not a shred of mourning on your clothes, and refuse to talk about his child! You are inhuman!'

'Don't talk to your mother in that way, Henry!'

'Father, she's only hurting herself.'

His mother stood up abruptly. 'If you insist on prolonging this distasteful conversation, let us retire to the drawing room. I will explain to you, once, Henry, my reasons.'

She swept out of the room, the butler Kemp opening the door for her. 'Is there anything else, sir?' the man asked.

Mr Endersby waved him away. 'No. That is, bring some brandy to the drawing room. We'll go there now.'

Henry followed his father into the green drawing room, where Mrs Endersby was ensconced in a chair near the deep window bay. The view was magnificent, facing westwards and overlooking a steep-sided valley. The sun was setting gloriously, and in summer they often had their coffee beside this window and watched it.

Henry waited impatiently while his mother poured coffee and handed round the delicate cups which the Endersby pottery had only recently brought into production.

Kemp came and placed the brandy and some glasses on a small table beside his father, then silently withdrew. Henry looked unblinkingly at his mother. Suddenly she turned to him.

'Your brother was dead to me from the day he went through a form of marriage with this trollop. I do not accept her as his wife, and I certainly do not accept her child as his son. How can anyone have the slightest idea who fathered the brat? Richard was deceived into believing he had, but instead of appealing to us for help he allowed himself to be tricked into offering marriage!'

Henry was white with anger. 'Marigold is no trollop, even if she was a servant. You'd know that if you'd seen her!'

'I have seen her, Henry! You forget, he had the impertinence to bring her here, into my presence, without so much as asking my permission. He knew, of course, I would not under any circumstances accept his fancy woman here.'

'Richard loved her, and anyone seeing them together would know she adored him. He is gone, though you haven't the common decency to pay him normal respect, and you should be glad he left a son behind, something to remember him by!'

'Henry, if you continue to speak to me in such a manner, I shall lose both my sons!'

'Father, have you nothing to say? You let Richard go without making the slightest effort to understand. You didn't even see him, discuss it with him, or write to him!'

'I've always left the children's upbringing to your mother,' Mr Endersby blustered.

'Richard wasn't a child; neither am I. We're both adults, we're both full partners in the business. Surely –'

'Richard is dead! Don't talk as if he were still alive! He's dead, and I had to hear it from her! I'm his mother but they couldn't tell me! She robbed me of him, and at the end she stole that from me too. She isn't anything but a whore!'

She fought to keep control, but great tearing sobs erupted. When Henry and her husband went to her she pushed them both away, the new porcelain cups falling unheeded to the floor, and, waving the men aside when they would have accompanied her, almost ran out of the room.

'Father, I didn't know she was like this,' Henry said, aghast.

Mr Endersby sighed and shook his head. 'Sit down, Henry, there's nothing we can do for her. She needs an hour or two alone, then she'll reappear as though nothing has happened. If no one mentions Richard she's able to manage, but I'm afraid there have been so many letters of condolence since people heard it's upset her a great deal. She's very – on edge.'

'Does she really not accept they were married? Or believe the child isn't his?'

'She was wild with rage when Richard married that girl. I'm not sure if she believes it was a sham or not, but it's what she says.'

'I was there, and I promise you it was no sham.'

'Perhaps she'll admit it one day. But please bear with her, don't leave in anger. That would be the end. She loves you both so much, beneath her – well, rather odd manner.'

'I won't go, I promise, whatever she says. But Richard might still be alive. He could be a prisoner somewhere. Doesn't she hope for that?'

'She won't talk to me about it. I suspect she believes he is no longer her son for he belongs to this girl, and if he came back it would not be to her.'

'Does that matter if he's still alive? I believe he is, and you know we were almost like twins at times, able to read one another's thoughts. I'm sure I'd know if he were dead.'

It was the middle of July before Marigold had the courage to think about the future.

'You're welcome to stay here with me for as long as you choose,' Lexie said to her.

'I can't. It's so good of you, but it wouldn't be fair on you. I must make a home for Dick and myself, somehow. Perhaps I'll buy a small house in Hednesford and Mom and Dad could come and live with me.'

'And Dick? Do you want him to live there, having the same sort of life you did, even though it could be a lot easier?'

'No. But at the moment I can't think of anything better.'

'Then you must stay here until you are able to make proper plans. You know I can't have children after the one I lost,' she added quietly, 'and I love having you and Dick here. If you'd like me to come and see Richard's solicitor, to find out exactly what the position is – whether you get a war widow's pension, for example, since Richard is posted missing, and only presumed dead, and how much money you'll have to live on – I'll gladly do it. Or perhaps you'd prefer Archie to go with you?'

'I'll write tomorrow. I'd rather you came, I think, Lexie.'

That very afternoon, however, a letter came for Marigold, requesting her presence at the solicitor's office in Temple Row the following morning.

Dick was left with Janie, who adored him and had become an unofficial nanny, while Lexie and Marigold took a cab to the office.

Mr Thane, the elderly solicitor, ushered them in and busied himself arranging chairs for them. 'Mrs Endersby, thank you for coming so promptly. I didn't know – what with the baby, that is – well, you too, Mrs Cranworth, I am delighted to see you, although – But first I must express my condolences at the death of your husband, Mrs Endersby.'

'He isn't dead.'

Marigold had wondered sometimes if her inner conviction that Richard was still alive, somewhere, was the sort of fantasy all women had. But the solicitor's apparent certainty stiffened her resolve never to admit that there was no hope left.

Mr Thane coughed nervously. 'No, no, of course not! That is, naturally you will feel – wish – to believe he is still alive. There is a difficulty, though.'

'What do you mean? Difficulty? How is this?' Lexie asked, seeing that Marigold was not listening.

'It relates to the ownership of Endersby and Sons. Under the terms of the agreement when the partnership was established, both Mr Richard and Mr Henry Endersby had twenty per cent of the capital, as did their mother, with the remaining forty per cent belonging to Mr Endersby, their father,' Mr Thane said fluently, thankful to be talking about matters he understood.

'Yes, I know this,' Marigold said, dragging her attention away from thoughts of where Richard, if he were alive, could be.

'Well, Mr Richard Endersby made a will before he went to France, leaving everything he possessed to you. But I am afraid that under the terms of the partnership agreement he was not free to dispose of his share of the firm without a majority agreement by the rest of the partners. In the event of that agreement being withheld, and without his guarantee that he would not dispose of his share, his share would revert to the remaining partners in equal proportions.'

'That's monstrous!' Lexie exclaimed.

'So Richard is not here to give such a guarantee, but it is because he is not here that the terms of his will are being put into effect,' Marigold said thoughtfully.

'Precisely,' the unhappy Mr Thane had to agree. 'My dear, I am most terribly sorry, for I know it is not what your husband intended –'

'Surely we could fight this?' Lexie interrupted. 'It's quite unreasonable and, as Mrs Endersby says, illogical.'

'You could bring an action, but in such a case who knows what the law would decide? It's possible they might refuse a judgement until all likelihood of Mr Endersby still being alive is gone. They could order the income to be frozen so that no one benefits from it. I asked you to come here so that I could suggest, with the greatest respect, that you permit me to approach Mr Endersby's parents with a view to asking that you be allowed to continue using the income, as you were able to do when he was alive, until the matter can be finally resolved.'

'They have power to do that?'

'Yes, if they do not seek to declare him dead. If they did that the matter would change to your detriment.'

'They'll do anything to disown me,' Marigold told him. 'His brother came to see me when he returned to Whittington, before he went to France. Richard's mother hates me. She even tried to say we were not properly married. I can prove we were, so she will declare her son dead rather than see me have his money.'

'But that wasn't Richard's only income, was it?' Lexie asked.

'No. He had invested a small legacy from his grandfather, and surplus income from the firm, which could bring in about two hundred a year.'

Marigold laughed harshly. 'That's more than my father ever earned. More than the whole family earned. I don't want riches, Mr Thane. I married Richard because I loved him. I want to give his son everything he had – and a loving mother too! We can live on four pounds a week, and I'll work too. Somehow I'll send Dick to Eton, and Oxford! He won't suffer because a bitter old woman hates me. Thank you for telling me. Lexie, shall we go?'

'That damned dog! Poppy, look at him, he's got my drawing again!'

'You must have left it on the floor. He's too little to climb up on a chair.'

'He doesn't when we're here, but I'm sure he does when we're all out.'

'Then he'd steal food, not measly bits of paper with scribbles all over them!'

'They are not scribbles! They're not! My teacher says I'm the best artist she's ever seen at any school.'

'I suppose she's been to every school in the world?'

'You're a spiteful, jealous cat! You think because you go out to work now, you can do what you like. Well, you can't with my things.'

Poppy shrugged. She was used to Ivy's sudden flares of rage, Just as she was used to Ivy disappearing whenever there was work to be done.

Ivy ran towards the Chase. It was one of the evenings when she met Sam and his brother and Eddie after they'd finished work, and she was late.

They'd found a secret hollow on Brindley Heath, overlooking the Tackeroo Railway, which was being constructed to carry building materials to the army camps, and met there. Ivy had been intrigued to see that rubbing in the cream had the same odd effect on Billy and Eddie as it did on Sam. Boys were peculiar, she decided, but if their strange predilections produced money for her, why should she object?

When she reached the hollow she heard laughter, and slowed down. Perhaps it was someone else, not Sam. She crept up the bank, slithering on her stomach for the last yard or so, until she could peer through a screen of gorse down into the soft, moss-strewn dell.

Sam and two soldiers were sitting on fallen logs, smoking.

'Sixpence apiece, I tell yer. 'Er's a cute wench. Ten, but looks younger.'

'Sixpence, just ter look at a kid's boobs?' one of the soldiers laughed.

'A shillin' fer aase as well,' Sam offered.

'Nah. Plenty o' gals in Hednesford an' Rugeley willin' to lift their skirts for no more'n a shillin' all the way.'

'But them's not innercent li'l virgins,' Sam winked. 'I'll promise that, or yer can 'ave yer money back. Five bob, all the way?'

The soldiers shook their heads, laughing at the crestfallen lad.

'Never thought virgins anythin' ter write 'ome abaht, anyroads,' one said, rising to his feet. 'Gi' me a good inventive whore any day. Damn sight more fun.'

'Good try, lad, but keep 'er ter yerself!' the other said.

Ivy could scarcely contain her anger until they were out of earshot. Sam threw himself down on the ground when the soldiers left, face down with his head on his arm. When she thought it was safe Ivy crept down towards him.

'I hate you, Sam Bannister!' she shouted suddenly, at the same time unleashing several sharp kicks at his ribs.

'Eh? What the devil? Ivy, what's got inter yer? Leave be, yer little besom!'

'How dare you only give me threepence extra from the others! I expect you make Billy and Eddie pay you sixpence, and keep half of it yourself! That's why you wanted to get all your other pals as well! You're a cheat, Sam Bannister!'

'Eddie's sick an' Billy won't come no more,' Sam said gloomily. ''E's found 'isself a wench up in Cannock, says she don' charge at all, an' gi's 'im a better time.'

'Then if you want to experiment with your pesky cream, you'll have to give me a shilling each time! It's you being greedy drove Billy away, and fancy asking those soldiers for five whole shillings! What on earth made you think they'd pay that much?'

Sam almost told her, but his timorous nature balked at having to put it into words.

'It's no good anyway,' Ivy declared, and turned to stalk away.

'Ivy, don' go, I'm sorry, I'll gi' yer a shillin, 'onest!'

Sam at that moment envied his brother Billy with all his heart. No one wanted to walk out with him. They all reacted as Poppy Smith had done when he tried to show he admired them. Yet Billy, three years younger, already had a wench who, if Billy's claims could be believed, provided him with undreamed-of delights as often as he wanted.

It was, he recognized with sick despair, only his trickery with the cream that obtained for him Ivy's compliance. And that, after all, wasn't very satisfactory any more. It had been a thrill, at first, caressing her body, especially when she'd permitted him, on pretence of rubbing in cream, to fondle her bottom.

But now, when her breasts were beginning to be obvious, he wanted more. Yet he didn't know how to suggest it. Somehow he knew she'd refuse. It was with a muddled sense of introducing the idea to her through someone else that had made him approach the soldiers as they walked towards Hednesford for their evening's entertainment. That had got him nowhere, had probably lost him the little he had.

'A shilling, each time?' Ivy said now, after a long silence.

Sam almost gobbled in excitement as he agreed. He'd find the money somehow, filch a few more pennies from the till, or fill up some of the jars of cream with cheap substitutes, and sell the real stuff by himself.

'But I 'ain't got a shillin' ternight,' he remembered.

'Then you'll have to wait till Sunday.'

Ivy turned and walked away, and despite Sam's pleas as he followed her right back into the town, she was adamant.

She was also furious. He'd been cheating her, and through his stupidity she had no money tonight. And by going to see Marigold she'd lost Sunday as well.

Her anger turned towards Poppy, and Scrap's misdemeanours. He was a horrid dog, and Poppy was far too silly about him. Her mind began to weave plots, and by the time she reached home she was cheerful once more.

Richard felt himself falling, then his headlong descent was slowed by the upper branches of the trees. Surely he couldn't be making all that noise? The roaring and crackling of branches being torn asunder was far more than could be caused by one body.

The moment of unconsciousness vanished. Of course, the plane had crashed. Was crashing, to judge from the noise, into the belt of trees surrounding the field he'd been aiming for. He must have been thrown clear.

He felt some anxiety about where the plane was in relation to himself. Was he above or below it? And where was Frank?

Desperately he tried to see what was happening, but apart from sensing that the plane was some way to one side, he could see nothing. He concentrated on trying to control his hitherto somewhat haphazard descent, and managed to halt his progress by grabbing a substantial branch.

He tore off his goggles and looked round, spotting the aeroplane some twenty yards away, upended in the top of another tree. Frank, apparently unconscious, was caught up on a propeller blade and hanging helplessly upside down.

Richard surveyed his own position. He was no more than twenty feet above the ground, in what he thought was a hornbeam, but he never had been much good at recognizing trees. It didn't look a difficult climb, though, and he soon slithered down from branch to branch, jumping the final six feet or so and rolling over as he landed.

Now to get to Frank. As he stood up and took the first step towards the aeroplane, a dull whooshing sound thumped into his ears, and flames suddenly erupted from the damaged fuel tank. Within seconds the flimsy structure was a blazing bonfire. He had no hope of reaching Frank, even if he'd had ladders and people to help.

The shock of this explosion made him step back, and only then did he notice his leg was bleeding badly. His flying suit was torn from knee to shoulder, but whether it had happened during his contact with the tree or earlier he couldn't recall.

Limping, and beginning to feel the pain, he turned and moved away from the burning plane. The flames would bring people soon enough, and if they were Germans he didn't want to be nearby.

He made it round two sides of the enclosed field before the pain and weakness through loss of blood forced him to stop. As he looked back to where the plane now smouldered, there was a sound behind him. He turned, and beheld two villainous-looking men covering him with a rifle and a revolver.

Chapter Eleven

It was a broiling hot day, and even now, in the late afternoon, Poppy wilted. It was too hot even to take Scrap for his walk, disappointed though he'd be. Thinking of the puppy, Poppy smiled. He was so changed from the pitiful bag of bones he'd been when she found him. Now his coat was glossy, he was fat as butter, and full of energy.

Poppy opened the back door. All was silent. Was Scrap too hot to come and leap all over her in his normal effusive greeting? Or had Ivy let him escape? Poppy felt a surge of such fury at the idea that had Ivy been there she would have done something dire to her sister.

She went into the scullery and saw Scrap stretched out on the pile of sacking where he slept. 'Scrap, what mischief have you been up to?' she asked, wondering why he should be so uncharacteristically tired.

Then she looked closer. His head was lolling back and his tongue protruded oddly. Poppy, a nameless apprehension gripping her, knelt beside him. She stretched out her hand, and paused. He didn't seem to be breathing. 'Oh, no! Scrap, what is it?'

She touched him, but his body was cold. Frantically she picked him up, but the tiny body was stiff and she felt a stickiness on her hands. Looking closer she saw he had vomited in his bed before collapsing. Her beloved Scrap was dead.

Poppy sat there weeping helplessly. She rocked backwards and forwards with the pathetic body in her arms until Mary came home.

'Poppy, love, what is it?' Mary asked in alarm, and Poppy mutely held out the puppy's body. 'Oh, my dear! I am so sorry. How did it happen?'

Suddenly a flood of grief overwhelmed Poppy, mingled with helpless fury. 'Look, he's been sick! He's been poisoned! It was Ivy!'

'Ivy? Poppy, darling, what do you mean?'

'She hated him, she was jealous because I loved him! She said he tore up her drawings and he didn't! She left them on the floor! She's killed him!'

'Poppy, no! Not Ivy! Not your little sister! She couldn't be so wicked!'

'Couldn't she? She's always messing about with those herbs of hers. Some of them are poisonous. She gave him something, I know she did!'

'I know she thinks she's making medicines and such, but she doesn't really know much about those plants. Even if she did, she wouldn't kill your little dog! She's not wicked, and she knows how much you love him.'

'That's why she did it, she's jealous,' Poppy insisted. 'He's the only thing that was ever truly mine!'

'It could have been rat-bait someone put down. You know he's always rooting about in the gardens. Or he might have found something up on the Chase.'

'You'll never believe me against her,' Poppy said bleakly, and rose to her feet.

'Poppy, that's not true, but it's a wicked thing to suggest she'd deliberately poison your dog. Where are you going?'

'To bury him.'

'In the garden? Shall I help you?'

'No, I'm taking him up on the Chase, where he was happy, poor mite. Somewhere Ivy can't get at him again!' she added under her breath, and heedless of Mary's pleas to wash her hands first and clean her skirt, she walked away.

Ivy vigorously denied having anything to do with the dog's death. 'He was perfectly well when I let him out at dinnertime,' she insisted. 'He probably ate something then, from the garden. Anyway, why all the fuss? It's only a dog. You can always have another if you're so fond of them.'

'I'll never have another dog for you to kill!' Poppy shouted at her. 'You did it because you knew I loved him!'

Ivy shrugged. 'You're mad!'

When Poppy carried her woes to Marigold her older sister was incredulous. 'You can't believe that of Ivy!' she exclaimed.

'No one does,' Poppy sighed. 'Especially as she's been all sweet and helpful lately. I don't really believe it myself when I'm not mad at her, but there's always a niggle of doubt.'

'Forget it,' Marigold advised. 'She's growing up, her moods change.'

It was not mentioned again, but Poppy reverted to her former apathy, apparently uncaring. Mary worried, but never guessed that under the apparent acceptance Poppy burned with an even more fierce determination to get away when the first chance offered.

'You come with us.' He spoke a guttural form of French, but by concentrating Richard could understand him. He needed something to divert his mind from the horror of Frank's death. He hoped the poor fellow had been unconscious before the fire broke out.

The man with the rifle, a plump man in his sixties, gestured to Richard to follow him. By now feeling faint from loss of blood, Richard walked behind him. He was followed by the second man, who was not much above his own age, and who covered him with the revolver.

To his relief it was not far, just across a couple of fields where cattle, oblivious to the guns pounding relentlessly a few miles away, peacefully grazed. They came to a small farm, built of stone with a grey slate roof, steeply pitched. Round it were various outbuildings forming an irregular-shaped yard.

The older man turned and spoke. 'You are English? That was your aeroplane?'

'Yes,' Richard answered. 'To both questions.'

'Come, you must lie in the barn, we dare not take you in the house. Go and fetch water and bandages,' he ordered the younger man – presumably his son, for now Richard could see a distinct resemblance in the broad, flat faces and bright blue eyes.

He took Richard inside and helped him climb a steep ladder into a loft, where he swiftly arranged some bales of straw to form a barricade in one corner. He led Richard behind this and told him to take off his clothes and lie down.

'We will find you some old clothes to wear, but first my son will deal with that cut. It looks bad.'

'Just a bit deep,' Richard replied, breathing heavily after climbing the ladder. 'I am most grateful to you, but you must not endanger yourself or your family by helping me.'

The old man spat contemptuously. 'These Prussian devils attack little Belgium. I fight them any way I can.'

Richard was dealt with most efficiently. The son, by name Gaston, cleaned the deep cut in Richard's thigh, pronounced no muscles torn and, with Richard eyeing the preparations somewhat apprehensively, inserted several stitches.

'I stitch up the animals if they need it,' he explained, grinning as he saw Richard's expression. 'Now eat this food while I fetch some blankets. You must try to sleep, it's past nine o'clock. I will come to you after we've done the milking in the morning.'

To his surprise, Richard slept heavily. He felt rather muzzy when the clatter of milk churns below awoke him, and he suspected the Belgians had dosed his food with something to dull the pain.

Gaston clambered up the ladder soon afterwards. 'Good, you have slept well,' he approved. 'Here is bread, sausage, cheese, and a jug of coffee. I cannot come again until this evening, for any unusual movements would alert the Germans. They are about all the time, one never knows when they will come spying on us. Stay here behind the straw bales, and if one of them pokes his head into the loft he'll never guess you're here.'

'Do they suspect I wasn't killed in the plane?' Richard asked.

'Perhaps, but by this evening I shall know. My brother works at the café.'

Richard slept again for much of the day. It was dusk before Gaston returned.

'Here, eat this while I dress the wound,' he said abruptly, handing Richard a bowl filled with delicious rabbit stew.

'What did your brother discover?'

'It's not good news, I'm afraid,' Gaston explained as he tended Richard's gashed leg. 'They know there were two men in the plane, but only your friend's body was found. They have been searching the area all day. We need to move you tonight, before they begin to search the buildings nearby. They are aggrieved because you shot down two of their planes.'

'I'm strong enough to walk now, thanks to your care,' Richard said swiftly. 'I cannot put you in danger. I will leave when it is dark and see if I can get to the coast.'

'You would be picked up by a patrol before you had gone far. No, we have friends to the east, which is the last direction they would expect you to go. They will hide you tomorrow, and take you further away from the lines the next day. Then you should be safe. You speak good French, you could pass for one of us with those ignorant Germans.'

He would not accept Richard's arguments and in the end Richard was thankful. From imagining himself a prisoner, at the very least, of the Germans, he was beginning to entertain hopes that he might somehow get back to France and rejoin his squadron.

'You must promise me that if we are challenged you will leave me? I would not be easy if I had brought harm to your family.'

'It is my war first,' Gaston, dignified and calm, reminded him. 'We are grateful for all your help, you British, but it is Belgium which has been violated. I am prepared to fight too.'

They set off an hour later, and Richard was soon aching all over. He hadn't realized how weak he felt. Gaston set a steady but easy pace, for which Richard gave silent thanks. They walked along little-used paths, keeping to the woodlands or beside hedges to take advantage of the slightest cover. After an hour Gaston called a halt. He produced a flask. 'Drink this, my friend. It will give you strength.'

The raw spirit burnt Richard's throat, but also poured strength into him. For the next half-hour he felt equal to anything. Once they almost stumbled over a drunken German, sleeping off his excesses in a ditch, and Gaston silently produced a knife. Richard caught at his arm. 'No! It will only arouse suspicion and point to the way we're taking,' he hissed.

Gaston shrugged, but put away the knife. 'Perhaps, but there are many of my countrymen who would kill any German if they had the chance. You are too squeamish, my friend.'

Richard acknowledged it. Killing a soldier who would, if he had the chance, kill you, was one thing. He found he could not bring himself to kill a helpless man unable to defend himself.

After that Richard had little recollection of the journey. He vaguely remembered wading through streams. Once they climbed a tree to swing across a narrow river on a rope Gaston had come prepared with. Often they had to dodge sentries, and on the one occasion they had to leave shelter to cross a railway line they were shot at, but managed to get away.

He could barely speak when Gaston thrust him into a disused stable and told him to wait while he roused his unsuspecting host-to-be.

'My cousin Mathilde,' Gaston said briefly when he came back and shook Richard awake. 'She will dress the wound, and her brother will take you further tonight. Sleep well, and good luck!'

He was gone before Richard had time to say anything but an inadequate 'Thank you'.

'Would you like some food now, or in the morning?' Mathilde, a buxom blonde woman of about thirty, asked matter-of-factly. 'You look exhausted.'

'My pardon, madame. I forget my manners,' Richard said, struggling to rise to his feet.

She pushed him back. 'Sit there. I'll fetch a hot drink, then you must climb up into the loft. On second thoughts you'd better get up there now, you won't stay awake long enough to wait for a drink.'

'What time is it?'

'Two o'clock.'

'Only two? I thought it must be nearly morning!'

'Gaston has to be back for the milking. Now, up the ladder with you, unless you want me to carry you.'

Richard laughed. It was the first time he'd been amused since the plane had crashed.

'I could if necessary,' she said with an answering grin, 'but I confess I'd rather not.'

Richard scrambled up the ladder, and rolled himself in the blankets Mathilde threw after him. He knew no more until she woke him late the following afternoon.

'You must eat as well as sleep,' she told him briskly. 'I need to dress your wound and put on some of the ointment Gaston left for you. He uses it for the cattle. It's very good,' she added with a twinkle in her blue eyes.

He was ravenous, and swiftly demolished the bread and cheese she brought him.

'There will be a hot meal before you have to leave, and I will pack some food for you. It's a longer journey tonight, and Jean will have to stay there tomorrow.'

'Won't he be missed?' Richard asked, frowning.

'He has a sweetheart in the same village, he often goes to spend the day with her. If anyone asks, that is where he is.'

That night Richard was called upon to exercise great endurance once more. He braced himself with the thought that all the time he was getting further away from the area of the crash, and therefore further away from discovery.

This time they arrived at a small village just before dawn, and Richard was astonished to be led to the neat square house alongside the church.

'The priest will hide you for as long as necessary,' Jean told him, seeing his surprise.

'A priest?'

'Why not? Belgium is his country as much as ours.'

Wondering whether he was to spend the next few days, until he recovered sufficiently to attempt to make his way back across the lines, in a church crypt, Richard waited with interest to see this man.

He was old, incredibly old, with long white hair and twisted, gnarled hands. But his face was unlined, the innocent, untroubled face of a child, and his grey eyes as guileless as a baby's.

The thought made Richard think of Marigold's child. He must get back across the lines and let her know he was safe before the child was born. He'd have been reported missing, and she must be frantic with worry.

The priest, Father Matthieu, beckoned them into the house. There were just the two rooms downstairs, a huge kitchen from which the enticing smell of coffee was already drifting, and a big room used as both sitting room and study.

'Welcome, my son. Take the armchair, I am just going across to the church to say Mass. My housekeeper will bring you breakfast and we will talk later. Jean, will you come with me? Have you been to confession? I need someone to serve, none of the lazybones is up early enough this morning.'

Jean cast Richard a wry grin and shrugged. 'I'll explain to him later,' he said as he followed the priest out of the room.

'I'm coming! Can't you wait a minute?'

Janie muttered impatiently as she answered the strident peal of the doorbell. She had a lot to do and wanted to get on with her packing. She was off to London tomorrow to work in one of the big hospitals there. She rather fancied being a nurse with all those handsome wounded officers to look after. Mrs Cranworth had been very understanding.

'It's not as if we ever do any entertaining now, it must be very tedious for you. I've been thinking of shutting up some of the rooms. Emmie wants to go too and the rest of us could manage easily. In fact I'm wondering whether I ought to volunteer myself,' she said. 'I could be with Mr Cranworth if I did.'

'But you can't leave Mrs Endersby and the baby,' Janie replied. 'He's only four months old.'

'No, and to be honest the sight of blood upsets me too much. But there must be some way I could help. I think you're very brave, and if you want to come back afterwards you know there'll always be a job for you here.'

By the time the war ended she hoped she'd have better prospects than being a parlourmaid, Janie thought. She'd heard of girls who'd married officers, men they'd never have met before the war. Look at Mrs Endersby, though Janie didn't envy her much, with her husband probably dead and a baby to bring up.

She opened the door and stepped back slightly. A tall, imperious woman, swathed in black crêpe, stood on the doorstep. A large motor car with a uniformed chauffeur was parked on the gravelled drive.

'Please tell Mrs Cranworth Mrs Endersby is here,' the newcomer said, sailing past Janie.

'Mrs – Mrs Endersby?' Janie gaped.

'Do shut your mouth, girl, it makes you look a lunatic leaving it open like that. Well, are you going to show me where I can wait for your mistress?'

Flustered, and furious with herself for being so, Janie opened the door of the drawing room. 'Please wait here while I inform Modom of your arrival,' she said in her best accents, and stood back while the other swept past her.

Janie abandoned decorum the moment the door was shut, and raced up the stairs. Mrs Cranworth was in the room they had made into a nursery for Master Dick. She and Mrs Endersby had begun to sit there in the mornings because it caught the sun, and sew the endless shirts they made for the troops.

'Mrs Cranworth!' she gasped. 'Mrs Cranworth, Mrs Endersby!'

'Janie, calm down, we're both here,' Lexie said with a slight laugh.

'No, I mean it's the other one!'

'Janie, what is the matter?'

Janie took a deep breath. 'It's her. Mrs Endersby. Mr Endersby's ma, by the looks of her. Wants to see you.'

Marigold paled. 'Do you think she's heard something?'

'Let's go down and find out. Do you want me to see her first?'

'No.' Marigold shook her head firmly. 'If it's bad news I'd rather know straight away. Lexie, could she have heard something?'

'There's one way to find out. Janie, stay here with Master Dick, will you?'

Richard's mother was standing by the window, looking out over the garden. She turned slowly as they entered the room, and when Marigold saw her deep mourning, she clasped Lexie's hand convulsively.

'Mrs Endersby, please sit down,' Lexie said calmly, squeezing Marigold's hand tightly and drawing her over to a sofa where they could sit side by side. 'You wished to see me?'

Sophia Endersby sat facing them. She threw back her veil, and Marigold was shocked. The beautiful woman she recalled was gone, and she was looking into a ravaged, haggard face.

'I came to give you some bad news, and I hope to make my peace,' the older woman said.

'Richard? Have you heard? Is he –?' Marigold could not finish.

'I have heard no more. He must be dead. Now it's Henry too. We had the telegram saying he died in action a few days ago.'

'Oh, poor Henry, he was so kind! I am sorry,' Marigold said impulsively, suppressing the ignoble relief that it wasn't bad news of Richard.

'Both my sons dead. For a war that isn't theirs.'

'I don't believe Richard's dead!' Marigold declared vehemently. 'I'd know if he were!'

'Don't you think I would know too?' his mother said quietly. 'He is dead. But I came to apologize. I acted hastily that day. I was astounded, taken by surprise, and afterwards too proud to make the first move. Oh, how I wish I had! How I wish we hadn't parted on bad terms! Can you forgive me, my dear? Of course I know you are married, and the child is Richard's.'

She held out her arms and Marigold went to her, kneeling beside her and returning her convulsive hug. 'I'm so sorry, about Henry,' she said softly. 'I barely knew him but he was kind to me.'

Sophia drew a deep, rather ragged breath. 'I know you have been under some pressure financially, with the reversion of Richard's share in the partnership to us, but I would like to make it up to you. I want to invite you to come and live with us at The Place. I want you to be able to bring up Richard's son as he would have been raised had Richard lived.'

It was two weeks since Richard had been deposited with Father Matthieu. Ensconced in a tiny attic bedroom, he doubted whether anyone else in the village apart from the priest and his housekeeper, the elderly Madame Cotier, knew he was there.

She had once been a nurse and she made disparaging remarks about Gaston's cobbled stitches. They looked perfectly adequate to Richard, and had withstood the rigours of his journey.

'But you will always have a scar, for he pulled the flesh together irregularly,' she explained as if to a child.

'I don't mind a scar when he saved my life,' he replied mildly. 'The wound has healed perfectly, thanks to your salves, madame. Is it time to remove the stitches?'

'Yes, we can do that now, but you must not take violent exercise for a few days.'

Exercise was the only thing lacking, Richard thought. Apart from Marigold, that is. Madame Cotier's cooking was better than that of many acclaimed chefs, and the priest had a remarkably fine cellar of both French and German wines.

'I see nothing unpatriotic in drinking what I bought years before this débâcle,' he chuckled when Richard expressed surprise that he would choose to open a fine hock. 'Let us hope that before my cellar runs dry I will be able to purchase freely once more.'

'You live well, Father,' Richard said after one particularly fine roast goose.

'And you are wondering what became of my vows of poverty, eh?'

Richard grinned. He now knew the priest well. 'It had occurred to me to wonder,' he murmured.

'Village pastors do not take those vows, in fact. That is for the monks and some of the orders. We should not live ostentatiously, it is true, but when my parishioners, knowing my love of good food, present me with bottles of wine and fowls and fruit and sides of bacon as part of their offerings, should I refuse?'

'That would hurt their feelings,' Richard said gravely.

'Precisely, and now I am going to hurt your feelings, my son, by having my revenge for last night over the chessboard.'

As he said goodnight an hour later, Father Matthieu looked up from where he was bent over the chessboard, puzzling over the endgame, trying to see what he could have done to prevent another victory by Richard. 'Tomorrow I have a visitor for supper. Madame will bring you a tray. Have you enough books to keep you occupied?'

'Yes, thank you. There are enough here to keep me occupied for years!'

'Much as I enjoy your company, I trust you will not have to remain here that long. Goodnight, Richard. God go with you.'

Two days later he explained his plans to Richard.

'The man who came last night brought me some things. He does not know why. Most people prefer to know nothing apart from what they must. This is what we are to do. Here is a map. Destroy it after you have memorized it, for it could be traced back to my friend. Early tomorrow morning he will take you with him on his cart as if going to market. He will be going, but he will set you down in these woods here.'

'He takes a great risk. Would it not be better if I were just to slip away one night, and then nothing could connect me with you?'

'You would not get beyond the village unchallenged. You arrived here only because Jean is known and was not stopped, but I had word of you ten minutes before you arrived. You have not been betrayed because you were with him, but if you were alone it would be a different matter. We are suspicious of all strangers. He will say you are his wife's nephew. You are on your way to a new job in Ghent, if anyone asks. But they won't. In the valise he will provide for you will be a German officer's uniform, and a civilian driving coat.'

'A German uniform?' Richard exclaimed. 'Is that necessary? Or wise?'

'It is the best plan we could devise. Now see here on the map, this is where the nearest French soldiers are. We are too far east for the British, I'm afraid. You must behave on this side as if you are a German, and when you can take your opportunity to slip over to the French lines, covering up the uniform until you are safe, and no one will shoot you.'

Richard had several objections to this plan: he would have no English identification, and would have to rely on getting someone to verify who he was; but they could think of nothing better.

'It is too far, and too uncertain, to head for the sea. You have no friends to help you and could be betrayed by the first person you approach. This way you could be back with your squadron in a couple of days.'

'I shall be everlastingly grateful to you for your help, Father. I wish I knew how to repay you,' Richard said as he was about to climb on the cart.

'God go with you, my son.' His eyes twinkled irrepressibly. 'Our rewards will be in heaven, but if I should happen still to be alive when this conflict is ended, and you happen to think of me, a few bottles of a good wine would recall our happy evenings together.'

'You shall have a dozen cases of champagne, Father!'

Twenty-four hours later Richard thought longingly of the

comfortable house he'd left. He had parted from the rather taciturn driver in a thickly wooded area, and after changing into his German uniform and burying the jacket and trousers Gaston's family had provided him with, he cautiously made his way towards the German lines.

He kept in cover as much as possible, and blessed Father Matthieu for selecting such an area where there was a great deal of it. When it was impossible to move under cover, as through villages, he marched confidently forward. As he had seen the Germans do he ignored everyone, and much against his natural instincts walked as though he expected women and children and crippled ancients to step aside for him.

By nightfall he was within a mile of the nearest trenches, and in the faint moonlight he crept nearer, looking for a place where he might steal across.

It was all too heavily guarded. Several times sentries rose from holes as if from graves, and challenged him. With a few curt words in German he calmed their fears, but he dared not risk going past them towards the French lines, so tantalizingly close. That was to invite being shot in the back as a deserter.

Just before dawn he found a convenient tumbledown shed where he hoped he might remain hidden during the day, while he tried to work out some alternative strategy. He was desperately in need of sleep. The enforced idleness, on top of his injury, had taken more toll than he'd realized. He'd been walking, hoping, searching, for a whole day and night.

He wrapped himself up in the driving coat, lay down on the ground in the shelter of the part-ruined shed, and slept.

Some hours later, refreshed, he began to plan anew. He'd heard planes during the day and they seemed to be landing not far away. He would try to steal one and fly it back home. Of course there was a risk of being shot down, but that he had to take. He had to get round, under, through or over the German lines. The first three were improbable, which left the last. It had the advantage of an element he was used to.

He unwrapped the sausage Madame Cotier had given him, which, she'd said, would keep as long as he needed it. He bit off chunks to eat with the last of his bread, then went to drink from a stream nearby. The day was warm and the stream enticingly deep and cool. A track ran alongside the stream, but it looked unused. No one, walking or otherwise, had used it while he'd been thinking and eating. He stripped off his heavy uniform and plunged in.

Having dried off simply by lying naked in the sun on the soft grass beside the stream, he was almost dressed again when he heard a plane overhead.

Startled, he looked up. It was a Blériot, one of the French planes, flying low. The noise covered the sound of a motor bike tearing along the track. Then there was another sound, a slow, swelling medley of thumps and cracklings and booms, pierced by a shrill scream. Richard had time to realize that the plane had dropped a bomb just yards away from him before the motor cyclist was lifted from the saddle, and came hurtling towards him in a confusion of clumps of earth, twisted metal, and whirling branches. Richard knew no more.

'Lexie, I must. It's what Richard would want.'

'The old hag only wants you because little Dick is the last male Endersby left.'

'Perhaps. If Richard is not still alive,' Marigold said quietly.

'Oh, my dear, I'm sorry! You still feel he's not been killed?'

'I'd know if he were dead, Lexie. Something inside me would have died too, and it hasn't. Some day he'll come back.'

'But where can he be? Surely if he'd been taken prisoner we'd have been told by now?'

'Perhaps. Perhaps he's hiding in Belgium. Anyone there would help an Englishman. He may be trying to get home through Holland. It could take a long time, Lexie, to walk to the coast and find a boat. Are boats still crossing the Channel? Surely they are?'

'Yes, and I even heard of some people who were able to go and disport themselves in Nice, now the threat of France being overrun is less! How can they, when thousands of boys are dying to keep them safe?'

Marigold sighed. 'Like Henry. I must take Richard's son to The Place. It's what Richard would want, and she was sincere in her apologies. Besides, there are other advantages. They've turned over most of it for a hospital, and are living in just a few rooms. I shan't be overawed, like I was when Richard took me. I could do something to help.'

'You have Dick to care for.'

'There will doubtless be others, older women, to do that. I could help with the nursing. I'm used to hard work. I've been living in a sort of cocoon this last year, ignoring the war apart from how it affected me. I must do something to help. And if I went you could go to London to live with Archie.'

'He says he doesn't want me to risk being there.'

'And you know perfectly well, Lexie, that wouldn't stop you for a minute if you didn't feel obliged to keep this house open for me and Dick.'

'Wouldn't you hate it there?'

'Probably, if they lived in all those intimidating rooms. But they can give Dick everything I can't, Lexie. Mr Thane is sure I won't be able to force them to give me Richard's share of the firm. And in my heart of hearts I know how unlikely it would be for me ever to be able to afford to send Dick to a good school, let alone Eton. They will pay for him as a matter of course if he lives there with them.'

'You must promise that if it becomes unbearable you will come straight to me?'

'Of course. I don't know how I'd have survived this year if it hadn't been for you.'

'Marigold? Is Poppy with you?'

'No, should she be? If she came to meet me at the station I must have missed her. But how are you, Mom?' Marigold went to kiss Mary, then narrowed her eyes. 'What is it?' she demanded. 'Where's Pa?'

'He's going round all her friends, to see if she told any of them anything.'

'Told them about what? Mom, what is it?'

Mary sat down suddenly and burst into tears. 'I hoped she was with you. She went, yesterday. She's been very quiet since her puppy died, and I know she was unhappy, but she wouldn't talk about it. I came home from work to find a note, and she's taken her best clothes.'

'A note?' Marigold sat down beside her mother and began to chafe her hands. 'Where is it? What did it say?'

'Pa's got it. She said we weren't to worry, and she'd write soon, but she couldn't stand it at home any longer. Marigold, what have we done to turn her against us so?'

'You haven't done anything, Mom. Poppy was always dissatisfied. She's never content, and I don't suppose she ever will be, whatever she has. Some people are like that. She's almost certainly gone to get a job somewhere. She never liked it at Mr Downing's. Could she have gone to Lucy?'

'She's not there yet, and she went early yesterday. Pa sent a telegram. I didn't like to for I thought it would give Lucy a fright – you know everyone expects the worst when they get a telegram – but she's a sensible lass. She sent one straight back and promised she'd send to let us know if Poppy turned up there. But she hasn't. Where can she be?'

Marigold did her best to calm Mary, while pondering ways she might try to look for her sister. 'Have you told the police?' she asked tentatively.

'Pa reported her missing. They said they'd keep a lookout, but they didn't seem interested. Said she's over fourteen, and Pa said they seemed to think they had better things to do than look for a runaway girl. Oh, Marigold, they asked whether she went with men! Said lots of girls had their heads turned with all the workmen and soldiers on the Chase. Pa said he was tempted to knock the fellow down!'

'She'll be all right, Mom. Now let me make you a nice cup of tea. Here's Ivy. Have you been out looking for her?'

Ivy smiled at her older sister. 'Yes, I've been asking all her friends, but she didn't say anything to any of them.'

'I thought Pa was doing that?'

'He went to see the ones she works with. I wondered if some of the girls in her class at school might know. She still goes out with some of them, to the entertainment hall.'

'Did she have any money?' Marigold asked, practical as ever.

'Only her wages. I don't know if she's saved anything,' Mary replied. 'Are you going upstairs, Ivy? Bring me a shawl, I'm feeling cold.'

Marigold went to the scullery to fill the kettle. She was coming back into the kitchen when Ivy came rushing down the stairs, her face red with fury.

'The rotten thieving tyke! She's stolen my money!'

'Ivy! Don't use such language!' Mary protested.

'What money? Had you been saving up, Ivy?'

Ivy whirled round to face Marigold and burst into violent, angry tears. 'It was my money! How dare she! I'll kill her for this!' she stormed.

'Hush, darling!' Marigold hastily hung the kettle on the trivet, then seized the furious child and sat down with her on her lap while Ivy sobbed in bitter frustration. When she was calmer Marigold spoke again. How much was there? You couldn't have had a lot.'

Ivy gulped. 'I – it was just a few shillings,' she said bleakly, suddenly realizing that if she admitted to the real amount all sorts of unanswerable questions would follow. 'Money you've given me, Marigold. I was saving it up for some paints, and presents for Christmas.'

'Poor Ivy! Never mind, I'll buy you some paints, and when we find Poppy she'll have to pay you back.'

The kettle began to sing and Mary got up to make tea. She looked round in a rather dazed way. 'Did we have any dinner?' she asked. 'I can't remember.'

'We had bread and jam,' Ivy reminded her. 'You and Pa were out all morning, you said you couldn't cook.'

'I've brought some bacon, so let's have that now. You must be hungry,' Marigold said briskly. 'Ivy, go and see if there're any new eggs. Is there anything else, Mom?'

'I think there's some cold potatoes from yesterday, and some pork scratchings.'

'We'll soon have a feast.'

'What about Pa?' Mary asked doubtfully.

'He'll understand. You need something hot now, and he might be hours. He can have something when he comes in.'

'Marigold, what would I do without you? You're so sensible and strong. I haven't even asked how Dick is? And Lexie?'

Marigold told her the plans she had for going to live with

Richard's parents at The Place, but Mary wasn't paying much attention. She was listening for her husband's footsteps.

When John did come in Marigold was saddened to see the defeated look on his face once more. It was the look he'd worn so often since he'd been unable to do what he hoped for his family, and she hated it.

Soon she had to go. Dick would need feeding, and she couldn't help any more apart from promising to search for Poppy in Birmingham, hopeless though she knew the task would be in that teeming city. 'She'll write soon, no doubt to tell us she's got some marvellous job in a munitions factory. Don't worry, Mom, she can look after herself.'

'We are to retain the whole of this wing. It has a separate door and a private garden. In fact it was the original house.'

'It's charming,' Marigold replied, relieved to discover that this older part of The Place, which she had not seen on her first disastrous visit, was actually smaller than Gordon Villa.

Sophia, though, had made no concessions. She was as elegant as ever in her black satin evening gown and a profusion of jet mourning beads. Despite her fur coat Marigold felt gauche and out of place.

'It was built about a hundred and fifty years ago. It's very small, but since most of the menservants left to join the army, and the maids are all clamouring to go and work in hospitals or factories, it has been forced on us. Apart from wanting to do what we can, of course. Naturally I've stipulated officers only, and it will be mainly for convalescence. Well, that's the drawing room and the dining room, and the library is through there.'

Sophia Endersby led the way up the gracefully curving stairs. Marigold, with the sleeping Dick in her arms, followed. Her mother-in-law barely paused on the first landing.

'There are just four bedrooms and a bathroom here. I shall adapt one of the bedrooms for a boudoir, and we shall need a guest room, so I have put you on the nursery floor. I assumed you would prefer to be near young Richard.'

The rooms here were much smaller. A tiny night nursery, with communicating doors to a day nursery on one side and a small bedroom which was to be Marigold's on the other, occupied one corner of the attics. Sophia gestured to the other doors.

'Most of these had become storerooms. We've cleared two for Cook and the two maids. Kemp will learn to drive and take over the chauffeur's room above the garage when he goes. The wretched man enlisted, would you believe! No thought at all for our convenience! Betty, who is only fourteen and untrained, will be free to help you when she is not needed in the kitchen or elsewhere. Do correct her when necessary. I have little confidence in Joan's ability to control her. They are sisters, you know, and both a bit wanting. Betty was quite troublesome to her parents. It is a pity there is no bathroom up here, but you will be able to use ours when we do not require it.'

It was becoming abundantly clear to Marigold that she was to be treated not as a daughter-in-law but as an unpaid nanny to her own son, and a kind of superior maid who would train the others. She shrugged. In many ways she preferred to have as little as possible to do with the formidable woman who had persuaded her it was her duty to come here. She was here for Dick's sake, to give him the sort of life he would have had if Richard were here to order it.

'Would you like me to send supper up to you on a tray tonight?' Sophia asked.

Marigold tried to hide her relief at this reprieve. 'If it's no trouble, yes please. I must unpack and get Dick settled in.'

'You will need to be with him most of the time, I fear, since we could not find a suitable nanny. I had hoped you would be able to join us for meals, and learn how we go on,' she added smoothly, and Marigold could see no trace of embarrassment in her face. 'Perhaps later, if Betty proves reliable enough to be left in charge.'

Marigold moved to the window, which was partly obscured by the parapet in front of it.

'This is the side overlooking the private garden, I think?' she asked. 'When may we use that?'

'Any time, my dear. Unless, of course, we have visitors, when naturally young children should be out of sight.'

And their unsuitable mothers, Marigold added silently. But what did it matter? She would be happier that way. And the park, which no doubt the suitable officer convalescents would be permitted to use, was large enough for her and Dick to explore when he was old enough to walk.

She caught up her thoughts in dismay. That would be at least another year. She had fallen into a trap of assuming either that the war would still be dragging on for so long, or Richard would still be missing. It was not possible, and she vowed that from now on she would never look so far ahead, but treat each day as if it were the last before she saw Richard again. And she would see him. She knew he was still alive.

Chapter Twelve

FORTUNATELY he heard them talking before they realized he had come to. Even more fortunately, he realized they were talking in German, and replied in that language when they spoke to him.

'Good, you're awake. Name and number?'

Richard groaned. He was not acting. The pains in his leg and abdomen were excruciating. They deflected attention from the raging fire in his chest and arms, and the heaviness of his head.

'What? Who are you?'

'Name and number!'

'Why are we rocking? Where am I? What is it?'

'You are on an ambulance train, being taken back to the Fatherland. You have been wounded. Your identification tag was lost. Now, name and number!'

'I can't remember! God, what happened?'

He squinted up at the man, a hospital orderly by the look of his clothes. 'A bomb dropped by those damned French maniacs. It blew up in front of your motor cycle.'

'Motor cycle?' He was genuinely puzzled. He had no recollection of any motor cycle.

'The one on which you were riding pillion. The driver was killed. Where were you going?'

Richard shook his head, then wished he'd kept it still. 'I can't remember a motor cycle, let alone being on one or where I was going.'

Mercifully a doctor then appeared and injected Richard with some drug which sent him to sleep. He knew no more until he woke up in bed in a large room filled with other beds. The ceiling was rather incongruously covered with paintings depicting indecorously clad, suggestively frolicking nymphs.

The pain had subsided to a dull ache. When he tried to move Richard discovered that he was heavily bandaged from neck to knee, with another bandage wound round his head.

A nurse, dark and petite, came across to him when she saw he was awake.

'Good, I was beginning to think you would never wake up. How do you feel?' she asked in German.

'Terrible. What's wrong with me?'

'One broken leg, severe internal injuries, burns to your arms and upper torso, and a lump on your head which seems to have affected your memory. Can you remember who you are now?'

Richard stared blankly at her. 'I can't remember anything. Where is this place? What is it? A hospital?'

She grinned and glanced up at the ceiling. 'Some patients think they could be in heaven when they wake up and see that. It's a country house near Berlin, which has been turned into a hospital for officers. It was assumed you are an officer from your uniform. There was no form of identification on you or the motor cycle rider. He was badly burned and his papers also. They didn't know which unit you'd come from. So your name is Franz?'

Richard blinked. 'I don't think so. I've told you, I can't remember.'

'It will come back.'

'How long is it since – it happened?'

'A week. You have had several operations, and you have been unconscious for most of the time in between. Do you feel hungry?'

'Thirsty,' Richard realized.

'I will fetch a cordial. No tea or coffee for a day or so.'

After slaking his by now raging thirst, Richard feigned sleep. There was too much to think about before he decided what to say.

Clearly he had been mistaken for a German in his borrowed uniform. It would be wisest to continue to maintain an apparent loss of memory. If he tried to invent a name and background it would be far too easy to disprove anything he claimed. He just prayed his German would be fluent enough to disguise the truth.

With his injuries it would be weeks, probably months before he could hope to try to escape again. It was a blow to find he was so much further away from the Front, but he would have plenty of time to think of ways to overcome that. He must concentrate on getting well again.

He thought of Marigold, and wondered if her child had yet been born. Had he a son? When would he see his beloved again? Was she distraught at knowing he was missing? Did she think he was dead?

As he drifted off into actual sleep he concentrated on willing her to know, somehow, that he was alive, to believe he would eventually return to her, however long it took. Their love was too rare, too precious and new for it to be lost, buried and forgotten in the muddy Flanders trenches.

Marigold contemplated the dress-length of black silk which was her Christmas present from her mother-in-law. The elder Mrs Endersby had resented from the very beginning Marigold's utter refusal to wear mourning clothes for Richard.

'Richard is not dead,' Marigold insisted. 'If I wore black it would be admitting something I can't believe.'

'Something you won't accept, rather. You are a very stubborn young person. Being a mother does not give you experience and wisdom. You really ought to allow that we who are older and have been about the world for longer do know best.'

Christmas of 1915 at The Place had been a very different affair to that time – so long ago it seemed, but only three years earlier – when she had first met Richard. There were no parties for the servants, no entertaining even for the family. It could be excused either by the death of Henry and Richard's continued absence, or by the state of the war, for things were not going well in France. But surely some effort could have been made to be cheerful?

Not that The Place was ever a cheerful house. Mr Endersby went every day to his pottery, apart from Sundays which were spent mainly in his library. Marigold rarely saw him. If they happened to pass on the stairs he gave her an embarrassed smile, and at dinner he spoke only about his business.

Mrs Endersby ensconced herself in her boudoir, making no calls and receiving no guests apart from the local vicar once a month. Marigold had not the slightest idea of how she occupied her time. On Sundays she went to church twice, always swathed in deepest black, with a profusion of veils.

Marigold was expected to remain with Dick most of the time. For half an hour in the afternoon Dick was taken to see his grandmother, and she was politely but firmly dismissed. She had no idea what Sophia did then, or how she behaved with her grandchild, but Dick emerged from these sessions smiling and laughing, clearly content. Marigold wondered with some amazement whether Sophia relaxed and smiled and played with the baby. It was not easy to envisage.

In the evening Betty was delegated to watch over Dick, by then asleep in his cot, and she was summoned to join the others for dinner. She would have preferred to forgo even this restricted contact.

This was the worst part of the day, with Marigold tense and the older Endersbys making strained conversation, except when Sophia made grudging personal references to Marigold's behaviour or appearance.

'Your voice is quite pleasant, and your speech good,' Sophia had said to her when she had been at The Place a week. It was her first sign of unbending, a determined stretching of the smile on her lips. But she bit the compliment off short and Marigold silently added 'for a former servant'. That was what she meant.

'My mother always insisted we spoke correctly,' Marigold replied mildly.

'Your table manners are excellent, considering you have not had much opportunity to move in elegant society,' was another patronizing remark a week or so later. Or had she meant it to be complimentary? Marigold could not tell. With a rising sense of hysteria she wondered if she was expected to pick up the cutlet in her fingers and gnaw at the bone. Or how long, at this rate, it would take before Sophia catalogued all her virtues.

It was the ludicrous aspects of the situation which saved her sanity, she sometimes thought. Sophia was so isolated from ordinary feelings she had no conception of how offensive her remarks were.

And Marigold still could not decide whether they had in fact been intended otherwise.

Thus, apart from when she had to endure these agonizing visits to the dining room, Marigold was segregated in the nurseries with her son, with the company only of the dim-witted, adenoidal Betty. Marigold craved congenial or at the very least rational conversation. Her salvation had come when, bored with the formal paths which bisected the shrubbery at the end of the private garden, she had wheeled Dick in his perambulator into the large, now neglected park.

In front of the main section of the house was a spacious lawn, bounded by a belt of trees. Beyond these, out of sight of the windows, a path wound down through a wooded valley until it came to a stream. It reminded Marigold of her walks with Richard in Oxford, when they had first begun to discover the enchantment of being together.

She began walking there every day when it was fine enough. It was several weeks before she met anyone else. Then one morning she almost pushed the perambulator into the legs of a man who sat, heedless of the wet, cold mud, with his back propped against a fallen tree.

'Oh, I'm sorry, I didn't see you!' she exclaimed, and he looked up at her with lack-lustre eyes.

'I'm sorry,' he muttered, and shifted his legs out of the way without attempting to get up.

'Won't you get horribly wet and cold sitting there?'

'Wet? This is paradise after the trenches. It's almost as good as sitting in the sun beside the Mediterranean.'

'Nevertheless, it's a wet and damp and muddy English wood, and the doctors wouldn't appreciate your undoing all their work just because you are indulging in foolish comparisons,' Marigold said sharply. 'They have enough to do mending men injured by the Germans.'

He grunted, smiled at some private joke, but slowly rose to his feet. 'I suppose you are right. Who are you? I haven't seen you about the hospital.'

'I'm staying in the private wing. My son' – she indicated Dick – 'is their grandson.'

'What an odd way of putting it. I presume your husband is their son? Does he live there too, or are you visiting?'

'He's – lost somewhere in France. He was shot down, but no one found him. They all think he's dead. I know he isn't.'

He looked at her curiously. 'You are so certain?'

'Yes,' she said simply.

He was very easy to talk to, and Marigold was starved of friendship. Time passed unheeded as they talked until he glanced up at the sky, which had clouded over.

'Do you mind if I walk back with you? It's going to rain soon, you ought to get back indoors.'

After that first meeting, when she discovered he was not a patient, as she'd thought, but a doctor specializing in caring for the victims of gas attacks, they had frequently met and walked together briefly.

Dr Carstairs was in his thirties, had initially served at the Front, and witnessed horrors which still, he confessed, disturbed his dreams at night. 'People here cannot imagine what conditions those poor devils live and sleep and die in. I have to get away into the peace of the country for a short spell occasionally, to refresh my soul.'

'And I am disturbing you,' Marigold said remorsefully.

'Of course not. Do you think I could not avoid your company if I wished? But the talk amongst my colleagues in the hospital is all of war, and medical matters, and horror, gloom and death. You glow with life and optimism, both in your care for your son and your determination to believe your husband is alive somewhere. It's a refreshing change.'

His obvious admiration and the interludes of normality made Marigold wonder how she could lighten the gloom in the house. When she tentatively suggested that Lexie might come to stay Sophia fixed her with a pained stare.

'Surely you cannot endure the thought of gaiety so soon after your husband's death?' she demanded, scandalized.

'Richard is not dead. And having a friend to stay for company is hardly indulging in wild excesses,' she replied quickly, and Sophia barely spoke to her for the next week.

It was the same when she proposed taking Dick to visit her parents.

'Quite impossible for the moment, my dear. I cannot spare Kemp to drive you there, and you surely could not contemplate taking my grandson on the train, with all manner of rough people jostling and fighting for seats.'

'I shall take him for a few days after Christmas, then,' Marigold said quietly. She was determined not to bow to Sophia's domination in everything. 'One of the doctors at the hospital has promised me a ride in his motor as far as Stoke.'

Sophia was distracted from the purpose of Marigold's journey by her furious reaction to this information.

'When did you make his acquaintance?' she demanded.

'I met him in the park one day. He was at the Front for a while and we talk occasionally,' Marigold informed her calmly.

'You flirt with him!' It was an accusation, not a question.

'I do no such thing,' Marigold began indignantly, but Sophia ignored her, speaking in such a bitter, hysterical manner that Marigold stared at her in astonishment.

'Your husband, my son, is scarcely cold in his grave and you are seeking to replace him in your bed! I always said you were no better than a trollop, and how you ever enticed my boy into marrying you I can only guess! I forbid you ever to speak to any of those people again! We have to have them there! If I hadn't offered, they would have forced me, and probably sent uncouth privates who would have done untold damage to the house, and lived there like pigs!'

Marigold was incensed, both at her mother-in-law's insensitive response and her utter selfishness. 'Those uncouth privates, like my brother, are being killed in their thousands in France! When they're lying there, riddled with bullets, or choking on horrible gas, do you think it matters to them whether they were born to luxury and privilege or grew up in squalor? It's the same death for Henry and for the most rude enlisted man! Don't the ones who do survive deserve something better than your contempt, madam?' Marigold's voice shook with passion.

Afterwards she marvelled at herself. She, the placid, competent and never-ruffled Marigold, who had for years dealt calmly with Ivy's tantrums and Poppy's woes without getting flustered, had dared to tell the imperious Mrs Endersby some home truths.

It was an aspect of her character she thought about a great deal, later when she had leisure. She was uncertain whether to be horrified or gratified at this evidence of her willingness to fight back against injustice.

She had immediately apologized, but had been treated with polite coldness ever since. She thought with immense gratitude that it was only two more days before Dr Carstairs drove her to the station, and she would be with her family for a few days of blessed relief.

Poppy pushed some loose strands of hair under her mob cap, and eased on to her other foot. She had never worked so hard in her life. At least at home she'd been able to sit down when she wanted to, do an easier job if she felt like a change. Even Mr Downing's drapery shop was more interesting. Here it was the same monotonous motion of lean, push, twist, lean, push, twist, all day long.

She was so tired that although the other girls were friendly and asked her to go with them to the cinema, or the dance hall, she never had the energy. All she wanted to do was crawl back to her room and fall into bed.

When she'd left home, all those weeks ago, she'd been wildly miserable. Her puppy had meant so much to her; a creature she could call her own who depended on her and owed his life to her. And then had come his death, horrible and lonely, and her dark thoughts against Ivy.

It was fury and suspicion of her sister which had sent her to search Ivy's private drawer in their combined chest. They each had one, and it was understood the other would never look inside. But she had to find some evidence to prove to the others that Ivy knew about poisons. Perhaps she could find a recipe copied out, something she'd learned from all the reading she did in her plant book.

When she'd picked up the old tobacco tin and it rattled she'd been no more than mildly puzzled. It felt heavy, but she had her own few shillings saved towards Christmas. Then the tin had slipped out of her fingers and fallen to the floor, scattering its contents.

Poppy had been astounded, wondering how Ivy could possibly have come by such a huge sum – several pounds by the looks of it.

Then she had been seized with a bout of renewed fury at the deception Ivy must, somehow, have practised. It would serve her right if she lost it all!

With that thought the plan was born. Here was enough to keep her until she could find a job. She felt little compunction in taking what was Ivy's, telling herself Ivy had probably come by most of it dishonestly. It was justice; retribution for the death of poor innocent Scrap. Within days Poppy was installed in a cheap lodging house in the Nechells district of Birmingham, and had found herself a job in a small factory nearby.

She wasn't at all sure what she was helping to make, apart from the fact it was something to do with guns. She had a simple machine to operate, just a few moves to learn as she pushed and twisted levers, and it was all desperately, mind-numbingly boring. And the workshop was so noisy she couldn't distract herself by talking to the other girls.

The girl on the next machine laughed when Poppy complained once during their dinner break. 'I know. Me brother worked 'ere before 'e enlisted, an' yer should 'a' seen the fuss 'e created when 'e knew women were goin' ter do 'is job! Yer'd 'a' thought it needed a year's trainin' ter learn 'ow, not five minutes!'

On Christmas Eve they finished an hour earlier.

'Two days off!' she sighed. 'No more work till Monday! Yer goin' 'ome ternight, Poppy? Where d'yer live?'

'No,' Poppy said quickly. 'I – I can't. I live too far away.'

She smiled slightly and scurried out, avoiding the other girls who were calling cheery greetings to one another. She didn't dare go home. She knew that once she had Mary's arms round her she'd never find the courage to come back. Going home meant confessing failure; admitting she couldn't manage on her own. She'd have to face the accusations of stealing Ivy's money. Everyone would laugh at her, and Poppy could bear the thought of that even less than she could endure the prospect of endless tedious toil in the factories.

Her room was at the top of a tall, narrow house. There was a small fireplace, and she was permitted to have a fire, and cook on it if she wished, but she couldn't do much with just one saucepan. Most of the time she existed on bread and jam, and fish and chips she bought from the nearby fried-fish shop. She kept the fire for boiling water for tea, and to wash with.

Tonight, though, as she dragged her weary feet homewards, she thought of the two days ahead. Suddenly hungry for the sort of food she'd had at home she turned into the market, spending her wages recklessly without a care for anything else, buying some scrag end of mutton, bacon and onions, carrots, parsnips, potatoes and turnips. She would have a good stew for once, it would last her all Christmas, and probably several more days.

It would keep her busy, too; stop her thinking about what they were doing at home and whether they missed her.

She hurried to her room and left the food, then almost ran to the coal merchant's, where she bought the biggest sackful she could manage. She would enjoy Christmas, she would be warm and she would eat as much as she could. Why, then, was she crying silently as she dragged the coal up the four flights of stairs to her lovely, independent room in her life of freedom?

My darling Lucy,

It seems like two years rather than two months since I was with you. Leaving you again to come back to this hell-hole was the hardest thing I ever did, and the week we had together was wonderful. I'd hoped to have leave for our first anniversary, but it wasn't to be. And now we have endured our second Christmas apart. Thank you for the hamper you sent, your cakes and jam are the best food I've ever tasted, and certainly better than what we get here in the canteens. And unlike most of the chaps I eat at several different ones when I'm driving around, so I can truthfully say they are all as bad as each other.

I pray with all my heart that the stalemate which continues here will break soon, and I can be back with you for ever. Especially when I received your last letter with the marvellous news that you are going to make me a father! It's unbelievable, but every time I think of it I want to dance for joy.

You must not dream of continuing your job. You must give it up at once, and take care of yourself and little Lucy (or little Johnny, whichever it is to be) for my sake.

There is little to do here as a driver, in the way I expected at first. But I am driving an ambulance with the casualties to the hospitals. When I see what they have suffered I feel a sense of guilt that I am not enduring the same horrors, but then I know my skills in driving, and even more so in keeping the motors going when they break down, are better used in this way. Sometimes we would not make it if I weren't able to mend parts and contrive makeshift replacements from all sorts of oddments. Someone not used to the engines or the working of a motor, just driving one, would be unable to cope.

Has Mom heard any more from Poppy? I suppose she is in Birmingham, as her letter was posted there, but I wonder why she did not wish us to know her address? Perhaps she was afraid Pa would go and fetch her back. And it was very odd she didn't say more about what her job was, almost as if she was ashamed of it. I pray she has not fallen in with bad company. She's an odd girl, moody, and one could never tell what her thoughts were. Not like Marigold, who is so sweet and open with everyone, or Ivy, who can be loving when she wants.

I'm pleased she's coming to see you for a day or so. It was kind of you to ask her. But you mustn't let her tire you, demanding to see everything in the entire town. I know what she's like, she'll want to draw everything. She sent me a very clear drawing of little Dick for Christmas. She'd done it when he was a month old. I wonder how he and Marigold are enjoying their palatial life in Richard's mansion? Well, our child may one day be invited there! What a turn-up!

It's time for lights out, and I want to post this first thing in the morning, so I'll say goodnight, my darling, and God bless you both,

Your loving husband,
Johnny

'Everybody's left me, it's horrid now,' Ivy complained.

She and Marigold were sharing their old bed. Dick lay in a wicker basket beside Marigold.

'But we all have to leave sometime,' Marigold tried to console her. 'You'll want to leave one day, to get a job or get married. It's normal.'

'I don't ever want to leave home, and who'd want to marry me with my horrid scars?'

Impulsively Marigold turned to hug her, and Ivy snuggled close.

'Do they still bother you? They really can't be seen if you keep your hair the way it is,' Marigold said. 'I'm so sorry, I always blamed myself for leaving you alone. I want to make it up to you.'

'I do love you, Marigold. Better than Lucy, she can only talk about Johnny and their silly baby! And better than horrid Poppy, she was always cross and she stole my money.'

'But I gave you some to replace it, and I'm sure she only borrowed it to help her leave. You see, she'll come home one day and give it back to you.'

'Then shall I have to give you your money back?'

Marigold laughed. 'Of course not, love. It was a present. You'll be able to buy lots more paint and drawing paper.'

'I wish I could go to an art school,' Ivy said wistfully.

'But I thought you didn't want to leave home?'

'It's different with all of you gone. Johnny won't ever come home now he's got Lucy, Poppy will find someone else to love, and you love Dick better than me.'

'I love you all,' Marigold said firmly. 'Dick's my baby and of course I love him, but that doesn't stop me loving you and Mom and Pa just as much as ever I did before.'

'You haven't enough love to go round.'

Marigold thought for a moment. Was that true? Had she, in her passion for Richard and now for his son, ever reduced her love for her family?

'It's odd,' she replied slowly, 'but as you have more people to love, the amount of love you've got to share out somehow seems to get bigger.'

Ivy was growing sleepy. 'Stay here with us, Marigold. Stay with me for ever. I could help look after Dick. I like being an aunt.'

Marigold didn't reply, and soon Ivy was breathing deeply, fast asleep, cradled in her sister's arms.

'Miss Smith, you're not concentrating!'

'I'm sorry, I'm so cold.'

She remembered to turn towards the foreman so that he could lip read her words. The noise was fearsome within the workshop, and he, an elderly, bent, and perpetually bad-tempered man, was deaf too. Not surprising, Poppy thought, if he'd been forced to endure for years the clanging whirring and shrieking noises the machines made as they sliced through metal and transferred it with teeth-rasping clatters to the next stage where it was thumped and banged into shape.

'Then wear warmer clothes. We can't afford too many rejects or we'll never win the war.'

The foreman moved on, and Poppy's neighbour gave her a sympathetic grin.

'Don't let old grumps get to you,' she advised when they stopped for their midday meal, and had been able to escape outside to sit on the canal bank.

Poppy shivered. 'I'm freezing,' she complained, 'but I had to get away from that racket for a few minutes.'

'It's a lot warmer than it was back in February. Are you ill?'

'I don't know,' Poppy said miserably. 'I had a dreadful cold last week, and had to stay away from work for three days. I haven't been warm since.'

Too ill to fetch coal, too miserable to care whether she ate or not, Poppy had huddled under the inadequate blankets, wearing almost all the clothes she possessed in order to keep warm. No one else in the house had seemed to care; certainly no one had offered to help her or brought her food. She thought back longingly to the way neighbours would have rallied round at home. Mrs Tasker bringing in hot stews; others coming in to keep the fire made up. In big cities they didn't seem to care. In fact all her dreams of a life of freedom and happiness had withered long ago, and it was a struggle just to keep going.

Part of the reason she was still cold was that as she'd staggered, half-unconscious, home from work on that awful day when she'd felt too ill to care if she lived or died, her purse had been stolen with all her money in it. She always carried it with her, for she dared leave nothing valuable in the room, which had no lock. It was two more days until she had this week's wages, and she'd been living on what meagre stores she'd accumulated in her room. But stale bread and mouldy jam couldn't keep her warm. And now that was finished and she had nothing.

'Haven't you got any dinner?' her companion, a woman in her early twenties who lived in Aston, asked. Charlotte Harrison was the widow of a regular soldier, an officer who had gone to France with the Expeditionary Force and been killed within the first few days. Although she was much better educated than the rest of the girls in the factory, she never put on airs, and when they realized she was determined to work as hard as the rest of them she was accepted as an equal.

Gradually, as she made Poppy eat some of her own dinner, good beef sandwiches, she heard the story. She didn't comment, but Poppy felt more cheerful as well as warmer when they went back into the workshop.

At the end of the day Charlotte was waiting for Poppy when the girls poured out of the building. 'Poppy, will you come home with me for a few hours? For a meal and a chance to get warm? That will help you get better more quickly. I don't think you are properly well yet.'

The kindness was more than Poppy could bear. She began to sob, and went unresisting, snuffling into her handkerchief all the way to Charlotte's home on the tram.

It was a small house, one of a terrace, but better by far than her own home. Charlotte made up the fire, which had been banked down all day, and hung a kettle over the flames. 'We'll have a cup of tea first, and then you can tell me all about it,' she said cheerfully, bustling about and getting a large fruit cake out of her larder. 'This is just something to keep us going, we'll have a proper meal later.'

In the end, as she prepared potatoes and saw to an appetizing stew which had been simmering all day in the oven, she had heard all about Poppy's home, and the freedom which had turned into a worse prison.

'How old is your sister?' she asked quietly, after Poppy told her about Scrap's death.

'She'll be eleven now. It was her birthday in January.'

'I doubt if a child that age could know enough to prepare poisoned food,' Charlotte said thoughtfully. 'And it would have been a very wicked thing to have done. I just can't believe a young girl could be so evil.'

'You don't know Ivy,' Poppy said mutinously, but to hear the actions she accused her sister of called wicked and evil made her pause.

Had she been too hasty? Might Scrap have scavenged for food

and found some rat-poison? It would have been easy enough. The houses were plagued with rats and it was a regular chore to set bait. Not everyone was as careful as they might be to keep it out of reach of domestic pets.

Seeing the beginnings of doubt Charlotte took advantage of it. She liked Poppy; had admired her determination and her grim concentration on the task at work; and suspected for some time that she was younger than the seventeen she claimed.

'Your parents must be frantic with worry about you,' she said. 'Have you told them where you are?'

'I sent them a letter saying I was all right, soon after I got here and found a job,' Poppy defended herself. 'And I wrote again after Christmas.'

'Don't you think you ought to go home and see them? No doubt they are used to the idea of your being here now, and you have proved you can look after yourself, so they might be happy to let you stay.'

'But I can't, can I?' Poppy said bleakly. 'I can't look after myself. It's not at all how I thought it would be. I'm even too tired to go out to the cinema or anything.'

'Dinner's ready. Will you lay the cloth for me, Poppy? The knives and forks are in the table drawer.'

Charlotte judged it wiser to say no more yet. Poppy had admitted she was in need of help. Soon she might wish of her own accord to visit her parents. Undue pressure might make her stubborn.

Later, Poppy sat back, replete and licking her lips. 'That was even better than Mom's cooking,' she said with a shy smile. 'Thank you, Charlotte, for helping me. I'd better go home now.'

'Why don't you stay here for the night? It's getting late and your room will be cold. I've a spare bed and we can soon put some bricks in it to air it.'

Poppy knew she ought to refuse, but she suddenly realized she had no money for the tram fare, she didn't know where she was, and certainly couldn't find her way back to her room in the dark. She was warm, comfortably fed, and had the prospect of a good bed with a hot, flannel-covered brick to cuddle up to.

'If you don't mind? Yes, please, I'd love to.'

On the following day Charlotte insisted on giving Poppy a few shillings so that she could buy food and coal. Poppy vowed to repay her as soon as she had her wages. Charlotte had been tempted to ask Poppy to come and lodge with her, but restrained her impulse, feeling it would be better for the girl to go back to her parents. Now the cracks in Poppy's determination had appeared, Charlotte judged they would deepen faster if she had to return to her cold, cheerless attic.

Two weeks later Poppy gave in. Shyly she told Charlotte she had written to her parents asking if they would have her back, and received a letter telling her to come at once.

'When am I going to be able to leave hospital?' Richard demanded for the hundredth time.

The pretty blonde nurse playfully slapped his hand. She made no attempt to disguise her favouritism. 'Your leg is still not strong enough, Hans. You were fortunate not to lose it. If you'd had to stay in the field hospital they'd have had it off within days. They're nothing but butchers there, not surgeons at all. Besides, we don't want to lose our most handsome patient. Be thankful for your good fortune. And until we discover who you are, or your memory returns, where can we send you?'

He had been in one hospital after another for almost a year. He knew he'd been incredibly fortunate, both in the medical treatment he'd received, which was due to his borrowed officer's uniform, and his continuing ability to pretend loss of memory.

Sometimes he wondered if he talked in English in his sleep, or during the spells of fever he'd suffered during the bout of pneumonia he'd had that winter, but no one ever showed any suspicion. If they'd had the slightest doubt about him he would, he knew, be interrogated ruthlessly, injuries or not.

In other ways his luck had not held. His wounds had been extensive and taken a long time to heal, with many relapses. He had been moved, this last time, to a converted church in a small town on the Baltic coast. The sea air was supposed to be good for almost-convalescent officers, and many of the municipal buildings had been requisitioned for hospitals. But he was about as far as he could be from the Western Front, and the problem of how to get home was not made easier.

If he could reach a port he could attempt to stow away to a neutral country like Norway. He could demand, alternatively, to be returned to the fighting, but without an identity that might be difficult, and he was far from fit enough. Or he could somehow make his way overland to Holland or Switzerland. From there he would have a good prospect of getting home by going round the lines of trenches that stretched from the borders of Switzerland to the English Channel.

'Time for your medicine.' The pretty nurse had returned.

'What's the date? I lose track, every day's so like another.'

'The last day of March, 1916. When's your birthday, Hans?'

He frowned as if trying to think. 'I don't know.'

They were always throwing unexpected questions at him, in an attempt to surprise some recollection. He suspected that once he appeared to begin remembering things they would redouble their efforts, so he adopted a policy of utter blankness, even sometimes pretending to forget incidents which had occurred a few weeks or months earlier.

'Never mind, we'll celebrate your birthday on the day you were found.'

He shuddered, not pretending. The agony of that journey was still vivid, both the physical pain, and the mental torture at having failed to cross the lines back into France.

'Do you have a sweetheart, Hans?'

He covered his eyes with his hands. He could not disguise the distress it caused when he was suddenly confronted with the loss of Marigold. It would show in his eyes.

'I don't know! Why do you call me Hans?' he asked, to deflect her attention.

'We have to call you something,' she said cheerfully. 'If you do have a sweetheart she's a lucky one, and must be missing you. You'd better find that lost memory before she forgets you, though. Girls don't wait for ever.'

Marigold would, he thought confidently. But later that night, as he lay sleepless, he began to wonder if he could use the nurse's predilection for him to his advantage. It would not be gentlemanly, but it was wartime, and she was as much involved as he was. Once more he began to to weave plans for escape. Soon, he hoped in a few weeks, he would be fit enough to set out on his own. Perhaps he could trick her into helping him.

First, however, he must discover all he could about what was happening at the Front. What news they had was sparse, and he suspected heavily censored. It would be carefully contrived to be appropriate for civilian consumption. But if he could suggest that hearing about his former comrades might stimulate his memory, perhaps he could learn more.

Cheered, he turned over and went to sleep.

'Poppy's coming home! Poppy's coming home!' Ivy sang as she walked with her parents towards Hednesford station.

It was Saturday but John had a day off from work. He was dressed in his best suit, with the new cap Mary had given him for Christmas. Mary and Ivy had new dresses and boots Marigold had given them, and they were all three in holiday mood.

Poppy was fully forgiven for the pain she had caused when they hadn't known where she was. Ivy, secretly resenting the theft of her money, had prudently decided not to make a fuss. If Poppy disclosed how much she'd taken, there would be difficult questions. She would demonstrate, by her joyful greeting of her sister, that she bore no ill-will, and if Poppy referred to it privately she would say she'd found the large coins in a dropped purse.

They reached the station in plenty of time and went on to the platform, the sooner to greet Poppy when she arrived. Several people were waiting, going into Rugeley for the day.

'Look!' Ivy almost screamed with excitement, and there, in the distance, were puffs of smoke as the train rounded the bend and chugged slowly into view.

'Get down off the bench!' Mary said sharply. 'You'll tear your new dress. And watch it, it's still wet from the rain we had earlier.'

Ivy pouted, but knew better than to argue. She jumped down, and consumed with excitement began to get rid of her physical energy by hopping from one foot to another. This being unsatisfactory, she changed to an improvised form of hop-scotch, using the cracks in the platform as rough guides, and hopping over the many puddles which lay there.

'Oh, John, it's been so long! Will she have changed? Do you think she's been hurt?'

'Don't fret, love. She's proved she can take care of herself, even if she found it wasn't so easy as she thought,' John replied soothingly. They'd read far more into Poppy's short letter than she could ever have imagined she'd given away.

'But she'll be changed.'

'Of course she will. Girls grow fast at her age,'

'And she'll have to find another job,' Mary worried. 'Mr Downing won't take her back.'

'Perhaps she won't be so fussy now,' John laughed. Then his voice sharpened. 'Ivy, come away from the edge!'

Ivy, her attention concentrated on the intricate patterns she was jumping in her game, looked up and grinned at him. 'I'm not near the edge, and I can balance on one leg for ever and ever! Look at me!'

The train was approaching, and had almost reached the end of the platform. Several people were leaning out of the windows, and Mary thought she could see Poppy. She moved forward to get a better look, then swivelled round as there was a terrified scream.

Ivy, also turning to look for her sister, had slipped on the wet platform, and Mary saw her flailing arms as she fell sideways, infinitely slowly, on to the track.

People were shouting. Some were pushing forward to see, others straining to get back out of the way. The train was already braking hard, the horrified face of the driver looming up as the monster rolled inexorably toward them.

John plunged after his daughter moments after she had fallen. He leaped down on to the line, seized her limp form, and tried to jump out of the path of the engine. It was yards away, and no one afterwards was able to agree on the precise order of events.

John appeared to hesitate; half turned as if to try and regain the platform; then hurled Ivy away from him on to the other track. He turned again, but by now the front of the train was towering above him. He leapt after Ivy, but the engine caught him a glancing blow. As he fell, the great iron horse drew to a shrieking halt and hid everything from the watching crowd.

Chapter Thirteen

'I HAVE no choice. My mother cannot be left to endure this alone.' Marigold turned away from the opened chest of drawers and faced Sophia, who was standing just inside the door. Whether it was the size of the bedroom or the overpowering personality of her mother-in-law, Marigold found the room smaller than ever.

'She has both your sisters with her. Surely she does not need you also?'

'Ivy is still at school, and Poppy has to work. She's found a job in Walsall, at the George Hotel, and must live in, so she cannot help at home and in any case her money is not enough to support everyone.'

Sophia advanced to sit on the only chair. 'Let us discuss this calmly, my dear. Sit down – on the bed, I suppose. We don't want to disturb Dick.'

Marigold removed the clothes she had laid out on the bed, draped them on the open trunk, and obediently sat down. It would be over faster if she complied. Then she would be able to resume her packing.

'I thought your mother was a cook-general?' Sophia said, her nose turning up with distaste at having to recognize the fact.

Marigold held hard on to her temper. It would do no good to lose it. 'She was a cook,' she replied quietly, 'but she could not keep her job while she was going to see my father every day for months, and the Andrewses have shut up part of the house for the duration of the war. They do not entertain as much now, and don't need her.'

'Surely there are plenty of war jobs?'

'Mrs Endersby, if – when my father comes home, Mom will have to do everything for him. Can you imagine the problems in a house with only narrow stairs, no inside lavatory, and only a cold tap in the scullery? He can't move much by himself, he cannot be fitted with artificial legs, and he needs good food and excellent care. He almost died when the train ran over him. Sometimes, when I see how much he's suffered, I almost wish he had!'

'That is a wicked thought!'

Marigold sighed. 'I know, and I have not truly wished it, just wondered occasionally whether we would not all have been spared much anxiety and Pa much pain if the train had killed him instead of just sheering off his legs.'

'Many of our gallant soldiers have suffered worse injuries,' Sophia said sanctimoniously.

Marigold looked at her curiously. She could understand her mother-in-law no better now than she had when she first came to The Place a year ago. Sometimes she utterly refused to permit any mention of the war, citing her sorrow at the loss of two sons. When in this mood she contrived to ignore the presence of the recuperating officers in the main part of the house. At other times she dwelt on her losses, bewailing the sadness and futility of the fighting. And she could, as now, declare her patriotism by praising the heroes who were performing glorious deeds in the name of freedom.

Marigold had the occasional suspicion, which she thrust away as unworthy, that Sophia's reaction depended largely on how she could best contradict Marigold or make her feel in the wrong.

'The soldiers have people caring for them, hospitals like here, and lots of sympathy. Pa's injuries are regarded as just an unfortunate accident, the sort that happens every day to civilians, and as such not deserving the privileged treatment given to wounded soldiers! His agony and the wrecking of his life are just as great,' she added under her breath.

From the account she had been given when, summoned home by a frantic telegram, she had arrived in Hednesford, it had been a frightful, unnecessary accident. If Ivy had not slipped . . . If she had not been so close to the edge of the platform . . . If Pa had not caught his foot in the rail, which was what seemed to have happened . . . It was pointless, Marigold had fumed. If the train had been late, if Poppy had not run away, if the platform had not been wet, if hundreds of things had not happened to bring about that peculiar combination of circumstances, her father would still be whole.

Following the same logic it was foolish to blame Ivy. The child was distraught, blaming herself, and still had spells of hysterical weeping and dreadful nightmares. She refused to go back to school until Marigold, in despair, rashly promised to try and arrange for her to go to an art school when she was old enough.

'But only if you reach Standard Seven, Ivy, and unless you go to school and work hard all the time you won't do that.'

'You mean you'll pay for me to go?' Ivy demanded, and for the first time since the accident had, that evening, picked up a pencil and begun to draw once more.

Marigold had promised to pay the necessary fees. Her income was not large since the profits from Richard's share of the firm had been taken from her, but she spent almost nothing on herself. Since the accident she had sent Mary money, however, to make up for the loss of both her earnings and Pa's, and she had no idea what art school fees cost. There would be time enough to worry about that.

'Are you proposing to take my grandson to live in such squalid conditions?' Sophia's question broke into Marigold's reflections.

'Of course, what else could I do? Besides, he needs to be with me.'

'He is weaned, he is no longer dependent on you.'

'I'm his mother; of course he needs me.'

'So you would condemn the poor child to live in poverty, crawling about in the dirt of a slum, mingling with all sorts of riff-raff, when he is the heir to all this?'

'As you deny me the money from Richard's share in the firm, what other choice do I have?' Marigold asked calmly. 'I cannot provide anything better for him, but I will ensure he is brought up in the way Richard would want. He'll be taught to value people for what they are, not what money they have or what schools they went to!'

Sophia stared at her, then shrugged and went out of the room. With a sigh Marigold resumed her packing. If she were honest she didn't want to return to Hednesford. Lonely though she was, and however antagonistic Sophia was, she had become used to her life at The Place.

She revelled in Dick's company and progress, especially now he was toddling; she enjoyed the spaciousness of the grounds, and had come to terms with living almost entirely in isolation. The times when she must try to explain to Betty the correct way of doing something, or endure the formal dinners in the dining room, were amply compensated for by her discovery of books.

Mary had always spoken nostalgically of the reading she had done at Old Ridge Court. Marigold had read all that came her way when she'd been a child, but there had been little enough of it after she'd left school, and she'd worked so hard she rarely had leisure or energy in the next few years. When she was at Gordon Villa she had been permitted to borrow from the library there, and while living with Lexie had extended her reading. But she had never had a great deal of time to herself even then.

Here, though, with the long evenings when Dick had gone to bed and she had escaped from the dining room, she devoured books. Mr Endersby had collected all the Victorian novels, although he never seemed to read them. Most of the pages were uncut. Marigold lost herself in the cloisters of Barchester and the historical adventures of Scott. She marvelled at the way Dickens brought to life the appalling conditions of the slums or the prisons, and laughed at Becky in *Vanity Fair*.

Delving further into the library she discovered the Brontë sisters, Jane Austen, and Mrs Gaskell. A faint ambition to occupy herself with weaving a tale someday was born. Then she found the more recent books of Arnold Bennett, and perused them in the hope of learning more about the Pottery towns, so near, and yet for her virtually unknown.

She had just begun to explore the foreign writers when the accident happened. Then, much to the obvious if unexpressed disapproval of Sophia, she had travelled twice a week to the hospital to visit her father. Now he was almost well enough to return home. Mom could not manage on her own, and Marigold had to help.

*

Richard knew that if he wished to regain the Allied lines before the onset of winter, which would make travelling more difficult, he had to move soon.

He knew a little more now about the progress of the war – if it could be called progress. The opposing sides had remained holed into their trenches, firing away at one another ceaselessly. There had been occasional increases in activity, justified by the designation of specific battle titles, but almost no movement of positions.

The ill-fated Gallipoli venture had ended, and the German papers said that men were being conscripted in England to fill the gaps left in the lines by the thousands of dead and wounded. Now, for over two months since the beginning of July, the guns had been pounding away at one another across the Somme.

He had, very cautiously, appeared to remember a few details. The talks he'd had in Oxford with the German army officer, his fellow guest that long-ago Christmas at Gordon Villa, provided useful facts about the army. He knew Munich well from his pre-war studies there, and began to drop hints that he came from the town. If he could persuade them to send him there in the hope of restoring his memory, he would be much nearer to Switzerland.

He'd abandoned the idea of escaping by ship after seeing the precautions taken in the docks. Overland would be easier, and Munich was in the south.

He began the campaign when the blonde nurse Anna came to sit with him one day, as had become her custom when her duty shift ended.

'Where do you come from, Anna?' he asked casually during a lull in the conversation.

'Berlin. I lived there until two years ago. Do you know it?' she asked.

He shook his head. 'I can't remember. Is there a Prinzregenstrasse there?'

'I don't think so, but why? Can you remember that? Hans, do you think your memory is returning?'

'Who knows? I just had the name come into my head for no apparent reason. I can see a great new boulevard, nothing more, yet the name runs through my head.'

Watching her from under lowered eyelids, Richard saw she was trying to control her excitement. For a moment he despised himself for using the girl, then he reminded himself that he was at war with her country, her brothers were trying to kill his countrymen, and he had never responded to her covertly amorous advances.

She made an excuse to leave soon and he sat back to await the reaction.

The next morning, instead of a posse of doctors descending on him as he had half expected, Anna came alone.

'I managed to discover there is a Prinzregenstrasse in Munich,' she said casually.

'Prinzregenstrasse? Munich? What do you mean?'

'You mentioned the grand new street yesterday, don't you remember?' she said, her voice showing her disappointment.

'Did I?' Richard frowned, then shook his head. 'Oh, yes, so I did. Is it in Munich?'

'There is one there. Built not long ago by Prince Luitpold. Does that mean anything to you?'

Richard pretended to ponder. 'Sorry, it means nothing. It could be my home, I suppose, but the name is not important to me. And yet? No, it's gone, it could mean anything. You seem to have been busy researching on my behalf,' he added.

She blushed. Richard knew they tried to keep all attempts to jog his memory apparently casual. He wondered in some amusement how she would deal with this.

'I happen to have an aunt there,' she said awkwardly. 'I found a few old postcards she sent me. I thought you might recognize some other places in the town.'

She produced a handful of cards. Richard glanced at them, noting cynically they were almost all of them unused, and the rest were addressed to various people at different addresses.

'I was given some of them because I collect postcards,' Anna said hurriedly, her blush deepening, and Richard felt sorry for her. She was not a natural conspirator, and telling lies was obviously not easy for her.

He concentrated on the cards. After a while he selected one of a huge palace, similar to Versailles in appearance.

'I believe I've been there,' he said slowly, 'but I don't recognize the name. Herrenchiemsee, is it?'

Over the next few days, on various pretexts, Anna produced items connected with Munich and Bavaria: more postcards, books, and a map. Richard thanked her and spent hours poring over them, but in the end turned away in apparent frustration.

'None of it helps, I'm afraid. You've been so kind, Anna, but the only way is to go there myself. Do you think that could be arranged? Are there any convalescent homes there? They were talking some time ago of transferring me.'

Anna sighed, but she was a dedicated nurse. She would do what was best for her patient, even if it conflicted with her own wishes to keep him with her. Perhaps she might later on arrange a transfer for herself too, she thought, and cheered up. Hans was still far from fit, and even without the loss of memory it would be months before he was strong enough to be discharged.

Poppy flopped into the corner seat of the carriage. She was tired after her work at the George all week, but it was far better than the factory. She shuddered at the recollection. And now she lived in a warm hotel, ate good food, and had time and leisure to go out with the friends she had made in Walsall, mostly fellow waitresses and chambermaids at the George. With Marigold living at home again, and the money she contributed to the family budget, life was easier than for years, and she only had to go home on her day off.

Poppy caught her thoughts guiltily. Of course it wasn't better with Pa crippled, with no legs and no chance ever of working again. His mind would never recover, even though he'd been hailed a hero for saving Ivy's life.

Poppy shivered as she recalled that appalling homecoming. She'd leapt down from the train eager to greet them all, and found Mary collapsed from shock, Ivy lying bruised but otherwise unhurt on the other side of the track, and her father surrounded by frantic men trying to stop the bleeding from the severed stumps of his legs.

It was a miracle he hadn't died, they'd said. He'd spent months of agony in hospital, Mom had gone white haired overnight, and Ivy was changed utterly. She was no longer pert and selfish, absorbed in her own concerns. For weeks she refused to go to school and clung to whoever had time to comfort her, and she hadn't touched her drawing until Marigold had promised to find a way of sending her to an art school. That was a ploy, Poppy knew, to get her back to school, but Ivy would demand the promise be kept.

'Excuse me, but are you all right?' a voice opposite asked diffidently.

Poppy looked up, startled. A young man in soldier's uniform was looking at her worriedly.

'Yes. Why?' she asked, genuinely puzzled.

'You were shivering, I thought you might be cold, and then you looked so pale I was afraid you might faint.'

'No, just a horrid memory,' she said and smiled determinedly. 'Are you on leave?'

He laughed ruefully. 'I haven't got as far as France yet. I was at Whittington Barracks, training there, but now we have to move to the transit camps on Cannock Chase. I've just been for forty-eight hours' leave to my home in Walsall.'

'Is it beastly in those camp huts? We saw them being built.'

'I'm not looking forward to it. It's beginning to get cold at night, but we're better off, from all you hear, than the poor devils in the trenches. Have you anyone out in France?'

'My brother, but he's a driver and a motor engineer. He seems to spend his time keeping ambulances and trucks going. And my sister's husband was killed, he was a pilot.'

'A pilot! That's what I wanted to be but I didn't get in. I'm sorry. Had they been married long?'

'Just a few months. Are you married? Do you have brothers there, or anyone?'

'Definitely not married. My two older brothers went a year ago, I had to wait till I was eighteen in the summer.'

'You look older,' Poppy said frankly. He was dark-haired, with a thin, intense-looking face, and a narrow, dashing moustache.

'Yes, but when I tried to enlist two years ago they found out – my older brother told them, the wretch, and ever since I've been given dozens of white feathers by helpful ladies.'

They chatted until Poppy left the train at Hednesford. She marvelled at the freedom which had arisen since the beginning of the war. Beforehand no one would have dreamed of talking to a strange young man encountered on a train, but now it was normal. The common interest of war, she supposed, as well as the fact that women were doing so many of the jobs while the men were all away in France.

As she walked home she hummed a tune she'd heard in Walsall market that day. She didn't often sing, she'd not felt like it in recent years, but she still had a sweet, true voice. She recalled her fervent desire when she was much younger to join a choir and go on exciting outings.

Then the idea hit her, and she stopped so suddenly that a boy walking behind bumped into her. After they'd sorted themselves out she walked on slowly. Several of the local people had formed concert parties and were entertaining the soldiers. She would join one in Walsall. She could sing well enough to be accepted, she was sure, and that would be far more enjoyable than the endless hymns of a church or chapel choir. It would also be something to do which did not cost money. That was always a consideration.

He was to go by train and Anna, to her unconcealed delight, was to accompany him. She had asked for a transfer and proposed the plan, once it was agreed to try stimulating the patient's memory by the sight of the only place he appeared to have any recollection of.

'So, Hans, we go in three days, but not by the most direct route.'

Richard stared at her, his eyebrows raised. He dared not admit his excitement at the news. 'Which way do we go then?' he asked quietly.

'Here, let me show you.' She opened one of the maps lying on the table beside his chair. 'Look, we go first to Frankfurt, with a group of soldiers who are fit enough to return to the army of the west. That will be the easiest part of the journey for me, I shall have no duties.'

Richard was calculating busily. About three hundred kilometres, roughly two hundred miles. 'A day's journey?' he hazarded.

Anna shrugged. 'A long day, for there are many delays on the railways as supply trains are given priority. We shall sleep overnight on the next train, which is a hospital train with berths for the wounded, then go on the following day when they have been loaded; a slow journey, but not so far, to Munich. We shall be stopping on the way to deliver men to various hospitals. I shall be busy then, looking after them.'

'Have you a map? A bigger-scale one than this?' he added hopefully.

'I could get one? But why?'

'If I come from that region, and it seems a possibility, seeing a map and the names of towns and villages might help me remember something else.'

'I'll see what I can do. Now I must go. What will you do today?'

'It's sunny outside, though cold. I'll go for a walk.'

'Don't overtire yourself. You are still far from fit; your muscles are weak.'

Richard knew it only too well. He was working secretly, for hours when they thought he was sleeping or on his solitary walks in the grounds of the clinic, exercising the damaged muscles of his leg to make them stronger. He would need all his strength during his escape attempt.

The following day Anna brought him a map, apologizing that it was on a smaller scale than she thought would be useful.

'No, it's fine, it shows all the route from Frankfurt to Munich,' he reassured her.

Inwardly he was gloating. The map also showed parts of Austria, Switzerland and France, and would be of immense value whichever of those countries he managed to reach.

His next task was to plan where best to make his bid for freedom. He could wait, and hope to vanish from the clinic in Munich. But then a search might be made, swiftly and locally, before he could get far enough away.

The alternative was to attempt to leave the train at some intermediate station, and hope he would not be missed immediately so that they did not know where to begin a search. They might not even bother in those circumstances. It could be assumed he had simply got on the wrong train and would be discovered before long. Whereas in Munich it would be thought he had gone to find a place he knew, and they would feel more obliged to start searching for him.

He would have to leave the train, but where? Certainly not before Frankfurt, which was close to the French border. He might be able to give Anna the slip then, where there would be some confusion and he might be thought just to have gone on with the party of soldiers returning to the front.

Afterwards there would be many stops, but with wounded men on stretchers to be dealt with there would be many people milling about on each station, and he could not decide whether it would be easier or more difficult to slip away in the confusion.

If he were seen walking in any German town in his officer's uniform, it would be regarded as odd. He would be noticed and remembered. Officers had privileges and rode in motor cars. The first priority would be to exchange his uniform for the clothes of a civilian or a lowly private.

He pored over the map that night, once more thankful that his officer's status had provided him with a single room. If he left at Frankfurt he could follow the Rhine valley, and when the river crossed the Swiss border he would be close to France, beyond the end of the trenches. From there it would be simple to get back home.

He found himself dwelling on thoughts of Marigold. She was always there, spurring him on in his long, tedious contriving, but he dared not often permit himself to think in detail of the joys they had experienced together or her loving tenderness. His child would be almost eighteen months old, he realized with a shock, and he didn't even know if he had a son or a daughter.

Such thoughts were dangerous. Firmly he thrust them away. If he talked in his sleep or permitted his longings to control him, he could so easily betray himself. Only when he crossed the border to freedom would it be safe to give rein to his frustrated need to think of her, to look forward once more to the bliss of holding her in his arms.

'Look, Pa, I've found a piece of wood that's almost the shape of a fish,' Marigold said cheerfully, going into the parlour which had been turned into a bedroom since her father came home.

He was propped against the pillows, the blankets pathetically flat where his legs should have been, and she had to swallow hard.

Even after all these months it hurt with renewed pain each time she saw the wreck he had become.

He made a pitiful attempt to smile. 'Hello, love. Where's my grandson?'

'Mom's taken him down to the shops. Do you want a cup of tea?'

'I'll wait till she gets home.'

'Why don't you see if you can make a proper fish out of this?' Marigold persisted, holding out the wood.

'I lost my pocket knife – along with my legs,' he replied with a wry grimace.

'I wondered where it was,' Marigold said as matter-of-factly as she could. 'I bought you a new one, but was waiting till I found a suitable bit of wood before I gave it you. Do you think you can do anything with it? The man in the shop said people often swear by the one they've used for years, claiming they can't manage with another even if it's better.'

'I suppose that's true,' John said. 'I haven't felt like carving anyway.'

'Surely you're good enough to adapt to a new knife? Mom has to start with a new kitchen knife when the old one's lost or broken. Cooks have no choice,' she added lightly.

'But what's the use? I don't feel like carving.'

'You did it all the time before and always gave the best away,' Marigold reminded him. 'You did it for pleasure then, but I've got a scheme.'

'A scheme?'

'Yes. There's a shop I know in Birmingham, I often used to go in when I was staying with Lexie. They sell all sorts of things and I'm sure they'd love to have your carvings.'

'That's nonsense, girl!' John interrupted. 'Who in their right mind would pay good money for a bit of carved wood? I've had no training, like Ivy wants. I don't know how to do it properly.'

'That's where you're wrong,' Marigold said with satisfaction. 'I went there the other day and took them all the carved animals you'd ever given me, as well as everything Poppy and Ivy had. They agreed to take a dozen to try them. They would pay you if they sold them; they said it would be about half a crown a time.'

'Half a crown! But it only takes an hour or two to do them, if the wood's already roughly the right shape!' John said in astonishment.

'So instead of lying there feeling useless, you could help earn the money we need to send Ivy to art school,' Marigold told him. To her secret relief he reached out a hand for the piece of wood. 'I can hear Mom now, I'll go and make some tea,' she added, putting the knife down beside him.

That was one small success, one step forward, she thought later that night as she lay sleepless in the bedroom above the parlour, which had once belonged to her parents but was now for her and Dick.

She was determined somehow to get her family out of the present awful situation. She desperately wanted to give them all a better life, especially now that she had Richard's son to consider and a father brought down by constant pain. Above all she couldn't bear the effect on her mother and Ivy. Mary was not working now, living off Marigold's widow's pension and the interest from Richard's private fortune in order to stay at home and look after John. But the constant strain was beginning to tell and she had aged ten years since the accident. If she sought for a solution hard enough she would find one.

There had been no opportunity to leave the train before Frankfurt. It was crowded with men returning to the front. Many were reluctant to face the mud and boredom of the trenches, a few were frankly afraid, but the vast majority were eagerly looking forward to joining in the fighting which had become more intense.

'We'll push those damned British back into the sea and watch them drown!' one of the more bellicose gloated. 'The ones we don't shoot like wild ducks or spit like chickens first!'

For the thousandth time since he'd been injured Richard thought of the fate which would undoubtedly be his if his identity were discovered. If he were fortunate, and there were officers around who wished to and could restrain the men, he might be shot quickly and cleanly by firing squad. The dire alternative of being torn apart by an enraged enemy who would assume he was a spy was too horrible to think about.

Eventually the train rolled into Frankfurt, and Richard thankfully got out of the cramped carriage and began to stroll along the platform. He needed money and civilian clothes, and had decided that in a large city it would be easier to obtain both than in the smaller towns between Frankfurt and Munich.

Long ago he had argued with his conscience about the necessity of stealing money. It was enemy money, probably earned by making war. He was already stealing by accepting food and clothing and medical care from his enemy, of a standard they would not accord him as a prisoner of war. So why did he shrink from stealing money to finance his journey to freedom?

It belonged to an individual, his conscience reminded him. It might leave that person in difficulties. In that case he had to steal from a shop or a bank, he replied, and that had quieted his conscience as much as it was prepared to be subdued.

It made his task harder, though. He might easily filch a wallet left carelessly in view, but he could not imagine himself rifling the till of a shop. Besides, shops belonged to people too, and they were individuals.

He had a small amount of money provided for the essentials of the journey. The authorities, with relentless logic, had decided that they could not pay an officer's salary to a man with no name.

'How could we enter it into the records?' they asked when Richard had tentatively mentioned his wish to make a few modest purchases. 'All your needs are being met in the hospital. If they are not you must inform us and we will do our best to provide whatever you want.'

They had given him a small amount for the journey, enough to travel a few miles on a tram, perhaps. Not enough to get to the Swiss border.

'Hans, there you are.' It was Anna. She had travelled in a different compartment with the other nurses, for several of them were transferring from hospitals in the north to the south.

'What happens now?' Richard asked.

'The train we are to sleep in, the one we will use tomorrow, is already in the sidings for the night. Let's take our luggage across and settle in.'

It was not going to be possible to walk away and lose himself in the crowd. Anna treated him as her personal property and Richard, with a mixture of amusement, pity for her, and growing fear that her presence would hamper his attempt to escape, resignedly picked up his valise and followed her.

'Let's go and explore the town after we've found where we are to stay,' she suggested, linking her arm possessively in his. 'We could even have dinner in a restaurant. That would be a change from hospital food!'

'I have very little money, as you know,' Richard reminded her.

'I have plenty and it is my present to you. For your birthday, whenever it is,' she added swiftly, forestalling his protest. 'You have been lost for well over a year now and may have missed two birthdays. How old are you?'

Richard grinned inwardly. She never gave up her attempts to shock him into some recollection.

'I'm not a horse,' he replied. 'You can't look at my teeth. I assume I'm over twenty and under forty.'

'About my age, I would guess,' Anna said cheerfully. 'You are not much above twenty-five. I am twenty-three.'

He asked polite questions and she seemed more willing to talk freely than before. Theirs had been a largely professional relationship of nurse and patient at the hospital. Now perhaps she was in a holiday mood.

'Here is our train,' Anna said at last, having led the way along a narrow, curving platform that snaked off into the sidings.

'How do you know?' he asked curiously.

'We had instructions on the other train. This first carriage is for the nurses, but you may choose a bunk in the next one which will be loaded with the wounded tomorrow morning.'

'Where are they now?'

'In a hospital nearby. And some will be coming on an early train from near the Belgian border.'

Briskly she led the way and Richard meekly followed, allowing her to select a bunk for him, but saying he would prefer to unpack later on. If he saw an opportunity to escape he didn't want to have his few possessions scattered all over the carriage.

'I'll go and claim my bunk then come back for you,' Anna said. 'In about half an hour.'

Richard was beginning to appreciate the problems of getting away. It would not be possible, as he'd hoped, just to walk away and mingle with the crowd. Anna was determined to spend all her free time with him, and if he vanished would give the alarm at once. He might have to take a sudden opportunity at any time.

Swiftly he abstracted the most essential items from his valise and distributed them about his pockets. Comb, soap, toothbrush, razor, handkerchiefs and spare socks were easy. A spare shirt and collar were necessary but would be bulky and sadly creased after any time in his pockets. But he could wear two, and two sets of underwear. Having made that decision he donned them rapidly, and decided they didn't make him look unexpectedly plump. He hoped that the weather would remain cool.

During their stroll about Frankfurt and a simple dinner in a small restaurant, Richard was abstracted, making plans. Anna was bubbling over with excitement and his silence went unnoticed. As they walked back to the station, however, she grew pensive too.

'This may be our last time together, Hans,' she said at last, halting and leaning back against a wall.

'What do you mean?' Richard was startled. Had she somehow guessed his intentions?

'When we get to Munich, I may not be nursing in the ward where you are,' she replied. 'It may be difficult to see one another.'

'Oh. I see what you mean. But shall I be in a hospital ward? Surely I will have a room of my own?'

He swung round to face her. He was concerned about privacy if he had to delay his attempt to escape until he reached Munich. Anna had different ideas.

'Yes, I expect you will, and if you wish I can come and visit you when I am off duty.'

'That will be pleasant,' he replied automatically, and Anna moved suddenly, reaching out and sliding her hands up his chest and round his neck.

'Oh, Hans,' she sighed, clinging to him.

Richard felt a quiver of desire as he instinctively put his hands on her shoulders. It had been so very long since he had held Marigold in his arms, and Anna was soft and yielding, sweet smelling and eager.

Then a wave of revlusion swept over him. How could his body betray him so? He pushed her away from him abruptly and almost shook her.

'Nurse! You forget your position!' he snapped in a fair imitation of the Prussian officers he had lived with in the hospitals.

Anna gasped, then turned away, struggling to control her sobs. Richard stepped towards her, appalled at the effect of his words, and realized at the final moment that this development might serve him well. It would rid him of Anna's fond surveillance.

'Go back to the train. I will follow later,' he said curtly, and forgetting that he was her patient, humiliated and rejected, Anna almost ran away.

Richard turned and made swiftly for the centre of the town. He had seen some motor cycles near the restaurant, some with army kitbags tied on the back. If he could steal one he would be well on the way south by morning.

Ivy sat huddled in front of the kitchen range. She had a fearful cold and no one had even suggested she go to school. Mom had gone shopping and forbidden her to go in to Pa.

'You mustn't give him your cold, he's still not well,' she'd said.

'I'm bored in bed,' Ivy wailed. 'It's cold if I sit up and you won't let me have a fire.'

Mary sighed. 'I've too much to do and can't keep bringing up coal,' she said wearily. John had been unusually restless and neither of them had slept much that night.

'But I can't draw lying down. I can't draw and I don't want to read. Why can't I come downstairs?'

'Because you might give your cold to little Dick, and he's only just got over the last one he had.'

Marigold, as so often, had come to her rescue. 'I was thinking of taking Pa's new carvings into Birmingham,' she said. 'I can take Dick, the trip would keep him interested.'

'It's very cold, won't he take harm?' Mary demurred.

'It's frosty, not damp. If I wrap him up well he won't be hurt. Then Ivy can spend the day in the kitchen if she wants.'

After an hour Ivy was bored with her own company. Life had changed so much since Pa's accident. She knew everyone blamed her, even if they hadn't said so, and she'd done her best to avoid them all. At school she spent playtime alone, and after a few weeks of taunting the others had left her to her own devices. It wasn't fun when she simply turned her back and never once retaliated.

Why couldn't people love her? First it had been the scars which made even her mother and father turn away from her in distaste. Of course they tried not to show it, but she was convinced it made them treat her in a special way. Pa made a great fuss of her, and she knew full well she was allowed more licence than her sisters. It was to make up for the ugliness of her blemishes; it wasn't because they loved her more than they did the others.

First Johnny had left, and although she could have borne that, for now she was older she could see he'd had to go, she'd felt betrayed when he married Lucy. He was saying he loved Lucy more than he did his family, more than he did Ivy.

Marigold's departure had hurt her even more. At the back of her mind she saw there had been advantages, but she still wished Marigold had loved her enough to find a job in Hednesford and stay at home rather than going to Oxford. She'd thought Marigold was the one member of the family least likely to go away from her, because she had always been able to persuade Marigold to do as she, Ivy, wanted.

In the end, in big things, she had found her power was limited. Marigold rejected her completely when she defied everyone and married Richard. For a long while Ivy simmered, resentful, longing for a way to hit back at Marigold and make her feel as unloved and rejected as she did herself.

Then Poppy had loved that wretched little puppy more than she loved Ivy, and when he was gone it hadn't changed matters. Poppy had left home and her parents hadn't turned to her as she half expected, they'd been distraught, unhappy, impatient with her. And this despite Poppy's theft of her money.

Even Sam Bannister didn't want her now. She'd revelled in the power she had over him, although she hadn't understood why stroking the creams into her flesh had turned him from a rough, abrupt lad into a pleading creature who quivered and moaned and, during the later times they'd met, declared in broken words, whispered into her hair, that he loved her and wanted her.

She'd offered, after Poppy stole her money, to let him bring his friends again, even soldiers if he could find any who wished to indulge in this strange, inexplicable occupation. She needed to replace her lost money swiftly, and if Sam's friends would pay she wouldn't object.

'But you can't keep most of the money, Sam,' she'd stipulated. 'I want tenpence out of every shilling.'

To her angry dismay he'd refused. He'd offered to pay her a shilling each time, and she had to be content with that. But one or two shillings a week nowhere near began to replace her previous hoard.

Then suddenly he vanished from Hednesford. 'They pushed 'im inter army, rotten coward!' Billy explained. ''E dain't wanner goo. They won' 'ave ter mek me, when I'm ode enuff.'

With him vanished Ivy's income, and before she could think of a way to get some of Sam's cream and suggest to Billy that even without his brother something might be arranged, Pa was injured. She'd been too withdrawn since to care and then, miraculously, Marigold offered to pay her art school fees. There was no more need for contrivance, or to endure Sam's rough hands as he rubbed in useless creams.

She had ceased to believe the scar ointment was any good two or three months after Sam's treatment began. And since he'd left her bosoms had grown at a faster rate than before. That seemed to prove the other cream had been useless too.

Ivy sighed. In one way it was a pity for she enjoyed the feeling of superiority over these silly boys. They became slavering jellies just through stroking cream into her body. She couldn't imagine losing control of herself for such a reason. It was laughable.

Her thoughts were suddenly distracted as Jim, the postman, came whistling through the yard. He'd been doing the job for just three months, when he'd been dismissed from the army because he suffered from chest injuries.

'Gas, it were, mekin' us all choke ter death. We couldn't breathe, 'ardly,' he'd explained cheerfully one day when he came in, as he occasionally did, for a cup of tea. 'Still, it got me out o' there, perishin' mud an' freezin' cold. They thought I oughter get a job outdoors, good fer me chest. 'Ow breathin' in smoke from factories an' pits is good fer me, I dunno, but it's a better way o' spendin' the days than down pit.'

She ran to the back door. To receive a letter was always an occasion. She'd waylaid the postman for years on her way to school just to see what letters there were. This one might be from Johnny, or Lucy with news of him.

''Oo do yer know wi' thick paper an' envelopes fit fer Buckingham Palace?' Jim said jokingly as he handed over the single letter. 'Why ain't yer at school?'

'I've got a cold,' Ivy explained, and sneezed several times as if to prove it.

'Aye, well, best shut door an' get back in front o' fire. 'Ow's yer Pa?'

'A bit better now he's started carving again.'

'Good. Gi' 'im me best wishes. Tara!'

He went off, whistling, and Ivy looked at the letter. It was addressed to Marigold and Ivy recognized the writing, spiky and elongated, with flamboyant flourishes on each capital letter. It was Mrs Endersby's, for she wrote occasionally demanding to know when Marigold intended to return to The Place.

Ivy turned it over and found the flap was stuck down very loosely. Within seconds she had it open and took the single sheet of paper out. She wished she could write like that, so different from the plain, rounded letters they were taught at school. It looked distinguished, somehow.

She seized her drawing pad and sat at the table, the letter spread out in front of her. Without troubling to understand the meanings of the words she concentrated on copying the form of the letters.

By the third time she was satisfied with her efforts. It was hard, apart from the different paper, to tell her copy from the original. She read out certain phrases under her breath, careful not to let Pa hear her.

> My beloved son Richard is dead, lost to me. You stole him from me, and now it appears you mean to steal my grandchild, the heir to our property, also. Our precious Henry is dead too, and little Dick is all we have, and you mean to deprive me of the joy

of seeing him grow up. You have not been to visit us once since you returned to Hednesford, despite my letters.

There was more, but Ivy heard Mary's footsteps as she came slowly along the yard. Hastily she put the original letter back in the envelope, sealed it, and propped it up on the mantlepiece against the clock. By the time Mary came in she was sitting beside the fire again, the pages of her pad turned over, and apparently so absorbed in drawing from memory a portrait of Dick playing with his toys that Mary had to speak to her twice before she realized her mother had returned.

They were gone. Just when he began to allow himself to hope freedom was within reach, the means was snatched away from him.

Richard walked slowly along looking for other motor cycles or cars he might steal. By now his scruples had vanished. He would take any means of escape that presented itself. None did.

He raged inwardly, impotently. Surely in so large a town as Frankfurt there would be an unattended car or motor cycle somewhere!

He was standing in front of the cathedral, oblivious to the incongruity of plotting a theft virtually within its portals, when someone touched his arm. Lost in his bitter thoughts he'd heard no sound, and started in surprise.

'Hans, I'm sorry! I should have known better. It won't happen again, I promise. I could have wrecked the progress you've made. I was distraught when I discovered you hadn't come back to the train. Oh, please will you forgive me? I'll go back to Berlin if you wish. I won't speak to you again, if only you'll come back to the train with me!'

By the time Anna had sobbed out all her apologies and self-recriminations Richard had recovered his wits. He would find it more difficult to elude her anxious vigilance now, and if she followed him and saw him stealing a vehicle the alarm would be raised immediately. The train would take him southwards, nearer to freedom although further from home. If he remained cool towards her he would be able to make plans once they got to Munich.

A spark of an idea came to him. If they thought he might recognize places round about, they might permit him the use of a motor cycle in order to explore the area. Even a horse or ordinary bicycle would be an advantage. With much greater cordiality than he had been feeling a few moments earlier he turned to Anna and nodded briefly.

'I needed some time alone,' he said, making his voice curt. 'I shall walk back along the riverbank. You may accompany me if you choose, but I prefer not to talk. Is that understood?'

She nodded and, as he turned away, fell into step a yard or so behind him. All Richard's natural inclinations warred against the image he must present. Now their relationship was reversed. Instead of being her patient he was her officer, and he must make sure he retained this authority.

Later, as he undressed on the train, he was able to smile at the astonishment she would have felt had she been permitted to undo the buttons on his shirt, only to find another underneath. Poor Anna, he thought. She had been useful, but was unlikely to be so in the coming weeks. He salved his conscience by telling himself she would soon transfer her affection to someone else.

By the following night he was installed in the Munich house which had been converted into a convalescent home. To Richard's astonished disgust the journey had exhausted him. He was still far from well. He wondered whether he would have been capable of riding a motor cycle far, and set himself with grim determination to restore his strength as quickly as possible. He must make an attempt to escape before the winter came.

He had in the end persuaded the hospital authorities that sitting in a house or walking in the garden would do little to bring back any possible memories of the area. They shook their heads firmly when he suggested borrowing a motor cycle, saying truthfully that there was no such thing available. Then the gardener, Gerard, an elderly gnome-like man who came every morning on an ancient bicycle, offered it to Richard while he was at work. The matron had reluctantly agreed they might try it.

Richard found the exercise beneficial, apart from the freedom to explore and find ways of possible escape. The nearest border with freedom was at Lindau, at the eastern end of Lake Constance. The borders of Germany, Austria and Switzerland were very close together around the town of Bregenz. He had only to cross into Switzerland and his problems would be over. He could wait there while he arranged for money to be sent, and then travel home.

He even had civilian clothes and a map. Pointing out that it was not suitable for an army officer to be seen on an ancient bicycle, he had been provided with riding breeches and a jacket. He had a small amount of cash, jealously hoarded, and was almost ready to make the attempt.

He might take the bicycle and sleep rough for a couple of nights, but the terrain was hilly, the bicycle old and ramshackle, and the gardener his friendly benefactor. With a car or better still a motor cycle he could cover the hundred or so miles in a day. He would not be missed until he had left German soil.

He knew of a motor cycle always left unattended at a nearby house. He could even walk there so that he would not have to abandon Gerard's bicycle. Then on one of his intended final cycle rides a new possibility presented itself.

At the beginning of November, on a gloomy but so far dry day, he was riding along a narrow, unfrequented track. It led only to a couple of farms but was a short cut to another road. He skidded to a halt when he saw a small aeroplane sitting in a field. There was a barn nearby, not large enough to be a hangar, and the farmhouse was some distance away, invisible behind a low hill. This field was the only one flat enough for landing in.

After a hasty look round to ensure no one was in sight Richard thrust the bicycle into the cover of a clump of trees, and cautiously crossed over to the barn. The door was unlocked and inside he found a stack of tins full of petrol. On a peg nearby was a flying suit and goggles. His heart beating furiously he went to the plane and inspected it. It was in good condition, a newish two-seater bi-plane.

He had to go now. The low cloud made flying conditions hazardous, but he did not need to reach a high altitude and in an hour or so the aeroplane might have vanished.

Working feverishly Richard fuelled the plane to capacity, then he retrieved Gerard's bicycle. Although returning it would give away his own actions, he wrote Gerard's name and the address of the hospital on a piece of paper and left it attached to the bicycle in the barn. He dragged on the flying suit, found gloves in the pockets, and hung the goggles round his neck.

No one was in sight. Praying the engine would start first time he swung the propeller. It fired, spluttered, and fired again, and in seconds Richard clambered aboard.

He taxied round until he was facing into the wind, blessing his good fortune that this gave him the full length of the field in front of him. He would not have to remain on the ground for any longer than necessary.

As the aeroplane lifted, clearing a small wood at the end of the field, Richard could see the farmhouse on his left. Two men had emerged from a doorway and were pointing excitedly at him. Richard waved back, and full of exhilaration turned towards the west.

He soon picked out the railway line which led towards Lindau and followed it. He was singing at the top of his voice, feeling a little mad both at being in the air again and the prospect of freedom, so suddenly presented.

It took two hours to reach the lake. He saw it as the railway turned southwards for Lindau, a long narrow stretch of grey water, grey clouds scudding along above. He flew over it midway along, where the two arms of the lake divided, and although his map did not extend so far he knew that he was heading for Zurich. So long as he kept to the south of the Rhine and landed in one piece, he would within days be holding Marigold in his arms once more.

He glanced at the fuel gauge and saw it was still reading full. That could not be right, and he tried to calculate how much further he could go. Without any idea of the capacity of the tanks or the wind speed, however, this was an unprofitable exercise.

Richard debated inwardly. Should he come down as soon as he saw a suitable field, or try to get nearer Zurich and risk running out of fuel in an impossible area? He glanced down. At the moment he could see a fairly large number of possible landing sites. The hills here were low and there were plenty of meadows. It was probable he still had a good amount of fuel left, and he wanted to get as far away from Munich as possible.

He followed a river valley going almost due west. The River

Thur, he thought, which flowed into the Rhine below the Falls at Schaffhausen. He would need to turn south before he got there or he would risk flying back into Germany.

The clouds had come even lower and were hiding the hills, but the silver gleam of the river below was sufficient guide, and he would have plenty of chances of landing in the valley. If he reached the Rhine he could turn south with it and be heading for Zurich.

And then it began to snow. Almost without warning the heavy, soft flakes descended, and within minutes the surroundings were blotted out.

Richard lost height until the ground was once more visible, a grey blur beneath him. He spotted a road which crossed the river and led southwards, and turned to follow it. He had no idea how near the German border he might be, but under no circumstances would he risk flying back to be recaptured by his enemies.

Within minutes he was completely lost. The only course now was to land. He came as low as he dared, searching for a flat area. To his immense relief he spotted one on his left, and with the weight of the snow and the blinding vision he had no time to do more than point the nose of the aeroplane towards it and drift down, fighting to control the speed of the descent and keep the wings level.

He touched down in a series of jerks and bumps which would have had his flying instructor gibbering with scorn and fury. But he hadn't learnt to fly on a ridged, tussocky meadow. It was a miracle he kept the plane the right way up, and shuddered to a halt only five yards short of a massive stone barn.

Shelter from the snow was imperative. During the struggle he hadn't appreciated how cold he was. Without the flying suit he would by now be incapable of moving. As it was his feet, in ordinary shoes, were numb.

He stumbled round the corner of the barn and tugged open the heavy wooden door. Inside was a pile of sweet smelling hay, and Richard breathed in great gulps of the welcome aroma. Here were warmth and comfort.

He burrowed beneath the hay, leaving a space just for his nose. It was warm and soft, and the smell of it evocative of boyhood days when he'd escaped with a book and a pocket full of apples to hide away from his mother's importunate demands. Within minutes he was asleep.

Chapter Fourteen

HE was there, in the audience! Poppy saw him as soon as she walked on stage behind the other three girls.

She had been rehearsing for several days a week, since she'd joined a small group of girls and older men who gave concerts every week in the church hall for the soldiers home on leave.

This was her first appearance, and she had been incredibly nervous. For the time being she would sing in a group, for she hadn't had time to learn all the songs, and soloists needed to know a lot of different ones, Mr Thwaite said. 'You've got a good voice, though, lass, and soon we'll give you a spot.'

Looking at the sea of faces below, Poppy wasn't too sure she wanted to face the whistles and cheers of the soldiers all by herself. She'd listened to the joking and the repartee of some of the more experienced performers as they responded to the comments of the soldiers, and thought she'd never have the nerve to do the same.

But he was there, sitting at one of the tables at the front of the hall, and it was clear he recognized her.

She'd looked for him on the train every time she went home, but fruitlessly. It could have been a dream that he'd ever spoken to her. She thought him handsome, with his dark hair and small, dapper moustache. He'd been kind, and he seemed to admire her.

Now she sang as well as she could, glancing occasionally at him, but apart from a slight smile which hovered on her lips, which she could not control, she tried to give no indication she knew he was there.

They had solo singers, a man who played a violin, another with a trombone, and one who told a series of funny stories. At the end, the whole company came on stage and the soldiers joined in several of the songs until it had become a general chorus.

'"Rugeley! Sing "Rugeley",' they shouted, and the chant built up until, the pianist complying, they began the latest ditty which had swept the camps on the Chase.

> Rugeley, Rugeley, we're all enjoying it hugely.
> To and fro we gaily go – we're always on the tramp,
> But if you think that Cannock Chase
> Is a lively and attractive place,
> You'll be Rugeley awakened when you get to Rugeley Camp.

They insisted on repeating it several times, and only stopped when the ladies who prepared the tea and cakes came in. Then the concert party left the stage and went to sit at the tables.

Poppy hesitated, but he was waiting for her.

'Come and sit with us. How lovely to see you again. Perhaps I ought to introduce myself this time. I'm George Grierson, I live here in Walsall.'

Shyly Poppy responded, but by the end of the evening her shyness had been overcome by the friendliness and obvious admiration of George and his companions. Perhaps after all she might one day be able to exchange witticisms with an audience.

'May I walk you home?' George asked as the evening ended, and they began to leave.

Overcome with a mixture of pride and nervousness, Poppy assented. It was the first time an attractive, older boy had shown any interest in her. She recalled Sam's advances with a shudder. This was totally different. For one thing, George treated her with respect. He showed his admiration in unexceptional glances and words; he didn't try to maul her. He was well spoken, too, and she soon discovered he'd only just left school.

'I should have gone up to Cambridge,' he said with a laugh as they walked back down Digbeth towards The Bridge and the George Hotel, close but not touching one another. 'But how on earth could I have concentrated on law while this was going on?'

'Law? You're going to be a lawyer?' she asked. Dreams and aspirations and wonderful prospects swirled round in her brain. A lawyer was better even than a pottery owner, for it was in no way connected with trade. Instantly, Poppy became a vehement if silent supporter of Cambridge. It was, it must be, far better than Oxford.

She felt ashamed, for a moment, remembering that Richard, despite Marigold's unwavering belief, was certainly dead. But her own newly awakened tremulous hopes could not be kept at bay. When George suggested taking her to a dance on the following evening, she could scarcely reply for happy excitement.

'I have to go back in a couple of days, then we'll only be in camp for a short while,' he explained diffidently. 'We've lost so many men on the Somme they want to send us out as fast as possible to replace them. I'd like to see you as much as I can before I go. If, that is, you are agreeable.'

Poppy was decidedly agreeable, and for the next few days lived in a pink cloud of happiness. When George tentatively kissed her she felt there was nothing else in the world she ever wanted. She promised to write to him, and such was her euphoria she was only mildly unhappy when he finally departed for France.

She knew she loved him, but the sensible part of her reminded her she was not quite sixteen, and he would have to train for his profession when he came out of the army, when this horrible war was over. It was sufficient for the moment to hug her secret to herself; to lose herself in dreams and not spoil it by introducing reality: the questions and arguments and plans which would be voiced if she shared her happiness with anyone else.

It was pitch dark when Richard woke. Outside the barn it was snowing heavily, with neither stars nor moon visible. He was hungry and thirsty, but could slake his thirst at least on a handful of snow. He went back to his snug nest in the hay and lay contentedly thinking of Marigold, his unknown child, and how soon he would be able to see them. He drifted off to sleep again, and when he awoke some hours later bright daylight showed through cracks in the barn door.

He went to look out, and gazed on a scene of incredible beauty. The snow, crisp and fresh, lay several inches deep. Today there were no threatening clouds and a bright sun, a deep orange-pink in colour, had just risen over the far horizon. Spruce and pine trees, their branches loaded with the snow, dotted the white slopes of the hillside on the right. Far below the river he had been following glittered silver, shot through with ice-blue shards. A road snaked up towards him, passing within half a mile of where he stood.

Richard discarded his flying suit, for it would give rise to difficult questions, and struck off across the fields. He scrambled down on to the road. The tracks of vehicles showed in the fresh snow, and with luck he would soon be able to beg a ride towards Zurich.

Within minutes a large truck stopped for him, and the driver cheerfully said he could take him some of the way. 'I'll drop you by the railway. There should be a train soon. I want to stop for breakfast first, though. Do you mind waiting?'

'I could do with some food too.' Richard realized how hungry he was, and then belatedly began to wonder whether he would be able to use his German marks, the only money he had.

'Where did you get those?' the driver asked suspiciously when Richard explained his problem.

'I've just escaped from Germany. I'm a British pilot.'

'You speak German very well.'

'I spent some time in Germany before the war, and I've spoken nothing else for months.'

The driver said no more, but when he stopped and they entered an inn he excused himself and Richard saw him talking to another man, both of them glancing frequently in his direction.

'I'll pay. You can give me the marks afterwards,' the driver said brusquely when he returned to the table where Richard sat.

The rolls spread thickly with butter and plum jam were delicious, and so was the coffee. Nothing in Germany had tasted half so good as this simple meal eaten in freedom.

'I'll be out in a minute, go and wait by the truck.'

Richard nodded and walked outside. The truck was parked alongside a large shed, and he strolled towards it. As he rounded the corner of the shed a noise behind him made him turn swiftly, but he was too late to save himself from the vicious blow which connected expertly with his skull.

When he came to he found himself sitting in the truck, his wrists and ankles tightly bound, the rope securing him to the seat.

'So you have a hard head?' the driver commented.

'What happened, and why am I tied up?' Richard demanded.

'A precaution. I don't like the Germans, and I mean to turn you over to the authorities who will test the truth of what you say.'

Richard couldn't judge the time, for the sun had disappeared behind some clouds, but it was starting to get dark. There was almost no other traffic on the road, and what little there was went in the opposite direction.

'Where are we? Near Zurich?'

'I haven't the time to go there. The pass won't be open after tonight, for there is more snow to come soon. I'm taking you to St Moritz, where I live. If you can prove you are who you claim to be, you might be able to get to Zurich before the passes are all blocked for the winter,' the driver said cheerfully.

There was nothing he could do, although he fumed at the mischance which was taking him in the opposite direction to that he wished to go.

The roads were icy and treacherous. The driver was navigating a relatively gradual slope, with a bend at the bottom, when a horse-drawn cart appeared. It was being driven utterly recklessly, approaching him erratically with no indication that it would get out of the way.

With an oath the driver steered for the wall of rock to the side, but the jarring shock as the truck hit it sent him falling helplessly out of his seat and on to the road. If he had not been tied to the seat Richard would probably have been flung out too. The truck careered on for some yards, scraping against the wall of rock, coming to rest several screeching, shattering seconds later, leaning drunkenly against an outcrop which halted further downward progress.

A girl's voice was calling frantically for help, and it was some minutes before Richard could attract her attention.

'I can't help until you untie me,' he shouted down to her as she ran towards him. 'There's a knife in my jacket pocket.'

She was shaking and sobbing wildly, but she managed to find the knife and cut the rope round his wrists. Swiftly Richard freed his legs and scrambled out of the wrecked truck, thankful they had not been alongside a sheer drop.

It was none the less a scene of carnage which met his horrified gaze. The truck driver had fallen under the wheels of the truck, and a quick inspection showed he was beyond help.

The cart had been halted but the girl who had freed him was back beside it, staring down in horror at her companion, lying frighteningly still on the road.

'He was flung out!' she sobbed. 'Oh, please help me! Is he dead?'

Richard was already kneeling beside the man, an elderly peasant from the look of him, and feeling for his heartbeat. 'No, just stunned I think, from the fall. But his leg may be broken.'

'Can we move him? He'll die of cold if we leave him there. Please, can we get him into the cart? Should we take him home or to the town? It's too far away, we'd never reach it before dark! What shall we do?'

'You have a house nearby?' Richard cut into this torrent of words ruthlessly and she looked at him blankly for a moment, then took a deep breath and pulled herself together.

'Yes, a short way along the track. If he isn't badly hurt we'd better take him there. My aunt can look after him. She used to be a nurse, I am sure she can set his leg.'

'Tie the horse to something. That tree will do, and then come and help me lift him.'

To Richard's relief she obeyed without delay. The cart was too small to take the dead man too, and Richard knew he would have to return later to move his body, unless there were local officials to whom the task could be left. They were soon driving back along the track, the horse now docile. The girl explained he had been frightened by the gunshots of a hunter too near the track.

'It was probably Dieter, the fool. He's always coming too far from his own house. We'd been going to collect a last pile of wood before the snow covers it up, and the idiot horse got the bit between his teeth and ran away. Is Uncle Friedrich all right, do you think?'

'Apart from his leg he's just stunned,' Richard assured her, hoping he was right.

It seemed a very long way before they reached a house, but once there a motherly woman took control. She gave brisk orders, fashioned a competent-looking splint for what she declared was a simple fracture of the tibia, and seemed quite unperturbed by the disaster. Soon after they had put Uncle Friedrich to bed he recovered his senses, but was promptly forced to drink a herb sedative by his dominating wife.

'We will keep him quiet tonight,' Frau Müller said firmly.

'I must do something about the driver.' Richard said. 'Is there a village, someone I should report to?'

'It's too dark for you to find your way; these tracks are difficult for strangers. And it's too late to get to the town tonight, but in the morning we will see what is to be done. There is a bed in the other room for you, sir.'

By the morning, however, there had been another heavy fall of snow. Frau Müller was busy in the kitchen when Richard appeared.

'How can we get out? It's too deep for the cart,' he said after enquiring about her husband.

She shrugged. 'We can't. We will be snowed in for several months now. The poor man will have to lie there. The only way out, if you can use them, is on skis.'

When Marigold returned from shopping she found Mary slumped in a chair beside the kitchen table. She was shaking uncontrollably.

'Mom, what is it? Are you ill?'

Mary looked up at her, eyes blank. 'The rent collector came,' she said tonelessly. 'The landlord sent a message.'

'Well? What was it?'

'He wants us out.'

'To leave here? Mom, he can't! We're never late with the rent!'

'He says it's meant for miners. He's offered us a back-to-back, two rooms, the same rent. It seems he can get more now.'

'Have you told Pa?'

Mary shook her head. 'I daren't. You know how quiet he goes, not speaking for days when something upsets him. This would finish him – to be turned out of the house he's been so proud of and be pushed into a slum.'

'That won't happen!' Marigold declared. 'With my money we can afford something better anyway. How long have we got?'

'A month. But your Pa and I couldn't afford a good house,

Marigold, and it's not right to depend on your money. You need it for youself and Dick.'

Marigold waved aside her objections. 'Don't say a word to Pa. I'll arrange something before he has to know, and make it look as if it's planned and meant to help rather than forced on us.'

Marigold had been thinking hard even before this latest calamity. Sophia's letters had been growing more desperate, more pleading even, as she wrote how much she missed Dick. Also Marigold was concerned for the child. He seemed more delicate than he'd been at The Place, and succumbed to colds and other infections too readily. It really wasn't a good place for a child, this damp and cheerless house, but she couldn't desert her mother, especially now.

Mary had grown suddenly old, her previous boundless energy gone. She could see to do her sewing, her sole way of making money now, only in bright daylight. Pa had more frequent and longer spells when he seemed oblivious to everything, not speaking for days on end. Without Marigold's help and support her family would be doomed.

She spent a day in Birmingham and then was ready with her plans.

'I ought to take Dick to The Place,' she said that evening. It was shortly before Christmas. 'Mrs Endersby misses him so. Could you manage if I went for a few days?'

'Of course, we mustn't be selfish and keep him all to ourselves,' Mary said at once. 'Ivy is much more responsible now, and helps a great deal. And Poppy doesn't seem to have so many rehearsals lately on her days off for that Christmas show she's involved in. Of course we can manage.'

Marigold set off for the Potteries. She'd sent a telegram to announce her time of arrival, and Kemp was at the station to meet her.

They settled into their old rooms and Marigold left Dick with his grandmother while she unpacked. Then he was put to bed, Betty once more in charge, and Marigold donned her best dress for dinner. It was important for her plan that she looked and felt confident, and did not give Sophia any chance to criticize her.

The dress was one Richard had bought her, of soft hyacinth-blue silk, with a modest neckline and short sleeves. It didn't have the wider skirts and shorter hems now fashionable, but Marigold did not intend to waste her limited income on frivolous clothes for herself when her family needed so much.

She chatted easily, giving Sophia details of Dick's progress. Out of the corner of her eye she saw that Mr Endersby, while trying to appear indifferent, was listening just as eagerly. Good, that boded well.

Kemp left the room once the dessert of apple pie and cream was served, leaving cheese and nuts on the table for them to help themselves.

'I have a proposal to make,' Marigold said at once, before she could change her mind.

Sophia looked at her in surprise. Marigold had altered since leaving here. Before she had been a pliable girl still, now she was a woman with a steely determination shining from her eyes.

'A proposal? What can you mean?'

'A bargain, perhaps,' Marigold said quietly. 'I need to provide for my family; I am the only one with the means to help them. I believe that in justice I should have the share of the firm that was Richard's, and it is possible a court would agree with me. But I have no money to start a legal battle, and no wish to do this for it would distress Richard.'

'Richard is dead!' Sophia said harshly. 'Why can you not accept that and come here, where we have offered you and his son a home?'

'I would, I did, but now my parents need me more. I cannot be in two places. The income I have is sufficient for us all at the moment, but it may not remain so, with rising prices and the sort of expenses that are necessary for helping my father. Besides, we rent the house from the colliery owners, and they want it back. I would like to set up a business which could provide us all with some income, but I have no capital and no way of borrowing money.'

Mr Endersby was looking at her with open interest in his face. 'What do you propose?' he asked. Any matter of business caught his attention as nothing else could.

Marigold took a deep breath. 'There is another consideration. Dick has been sickly since living in Hednesford.'

'Dick? Ill? You never said!'

'I didn't wish to worry you. They were minor, childish ailments, but I can see it is not as good for him living there in crowded conditions as it was here at The Place.'

'I should have been told! How could you be so unkind as to keep me in ignorance! Marigold, whatever our differences, whatever I thought of Richard's marriage, I love his son! He is the only thing left to me!'

'I thought it kinder not to worry you. And as you have seen, he's in perfect health now. But please let me explain my proposal.'

'Yes, Sophia, let her go on,' Mr Endersby said, quite sharply for him.

'I need money, you want Dick. I'm not suggesting a cold-blooded trade. I've agonized over what's best for us all. But if you will give me, outright, the money representing Richard's share of the firm, I will allow you to have Dick here and bring him up as you would wish Richard's son to be brought up, in his old home.'

'You'd give up the child?' Sophia spoke haltingly as if she could not believe her ears.

'Not legally, and not completely. I would want to visit him frequently, and be consulted before any major decisions, such as employing a new governess or sending him to school, were taken. I would want to know the people in whose charge he was placed; his nanny, and so on. I would not agree to Betty looking after him, for instance. And I would want him to visit me frequently. I would sign a paper agreeing to leave him in your charge until he is twenty-one, of age, and able to choose his own life, on those conditions.'

'Of course. Oh, Marigold, thank you! You don't know what this means to me!'

Don't I? Marigold thought. I'm giving you my child. I'm voluntarily separating myself from my own son, the only reminder I have of Richard, for money. It's been a hard, agonizing decision. I am ashamed of myself, but it's the only way I can help Mom, take her and Pa out of the despair and ever-threatening poverty of their life. It's the only way I can make up to Ivy for the scars my negligence inflicted on her. And it's best for Dick himself, in the end, to escape from the sort of life I could provide for him. It would be difficult for a child while she was coping with a business venture, and he would have a better life here, a life he would have been born to had Richard still been at home.

'If – when Richard himself returns, of course, the agreement would be finished, for he might not wish it.'

'You're not still deluding yourself he's still alive, are you?' Sophia asked, and it was the kindest tone she'd ever used to Marigold. 'My poor child, don't you think we'd have heard if he were a prisoner? He's one of the thousands whose fate will never be known.'

'But if he's not dead? In time I hope to have made enough with my business to pay you back. But if Richard came home he must have a right to claim his son. And the share of the business would surely belong to him then anyway.'

'Of course. Now to details,' Mr Endersby cut in. 'It will take a few weeks to raise the cash, but I could borrow on the strength of it if you need it immediately.'

'I think your guarantee would be sufficient, thank you,' Marigold said gratefully. The worst was over. 'I have been consulting Mr Thane, my solicitor in Birmingham, and he agrees with me. He has drawn up various papers and is willing to discuss them with your legal advisors at any time.'

'But what sort of business do you mean to start? A shop?'

'None of us knows how to run a shop,' Marigold said with a slight smile. 'No, there is a house for sale in Birmingham, in the Hagley Road near Five Ways. It is already let out in apartments, and I mean to convert it into a superior hotel. After all, Mom and I both know how to cater for the gentry, and Poppy is an excellent cook, besides having worked at the George Hotel. Are we agreed?'

Ivy walked along Colmore Row. She'd just come from the Art Gallery and was eager to do some sketches of the Grand Hotel. It was amazingly difficult to get it just right, and if she didn't get the spacing between the windows really exact the balance was wrong. It was far easier to draw something more elaborate like the shops in New Street or the huddles of mean houses in the dark, depressing courts in the poorer areas of the city.

Standing in the lee of St Philip's Cathedral opposite the Grand, she leaned back and steadied her pad, then squinted up at the façade. After several attempts she was satisfied, and with a deep sigh moved on across the churchyard towards the Bull Ring which was her main objective.

She hadn't noticed the cold, and had been sheltered from the bitter March wind which blasted across the open space. But as she cut through Cherry Street she shivered violently. Even in the thick woollen coat Marigold had bought her she felt cold. She would draw inside the Market Hall today. The stallholders with their vast arrays of brightly coloured food offered another challenge.

Ivy had found a host of new subjects during the weeks they had been in Birmingham. Although she returned still to her plants, and drew dozens of faces of the people she saw about her, she was fascinated by the variety of buildings in the city. At every opportunity when the weather permitted she was out of doors, drawing whatever took her fancy.

'When can I go to the art school?' she had demanded the day after they had moved into the new hotel.

'They won't accept you until you're a little older,' Marigold replied. 'But I asked Mr Thane and he suggested a school where they have a very good art teacher,' she hurried on, seeing Ivy's mouth droop ominously.

'I don't want to go to school. They'll hate me. They'll make fun of my scars.'

Marigold was prepared for this argument. 'I'm willing to make a bet with you,' she said calmly. 'If you wear high-necked blouses and keep your hair forward no one will know. If you can hide it from them for a month and no one says anything about it, I'll buy you a proper easel.'

The struggle in Ivy's face was sharp but brief. 'A proper easel? And an artist's palette?'

Marigold breathed a sigh of relief. 'Yes, if you want one. Do you want to do proper oil painting now?'

'I couldn't afford the paints very often before, just pencils and crayons,' Ivy replied, and for a moment the memory of Poppy's theft of her hoard threatened her new happiness. Even though she could now have all she wanted that episode still rankled. 'What school?' she asked almost perfunctorily.

'Miss Dawson's,' Marigold said. 'It's in Church Road, and there are girls from some of the best families in Edgbaston there, daughters of gentlemen. I want you to have the best there is, Ivy.'

Ivy had been at the school now for more than the stipulated month, and her easel was in pride of place in the small bedroom which was her own. The bed had been pushed to one side, and she referred to the room as her studio, grumbling that the window did not have a skylight with a northerly aspect, but vowing to herself that one day she would obtain that too.

She was absorbed in her copying of the scene in the Market Hall, and didn't realize for some time that someone else had set up a small portable easel a short distance away, slightly behind her. As she stretched to relieve the stiffness in her shoulders he spoke.

'Who taught you to draw?'

Ivy swung round. He was elderly, with a flowing white beard and pale blue eyes. His ancient shabby Ulster was spattered with specks of paint, and a wide-brimmed hat was flung carelessly on the floor at his feet.

'I taught myself, mostly.'

'Remarkable. But do you have lessons? At school, for instance?'

'I want to go to the art college. Are you an artist?' Ivy asked instead, and stepped back to look at his painting.

She gasped with admiration. It was bold, in vivid colours, and though to a casual observer might seem rough and unformed, Ivy saw the intense feeling which had directed the brush strokes.

'I teach at the college. Do you have lessons at school?' he persisted.

Ivy shrugged. 'Miss Burton teaches us but we don't use oils, just watercolours. That's good for my flowers and some of the people I do, but I want to start with oils and I can't get it right yet.'

'How old are you?'

'Twelve.'

'Too young yet, I'm afraid, for the college, but we might be able to do something. You have a rare talent. Where do you live?'

'In the Hagley Road. My sister is turning our house into an hotel.'

'May I come and see her? What's her name?'

'Marigold Endersby. Would you really teach me? Do you mean it?'

'I am not used to my word being doubted, young lady. Have you finished for today?'

Ivy nodded. She was far too excited to continue. It looked as if her dream was coming true, and at last a real artist would soon be giving her lessons.

'Come on, let's go and find her straight away.'

Marigold surveyed the hall proudly. The last workman had just left, the last of the floors were polished, the last piece of furniture put in place.

Sometimes she had wondered if her dream would ever be realized. The first obstacle she had met, unexpectedly, had been her family's opposition. It had taken more cajoling, pleading, and persuading to convince them her plan was feasible than it had done to get the money from the Endersbys.

They, oddly, had seen nothing strange in her wish to start a business, and had indeed helped her by introducing her to people who might be useful. Perhaps it was that they were already in business, whereas for her parents it was a frightening new venture totally outside their experience.

Mary had wept and pleaded with her not to give up Dick. 'He's had a few colds, but everyone does. You all used to, and look at you now, strong and fit. Dick will be the same, you'll see. Besides, it's not right for a baby to be separated from his mother.'

'I don't want to give him up, but he isn't thriving here, and he wouldn't be any better in any other house I could afford for us all. I've thought about it until my head's ready to burst, and I know it's the only way. He'll have the sort of life Richard would want for him. How can I face Richard when he comes back and say I was selfish, depriving his son of what should be his?'

John had sunk into one of his blackest moods, hardly speaking for more than a week. When he did it was only to blame himself bitterly for bringing his family to such a pass.

'How on earth shall we know how to go on?' Mary asked fearfully when she saw how implacable Marigold was.

'Mom, it'll be no different from running a house like Old Ridge Court, except we shall be paid a great deal more for doing it!' she had explained.

Mary remained unconvinced. It was too great a risk, it would swallow up all the money Marigold had so unexpectedly acquired. 'We've never done anything like this before, neither Pa's family nor mine,' she said dubiously.

'I don't like it, but I'm a helpless cripple, and you will do what you like with me, drag me all over the country, and I won't be able to object,' John said dolefully, and Marigold wanted to scream with frustration.

She didn't. She told him that the colliery owners were making them move out to provide room for some of the Belgian refugees who were now working in the pits in place of the young men who had preferred to enlist. They would have to find somewhere else anyway.

She won Poppy's support by pointing out that she would no longer have to work for someone else, but if they did well would soon be able to employ others to do the hard work and just supervise them.

Ivy, her eyes on the art college in Birmingham, very close to the Hagley Road, didn't need winning over, and it was, in the end, her enthusiasm which swung Mary into reluctant acceptance. 'I hate leaving Hednesford, it's been home almost all my married life,' she said one evening as they sat round the fire. 'But I mustn't stand in your way. And Ivy will be able to go to drawing classes. Leave Pa to me, I'll persuade him.'

'Mom, you won't regret it, I promise!' Marigold flung her arms round her mother's neck. 'It's the start of a better life for all of us, the chance to get out of this drabness and make more of our lives.'

'Even Pa?'

'Yes, even Pa!' Marigold declared. 'I know he's crippled but he's still alive. He'll be better when he has something to look forward to. He can do his carving; why, he might go to art classes too! And although he has his pals here from the pit, he'd make new friends. He's that sort of man. And in Birmingham there'd be a different sort of people, more like what you wanted us to be long ago when you taught us to speak properly and wouldn't let us copy everyone else.'

'Are you being a snob?' Mary asked.

'No, I honestly don't think so. I like some of the people round here, such as the Taskers, and I heartily disliked some of the people I met at Oxford! But there's nothing wrong with ambition, and wanting to live better is an ambition, like wanting to become foreman or go on the stage and become famous.'

She had prevailed. Even her father became involved in the planning, and as soon as the house was hers they moved in to supervise the necessary alterations.

Now they were ready to open. With Mr Endersby's help they had advertised in the Birmingham papers, as well as the county ones, and this brought several replies.

'I'd advise against permanent guests,' Mr Endersby suggested. 'However much you ask for references there will always be people who prove difficult, and other problems too. After a while they begin to expect privileges and you are not yet experienced enough to face up to that sort of pressure. It may mean you have to advertise more frequently, but you will be able to charge more and people will come back. If you make a few mistakes and lose a few customers, that cannot be helped. Better lose a casual visitor than one who has lived in the hotel for many weeks or months.'

Marigold had been astonished and delighted to find that in her father-in-law, who had always been silent and withdrawn with her in his own home, she had found a friend. He developed a keen interest in her own venture; indeed he confided that to some extent he was bored with the pottery business and would like to try his hand at something else.

'I need a challenge,' he said with an embarrassed laugh. 'But there is one thing you must let me do. Don't object, for it will be an advertisement for me. I shall equip the hotel with Endersby china. It will be a feature: Mrs Endersby the proprietor, with Endersby china in her hotel.'

Marigold immediately saw the value of this and thanked him warmly. 'It will be something for people to talk about. I wonder . . . You make many things other than plates and cups, ordinary tableware. The figurines, for example. Like that marvellous collection you have in the library at The Place. Would you let me have a showcase and sell them?'

'There's no call for such figures now,' Mr Endersby said regretfully. 'But I'll get my designers working on something small, which we can try in single pieces first, and if they are successful we can expand production.'

He had made some decorated plates and mugs, with pictures of Birmingham notables such as the Chamberlains. They occupied pride of place in the entrance hall, in a special cabinet with a discreet price list and a notice explaining they had been specially created for Endersby's Hotel.

'If people believe they are buying something rare they will pay a great deal more for them,' Mr Endersby insisted, and settled on a price Marigold thought outrageously high. She could always reduce it if no one bought, she consoled herself.

Tomorrow they opened the doors to the first guests. Poppy would supervise the kitchens, Mary the bedrooms, while Marigold was in charge of the public rooms. John, surprising himself as much as his family, asked Mr Endersby to show him how to keep accounts, saying it was the only thing he could usefully contribute, and once he grasped the basics of bookkeeping he became surprisingly adept.

For the moment they had only two other staff, a young man invalided out of the army with gas poisoning who was to be porter and waiter, and a girl who would help both in the kitchens and as a chambermaid. Two women came in daily to do the main cleaning.

Marigold was certain, as she looked round, that she had forgotten something. But now it was too late. It was time to go to bed, ready for the day that was to make their fortune.

'Mrs Endersby, I assure you it would give me great pleasure if you allowed me to teach your sister. She has a remarkable talent and so far as I can tell almost totally instinctive. She seems to have had no tuition of merit and it is a wonder, from what she tells me, that her talent was not perverted by ignorant teachers. As for the one she has now, Miss Burton, she is adequate I suppose for the average girl, but not for Ivy!'

Silas Frome stopped talking abruptly, bit a huge chunk out of the slice of fruit cake he held in one hand, and gulped some tea from the cup in the other. Marigold and her mother looked at one another, perplexed.

'I know nothing of the techniques of painting, Mr Frome,' Marigold said slowly. 'You say you teach at the art college? I am hoping to send Ivy there when she is old enough, if she is good enough to be accepted –'

'She's far too good!' he snorted, rudely interrupting. 'She can do more already than some of our prize students. I despair of the general mediocrity but it is the same everywhere. What I am suggesting is that she comes to me for a lesson once a week. Or I will come here if you prefer, although in my own studio I have all my equipment and can do more, obviously. I do not ask for payment,' he added.

Marigold flushed. 'I can afford your fees if you teach Ivy, Mr Frome,' she said sharply.

He smiled suddenly, and at once she found her antagonism melting. He had a charming, almost puckish grin which transformed his face. 'My dear young lady, I did not mean to imply differently! I understand you are in the process of converting this place into a select hotel? I am sure that, with such charming proprietors' – he bowed slightly towards Mary – 'it will be a great success. I meant that I would feel privileged to help Ivy. If you insist on payment, may I ask for a meal in lieu? I detest cooking and am always forgetting to eat. If what comes out of your kitchen is even half as good as these cakes it will be a feast fit for a king. Well, are we agreed? Today is Sunday, but she could come one evening during the winter months, for she must use what free time she has in daylight on her own work. How about Tuesday? I live nearby, just across the Hagley Road, in Ladywood. A shack of a studio, but ideal for me. Naturally one of you must accompany her as a chaperone, for I know artists are regarded as monsters of depravity by ordinary mortals.'

Marigold managed to stem the flow. 'It is so kind of you, and I'm sure Ivy would love to have some lessons –'

'Good, then I will expect you on Tuesday at five o'clock.'

'And perhaps you will come back here for your meal afterwards?' Mary asked faintly.

When Marigold saw that Mr Frome had a ground-floor studio, converted from an old conservatory, ideas began to flow.

Although she had taken a book to read she was intensely bored sitting listening to incomprehensible instructions. All Mr Frome seemed to be doing was showing Ivy how to draw lines and curves, and Marigold considered she already could do that well enough to satisfy the most exacting of tutors. Besides, she was so busy she could not afford the time every week.

She suggested her idea to Mary, who went with Ivy the following week, and then they proposed it to John.

'You have your wheelchair, Pa,' Marigold said. 'It's only a short distance and no steps to negotiate. Ivy can push you there and back and you could enjoy the lessons too. It would help enormously by giving me more time to supervise all the arrangements here.'

John was tempted, for his inactivity bored him and he was terrified he might descend into an even deeper mood of despair and frustration if he did not make some attempt to help himself. He spent his days either in the room which had been converted into a family parlour for them, on the ground floor next to the kitchen, or in the kitchen itself.

Mary added her persuasions after they had gone to bed, hinting she was worried about Marigold. 'She misses little Dick, and she'd maybe feel cheated if things don't work out right here. She's still hoping Richard is alive too, and she occupies herself all day long so as not to dwell on other possibilities. It's bad for her to have time to brood. I wish she would accept that after all this time, almost two years, he won't return alive. Then she could mourn, and get on with her own life.'

Half reluctantly, half intrigued, John took on the task of chaperoning Ivy, and found a great deal of satisfaction in learning for the first time to use his own drawing skills. Silas Frome encouraged him and introduced him to several other artists, and soon John had his own circle of friends and was selling all the wooden carvings he could produce. His spells of silence became shorter and fewer, and Marigold turned with renewed energy to running her hotel.

Chapter Fifteen

'It's going to be a marvellous success!' Lexie exclaimed, looking round the light and airy dining room.

'I hope so,' Marigold said more cautiously. 'We've been almost full all the time after the first two weeks, and people are already booking to come back.'

'Satisfaction. That proves it,' Lexie replied. 'They'll tell their friends, and soon you'll want to expand.'

'I've already had to employ two more staff, Mom and Poppy couldn't cope. Now, what will you have for dessert?'

Later, when they had retired to Marigold's sitting room which she also used as an office, Lexie became more serious.

'You're looking too pale and thin,' she declared bluntly, 'despite your fashionable clothes. I know you've been working hard to get this started, but it's more than that. You're strung up so tightly it's like a violin string about to snap.'

'It's been tough making everyone do the work on time, and I'm not used to directing a large house and a staff,' Marigold defended herself.

'You could do that without a blink,' Lexie opined. 'It's Dick, isn't it? You're missing him.'

Marigold sighed, then reluctantly agreed. 'It hurts more than I ever thought it could,' she confessed. 'I see him every Sunday at The Place, but he's beginning to forget me. He turns to Sophia when he falls over and hurts himself. He isn't quite two yet but I feel I've lost him. Yet what else could I have done? It wasn't right to keep Richard's son in the sort of damp, insanitary house I grew up in. I remember so many children dying. We thought it was normal and we were just lucky because we all survived, but Dick isn't as strong.'

'Darling Marigold, you did your best for him and you had to consider the rest of your family too. You were brave to let Sophia have him.'

'She does love him, more than she ever admits.'

'Sophia's a funny creature, more aristocratic than the bluest-blooded English duke! But underneath she's as soft as a blancmange. She'll care for him.'

'I know, and I'm glad for him, but I miss him so. We were together almost all the time until a few months ago.'

'You miss Richard too, don't you?' Lexie asked softly.

Marigold nodded, her eyes bright with unshed tears. 'It gets worse,' she whispered. 'I thought the pain would grow less in time, duller. But it's worse than ever, particularly when I think Richard is missing seeing Dick as a baby. He won't know him when he comes home. He probably doesn't even know he has a son.'

Lexie regarded her sadly. 'Do you still hope Richard is alive?' she asked gently.

'I don't hope, I know he is!' Marigold insisted. 'He's somewhere, and he's unable to let me know where, but he'll come back in the end. It isn't possible he won't. I'd know if he were dead,' she added more quietly. 'I think I'd die too if I knew he was dead. And I would know, Lexie, don't think I'm just feeding on hope. Richard and I – it was so perfect! I'd *know*,' she repeated with absolute confidence.

'It's the only thing that keeps her going,' Lexie said later to her husband. 'I'm afraid for her, either when we get news that he's dead, or when the years go by without us knowing for certain. She'll end up in Burntwood Asylum. No one can stand the sort of strain she's under without cracking.'

'Marigold has a strength none of us appreciate,' Archie said thoughtfully. 'That was partly the attraction she had for Richard, I suspect. His mother is strong and so is he. He responded to it in her, although she was so young when they met. You say the hotel is flourishing?'

'Yes. She has all sorts of people staying. There are some who are visiting the cathedral, on church business, or the university, or come on civic matters. It's in a good position: out of the main city centre and fairly quiet, yet near everything. And she is beginning to build up a regular clientele of commercial travellers, the better sort who can afford her prices. They will be one of the mainstays of her business, I suspect.'

'We shall have to stay there ourselves if we turn the rest of the house over to the army,' Archie commented. 'Have you finished packing up your clothes?'

'I'm giving most of them away. I can't wear evening dresses while I'm working in London, and by the end of the war they'll all be hopelessly out of date. They can have our rooms now as well as the others. Mrs Glover is coping marvellously. We can go back tomorrow but I'd like to see Marigold again before we catch the train.'

Early on the following morning they entered the hotel to find Marigold talking to an army officer in the foyer. He was tall, fair-haired, and ruggedly handsome. The scar on his cheek added to rather than detracted from his bold good looks.

Seeing them waiting he flashed them an apologetic smile, and took what was an obviously reluctant farewell of Marigold. Saluting smartly, he swung on his heel and left, a small valise in his hand.

'A guest?' Lexie asked as Marigold turned to greet them.

'Yes, he's been several times. A Captain Thomas. He's working on some sort of liaison, with the gun manufacturers, I think, but I'm not sure what. He has to travel a great deal and he says he can't tolerate mess food,' Marigold said rather abruptly.

She seemed rather flushed and Lexie was unable to decide whether it was from embarrassment or anger. The handsome Captain seemed to have been making his admiration too obvious, but did it annoy Marigold or flatter her?

Lexie had been convinced Richard must be dead until Marigold's utter confidence made her admit, reluctantly, that there might still be hope. Of course she wanted Richard to come back alive, she thought in some confusion, but more than that she wanted the uncertainty to be over. Seeing the Captain's attitude to Marigold made her realize that other men might want to court her friend, and Marigold would be placed in an impossible dilemma. Even if she came to love one of them, could she ever marry again? At the moment her love was all for Richard, but she was still very young, and would not want to spend all her life alone. Having lost Dick to his grandmother she might crave other children.

Lexie sighed and thrust the problem out of her mind. She only just had time to say goodbye before she left for London.

Richard vented some of his frustration on the logs he was chopping. It was already April, and it would be a couple more weeks before he could leave the Müller farm and travel home.

It had been a winter of horror and frustration worse than any he had known. The scenery in this remote Swiss valley was spectacular: incredibly beautiful with the soaring mountains in the distance; the deep crisp clean snow; and the sturdy evergreen trees covering the lower slopes with their dark, mysterious shades. But within the small old farmhouse everything seemed to have gone wrong.

In the first place his exertions had brought about a relapse, and for several weeks he had been too ill to move far. Even if he had been able to ski he could not have reached the nearest town with a railway, some twenty miles away.

The cold mountain air seemed to have an invigorating effect on him later, however, and he gradually recovered his strength. By Christmas he was able to chop wood for the voracious stoves which kept the house warm, and go out to shoot game, supplementing their diet of dried and smoked meat with the occasional fresh rabbit or partridge, and even venison.

Herr Müller had been more seriously injured than any of them had supposed. His leg was mending slowly, but the concussion seemed to have affected his wits. He had no recollection of events of the last twenty years, and thought Frau Müller was his mother.

The strain of nursing both her husband and Richard, with only the assistance of the willing, but not particularly bright Inge, finally told on even the indomitable Frau Müller. At the beginning of February her heart failed and within hours, despite all Richard could do, she was dead.

'What shall I do on my own?' Inge wailed piteously.

'We must look after your uncle,' Richard said patiently. 'When the thaw comes we'll be able to take him to the town and get professional help.'

And also bury Frau Müller properly, he thought, but didn't voice this worry. He had been able to scratch a pitifully shallow grave in the cultivated vegetable patch of the garden, and had covered it with all the small rocks he could collect, but every day he dreaded seeing that marauding animals might have dug through to the body. He hadn't been able to go and see what had happened to the truck driver's corpse, but he guessed it would no longer be there.

Inge, instead of helping, had taken to her own bed in a frenzy of despair and terror. Richard felt a weight of responsibility. He knew the accident to the truck and Herr Müller's injury had not been in any way his fault. Indeed if he hadn't been there Inge could not have brought her uncle back to the farm on her own, or they might all have gone over a cliff at the next bend in the road. He nevertheless was grateful to Frau Müller for her nursing of him, and could scarcely abandon her bedridden husband and distraught niece to themselves.

Gradually he induced Inge to do the cooking and housework. Most of his time was spent searching for wood. He began to question Herr Müller's competence when he realized the stack of wood under the deep overhanging roof would not last much beyond the end of February.

'Where is the wood you were fetching the day we met?' he asked one evening as they sat over a surprisingly appetizing stew. At least when she put her mind to it Inge could cook, he reflected gratefully.

'What wood? Oh, yes, I remember. We can't fetch it now, we can't use the cart.'

'There's a sled in the hut behind the house,' he pointed out patiently. 'Could the horse pull that?'

'Oh, yes, of course. I didn't think. But you can't ski. The snow's too deep to walk through.'

'I'm learning, slowly,' he replied. 'There's a pair of short skis which I think must be used for walking on, like snowshoes. I can manage on them quite well, but I can't bring a lot of wood back without some sort of cart or the sled.'

'Why do you want to bother? There's plenty outside, and soon Uncle Friedrich will be able to get some more.'

'There's only enough for a couple of weeks,' he told her bluntly. 'And Uncle Friedrich won't be able to walk again for a couple of months at the very least. He isn't even trying to walk with that crutch I made for him.'

'Poor Uncle Friedrich!'

She began to cry softly, and Richard ground his teeth together in order to stop himself speaking sharply to her. Poor child, she was simply unable to face the disasters of her life with any courage.

He thought of Marigold, and wished as he did a hundred times a day she were here with him. She would not give in so feebly. She would be devising ways of making life easier, always cheerful and always loving.

Soon, though, the thaw would come, they could get out of this valley and he could resume his journey home. At long last he would be able to hold Marigold once more, kiss her dear face and hear her beloved voice.

He tried out the sled, and with some urging the horse ploughed through the snow. They brought back, painfully slowly, small loads of wood, just enough to keep them going.

He would have to go to the nearest village as soon as the tracks were passable and try to discover where and what sort of help was available. He could also, he hoped, send a letter home. Only a few more days, but each one dragged more than the early months had done, every hour seemed longer.

He occupied the evenings writing to Marigold, explaining the reasons for the inordinate delay in contriving his escape. He poured out his love for her, promising tenderly that once they were reunited he would make up to her for all the unhappiness she must have suffered.

Inge sat and talked to her uncle, by now thoroughly confused after his wife's death. He mourned her as his mother and thought Inge was his sister, which was distressing for the child as his real sister, her own mother, had died five years ago.

Each night Richard went to his lonely bed praying for the thaw to come, to release him from this smothering white prison of snow and obligation.

Poppy paced nervously up and down the platform waiting for the train. She was wearing her new tweed costume with a belted, military style jacket and short, ankle-length box-pleated skirt. She also had a small fur-trimmed hat and dashing, buttoned gaiters over her shoes. At last, she thought with satisfaction, there was money for new clothes, and Marigold was generous, insisting they all dressed smartly.

George was coming on leave and spending a couple of days with her. More accurately he was staying in the hotel. She hadn't told her family about him and had been able to conceal their correspondence.

'Why are you so secretive?' he'd asked in one letter when she'd admitted they didn't know about him.

'I suppose it's silly,' she replied, 'but I can't help being superstitious. My dog Scrap died, and he was the only thing that had really been mine. I feel that anything I value will be lost to me. Besides, Ivy will be jealous. She made a tremendous fuss when Marigold got married even though she'd already left home. Everyone was deserting her, she said. I couldn't bear to have her constantly complaining while we wait for the war to end, and until we're old enough to get married.'

She hugged her secret to herself. George had written as often as he could, and since the waiting in the trenches was so incredibly tedious, and the men had little to do when they were off duty, she received a lot of letters.

Fortunately she could hide them from the rest of her family. The hotel received many letters and she had taken over the task of opening and sorting them.

George had proposed at Christmas, by letter, and this was the first time she had seen him since. She was both excited and shy.

> Despite the dreadful losses on the Somme [he had written], we are doing better. We've brought down the Zeppelins at home, and with Lloyd George now Prime Minister the war will be fought a little more vigorously, as everyone out here wants. It would not surprise us if the Germans sued for peace soon.

The peace proposals had been rejected, and Germany had turned their submarines, the much-feared U-boats, on to non-combatants. That had brought the Americans into the war just a few days earlier. With their fresh armies the war would be over within weeks, people said. Poppy would soon be able to plan her marriage.

She was tremulously happy. Here was someone who wanted her for herself. She did not have to compete with Marigold, always so capable and in charge. She didn't have to defer to Ivy, because she was the youngest and had suffered from the burns when she was a baby, so that everyone felt sorry for her. She would have her own house at last as she had dreamed all those years ago. George was a gentleman, so she would be looked after, she would always wear smart clothes and not have to work.

Of course she loved George. He admired her, he was handsome, and so different from the boys she'd known in Hednesford. A sudden remembrance of Sam Bannister's slobbering attempts to kiss her made her shudder involuntarily. That had been horrid. Poor Sam, though. He'd died a week or so after arriving in France.

The train came puffing in, putting a stop to her reflections. Lots of people were hanging out of the windows waving to friends, and Poppy saw George near the front of the train.

He opened the door and leapt down before the train fully stopped, and ran to catch her to him. 'Poppy! Oh, my darling Poppy! You can't believe how much I've missed you!'

He was swinging her round in excitement and she put her hands on his shoulders to steady herself. 'George!' was all she could say. Her voice seemed to have vanished.

He smiled, gently took her face in his hands and kissed her on the lips. 'Darling Poppy, that's the first time I've kissed you properly!' he said wonderingly. 'In my dreams I've kissed you so often. I feel I know you so well, but I've never kissed you properly before!'

She was blushing and laughing, clinging unashamedly to him. She loved him so much, he was hers and he wanted her. Life was wonderful.

'We'd better go to the hotel,' she said breathlessly.

'Have you told them about me?' he asked.

Poppy shook her head. 'No, I was – well, I explained to you, I'm superstitious. I don't want anything to happen to you, and when I love something it always seems like a bad omen!'

'But if they don't know how can we spend time together?'

'It would be difficult inside the hotel, but I'm having a few days off. Marigold said I could, we've worked so hard for the last two months. We can go for walks, get a train somewhere, or we could borrow bicycles and go out into the country. There's lots to see.'

'I wanted to buy you a ring,' George said. 'I can't do that unless I have your father's permission.'

Poppy was tempted. What a thrill it would be to flaunt a lovely ring. None of her friends had yet become engaged. She would be the first and the envy of them all when she explained what George was. But caution and an irrational stab of fear made her shake her head.

'Not just yet. I want you all to myself before we start discussing practical details,' she pleaded.

'You're not having second thoughts now you've seen me again?' he asked quickly.

'No! Of course not, George! I love you, I said I did in my letters and it's true.'

'Until my next leave then? Before next Christmas, I hope. Who knows, perhaps by then the war will be over!'

It was an enchanted two days for Poppy. They walked in the parks, rode bicycles around the nearby countryside, sat on the banks of the canal and talked until the chill spring air made them move on. They kissed under the shelter of the willows, hidden by the bright fresh foliage as the yellowy-green leaves burst into abundant life.

All too soon it was over and George had to return for the last few days of his leave with his parents. 'Next time we'll get properly engaged,' he said firmly. 'I want to shout my love to everyone; tell them what a lucky chap I am to have your love.'

Ivy was disgruntled. Silas Frome had gone to London for a few weeks and her lessons with him had stopped for a while. She had been doing, under his direction, several small drawings of the buildings about the city centre, and he had promised to sell them for her. But he wasn't here and she was impatient.

She was dawdling on her way home from school, for this was the day she would normally have gone for her lesson. Now she was uncertain what to do.

'Miss Ivy? I thought it was you!'

She turned round, puzzled, to see an elderly woman hurrying after her.

'I'm Mrs Glover, probably you don't remember me,' the woman said. 'Mrs Cranworth's housekeeper.'

'Yes, of course,' Ivy said politely. She could always recall faces, even if not the names which went with them.

'This letter came.' Mrs Glover fumbled in her capacious shopping bag. 'It's got a foreign stamp. I was going to take it round to Mrs Endersby, but you can save me a journey. I'm that busy nowadays with the house turned over to the officers, I don't have a spare minute.'

'Yes, of course I'll take it,' Ivy smiled at her and after a few polite questions about Marigold and the rest of the family Mrs Glover departed.

Ivy looked at the envelope curiously. Who on earth could be writing to Marigold from Switzerland? Surely the fame of her hotel hadn't spread that far yet? But it was far too thick a missive for a simple query about accommodation.

She continued on up Church Road into the Hagley Road. So absorbed was she in puzzling over the letter, she almost walked into a young man carrying a large flat parcel.

'Hello, Ivy,' he said cheerfully.

'Herbie. Hello.'

'Are you on your way to Mr Frome's?'

'No, he's in London,' Ivy said, her original cause for discontent resurfacing.

'Is he? Then I can use his studio. Good, I've been wanting to finish off the portrait of old Mrs Tucker. You know, the grocer's wife.'

'The one you're doing with her dressed up in Tudor costume?' Ivy asked, intrigued. 'Mr Frome told me.'

'Yes, just because they have a Tudor house near Alcester and he thinks it would be appropriate.'

'Does Mr Frome let you use his studio?' Ivy asked enviously.

'He lets a few of the senior class at the art school use it, but only when he doesn't want it himself. I know where he puts the spare key, and I could work on it now, but the problem is I haven't got a model.'

'I thought it was of Mrs Tucker?'

'Yes, but I've done the face and the hands, now I need to fill in the dress. Anyone could sit for me dressed in that.' He looked at her speculatively. 'Would you do it for me?'

'Me?' Ivy was wary. It might involve showing her scars, and no one in Birmingham, she was sure, knew about them.

'She's quite small and you'd be sitting down. It's just so as to get the folds right. They never look the same unless someone's wearing the dress. Come on, Ivy. Just for an hour?'

'What's the dress like?'

'Tudor dresses are very stiff, with ruffs round the neck and those pointed waists.'

Suddenly Ivy made up her mind. She wanted to mix with other artists, if only to display her own superior skill, but Mr Frome said she did not need to go to the art college even when she was old enough. She had met Herbie and a few other students at the studio on several occasions. Now she would sit for him.

She almost forgot the letter until Herbie put his brushes down and began clearing away. While she was changing back into her own clothes behind the screen she found it in her pocket, and curiosity consumed her. Carefully she eased up the flap, which was quite loose. She saw the beginning, 'My darling Marigold,' and with a sickening lurch of her heart turned over the many pages and read the ending, 'Ever yours, my dearest love, Richard'.

After all these years, during which she had got Marigold back with them, as well as money and a lovely house – even if they did have to share it with hotel guests – he was going to come back and spoil it all. Marigold would go away again, they'd probably have to move back to a horrid little house in Hednesford, and she would lose her lessons with Mr Frome.

'Have you finished? I must lock up now,' Herbie called, and Ivy thrust the letter into her pocket.

'Will you come again tomorrow?' Herbie asked. 'I still have quite a bit to do.'

'If you like,' Ivy said listlessly. 'What time? After school?'

'I may be a bit later. Look, I'll show you where Mr Frome keeps the spare key, then if I'm late you can let yourself in and get changed ready for me.'

Ivy nodded, watched where he hid the key, and set off for home. As she went an idea came to her. She must read the letter first before giving it to Marigold, and then she would know what had happened to Richard. It wasn't safe to read it at home, for someone might come in. She would creep back to the studio where she would have privacy.

Ten minutes later she was letting herself in and locking the door behind her. It was still daylight, and she sat by the window and pulled the many sheets of paper out of the envelope. She read them grimly, wondering why Richard had survived all those calamities, any of which could so easily have killed him. And now all he waited for was Marigold to arrange to send him money for the journey home.

Within days, a week, he could be here and her life destroyed. He would take Marigold away as he had before, and she would no longer love Ivy best.

Ivy raged against a cruel fate that had kept Richard alive when so many of their other friends had been killed. She didn't want him here. She wouldn't have him. Somehow she would stop him coming.

Having made that decision she became calmer. She looked round for somewhere to hide the letter, and in the end stuffed it into the depths of a wickerwork hamper in which Mr Frome kept various lengths of cloth he used for draping the throne. She would miss school on the following day and come here to plan what she must do. On the way into the hotel she went into Marigold's office, which was empty, and took a sheet of the handsome headed notepaper and some envelopes. Hurrying upstairs she decided that a bilious attack would be the safest excuse. On reaching her room Ivy sat down and hastily wrote a note to Miss Dawson to explain her absence the following day, copying her mother's writing. It wasn't the first time she had adopted this ruse to escape from school.

Ivy sealed the note, went out once more, and ran swiftly to the school in Church Road. It would be quite safe to put the note through the letterbox tonight, for once the school was closed no one looked there until the morning.

By the following morning, when she let herself into the studio again, she had made her plans. She had with her a supply of writing paper and various other items, including the copy she had once made of the letter in Sophia's writing.

She had thought very carefully about what she needed to do. Richard had said in his letter that he wouldn't write to his mother until he heard from Marigold whether they had begun to treat her properly. If she wrote a letter as if from Sophia it might prevent Richard from contacting them. This was essential because she was going to tell him Marigold and his child were dead. Then he would never come back and wreck her life.

'This is wonderful, Marigold! You've made it so elegant. Johnny will be amazed when he sees it!'

'Thank you, Lucy. When's he coming home on leave next? And how are you?'

'He hopes to be here in the summer. They're having leave every six months if possible, but I pray the war will be over very soon. Little Jack hardly knows his father, and now – well, Johnny was here just after Christmas, and I'm having another child.'

Marigold was honestly delighted for her sister-in-law, but she was surprised to feel a fierce pang of jealousy consume her as she thought of holding another baby in her arms. That would not be until Richard came home. If then, she thought, desolation in her heart. He must be seriously wounded, perhaps helpless, not to have found a way of contacting her all this time. Even when he did come home he might be an invalid or a cripple like her father.

They might not be able to have more children. Then she chided herself. She'd had Dick. Richard had never seen him, not known the infinite joys of each tiny new thing the miracle of a baby learnt.

Firmly Marigold pushed these gloomy thoughts away and concentrated on what Lucy was telling them. Then the child Jack was left with his adoring grandparents while Marigold took Lucy on a tour of the hotel.

'I do admire you,' Lucy said sincerely. 'It looks both friendly and efficient as well as terribly superior.'

'Good. That's what I aimed at,' Marigold said. 'One of those is no good without the others. Birmingham has some very big, grand hotels, and lots of small ones, but nothing in between. I couldn't have done any of it without Mr Endersby's help, or Richard's money.'

'Will you keep it on when Richard comes home?'

Marigold blessed her sister-in-law. Lucy was the only one who believed Richard was alive and spoke of it as a normal event, to be expected, that he would come home one day soon.

'That depends on what he wants. It's his money, after all,' she replied.

'But I've no doubt you're increasing it!' Lucy suggested, smiling.

'I've already had an offer to buy me out or go into partnership,' Marigold said with a pleased laugh. 'I can't believe it, we've been open for only a few months.'

'Who is this?

Marigold flushed slightly. 'It was actually an army captain. His family own hotels in Worcester and Northampton. He came here to stay, came back twice more, and on the last occasion he said we might perhaps do business.'

Lucy was aware of Marigold's heated cheeks. 'Was he impertinent?' she asked sharply.

'No. No, of course not. Why on earth should you think he was?'

'You seem agitated.'

'It was nothing. No, that's not true. I can tell you, Lucy. You're to be trusted. You'll understand.'

'Of course.'

Marigold smiled gratefully at her. 'He was just flattering. He admired me. Not the hotel or what I've built up here, although he did praise them too, but me as a person. I knew it although he was perfectly correct. I haven't noticed it before with anyone. It's a look in their eyes; an expression you can't define. I know he liked me and, Lucy, it was as if I'd been unfaithful to Richard!'

'Do you like this captain?'

'Yes, but not at all in the same way as I do Richard. It's laughable, as if I could ever feel the same about anyone else! But he was pleasant, polite, and he admired me. I didn't want his admiration, I felt threatened. Do you understand what I mean?'

Lucy nodded. 'I hear lots of women talking about the temptations when their men are away for a long time. They miss them, and some of the weaker ones confuse that with missing any man. I expect you're afraid of yourself, but you needn't fear, Marigold. You love Richard and you're strong. No one will come between you unless you want them to.'

'Thank you, Lucy. I'm not surprised Johnny loves you. It does me a great deal of good to talk to you. I just wish you lived in Birmingham.'

'Then I'd get on your nerves! No, Longbridge is my home, and unless Johnny wants to move that's where I'll stay. His old job is waiting for him when he comes back and he's already making plans. I hope it's soon.'

'So do I. I long for this awful slaughter to finish, and for us all to be happy again.'

'Happiness is God-given, Marigold. You and I have the capacity to receive it, I believe, but at times I wonder if Poppy and Ivy have. Forgive me for speaking to you like this about your sisters, but there are occasions when they worry me.'

'I know what you mean, but Poppy seems more content these days. She has a sort of glow about her.'

'She may be in love.'

'Poppy? But she's only sixteen!'

'How old were you when you met Richard?'

Marigold laughed ruefully. 'Fifteen! Younger, I know, but I felt much older. Not in dealings with boys, never that. I'd hardly thought about it. But I'd been looking after the house and the others for so long when Mom was out at work, I don't think I ever considered myself a child. Poppy's different, surely? She didn't grow up so fast.'

'We all grow up fast when necessary,' Lucy said drily. 'I guarantee Poppy produces a man before long. You'd best be prepared for it.'

It was a thick letter, but not Marigold's writing. Richard felt a tremor of unease as he stared at the packet from England.

By now some of the roads were open and Inge had fetched their neighbours, two sturdy brothers named Dieter and Helmut, to help. They lived a mile away, but across a couple of deep ravines which made communication impossible during the snows. A track similar to the one leading to the Müllers's house led from further along the main road to their farm and it was now open.

Horrified at the tale they were told, they had helped Richard bury Frau Müller decently, removed the pitiful remains of the truck driver's body, then took Inge to shop for stores, because some items were running dangerously low. She brought back the letter, a reply to the one Richard dispatched two weeks ago when he'd ventured to the village on skis for the first time.

'From England. You are going to leave me alone,' Inge said dolefully and began to weep big, slow tears. 'How will I manage without you? Uncle Friedrich is helpless! We can't take him to the hospital until the pass is open.'

'We'll arrange something,' Richard said soothingly. 'I must read my letter.'

Without apology he left her and went into his bedroom. He dared not open the letter except when he was alone. The premonition of disaster on seeing that unfamiliar handwriting was too strong.

He tore the envelope and found two letters, one on thick wove paper, wrapped round with the other, written on a sheet of cheap paper torn from a school exercise book.

With trembling fingers he separated them and with a shock recognized his mother's writing. He glanced at the signature on the other sheet. 'Mary Smith'.

Richard sat down heavily on the chair. His mother's letter fell unheeded on to the table before him, and he sat with the other sheet clutched convulsively in his hands. For a full minute he could not summon up the courage to turn the letter over and read it. His mind was numb, refusing to recognize the disaster this must mean. He was aware only of an unbearable weight pressing down on him, a blackness before his eyes, a need to crawl into some subterranean place and hide from whatever menace threatened him.

Eventually, his movements slow and precise, yet still clumsy as if there were no feeling in his fingers, he turned over the sheet of paper.

Dear Mr Endersby,

I am very sorry to have to tell you this, but I am afraid your wife, our Marigold, died giving birth to your baby in May 1915. The baby also died, I am sorry to say. Marigold had been very sick during her last months; partly, I truly believe, because of the way your parents treated her. First they asked her to go and stay at their big house, and then when she would not agree to give them the child they – well, I'd rather not say, but it was very bad the way they treated her. But she came home to us ill and already in labour, and it was plain to all of us that she was past caring whether she lived or died. There was nothing the midwife could do for her, although we had the best, we really did, sir.

We thought you were dead as reported, and though they didn't treat our Marigold properly I thought it only right to inform your parents that you were alive when your letter to Marigold was sent on to us from Birmingham. I know things weren't well between you, and you said in your letter (which we had to read, sir, please forgive us, and we are grateful to you that you loved our Marigold so much, but we wouldn't have read the letter otherwise) you wouldn't write to them until you heard from our Marigold, so I thought it only right to tell them that we had heard from you. Your mother wrote back to me and I enclose the letter for you to see. I do not want it back. To think any woman could behave like that to her own flesh and blood defies belief, it really does, but I should not speak ill of my betters.

We are moving from Hednesford shortly to go and live with one of my sisters, and I think that it would be better for you not to reply to this letter, all things considered, because although we know you loved Marigold it brought her nothing but misfortune to mix above her class. It is best for us all to try and forget and not be reminded of unhappy times.

I remain, sir,
Your servant,
Mrs Mary Smith

Richard stared down at the paper, and then his hands began to tremble. Slowly at first, then more rapidly, until the shaking spread to his whole body. Suddenly, fiercely, he reached for the letter from Sophia, lying ignored on the table in front of him. It was short and to the point.

Dear Mrs Smith,

Both my sons are dead. Henry died in the trenches, and Richard was dead to me when he was stolen by your daughter. I will see neither of them ever again.

I remain,
Yours very sincerely,
Sophia Endersby

Both letters fluttered to the floor and Richard sat still, incapable of movement or thought. He was for a while a mere vessel for a turmoil of feelings: anger, despair, regret, and above all an insufferable agony of loss.

When feeling returns to a numbed extremity, there is pain. As thought returned to Richard's mind, there was a mental anguish that seemed about to split his head asunder. He could not encompass, could not comprehend, such torture.

All this time, he'd been apart from his love. For two and a half years he had striven patiently against war, injury, sickness, and danger in order to return to her. But she was no more.

How had he not known? That was the first coherent thought in his mind. With such love as theirs, surely if one of them died the other must feel the wrenching pain of the loss? It should have been like losing a part of oneself. Instead there had been nothing, He'd even felt hope and happiness and joy. These were emotions he now could not even recognize, could not remember what they were like. He would never experience any of them again.

Two hours later Inge crept into the room and exclaimed in dismay when she saw Richard still sitting rigidly in the chair.

'Richard, is it bad news?' she asked timidly.

He didn't hear, and she approached cautiously and laid her hand on his arm.

'Richard?' she said again.

She stepped back in alarm as he turned slowly towards her. His face was ravaged, suddenly much older, but the look in his eyes terrified her. It was far worse than the petrified look in a rabbit's eyes when the dog had snatched it.

'What is it?' she persisted.

She had no experience of such emotion. Her only instinct was to talk and touch and gentle a frightened creature, which she recognized Richard was, as she would a petrified bird.

At last he responded. In a voice which seemed rusty with disuse he spoke.

'My wife is dead.'

Inge knew there was nothing she could say. She stood beside him and cradled his head against her breast, feeling the rigidity of his entire body. Slow, painful tears oozed out of his eyes and slid down his cheeks unheeded.

When her arms were stiff with holding him he gradually relaxed, and then took a deep breath. 'Thank you, child. I'm sorry.'

'No, I'm sorry,' she protested. 'Is there anything I can do?'

'Burn those letters!' he said harshly. 'I want no reminder, and I could not touch them again!'

'Who are they from?' she exclaimed, surprised.

'My mother, and my wife's mother. My wife and child are dead! And neither of them even thought to tell me how long the child lived! Or even if it was a son . . .' he added wonderingly. 'I shall never know.'

'You'll know when you go to heaven,' Inge said composedly. 'You'll be with them there, like we'll be with Aunt Gertrude and Mutti and Papa.'

He stared at her in astonishment. She had such a simple, certain faith, and it was comforting. 'I shall, shan't I?' he said. 'What time is it? How long have I been sitting here?'

'It's time for Uncle Friedrich's exercises, and then I'll cook dinner.'

He dragged himself back to the routine of the house, fetching wood, building up the fires, and making all secure in the outhouses.

After supper, during which neither of them had spoken very much, and Uncle Friedrich had been settled for the night, Inge looked doubtfully at Richard. 'What will you do? Will you leave me here alone now?' she asked anxiously.

Richard had not even considered beyond his present tasks. He glanced around the bright, cheerful room. He thought of the snow-covered slopes outside, invisible now through the sturdy shutters, and the first signs of spring which had followed the thaw.

It was beautiful here; there were no problems but those of day-by-day survival.

'I'll stay with you until Uncle Friedrich gets better.'

Chapter Sixteen

THE year of 1918 brought both joy and sorrow. As the peace negotiations took place and the survivors emerged from the horrors of modern warfare, there were unparalleled scenes of rejoicing across England.

Those men who were maimed and scarred, depending on their philosophy either thanked God for their lives at least, or cursed the misfortune which had put their face or their leg in the way of that particular shell or piece of shrapnel.

Marigold planned a gala evening to celebrate the armistice at her hotel, by now one of the most famous in Birmingham.

And then, two weeks before the date, Ivy succumbed to the influenza epidemic which was sweeping across Europe. Mary insisted on nursing her, saying Marigold was far too busy, and anyway she didn't want to risk either Marigold or Poppy being infected.

Poppy was ill the following day, however, and then John, who had insisted on sitting with Ivy while Mary rested, became ill too.

They all appeared to be recovering when Mary herself was stricken. Lucy immediately left her son and daughter with Mrs Kelly and came to Edgbaston to help Marigold nurse her parents.

'Mom is much the worst,' Marigold said worriedly a few days later. 'The others are nearly better, but she's so ill I'm scared. Pa wants to go and see her. Do you think he should?'

'It might help her, and surely he's almost better now?' Lucy replied.

'He would have been in already except he can't get upstairs on his own.'

'I'll find a couple of men to carry up his chair,' Lucy said. 'You go and get him ready.'

John was not in his room, although his wheelchair stood beside his bed. Had someone come and carried him? It had never happened before; he refused all except the absolutely essential help, determined to be as independent as possible.

Marigold went to her mother's room, and halted, aghast, as she opened the door.

John had somehow managed to drag himself along and climb the stairs, and was now struggling to clamber on to the bed where Mary lay. Before Marigold could rush to help him he succeeded, collapsing with a grunt beside his wife.

Mary was conscious, but unable to move. She smiled faintly as John took her gently in his arms and kissed her lingeringly on the lips. They were so absorbed they didn't see Marigold, who dared not move in case she disturbed them.

'I love you so much, and I've just been a burden these last few years,' John whispered. 'I meant to do so much for you. Please forgive me, love, and don't leave me. I can't manage without you.'

Tears were streaming down his cheeks, and Mary, with a great effort, lifted her hand and wiped them away. 'You've been the best husband ever,' she managed to say before her hand fell back and she closed her eyes.

They lay there, entwined, and with infinite care Marigold closed the door. She was leaning against the doorpost, silently weeping, when Lucy found her.

'What is it? Is she worse?' Lucy demanded.

'Hush! No, come away!'

Marigold went to sit on the window seat of a large bay window overlooking the main road, and described what she had seen to Lucy.

'Your pa climbed these stairs on his own? But he hasn't moved without the wheelchair for years!'

'He loved her so much.' And perhaps thought he might never see her again, she added silently.

'God must have helped him. But what should we do?'

'Leave them alone. It's all we can do for them. I'll take them both some food later.'

When she hesitantly knocked on the door two hours later Mary was dead, cradled in John's arms. He offered no resistance when they carried him down to his own room, but refused either to eat or speak. Marigold sat with him that night as he lay staring up at the ceiling, then as dawn neared he turned his head towards her.

His voice was strange, cracked and hoarse. 'I've been the most fortunate man alive, with Mary and her children,' he said haltingly. 'God bless you, love.'

They were his last words. He had no more will to live, and by evening he too was dead.

'They're together,' Lucy comforted Marigold. 'They loved one another very much. How are Poppy and Ivy this evening?'

'Both beginning to recover, thank goodness. I could not bear it if either of them died.'

There was a light tap on the door and Joan, the receptionist, came into Marigold's office cum sitting room.

'Mrs Endersby, I'm sorry, I know you don't want to be disturbed but the Colonel's here. He asked if you could spare him a moment.'

'Yes of course. Show him in, Joan.'

'Shall I go?'

'There's no need, Lucy.'

Colonel – once Captain – Thomas, as handsome as ever, came swiftly into the room. He smiled briefly at Lucy but went straight to Marigold and took both her hands in his.

'My dear Marigold, I've just heard. I am so very sorry. Your parents were both wonderful people and will be sorely missed.'

'Bill! Oh, Bill!'

Marigold, who had remained rigidly calm and dry-eyed since the first shock of comprehending her father's determination to be with his wife, and had coped grimly but sympathetically with Poppy's sobs and Ivy's wild hysterics, suddenly collapsed. Before Lucy's eyes she crumbled, and as the Colonel sat down beside her and gathered her into his arms, she wept.

Lucy signed to him that she would go, and crept out of the room. Marigold's unyielding composure had been unnatural. It would be good for her to weep. And Colonel Thomas seemed to be perfectly capable of offering comfort. Lucy went to see if there was anything she could do about the hotel.

It was so well organized, she discovered, that despite half the staff being struck down with the influenza there was little sign of anything untoward happening. Of course many of the bookings had been cancelled and there were fewer guests than normal for the staff to deal with, but Lucy was impressed with this evidence of Marigold's flair for business.

An hour later Marigold emerged, calm and dry-eyed once more. She came to find Lucy and say she had invited Bill Thomas to dine with them in the private parlour.

'He stays here often?' Lucy asked. 'He seems a very pleasant man.'

Marigold cast her a faint smile.

'He's a good friend, Lucy, although he's still badgering me to go into partnership!'

'Are you tempted?'

'No. Especially now. I could not bear to be without work. It stops me thinking. Now it will be more necessary than ever.'

Although Lucy still publicly accepted Marigold's belief that Richard was alive somewhere, privately she considered that they must have heard by now if he were. The next few months should be decisive. If he were a prisoner, but for some reason unidentified, surely with the ending of the war he would be discovered? Similarly, if he were hiding away from the Germans somewhere behind the lines, he would now be able to come back. If he did not, Marigold must accept the probability of his death.

Bill stayed for two weeks and quietly, almost without her noticing, relieved Marigold of the pressures of running the hotel while she dealt with the funeral arrangements. He supervised the gala evening which Marigold, although she did not attend, refused to cancel.

'It is not any business of my guests that I have been bereaved,' she insisted. 'It is my business to provide them with what has been promised.'

She became absorbed in work and continued to provide for the guests' requirements so effectively that less than a year after John and Mary died she opened a second hotel in Wolverhampton.

'Why are you calling it "Endersby's"? It should be "Smith's",' Ivy complained when Marigold took them to see the newly completed building.

'Marigold's name is Endersby,' Poppy said sharply.

'And it's Richard's money. I feel I'm doing something for him,' Marigold said quietly.

'For his memory?'

'No, for him. He will return one day,' Marigold insisted without heat. She was used to Ivy's frequent questions about why she didn't accept Richard was dead.

'He must be or he'd have come home by now. He would if he loved you as much as you say he did,' Ivy said once, and Marigold turned away to hide the hurt she felt at Ivy's cruel remark.

She was the only one who clung to her conviction that Richard was still alive somewhere. Even Lucy now had doubts. Sophia had never believed it, and despite Marigold's wishes taught little Dick that his father had gone to heaven to be with the angels. She didn't know what Richard's father thought. As usual, except in matters of business, where he was still very supportive of her, he kept his thoughts and feelings hidden.

Bill Thomas, no longer in a colonel's uniform, had on two occasions recently asked her to marry him.

'I respect your hopes that Richard might be alive still,' he said the second time. 'It looks increasingly unlikely, however, and it would be a wicked waste for you to spend your life alone.'

'Alone, with dozens of guests and all the staff as well as Poppy and Ivy?' she asked, smiling slightly.

'It is not at all the same,' he said sternly, and she nodded in wry agreement.

She and Richard had had just a few days of married bliss, of being together and loving one another. She had no idea what it would be like to live as his wife for months, years, a lifetime. She was certain, however, that she did not wish to live as anyone else's wife, although she was quite fond of Bill in a gentle, undemanding way. He was kind, helpful, and understood her business problems. But he wasn't Richard.

'I could never marry anyone else if I were not totally certain Richard were dead,' she said, trying to soften her refusal.

'It must be assumed after a time, there are ways of obtaining legal presumption of death,' he informed her.

'But I don't want to assume he's dead!' she said, impatient at last with this one streak of insensitivity in him.

Bill had not mentioned it again, but Marigold knew it would be only a few weeks before he returned to the subject. 'I believe in persistence,' he'd said once when talking about his business deals and how he persuaded one owner to sell a hotel to him. No doubt he would apply the same tactics when he wanted to acquire a wife.

Marigold believed in constancy, and she knew this would strengthen her when the pressures and the loneliness grew so intense that she was tempted to abandon all her dreams of business success and Richard's return.

The Hagley Road hotel was still home for Marigold and her sisters. It had become a very exclusive establishment, and the sisters had taken more space for their own use. Ivy had her own studio and she was selling her drawings regularly.

She still went to have lessons with Silas Frome, but now he only taught occasionally at the art college. He was often away, going to the south of France for months at a time. Ivy had the use of his studio along with a favoured few of the art school students, and felt she was moving in truly Bohemian circles.

After the first sittings for Herbie, modelling the Tudor dress, he often persuaded her to do the same again. 'I can charge higher fees if they don't have the bore of sitting too often,' he explained. 'I'll share the difference with you.'

Although Ivy now had no motive to hoard money as she had in the old days, her instincts made her agree. Marigold was generous but she tended to want to know what any large sums of money were spent on. Ivy considered it prudent to keep a secret hoard ready for a sudden emergency.

Soon Herbie's friends began to ask her to model for them, and provided she could hide her scars with high-necked dresses and sleeves she always agreed.

This peculiarity of hers attracted the curiosity of one student, Algernon Frobisher. He was older than the others and came from a wealthy family. Many of the students regarded him as an interloper, a rich man who could please himself what he did and was not struggling to earn a meagre living with his brush. Often he smoked expensive cigars as he worked, and the rich aroma wafted through the room. Ivy enjoyed sitting for him because he had his own studio at the top of his large house in Richmond Hill Road, and was very generous with his fees.

'Why do you always insist on high-necked costumes?' he asked one afternoon when Ivy was modelling an evening dress for a portrait he was doing and had insisted on wearing her own blouse to cover up the low neck of the dress while he worked on the skirt.

'I just do,' she said curtly.

'None of the other models insist. In fact they're all anxious to take off their clothes. You could earn much more if you were willing to pose nude.'

'I'm an artist. I just do this for friends,' Ivy told him loftily.

'Pity. You have an excellent figure,' he said consideringly, 'far better than the flabby, overblown charms of Maggie. And though Elsie's figure is probably better than yours, your face is prettier.'

Ivy scowled. She did not choose to admit that anyone was her superior in anything.

Algernon did not refer to it again, but a few days later when Ivy arrived at the studio just as Elsie was leaving, she saw him give the model a sovereign.

'You don't give me nearly so much!' she accused him immediately.

'Elsie poses nude,' he returned with a shrug. 'Are you going to get ready? I haven't much time, I must leave early today.'

Ivy sat and glowered.

Algernon did not talk while he painted as he usually did. He appeared abstracted and after half the usual time sighed and turned away. 'It isn't going well. I'm stale on this portrait. I think I'll have a rest from portraits for a few months. You can get changed.'

'Won't you want me again?' Ivy asked, annoyed.

'You won't pose nude. Perhaps you're too young. I shouldn't ask you,' he said with a smile. 'Go on, get changed.'

She flounced behind the screen and dragged off her blouse and the evening dress. She twisted her head to look at the scars on her shoulder and neck. Why couldn't she be as perfect as Elsie and the others? It wasn't fair! She was becoming even more conscious of the unfairness when she saw the new fashions with the low-necked gowns, and knew she'd never be able to wear them.

'So that's it! You poor child!'

Ivy swung round to see Algernon gazing at her. She tried desperately to pull the neck of her chemise higher to cover the scars, but he took her hand and stopped her.

'How did it happen?' he asked, and his tone was so sympathetic that before she realized it Ivy was telling him all about the childhood accident.

'I could paint them out,' he suggested. 'I've wanted to do a portrait of you for so long, but not all muffled up in the old-fashioned clothes you wear.'

'You said you were stale,' Ivy recalled gruffly.

'Of that silly thing. It would be different if I were painting you. May I?'

They spent every hour they could working on the painting, with Ivy dressed in skimpy flowing Greek costume. When Algernon allowed her to see it she was amazed at this idealized view of her. 'I wish I could paint them out on my skin!' she cried, and when he put his arms round her she rested against him, sniffing the mixed aroma of cigars and the heather-scented soap he used.

'There are cosmetics which might work,' he suggested quietly. 'It would have to be a thick application, like the greasepaint used on stage, but it could be worth trying. Would you like me to get some for you?'

He did and she was gratified with the result, although she knew it would not be possible to deceive people except from a distance.

She developed a new confidence in the privacy of the studio, preening in flimsy, delicate draperies. Eventually Algernon persuaded her to pose for him in the nude, a modern version of Venus arising from the sea, and Ivy was intrigued to see that while he was painting this picture he reacted in the same way as Sam Bannister had done so long ago, his lips wet and slack, his breath rapid and shallow.

At last the painting was finished. Algernon touched it for the last time, then threw down the brush in exultation. 'It's perfect. It will be my masterpiece!' he cried. 'Come and see what you've helped me achieve!'

Ivy stepped down from the dais and stretched her aching arms. By now she had lost all self-consciousness, knowing that with the heavy greasepaint her scars were hidden. She walked to look at the painting and Algernon threw his arm across her shoulder.

'It's beautiful, and so are you!' he exclaimed, turning her towards him and kissing her soundly on the lips.

Ivy reflected with interest that he really did behave remarkably like Sam Bannister. He was breathing heavily, stroking her back, her hips, her belly. Then his hands found their way towards her breasts, and she wriggled slightly at the unaccustomed touch. It was very different from Sam Bannister's rough stroking.

'Ivy, my darling, let me love you!' he gasped, bending to bury his face in her soft flesh. Before she could reply he was sucking greedily at one breast and kneading the other with trembling fingers.

If this was what people in love got up to, it was a most peculiar business, Ivy thought dispassionately. In love? Why not; he'd said he loved her. She wondered whether her prim Marigold had been mauled and sucked in such a fashion and decided the man would have to be decidedly rich to make it worth while.

Marigold had married a rich man, an inner voice whispered. Algernon was rich, probably even more so than Richard Endersby. If she could persuade him to marry her she would be independent, she would have as much money of her own as she wished. And Algernon, despite his decidedly odd way of showing it, said he loved her.

Ivy had always craved love. And the sudden and shocking deaths of her parents, when they might have lived for many years yet, had had a profound effect on her. Algernon might provide a substitute, and if she had to endure this slobbering, sweaty creature so be it. She would demand her own idea of love in return.

The same epidemic of influenza which killed John and Mary Smith also carried off Friedrich Müller two months earlier. Inge had been panic-stricken.

Richard decided she really mourned her uncle, but her main concern had been for her own position.

'What shall I do?' she asked time and time again. There were no other relatives, she was completely alone.

'You own the farm now, could you not sell it and use the money to buy a small house in a town, where you could get a job?' he suggested.

'I would be afraid to live in a town on my own,' she answered, and he knew she was quite unfitted to take care of herself.

'It is not right we should live together in the same house, and be snowed in for months on end during the winter,' he said firmly.

'I don't mind being snowed in, I am used to it,' she replied.

'What could you do if I fell and broke my leg?'

'Oh. I don't know,' she said in a small voice.

'You see?' He concentrated on the practical difficulties for he could see she would not comprehend the other aspects. When Dieter's father offered her a very good price for the farm Richard advised her to accept.

'What shall I do then? Where can I go?'

'I've been thinking about that. The war will be over within weeks, and then people will wish to travel all over Europe again. It's popular to visit Switzerland; winter sports are growing. Why not buy a large house in St Moritz and turn it into an hotel?'

'I couldn't possibly run an hotel all on my own,' Inge exclaimed.

'No, and it would not be fitting for a young girl to do so, but you could employ a manager.'

'Would you manage it for me?' she asked at once.

'I know nothing about the business,' he reminded her.

'You could learn, Richard, you are very clever,' she pleaded with him.

He would not go home, to unyielding parents who had spurned his wife and possibly contributed to his beloved Marigold's death. Let them continue to believe he was dead, he thought bitterly. The army must have reported him so. Therefore he would have to find a job, being penniless without his share in the firm. Why not start helping Inge with her hotel? When it was running smoothly he could find another manager for her and move to something more congenial himself. Exactly what, he didn't know.

So they moved into the pretty town of St Moritz, and by spring of 1919 were welcoming the first guests to their modest hotel.

Inge found, after the first few weeks of strangeness, that she was happy supervising the shopping and cooking. She left all other details to Richard, who threw himself into the task with such energy that by the following Christmas they were able to buy the house next door and expand.

Summer and winter, visitors flocked to the town, and more than once Richard saw familiar faces. He avoided contacts with old friends, however. He would not risk news of him getting to his unnatural parents, in however roundabout a way.

There was no chance of them recognizing him, he thought wryly. He was tanned with the open-air life, had grown a beard, and in summer wore the Tyrolean lederhosen, for the benefit of the visitors as well as because they were practical garments.

In summer he walked miles along the mountain trails, or followed the valley of the River Inn. In winter he learned to ski properly and found he had an aptitude for it. It was in some ways akin to flying. He would go for long expeditions on his own: his sole relaxation.

Away from the hotel he had leisure to think of Marigold and dream of what life could have been like had she survived. By now they might have had another child.

He had vaguely expected the pain of her loss to diminish with time. That was what he had always been told. Time heals; it soothes the raw pain of wounds into a dull ache. One can even forget at times. It was all false. After the years in Germany when he'd had to force himself to put all thoughts of Marigold to the furthest recesses of his mind for fear of betraying himself, he was now free to think of her as much as he wished – and with a never-diminishing regret. Their time together had been so brief, but he recalled every minute, and relived over and over again every step forward in their relationship. He dreamed of what might have been, and reality became swamped and lost in desires.

Poppy insisted on a July wedding. 'It's so much more cheerful in the summer,' she declared, 'and I want lots of flowers.'

Marigold wept a little as she stood where her mother had once stood at her own wedding. It was a year and a half since Mary and John had died. Their daughters would all have to have someone else give them away. But Johnny looked very smart in his morning coat and topper, behaving as though he wore them every day.

Ivy stood beside her, aloof and elegant in her perfectly straight ankle-length gown of grey satin, the only touch of colour a vivid lilac ribbon on her wide-brimmed grey hat.

'You look as though you're still in half-mourning,' Poppy had said crossly before they'd set out for the church. 'And your hat is years out of date, so wide.'

She looked radiant herself, in a slender gown of shimmering ivory silk. The gown was low necked and long sleeved, with a scalloped ankle-length skirt and long silk train embroidered along the hems. She wore matching gloves and shoes, the double strand of pearls Marigold had given her, and on her crimped hair had a pearl-beaded lacy cap.

'It's less than two years since Mom and Pa died,' Ivy said with what Marigold considered an unjustifiably smug air. She hadn't worn mourning clothes for above six months. 'And you can wear hats absolutely any shape this year, they say in London.'

Poppy turned away angrily. Ivy had raged and fumed when she and George announced their engagement two months earlier, saying Poppy had no right to desert them now the sisters were alone, and she utterly refused to be a bridesmaid.

She had then taken herself off to London, leaving a note to say she was going to see the Summer Exhibition and at the same time visit Silas Frome. Poppy was so angry at the outburst she had hurried to ask two of her friends to be bridesmaids, and ignored Marigold's pleas to wait until Ivy, her temper restored, came back and agreed.

'No, she's a selfish little cat and always was. She won't spoil my wedding!'

Ivy came home a week later, full of satisfaction at the number of museums and galleries she had managed to visit, and the wonderful paintings she had seen. 'Silas says they'll hang me at the Royal Academy one day,' she boasted, but Poppy was unimpressed.

'Hanging would be too good for you,' she muttered, but under her breath. She didn't wish to incur Marigold's displeasure by spoiling Ivy's miraculously restored sunny mood.

It was for the same reason she didn't mention George's report that he had seen Ivy dining at the Savoy with a young man. He hadn't spoken to her, being there with his own parents, and just possibly could have been mistaken. And if it had been Ivy, perhaps she was with Silas and his friends.

Marigold had worried when Ivy disappeared, but not unduly.

They'd known Silas for a long time and Ivy would be safe with him. She looked older than fifteen and was very competent when it was a matter of securing her own comfort.

Ivy had shrugged when Poppy rather defensively told her she had arranged her bridesmaids, and never again mentioned the wedding. Poppy even wondered if she meant to attend, especially as Ivy vanished somewhere the previous day and did not return until almost midnight.

The reception was to be at the hotel; Poppy didn't want a big affair. It seemed more like a reception at a family house, which would impress George's family, than if they held it at a bigger, impersonal hotel.

To Marigold's secret relief, for she had feared sulks, Ivy behaved charmingly, even helping to hand round the food.

Everything went well – until it was time for Poppy and George to leave. Poppy went up to her room for the last time to change, and while Marigold was helping her the best man came to knock on the door, a worried look on his face.

'It's George, feeling rather under the weather, poor chap.'

Marigold slipped outside to see what he wanted. 'What do you mean? He isn't drunk, is he?' she demanded incredulously. George always appeared to be a perfectly well-behaved young man and she'd been thankful Poppy had chosen so sensibly.

'No, no, nothing like that. But he – it's rather delicate – he –' The young man stopped and wiped his brow. 'He seems to have eaten something – well, bad, which has disagreed with him.'

'I'll come and see,' Marigold said, unsure whether to be sorry for George or angry at the imputation that her staff would serve tainted food.

Whatever the reason, George was very ill, and clearly it was impossible for them to travel to London that day. Marigold put him to bed, summoned a doctor, then went to break the news to Poppy.

Poppy behaved very well, being calm and sensible. She insisted on sitting in George's room during the night, saying she could nap in an easy chair but would be there if he needed her.

She was far from composed at five the next morning when she ran precipitously into Marigold's room and shook her sister awake. 'George! He's been dreadfully sick and I'm afraid! I think he's dead! Oh, Marigold, come quickly!' she cried. Marigold was still pulling on her dressing gown as Poppy dragged her, her feet still bare, along the corridor.

It was true. George had been violently ill but it was too late for anyone to save him. Poisoned, the doctor reluctantly opined, by mushrooms.

Aghast, trying to calm her distraught sister, Marigold wondered how it could possibly have happened. The kitchen staff were always especially careful when using mushrooms, and there had anyway only been a few in the vol-au-vents. Perhaps the new kitchen maid hadn't thrown out one which had gone bad.

In between all her other worries she waited to hear whether any more of the guests had been stricken, but none had. Only George. Poor innocent George, and poor, lost Poppy, widowed before she was truly married.

Was the whole family cursed? Marigold began to think the unusually large number of calamities which had befallen them owed something to a malignant deity.

She put Poppy to bed, heavily sedated, and set about the melancholy task of informing George's parents, who had returned to Walsall the previous night under the impression that their son had perhaps indulged too well in the excellent champagne.

The next few days were fraught with niggling little problems concerning the hotel, but Marigold watched Poppy descend into a mood of despondency deeper than any she'd ever known before, and even Ivy seemed preoccupied about something.

Two weeks later Poppy was induced to rise from her bed and join her sisters for dinner in the private parlour. It was the first time she'd ventured out of her room. She refused even to go to George's funeral, leaving Marigold and Ivy to represent her.

Now she picked at her food, although she drank deeply of the wine Marigold poured for her. Marigold tried to maintain a normal conversation but Ivy refused to respond, and Poppy said nothing at all.

After the maid cleared the dishes and they moved to sit beside the fire, coffee cups at hand, Ivy at last spoke. 'Poppy, Marigold, I have something to tell you.'

'What is it?' Marigold asked, her attention mainly on Poppy.

'I hoped you'd never have to know. Especially Poppy. But it's no good, I have to tell you. I need help.'

Marigold looked sharply at her. Was that a smile on Ivy's lips? No, she was trembling. She was afraid of something. All Marigold's protective instincts rose.

'What is it?' she demanded more urgently.

Ivy took a deep breath and glanced across at Poppy, ignoring the conversation, lost in her own deep misery.

'I'm going to have a baby and George is the father.'

'It happened in London,' Ivy explained. 'George bumped into me at one of the exhibitions, and asked me for tea afterwards. I thought he was taking me to an hotel restaurant, but before I knew what had happened we were in a lift and he dragged me into his room. I tried to get away but I couldn't. It was horrible, unspeakable!' she shuddered.

Marigold marvelled at her sister's self-possession. At fifteen and a half most girls would have been prostrate with fear and anger to be in such a situation. Ivy was disgusted, distressed even, but calm and lucid, quite devoid of tears and wailing protests.

Poppy listened with angry incredulity as Ivy repeated her accusation, and then burst out in defence of her dead husband. 'You're lying!' she said furiously, shaken out of her misery. 'George loved me, he wouldn't have touched a trollop like you!'

'He did more than touch!' Ivy flashed back at her.

'He told us he'd seen you with a man,' Marigold tried to calm the discussion. 'Why should he even admit to having seen you if he had – done this to you?'

'To throw the blame on whatever man he said he saw,' Ivy said swiftly. 'Apart from Silas Frome I was alone with no other man, and I thought we were going to a restaurant in the hotel. You don't think I'd let any man do that to me, do you, especially Poppy's fiancé?'

'Why didn't you tell us before the wedding?' Marigold asked.

'Because it isn't true!' Poppy spluttered with fury.

'I didn't want to admit such a shameful thing had happened,' Ivy whispered, hanging her head. 'Not until I knew it was going to be obvious soon anyway! And I knew you loved him, truly loved him, Poppy. I thought I'd be ruining your life if I accused him. Besides, he'd have denied it. You'd have believed him. You don't believe me now.'

'You wouldn't care a jot about ruining my life! You hate anyone else to be the centre of attention and you hate to think we might love someone else more than we love you! Look what happened to my puppy! You were jealous of poor little Scrap and I fully believe you poisoned him! You know how to well enough, with those everlasting weeds you keep digging up! In fact I wouldn't put it past you to have poisoned George! No one else –'

'Poppy! You don't know what you're saying!' Marigold interrupted angrily, shocked that Poppy could even think such evil things, let alone say them.

Poppy stared at her, then collapsed into hopeless tears. 'You always loved her best and believed her rather than me,' she sobbed, and before Marigold could reject the accusation she ran from the room.

Marigold followed her, but Poppy locked her door and refused to open it or even answer. At length Marigold gave up and went back to find Ivy, pale but composed, where she had left her.

'What are we to do?' she said slowly. 'You'll have to go away, but where?'

'I've been thinking about it,' Ivy replied slowly. 'Truly, Marigold, even if Poppy won't believe me, the baby is George's. If we said she needs to get away after George's death, and the two of us went abroad somewhere, we could write home in a little while and say she was pregnant. She could pretend the baby is hers. And it would be George's. It's possible,' she went on eagerly, warming to the idea. 'They did spend the night together, no one else knows how ill he really was, and anyway they could have slept together before the wedding. George could hardly wait. I wouldn't be surprised if they did,' she added as if to herself, and shuddered.

'You've planned it all,' Marigold said slowly.

'I've had several weeks now to think about it and plan. The fact George died gave me the idea of pretending the baby is Poppy's. Surely she would accept a child that was his?'

'I doubt it, but it's possible. She'd be very angry with you. If she agreed could you live with her for several months, alone in a strange place?'

'I would have to. What else can I do? I can't get married, there's no one to marry me. And why should a man accept another man's child? At least Poppy would be taking her husband's child.'

For several weeks Poppy refused to consider the idea, but then she sank back into the lethargy which had gripped her before Ivy revealed her condition.

'For goodness' sake stop badgering me!' she exclaimed one morning in a rare show of animation. 'What do I care? If it will stop your everlasting mythering I'll go with Ivy. I'll bring the brat back, but I won't admit it's George's. People can think what they like but I'll employ a nurse. At least I have the money to do that as George's parents have insisted I have what he owned.'

'So where would you like to go?' Marigold asked Ivy. 'You'll have to go soon, you are beginning to show and the new-style clothes won't be much help for many more weeks.'

'I heard Lydia Makepeace talking about a lovely little village in Switzerland,' Ivy suggested. 'She and her family went there in the summer. She says it's very quiet but the hotel is good.'

'You'd prefer Switzerland and all that snow and ice to somewhere like the south of France?' Marigold asked in surprise.

'We might see people we know, like Silas Frome or hotel guests, in the south of France,' Ivy pointed out. 'It's not so likely we'll see anyone in a small Swiss village. Besides, I'd like to paint snow scenes and mountains for a change. It's so flat round here!'

By September Marigold was in London to wave them goodbye. She had insisted on buying furs and boots, making sure they were both well equipped for the Alpine winter. She had been so preoccupied making all the arrangements as well as negotiating for another hotel she hoped to buy, this time in Coventry, it wasn't until she was on the train going home she had time to reflect.

Then Poppy's wild accusations kept ringing in her head. They couldn't be true! Ivy was a child still. Poppy was distraught. Poppy – yet it should have been Ivy, the wronged innocent, having hysterics and begging everyone to help her. Instead she'd been unnaturally calm. She'd had suggestions all ready, and appeared to have worked it all out carefully.

Poppy had raved about her dog's death and that had indeed been strange. She had also revealed how much money she had taken from Ivy's secret hoard when she ran away, but that was so large a sum Marigold at first refused to believe it. When Poppy insisted she was right Ivy was challenged, and rather ruefully admitted she had found and kept a purse someone had dropped.

'I'd no idea whose it was, Marigold. I should have told Pa, I know, but it gave me such a thrill to think I had some money I could use for drawing materials, or perhaps to buy us all treats.'

It was all reasonable but the nasty, niggling suspicion remained, however hard Marigold tried to thrust it away from her. During the long journey back from London she found herself recalling incidents from their childhood when Ivy had managed to wheedle Mom or Pa into doing things she wanted. She'd almost always got her own way, whether it was getting out of school or going the direction she wanted on their walks.

Shaking her head in disgust at her own suspicious nature Marigold turned her attention to the problem of the new hotel. It would need extensive rebuilding and Bill was eager to form a partnership and share the cost of this. Until now Marigold had refused even to consider it, but this venture would be expensive, and she wondered if she would be wise investing so much of her capital into one project.

As the train drew into New Street she thrust her worries about Ivy to the back of her mind. There was simply no point in dwelling on suspicions that could never be proved.

Poppy made it perfectly plain, as soon as they left Marigold, that although she had to be with her sister she would spend no more time than absolutely essential with her. 'So don't think that because you've got your own way in coming I shall be your slave for the next five months,' she said curtly.

'More than five months,' Ivy said gently.

'What do you mean? You'll have the brat in less than five months, and then we'll be able to go home.'

'But you will not have been married for nine months then,' Ivy said softly. 'I can add up, Poppy, even if you can't. We'll have to say the baby was born later than it will be. Unless you want people to nudge one another when you try to claim it's a seven-month child?'

Poppy bit her lip furiously. She had totally forgotten the discrepancy in time.

'The fact remains,' she retorted, 'I shall take my meals with you for the sake of appearances but I don't want you to be everlastingly plaguing me.'

Ivy smiled a secret smile and Poppy fumed inwardly. Why was it with her younger sister that she always had the feeling she was being manipulated?

Poppy's determination to avoid all unnecessary contact with Ivy suited the latter perfectly. She had chosen the village a few miles outside St Moritz deliberately. She intended to discover, if she could, what had happened to Richard. Her letters appeared to have had the desired effect but Ivy always wanted to be certain. Only then could she make foolproof plans. She'd intended to come anyway, but this inconvenient pregnancy had provided her with an excellent excuse.

Ivy went to St Moritz as often as she could, noting the layout of the town and studying maps of the area. Her first task was to locate the farm to which she had written.

She was rather dismayed to discover it was so far away, much further than she could comfortably travel in a day. It was also high up in the mountains so that it would soon be cut off for months. If she didn't find it almost immediately she might have to wait until the spring.

They had been in St Moritz for a month and Ivy had become resigned to waiting. She could ask questions in the meantime. Several of the local people were happy to practise their English. More and more foreigners were coming to Switzerland in both summer and winter, and to know something of their languages was always useful.

Until now Ivy had discovered nothing and met no one who knew the Müllers. This morning she was sitting in a café, indulging in a rich cream cake with a girl a few years older than herself, Margarethe Pohl, whom she had met the previous day.

'You know someone here?' Margarethe said carefully.

'I think so,' Ivy replied cautiously. 'A friend, someone my brother knew at school. We heard he had settled with some people called Müller, on a farm in the mountains to the south.'

'An Englishman? He is young?'

'Yes. He flew aeroplanes,' she added suddenly, and Margarethe's frown cleared.

'Ah, yes, I know!' she exclaimed in delight.

'You do? Where is he? Is he still at the farm?' Ivy asked eagerly.

'No, no, he left some time ago. A year, two years, I forget.'

Ivy felt a stirring of apprehension. 'Where did he go?'

'They died.'

'Richard died? How? When? How could he have gone if he's dead?'

'I am muddled. I don't speak so well. Inge's parents – no, that is not right – her aunt and uncle, yes, that is it, her aunt and uncle died.'

'Inge? Who is she?'

'The girl. The girl who lives with the Englishman.'

'They are married?' Ivy smiled slightly. So much for Marigold's faith in Richard's love.

'No, not that. I will explain.'

Haltingly, often searching for words, she did so. 'The Müllers died, the winter the Englishman came, I think. Or perhaps the next. I don't know how, but Herr Müller was ill for many months before he died. Then Inge sold the farm and bought a house here in St Moritz, which the Englishman manages for her as an hotel.'

Ivy stared at her in astonishment and then burst out laughing. How strange that both Marigold and Richard should have become innkeepers.

'Where is this hotel?' she asked, controlling her laughter when she saw Margarethe looking at her in astonishment. 'Shall we go and look at it?'

'You want to meet him?' Margarethe asked eagerly. She had a romantic soul and scented some mystery.

Ivy nodded, signalled to the waiter, and paid their bill. Then she and Margarethe strolled through the town until they came to a trim, neat little hotel, the balconies still colourful with pots of geraniums, the shutters newly painted in green.

'That's him,' Margarethe breathed, and although after so many years it was unlikely Richard would recognize her Ivy pulled up the collar of her fur coat until it almost met the brim of her fur hat.

'Is it the same one?'

'Yes.' Ivy nodded. He was older, naturally, and bearded. There were lines round his eyes and streaks of grey in his dark hair which aged him beyond his twenty-eight years.

'What is Inge Müller like? How old is she?'

'Almost twenty, I think. She is pretty, dainty, and rather silly, from what people say. Of course her name is not Müller. It was her mother's brother who died. She is named Schwarz.'

'Do you know her?'

'No, we have never met. Do you want to meet her?'

'I don't think so. Margarethe, don't say anything about this. It would be embarrassing if he were to discover I'd been asking questions about him, and not been to see him. But I think he and my brother had a quarrel.'

Margarethe promised, and Ivy was well satisfied with her discoveries. During the next few months she observed Richard from afar, and saw Inge when the girl went shopping.

To her disappointment they did not appear to be other than hotel owner and manager. Certainly on the few occasions when Ivy saw them together there was nothing lover-like in Richard's behaviour, although he did occasionally appear to escort Inge to social events in the town.

Further discreet enquiries by Ivy led to a middle-aged woman who had known Frau Müller, and she gave Ivy more details of the tragedy up in the mountains.

'It would be so suitable if the poor child married the Englishman,' this lady sighed. 'He was so good to her, and she needs a man to care for her as well as to run her business. They are very circumspect but it is not right they should be working so closely together.'

'Does he live in the hotel then?'

'Yes, and though I for one would believe no evil of dear Inge, people talk. They certainly do talk.'

Chapter Seventeen

THE child was due at the end of February, but Marigold did not expect her sisters to return to England until May at the earliest. She decided to go into partnership with Bill just for the hotel in Coventry, and the winter was fraught with problems getting this latest hotel ready for opening. She was thankful not to have to worry about Ivy and Poppy.

The last letter had been from Poppy at the end of January, saying the doctor in St Moritz expected the child to come early. Marigold heard no more but was too busy to be concerned. Then on the first of March Poppy and Ivy arrived in Edgbaston.

'Where is the baby? What happened?' Marigold demanded of Poppy, for Ivy had retired to bed before Marigold reached home.

'It was born three weeks ago and died almost at once,' Poppy said brusquely.

'Poor mite! Was it small or weakly?'

'It was large and seemed quite strong; had lusty lungs, anyway. Ivy refused to feed it herself, gave it a bottle, and in the morning it was dead in its cradle. Apparently it happens sometimes like that, especially in the valleys where people are rather backward.'

Marigold was puzzled by Poppy's tone. 'You sound cynical,' she said questioningly. 'Which valleys, and what has that to do with Ivy and her baby?'

'Valleys in Switzerland, everywhere. Villages and towns where people have too many babies and cannot feed them all. They take care to smother those extra mouths they cannot feed, the inconvenient children.'

'Poppy! Are you suggesting that Ivy – no, it's impossible!'

'Is it? She never wanted the baby. She managed to make you believe it was George's child and tried to foist it off on me.'

'You still believe it wasn't his?' Marigold asked gently.

'Of course it wasn't! But it was very convenient for her that he'd been in London at the same time, and then that he died and couldn't deny it!'

'Perhaps she was frightened to admit anyone else could be the father. Oh, Poppy, she was so young!'

'She knew exactly what she was doing, believe me. She wasn't the slightest bit interested in it while she was carrying it, and never once said anything about what we might do once it was born.'

'Perhaps she dreaded having to give it up,' Marigold suggested.

'You always try to see the best in people but there isn't any best in Ivy! She never had a moment's feeling for the poor little child. Perhaps it's as well it died, with a mother like her!'

'What happened?'

'She insisted on having it left with her the night it was born, even though the nurse wanted to take it out of the room for her to have a good sleep. In the morning it was dead. She maintained she had slept heavily all night and not heard a sound. Why did she want it left with her when she didn't care a jot for it? She didn't shed a tear and immediately began planning the journey home. She is an unnatural monster,' she said quietly.

Marigold shook her head quickly. She could not – would not – believe this of her little sister, but obviously Poppy did. Refusing to follow this train of thought: 'Have you decided what you want to do now?' she asked instead.

'I don't want to stay here with Ivy.'

'I wonder if she'd like to go to an art college in London?'

'No. I asked her that when we on the way home, but according to her she knows more than they do and it would be a waste of time. She has a crate of paintings coming, that she did while we were away, and she talks of opening a gallery here to sell them.'

'That might be quite a good idea,' Marigold said thoughtfully. 'She would have responsibilities and be independent. But she would need a manager. She doesn't know how to run a gallery and she wouldn't have time to paint if she did. But what about you?

You have enough from what George left to buy a small house somewhere, and probably enough left to live on.'

'I want to work. Could I do something in one of your other hotels?'

It was eventually decided that Poppy would move to Coventry and supervise the work there until the new hotel there was ready for opening. Afterwards, if she thought she could cope, she would manage it. Bill, anxious primarily to please Marigold, readily agreed.

'I will be able to go over regularly and lend a hand if necessary,' he said later to Marigold, and she smiled gratefully at him.

'I'd do anything to encourage her to forget George. She's been so good.'

'The holiday in Switzerland was a good idea, it helped her get over the shock,' he agreed, for that was the story everyone had been told.

Ivy herself never mentioned the baby and Marigold forbore to ask. She thought it was too painful a subject, perhaps, although try as she might she could not quite push Poppy's accusations out of her mind.

The next few months were busy. The Coventry hotel was nearing completion and Poppy was grappling with the many problems there and finding some satisfaction in it; Ivy had found a suitable shop and was planning her gallery.

'Will you buy it for me and let me live in a flat above it?' she asked Marigold. 'There are two floors above, it would make a very good flat.'

'You're too young to live on your own,' Marigold replied. 'And it would not be a good idea to buy until we see whether the gallery is successful or not. If it is we'll think about it, but for the moment I'll rent the shop and we'll let the flat.'

Ivy protested but in vain, and when Marigold, exasperated, asked her if she wanted to forget the whole idea she shrugged her shoulders and agreed. 'You all go away from me whenever you want, but you won't let me leave,' she complained. 'Poppy's gone again and we hardly ever see her. And you go to see Dick every Sunday. I never see you at weekends and you're too busy in the week to talk to me. What's the point in living here?'

*

'I admire you for the patience you show,' Bill said. Ivy had just flounced out of the room one evening after trying unsuccessfully to enlist his help.

'She's very young,' Marigold excused her sister. 'She's the baby of the family and after she was burnt everyone gave in to her, I suppose, so it's mainly our fault if she thinks the whole world revolves round her.'

'There you go again, blaming yourself. She has some responsibility for her own actions.'

'I know, but I've been in charge so long I can't let go.'

'You could if you married me. I want to take care of you, Marigold. Surely by now you must have given up hope of Richard being alive?'

Marigold shook her head vehemently. 'I know he's alive somewhere. I just do. If he were dead something in me would have died.'

'That's hope, or just superstition. He would surely have come back by now. It's six years since you last heard from him. He must have died when his aeroplane crashed.'

'What does the length of time matter? Six days or six years, it's all the same. I love him just as much, Bill. And apart from the fact that I could not love you, I'd feel disloyal; I would be doing something wrong if I were to marry you.'

Ivy roamed restlessly about the new hotel. The first wing had been open for a week and they would open the rest in stages, for it was the largest yet and there was still work to be done. She had come to fetch some clothes Marigold had left behind after the grand opening.

Eventually she went and ordered tea and occupied herself with a small drawing pad, sketching a border of entwined leaves and flowers round the edges.

Poppy was engaged with a visiting representative of a pottery firm who was trying to persuade her to buy china for the restaurant from his firm, and who did not appear to understand that the family connection with Endersby's Pottery meant they did not wish to buy elsewhere. 'So you see, Mr Travers, it's impossible,' Poppy said firmly. 'Now, can I offer you some tea before you go?'

He gave in, accepting his dismissal and the tea. Poppy felt uncomfortable about entertaining him in her office so she led the way into the café where a small orchestra played softly at the far end.

Ivy saw them come in and waved vigorously. Poppy had hoped to avoid her but it was impossible, and she had to lead Mr Travers across to Ivy's table and introduce them.

He looked casually at the pad Ivy laid down and raised his eyebrows. 'I say, this is good!' he exclaimed. 'It looks like the border of a plate. Is that what the design is?'

'It could be, I suppose,' Ivy said. 'I just like drawing flowers.'

'May I take this to show my boss? We want some new designs and this is the kind of thing he's looking for. The shapes are so natural and yet so vital, they could be alive. Would you like it if he offered to buy something?'

'Ivy already sells lots of drawings and paintings,' Poppy said.

'But I could always sell more,' Ivy said quickly. 'I've never thought of doing designs for pottery, that's all.'

Mr Travers arranged to contact Ivy in Birmingham the following week, and when he did he told her his boss wanted to see some finished paintings suitable for repeating on china. 'Just two colours and gilt edging,' Mr Travers told her.

A month later Ivy's gallery was open, with Herbie installed in the flat above. Ivy was busy with commissions and Mr Travers often came. By chance when she went to check on the Coventry hotel Marigold discovered he was a frequent visitor there too.

'He's nice,' Poppy said defensively. 'Do you think I'm wrong to see him? It's almost a year since George died and it wasn't as if we were really married.'

'Of course I don't think you're wrong,' Marigold reassured her. 'I'll be glad if you can be happy again.'

Would she be able to think about another man if she'd seen Richard die? she wondered afterwards. She doubted it, but if they hadn't had the bliss of loving perhaps it would have been different.

'Will you bring him home? To Edgbaston?' Marigold asked.

Poppy shook her head swiftly. 'No . . . It would be too painful,' she added after a pause when Marigold looked startled at her abrupt negative. Then Poppy begged her not to tell Ivy. 'I can't bear her everlasting questions and comments, and David hasn't spoken yet anyway. Please don't say anything, Marigold.'

'If you don't want me to of course I shan't,' she promised. 'Ivy's found a manager for her gallery, did she tell you?'

'No. Who is it?'

'Some student from the art college, Herbie Cole. He used to study with Mr Frome and is quite a good painter, I believe. But not many people can make a living from it like Ivy does,' she added proudly.

Poppy sniffed. 'She earns more money than most people but it still isn't enough for everything she wants,' she commented. 'She says the clothes here are too dowdy and the dressmakers too inferior, she plans to go to Paris to buy some.'

'Paris! She hasn't said a word to me.'

'She'll probably go off one day with her secret hoard of money and bring a trunkful back. Either that or she was making some subtle criticism of my clothes, for she said they looked dull. I'm still in mourning so what does she expect? And I wouldn't wear bright colours and these new flimsy materials for work anyway!'

'Of course not. I must go now, Poppy, but will you come up to The Place next week for Dick's birthday party?'

'Is Ivy going?'

Marigold's face clouded over. 'No, she says children bore her . . . So you can safely come, she won't be there,' she added, refusing to let Ivy's attitude to her son depress her. 'Bill's coming too, he's never met Dick.'

Sophia Endersby welcomed them graciously. Since the end of the war they had moved back into the main part of the house, and the party for Dick was to be held in the largest drawing room, and if the weather were fine on the terrace outside.

Dick, six years old, was a tall, handsome child. He was becoming so like Richard that Marigold's heart turned over with longing for her husband every time she saw him.

A dozen children were there, being carefully shepherded by their nannies or their mamas, and eagerly awaiting the conjuror who had been booked.

'I thought we could have the entertainment first, then tea, and they can go and run about and work off surplus energy outside afterwards,' Sophia explained.

Mr Endersby, an unwilling participant in the revels, soon became engrossed in business talk with Bill. Marigold was not surprised to see them slide guiltily out of the room as soon as the conjuror began pulling playing cards and long gauzy scarves from improbable places.

'Mr Thomas seems a very pleasant young man,' Sophia said to Marigold as they sat and watched Poppy and some of the younger nannies organizing games for the children on the terrace after tea.

'He's a very helpful partner. We are thinking of expanding again and opening another hotel in Walsall.'

'That might not be wise, my dear. Mr Endersby says the post-war surge of prosperity has reached its peak and there will almost certainly be a recession soon. Then your hotels will not be so busy.'

'Bill is confident it will not be severe when it comes.'

'I trust he is right.'

There was silence for a while. It was a companionable silence and Marigold marvelled that she and this woman now got on so well. Sophia had mellowed, and her gratitude to Marigold for letting her have Dick showed itself in all sorts of thoughtful ways.

'Have you ever thought of marrying again?' she asked abruptly.

Marigold glanced at her but Sophia was busy brushing a speck of fluff from her pleated skirt. 'Richard is still alive,' she said softly.

'You know all hope of that vanished when he didn't come home after the war,' Sophia said wearily. 'If he'd been hiding somewhere he'd have been able to get out. If he was injured he'd have been found in a hospital somewhere. No, my dear, you must accept that he's dead. He wouldn't want you to waste your youth in this vain wait for him.'

'I don't consider it a vain wait. I have no desire to marry again whether Richard is dead or not.'

'But this man Bill, it's clear he adores you. He could make you very happy and be a father to Dick. Mr Endersby and I will not be here for ever, my dear.'

'You're not trying to tell me you're ill, are you?' Marigold asked in alarm.

Sophia laughed. 'Of course not, child, though who can tell what disaster might strike at any time? But we are older than you and may die before Dick is able to take over the management of the firm. He will need a friend and some good advice then.'

Marigold laughed aloud. 'You want me to marry Bill so that I can provide Dick with a business advisor!' she accused Sophia, smiling.

Sophia shook her head quickly. 'Not altogether,' she protested. 'I want you to be happy again too.'

Marigold pressed her hand. Their relationship had progressed a good deal since that first disastrous meeting. 'I think Poppy may have found someone else,' she said. 'He works for one of the other pottery firms; a salesman only, but she seems to like him.'

They chatted about other friends and soon it was time for the children to depart.

'I've had a lovely party,' Dick said sleepily later as Marigold tucked him into bed. 'I like living with Grandpa and Grandmama, but I'd rather be like the others at school and live with my proper mummy and daddy.'

'One day, perhaps,' Marigold managed to say, blinking back the sudden tears.

It was the first time Dick had expressed such a wish. She'd always felt jealous of the love he showed Sophia, but now he was old enough to understand and had friends who lived in normal families he was beginning to question his own situation.

Would Sophia give him up if she were married again? She appeared to approve of Bill and recognized that there might be advantages for Dick in having a father.

For the first time Marigold admitted to herself the possibility of remarriage.

Was she being stubborn, relying too much on her desperate hope that Richard would come back to her? All rational argument was against it. No one else believed Richard could possibly be alive.

Bill had remained faithful for years. He loved her but she could never love him in return. Her heart would always be faithful to Richard. But people did make successful marriages without the sort of passionate love she and Richard had enjoyed. Would that be fair to Bill? Would he settle for second best?

She was very quiet as they drove back to Birmingham in Bill's car. When he leaned over to kiss her lightly on the cheek she didn't draw away as she normally did.

'Good night, Bill. I'll see you at the meeting with the bank manager in the morning. Thank you for coming.'

'I enjoyed it. Dick's a grand little fellow but he could do with being amongst younger people more.'

A month later, before Marigold could bring herself to decide on her own future, Poppy forestalled her by telling her David Travers had proposed.

'Poppy, I'm so glad. You've accepted?'

'Yes, but he understands I don't want a big wedding. We won't marry yet, it's still rather soon after George, but I am happy, Marigold, truly.'

Ivy was openly contemptuous. 'All you want is a man and a ring on your finger,' she said scornfully. 'George is barely cold in the ground and you want another man.'

'That's enough, Ivy!'

'But, Marigold, it's true. She hardly knows the man – and what is he? A miserable commercial traveller. He'll either never be at home, up to all sorts of mischief rushing round the country, or he's hoping to be given a cosy little job in one of your hotels.'

'I shall go and live with David in Stoke-on-Trent,' Poppy retorted. 'He doesn't want a job with Endersby's and he doesn't want me to go on working after we're married.'

'That's what he says now,' Ivy muttered. 'Marigold, I haven't had time to tell you before but I'm going to stay with Johnny and Lucy for a few days.'

Before Marigold could reply she left the room, and her sisters looked at one another with rueful resignation.

'In other words she's mad at me and going to pour out her woes to Lucy, hoping for sympathy,' Poppy said with a shrug.

'Lucy can cope. She's one of the calmest, most level-headed people I know. Johnny was so lucky to find her.'

It was, therefore, a total surprise when Lucy appeared in Birmingham three days later.

'Is Ivy ill?' Marigold demanded before even greeting her sister-in-law.

'Ivy? How should I know? Marigold, what's the matter?'

Apologizing, Marigold led her to the private parlour and explained. 'She said she was going to stay with you, and we know she often does, so we let her be. Didn't she come?'

'No. Where can she be? Ought we to tell the police?'

A sudden suspicion entered Marigold's mind. 'Wait, let me get the diary and work it out,' she said and rooted in her desk. 'When did she last come and see you?'

'Before she and Poppy went away,' Lucy said promptly. 'Has she been telling lies?'

'It seems so,' Marigold said unhappily. 'She said she was staying with you three weeks ago, just for a couple of nights. I wonder where she goes? Lucy, what have I done wrong? Why is she like this? Surely it can't all be because of the scars?'

'*None* of it's because of the scars. She's just wicked!' Lucy declared angrily. 'Marigold, she's played on the accident and tried to make you feel guilty ever since she was a baby! It wasn't your fault but she makes you believe it was, and ever since she's had you doing exactly what she wants!'

'I've never heard you speak ill of anyone before,' Marigold said in astonishment.

'I hate doing it now,' Lucy said gently. 'I wouldn't if I thought there was the slightest good in Ivy. I believe that if a sinner repents God can forgive and we should forgive too. But Ivy only says she's sorry if she can see some advantage in it for herself.'

'No, she's not that bad,' Marigold said, distressed. 'She may be selfish and thoughtless, but not deliberately wicked. That I can't believe.'

'Then you're more of a saint than I am. Heavens, listen to me, all this talk of saints and devils! It must be my Irish ancestry coming out,' Lucy said more lightly. 'Perhaps Ivy is possessed of a devil. I'm sorry, Marigold. I'm teasing you but it's not a fit subject for jokes. Just wait until I see that little madam again, I'll give her a large piece of my mind. How dare she tell lies to you and use us into the bargain!'

'Let's forget her. How long can you stay?'

'Just an hour or so. We're going on holiday to Blackpool next week and I thought I'd come and see you before we went. I wish you'd open another hotel there. That would be very popular with your niece and nephew! They love the sand and the sea.'

The following day Ivy reappeared and Marigold tackled her about the lies she told.

Ivy turned an innocent gaze towards her sister. 'I didn't tell lies deliberately,' she said in an injured tone. 'I decided on the spur of the moment that I'd go to Stoke. I wanted to look at some things in the potteries there. Ideas for the paintings I'm doing for them.'

'Lucy was most upset and she says you haven't been to see them other times when you've told me you were there.'

Ivy frowned. 'I hate having to tell you every time I go out of the house!' she declared petulantly. 'I don't want to be spied on all the time! That's why I don't tell you where I'm going.'

'But need you involve Lucy?'

'You fuss so if I tell you I'm going somewhere on my own. Lucy is respectable, not one of my disreputable artist friends. I can't stand your fussing!'

She ran out of the room and Marigold sighed. Ivy was getting much too difficult for her to deal with. A thought crept insidiously into her mind: would Bill have any greater success?

Marigold was surprised when Mr Endersby was announced. She rose from behind her desk and walked to meet him, hand outstretched. 'How pleasant to see you! Will you have some coffee? Joan, would you bring some for both of us, please?'

Mr Endersby seemed ill at ease. He muttered inaudibly until Joan reappeared with the coffee and after Marigold had poured he heaved a deep sigh. 'I'm afraid it isn't a pleasant mission I come on,' he said at last.

'Dick? Is he ill?'

'No, no, nothing to do with the lad. Look, I'd best start at the beginning. It's an odd business.'

He paused, gulped some more coffee, and as Marigold remained silent reluctantly began to speak again.

'A few days ago I received some drawings in the post – designs for china – and with them a letter from a fellow called Travers. David Travers. Do you know him?'

'Yes. He's just become engaged to Poppy.'

Marigold waited, puzzled.

'He works for one of my rivals, and he wrote to say he'd acquired these designs and wondered if I would be interested in them. I was suspicious because normally designs are kept very secret and the employees of one firm don't approach another firm unless they're hoping to get a better job. He didn't ask for a job, however.'

He paused again, set down his coffee cup, and refused when Marigold offered more.

'No, thank you, my dear. Well, before I'd decided what to do about it I had a visit from this man's employer. He demanded to know if Travers had offered me some designs. He'd been sent a rough copy of the letter Travers wrote to me, and a single drawing of the design he'd just bought himself, the same as the one I'd been sent. Well, as soon as I said I had received the letter, he went raging off and promptly sacked Travers.'

Marigold looked at him, her eyes wide with pain. She had a dreadful premonition of what was to come. 'Go on,' she whispered.

'I sent for Travers. His employer had given him no chance to deny the accusation, no chance to offer an explanation. He admitted having found the designs, and of course you can guess they were Ivy's, but he utterly denied having written to me or sent me any of them. So who would do this? Who is capable of doing it, of forging his handwriting? Who wants to get him into trouble?'

'You think it's Ivy?' Marigold said dully.

'She had copies of the drawings. She is such a clever artist she can probably copy handwriting. I wondered why she should have it in for Travers but you've probably just told me. She's jealous of Poppy's engagement.'

Marigold did not try to defend Ivy or deny it. It seemed only too true. 'What will you do?' she asked wearily.

'If Travers goes to the police, as he talks of doing, it will cause a dreadful scandal. It won't get him his job back though; his employer is adamant. It will probably lose him Poppy and they'll both be unhappy. And that, I suppose would be exactly what Ivy wanted.'

'Can David be stopped?'

'I wanted to ask your opinion first. If there's some way of

bringing it home to Ivy that she must not do these things, I'm willing to give Travers a job providing he'll forget the matter.'

'Ivy no longer listens to me,' Marigold said reluctantly. 'Would you speak to her? Impress on her how criminal such behaviour is?'

'That is what I'd like to do, if you permit. You and her brother are technically her guardians, but if you give me permission I would willingly speak to her.'

'I'll see Johnny and perhaps we could all meet here in a week's time, whenever convenient?' Marigold suggested. 'Lunchtime on Saturday week, perhaps?'

Richard was more restless than usual. The challenge of setting up the hotel and expanding it into the neighbouring house had occupied him fully for a while, but now it ran so smoothly there was little for him to do.

He suggested to Inge that, with the profits, which were healthy and growing, she ought to move to still larger premises. He also had plans for offering instruction to potential skiers during the winter, as well as guided walks in the mountains during the summer, but she would consider neither suggestion.

'I am earning enough to live very comfortably, thanks to you,' she replied. 'Why should I want to earn even more money?'

He could not explain. It was not the money but the satisfaction of taking on a more difficult task and succeeding that he craved. She had the peasant mentality: satisfied with obtaining just sufficient for her needs, and then keeping her head down for fear of disasters.

If only he had the capital to buy her out. He knew she would retire quite happily to a small house now she was accustomed to living in the town, and enjoy the social round of tea parties and dances. If he could offer her a fair price she would be able to buy a house and invest enough to live on.

He had no capital. If he approached his parents he would be able to buy Inge's hotel a dozen times over with the money that rightly belonged to him, but he still felt as bitter towards his parents as he had the day he read his mother's letter.

His father would never have rejected Marigold if it had not been for his mother's attitude, he knew. But by remaining silent and ignoring her unreasonableness he was equally guilty.

Again the utter desolation of loss swept over him, and he resorted to his normal outlet of chopping wood. If any of the guests expressed surprise that the manager should occupy himself with such a menial task, he laughingly replied that it was an excellent way of getting exercise, and one which he could stop the moment a guest required his services.

An hour later he carried a basket full of logs through to Inge's private sitting room and found her sitting side by side with Dieter on a small, brocade covered sofa.

'Good afternoon, Dieter,' he said with a smile. Dieter had become a good friend, although he did not often come to St Moritz. 'How is everyone?'

'Well, thank you. I'm pleased you are here. Can you spare a few minutes?'

'Of course. You came alone?'

'Helmut is busy on the farm. He is planning to marry soon and will be living in Herr Müller's house. I have decided that farming is not for me. I prefer a livelier existence than that of the high valleys, shut in for months of the year.'

'Are you looking for a job in St Moritz?'

'Dieter thinks he could teach the visitors to ski,' Inge said importantly.

Richard regarded her quizzically. When he'd suggested the same she had not been in the least interested. He saw the shy but fond look she was turning on Dieter and suddenly understood. 'Would you be looking for a base here at the hotel?' he asked carefully.

'If it is possible. I would rent a room here, and, if Inge allows, use it also as an office for booking lessons and so on.'

'Of course you may,' Inge said swiftly. 'It will be pleasant to have someone here who knew Uncle Friedrich and Aunt Gertrude.'

'When do you wish to come?'

'As soon as possible. Helmut's wedding is next week and I would like to come as soon after that as I can, to make ready for the winter season. You are both invited to the wedding, by the way. It would be pleasant to see you again.'

'I'd love to come!' Inge exclaimed.

'I must decline,' Richard said slowly. 'It would not be possible for us both to be away for several days, and we cannot make the journey there and back in a day.'

For the next few days Inge was more animated than Richard had seen her for a long time. It was decided that Dieter would drive her back that day and she would stay with his mother until the wedding.

'And I can bring back my belongings afterwards, if that isn't too soon.'

After they had gone Richard spent some time musing on this development. It would not be long, he opined, before Dieter asked Inge to marry him, and from the fond looks she had been giving him she was bound to agree.

She had a year or so ago hinted that it would be suitable if Richard married her, but he had gently told her it would not do. Apart from her lack of intelligence, which he knew would be an insuperable barrier to happiness, he still felt married to Marigold. However long she had been dead he could never imagine taking another woman in his arms, or making love to anyone else. His heart would always be entwined with hers.

Dieter would doubtless consider it his right, after they married, to manage the hotel for Inge. There was not enough work for him alone and certainly not enough for both of them, even if Dieter spent all the daylight hours teaching visitors to ski. It was time to move on.

Inge had insisted on paying him a generous salary, saying he had spent long enough at the farm helping her for no more than his keep.

'I was not able to pay you then,' she'd protested. 'You must have what is fair. I have asked what other managers are paid and that is what I shall give you.'

He had few needs and most of his salary had been saved. Did he want to remain here or should he perhaps make a fresh start in America? Soon he would have to decide.

Mr Endersby came alone to lunch, saying he hadn't thought it appropriate to bring his wife. For similar reasons Johnny had not brought Lucy. Marigold greeted them and handed round sherry in the private parlour where they were to eat.

She dreaded the confrontation that was to come, but sadly realized Ivy had now gone too far and was beyond her control. She ignored all the pleas Marigold might make. She needed a shock such as the combined fire of Mr Endersby and Johnny to bring her to her senses.

Poppy was not yet there but Marigold expected her soon, and David was to come with her.

'Where is Ivy?' Johnny asked when they had exchanged polite greetings and Marigold had asked after Lucy and the children.

'She's at the gallery seeing some potential customers. She promised to be here by one o'clock.'

Mr Endersby grunted. 'Does she know we're here?'

Marigold shook her head, a distressed look on her face. 'I didn't dare tell her,' she confessed, ashamed. 'She does normally come for meals if she says she will, so don't worry, I'm sure she'll be here.'

There was a tap on the door and Joan came in with a letter. 'It's just been delivered, Mrs Endersby,' she said apologetically. 'The man said it was very urgent or I wouldn't have disturbed you.'

Marigold's heart was in her mouth. Had Ivy somehow discovered what was awaiting her and taken this way of avoiding it? She took the letter and paced across to the window, her hands trembling.

The same thought had occurred to Johnny. 'Is she running scared?' he asked bluntly.

Marigold, her fingers clumsy, had managed to open the envelope. She shook her head. 'No, it's from Poppy,' she replied, her tone puzzled. Rapidly she skimmed the letter, which was brief, and then felt behind her for a chair.

Mr Endersby was beside her at once, and guided her back to the chair beside the fire.

'Read it,' she said tonelessly. 'Read it.'

Johnny came to read it with him and exclaimed in dismay. 'America! Why has she gone without saying goodbye? Do you think they really have got married? And why does she say she's scared for David?'

'She says they were married at Gretna Green at the beginning of the week, and by the time we receive this they will be on a boat from Liverpool,' Mr Endersby said. 'That's plain enough, but why should she be frightened?'

'I didn't even know she wasn't at the hotel in Coventry. The staff there told me she'd gone out when I went on Thursday. I suppose she must have arranged for them to send this letter. They shouldn't have deceived me.' Marigold spoke tonelessly, and with a swift glance at Johnny Mr Endersby indicated the brandy decanter on the sideboard. Johnny fetched a glass and Mr Endersby forced Marigold to drink some.

While she was sipping the brandy, which brought some colour back into her cheeks, Ivy swept into the room, stopping short for a moment when she saw the visitors and then running with arms outstretched towards Johnny. 'Johnny darling! How lovely to see you! Where's Lucy? Did she come too, and the children? How are they?'

Johnny stepped back behind a chair and fended off her embrace. 'Don't come near me, you despicable little liar!' he said furiously.

'Johnny!' Marigold said warningly, but Johnny, normally slow to anger, was in a positively deadly rage.

Ivy halted and turned a wide-eyed stare towards her sister. 'What's the matter?' she asked, glancing around nervously. 'Is someone ill?'

Mr Endersby cut off Johnny's impetuous reply and took charge. 'Let's all sit down calmly. Johnny, sit beside Marigold. You, young lady, come and sit here beside me.'

Ivy approached slowly, looking from one to the other. Johnny was glaring at her, Marigold was staring down at the hands in her lap, twisting them together in agony, and Mr Endersby, a man she had up till now regarded as a rather amiable old buffer, had taken on the aspect of a stern and rather fearsome judge.

She wanted to defy them all, turn and saunter negligently out of the room, but to her surprised astonishment she discovered that with the old man's eyes fixed unblinkingly on her she dared not.

'Johnny?'

Mr Endersby's calm tones gave Johnny time to collect his thoughts. Raving at Ivy would do no good. In brief sentences and unemotional tones, he informed his sister that her habit of making use of his family by untruthfully pretending she was staying with them when she wanted to absent herself from home was despicable, abusing his and Lucy's hospitality and his brotherly love for her.

'I do not wish to see you at my home ever again,' he said coldly. 'I will not have Lucy subjected to such discourtesy and my children exposed to your corrupting influence. They are being reared to be honest and your company will contaminate them.'

Ivy, her face white, tilted her chin defiantly. She could see that this time tears would avail her nothing. Johnny was in no mood to be swayed by protestations of sorrow and remorse. Telling lies would serve no purpose either. Marigold could disprove them if she claimed she had not said she was going to visit Lucy.

She glanced again at Marigold. Always, before, Marigold had believed and supported her. Surely her sister would have sympathy with her, if only she could think of a convincing reason for her actions? But Marigold too looked stern and implacable.

'You also seem to have been instrumental in driving an honest young man out of a job and forcing him and your sister to flee the country,' Mr Endersby said evenly.

'What?' Ivy was shaken out of her stubborn calm. 'Poppy has – what do you mean?'

'After your inexplicable behaviour towards David Travers, which unjustly caused him to lose his job, he and Poppy were married earlier this week and have gone to America. She says to escape from you, for she fears what else you might do to anyone she loves. No doubt you understand the reference.'

'She didn't even say goodbye!' Marigold said, deep pain in her voice.

Ivy stared at her. 'Poppy's left us?' she whispered, and slid silently to the floor.

'Ivy?' Marigold ran to her sister, but Ivy was in a deep swoon. 'Fetch the doctor, please! Help me get her on to the sofa!'

Ivy had recovered her senses before the doctor arrived, but after examining her he left a sedative and advised she be kept in bed for a few days. Marigold and Joan helped her upstairs, and the moment she was in bed Ivy fell into a deep sleep.

'She'll be better in the morning,' Marigold said to Johnny and Mr Endersby, who were waiting rather uncomfortably in the parlour.

'Was she faking?' Johnny demanded harshly.

'No, it was a genuine faint. She seems quite distraught at the news that Poppy has gone.'

'But she didn't deny her actions. Marigold, my dear, will you be able to manage if we leave you?' Mr Endersby asked, worried.

'Yes, of course. She's asleep now, but I'll give her the sedative as soon as she wakes and that will ensure her a good night. She'll be able to take it in tomorrow.'

To her relief they soon left, and she sank down into her chair to absorb this latest disaster. Poor, unhappy Poppy, forced to flee from her family because of her fears of what Ivy might do. 'Thank God Pa and Mom aren't alive to see this!' Marigold whispered to herself. At the thought her control gave way and she wept piteously.

She didn't hear the tap on the door and was unaware Bill had entered the room until he gathered her into his arms. He stroked her hair, talking gently to her until she was able to sit up, blow her nose, and tell him what had happened.

'I don't know what to do with her,' Marigold said wearily.

Bill was about to reply when the door of the parlour opened and Ivy, her dressing gown wrapped tightly round her, came in.

'Ivy! You're supposed to be asleep!' Marigold exclaimed, standing up and taking a step towards her sister.

'I couldn't sleep,' Ivy whispered. 'Have they gone? They didn't want to listen to me. Everyone thinks the worst of me and never lets me explain.'

'What is there to explain?' Marigold asked sharply. 'You told lies about staying with Lucy, and you deliberately made it appear that David Travers was cheating his employers.'

'But I didn't mean it to get him the sack! I just wanted to frighten them! I didn't want Poppy to leave me again!' she wailed, casting herself into Marigold's arms. 'Marigold, don't be angry with me!'

'Don't be taken in by her!' Bill exclaimed.

Ivy swung round towards him, her eyes suddenly blazing. 'What's it got to do with you?' she demanded furiously. 'Poppy's my sister! She shouldn't have left me!'

'She was afraid for David,' Marigold said slowly. 'Ivy, what did she mean?'

Ivy gave a bitter laugh. 'I expect it was that stupid accusation she made when George died, that I poisoned him!' she exclaimed scornfully. 'Just because her wretched little dog died of eating some rat-bait and George ate a tainted mushroom, she has to blame me! Well, good riddance to her! America is welcome to her crazy ideas!'

'Poison? You poisoned George?' Bill was staring at her in utter amazement.

'Whether she believes that or not you've driven Poppy away from us, Ivy!' Marigold said deeply distressed.

Ivy turned on her, at last losing control. 'I haven't! She was always trying to get away from me!' she screamed, and although Bill tried to hold her she shook him off and stormed around the room.

He shrugged, hoping she would exhaust her fury the sooner if left to vent her spleen unchecked.

'You all tried to get away from me!' she gabbled, the words tumbling over each other. 'Why blame me for everything? It was your fault I fell on the fire, and Johnny's that Pa didn't get better, and he started it by stealing and having to be sent away from home! If he hadn't gone you wouldn't have had to go to that horrid Oxford, and you wouldn't have met beastly Richard and spoiled everything! I hate you! None of you love me, and you're always trying to get away! But Poppy had to come back from her horrid factory and you had to come back as well, I made you, but now she's gone again! I hate her!'

She was striding to and fro, while the other two looked on in amazement. Suddenly she seized the decanter and hurled it at the window. Then, as the shattered glass slithered crackling to the floor and Bill rushed to grab her, she tossed the glasses furiously into the fireplace, sobbing wildly.

'Be quiet!' he commanded. 'You can be heard all over the hotel! There's no need to display such a temper just because you've been told a few unpalatable home truths and for once cannot scheme or lie your way out of trouble, you little hell-hound!'

Ivy went limp suddenly, and he laid her on the sofa.

'Should we call the doctor again?' Marigold asked, habitual concern for her sister overcoming her revulsion at the girl's behaviour.

'You'd be better advised to forget all about her and leave her to her own devices,' Bill said soothingly, crossing to clasp Marigold in his arms. 'Give up, my darling Marigold. Marry me and stop worrying about her.'

Marigold began to say this was not the time or the place to discuss her future but Ivy, hysterical and beside herself with fury, shouted her down.

'That's where you're mistaken, Mr Colonel Thomas! Marigold can't marry you or anyone else because her beloved Richard's still alive, in a love nest in Switzerland!'

Chapter Eighteen

MARIGOLD looked about her with awe. The mountains, snow capped even in summer, were magnificent. They were unlike anything she had ever seen before, even in the days of working for Mrs Roberts.

She had booked into a small hotel, but it was almost dark when she arrived and there was no time to do anything more that evening despite her impatience.

When Ivy made that shattering announcement she at first refused to believe the girl. It was yet another way in which her little sister, incredible though it seemed, was trying to wound her.

Bill, however, had taken charge. He questioned Ivy relentlessly, ignoring her tantrums and protests and Marigold's own pleas to him to stop, until Ivy had given way.

'I didn't want you to leave us and go back to him,' Ivy repeated over and over again.

'How did you know he was in Switzerland?' Bill asked.

Ivy at first tried to maintain it was pure chance which took her to St Moritz, but Bill's repeated questions made her once more lose her temper and she mentioned his letter.

'Letter? What letter?' Marigold intervened, by now as determined as Bill to discover all Ivy had to tell.

'Did you ever have a letter from Richard?' Bill asked.

'No, of course not, or I'd have known he was alive.'

Sulkily, realizing that neither tears nor hysterics nor repeated swoons would let her escape now, Ivy was forced to admit to having opened the letter Richard had sent to the Cranworths's house.

'Why didn't he write again? Surely he could not have been so certain one letter would find me?' Marigold asked, anguish in her voice. Had he cared so little after all?

Bill was watching Ivy closely and saw the smirk almost of pride on her face. 'You copied the writing of David Travers easily enough,' he said thoughtfully. 'Did you send Richard a reply, pretending it was from Marigold?'

'Of course not!' Ivy retorted. 'He was so besotted he'd never have believed it if she'd said she didn't want him back.'

'Then how did you stop him coming here, or writing again?'

'He obviously wanted to stay with his little Swiss doll!'

'You can't have it both ways! If he was besotted he would hardly be in love with anyone else!' Bill said sharply. 'Did you reply pretending to be someone else?'

'I wrote saying she was dead, and the baby!' Ivy said defiantly. 'I didn't want him ever coming back and disrupting our life here! It was all going well for the first time ever, I was having drawing lessons, we had money, we were happy!'

'And you didn't care one jot for how Richard would feel to be told his child and I were dead?' Marigold asked in revulsion. 'You are a monster, Ivy!'

Bill forced Ivy, defiantly proud of her ingenuity in forging the letter from Mary, to tell them what she had done, although she kept secret the fact that she'd also forged one from Sophia.

Marigold still found it hard to believe the sister on whom she had lavished love and care could repay her in such a way. The blow of Poppy's loss and Ivy's deception, coupled with this latest news about Richard, had sent her reeling.

She had packed a few clothes and set off at once for Switzerland. She refused Bill's offer to accompany her, saying he would be of much more use in England watching over Ivy and the hotels, including the imminent opening of a new joint venture in Stafford.

'Why not tell Richard's parents? They could come with you,' Bill suggested, but Marigold vehemently shook her head.

'If he'd wanted to contact them surely he would have done so long before now?' she said. 'He never forgave them their attitude to me. He may not wish to be reminded; to have the hurt renewed. Besides, if . . . Whatever happens, I prefer to face it alone.'

Ivy insisted Richard was living with a girl and appeared happy with her. Marigold had to see for herself. She could not subject him to a sudden letter announcing, after all these years, that the previous one had been false. And if Ivy was wrong she wanted to be with him as soon as it was possible. She could not bear to wait for letters to pass, for him to journey home, for the agonizing delay.

She went to bed but barely slept. In the morning she made herself swallow coffee and rolls, and wait again until it was a reasonable hour to be taking the air.

Marigold had discovered from Ivy where Inge's hotel was, and when she could bear the waiting no more she set off in that direction.

As she drew nearer her steps slowed. What would she say to him? How could she minimize Ivy's responsibility? The old habits of protecting her sister and excusing all Ivy's faults still gripped her.

With relief she saw there was a café opposite, and she hurried to sit where she could watch the entrance of the hotel. Perhaps if she watched for a while she would see something that might help. Precisely what she had no idea, but as the moment for seeing Richard came closer she was suddenly as apprehensive, as shy and nervous as during their first few encounters, when she had had no idea what he really felt for her.

Slowly she drank her coffee. The waiter hovered, for there were few people about so early in the day. Marigold spoke to him hesitantly and smiled as he replied in English although with a heavy German accent.

She breathed a sigh of relief. It had made her journey so much easier to find the Swiss often spoke two or more languages fluently. St Moritz was in the area where Romansh was spoken, but German was the commonest language. However, she had always found someone who understood English.

Marigold waved her hand towards the hotel opposite. 'I was told an Englishman lived there,' she said. 'Is it not unusual for an Englishman to own an hotel in Switzerland?'

The waiter shrugged. 'There is a man, a foreigner, English or German. But he does not own the hotel. It belongs to Fräulein

Inge Schwarz, though she is supposed to be getting married soon, my sister says, and they are friends. Then no doubt there will be changes.'

'She is marrying the Englishman?' Marigold asked faintly. Had Ivy been right after all? Was Richard happy with this girl? Had he forgotten her? Did he believe her dead? Of course he must, after receiving Ivy's letter.

Her thoughts were in such a turmoil she missed the waiter's reply, but then she noticed he was pointing along the road. A small cart driven by a tall, dark-haired young man was bowling along. Beside him a pretty, fair-haired girl sat clutching a wicker basket in her arms.

'Fräulein Schwarz,' the waiter said briefly, and moved away to attend to a new customer.

Marigold shrank back and instinctively raised her hand to shield her face. Then she gasped, half rose from her chair, and sank back again as her legs, quivering like jelly, refused to support her. Richard, more handsome than she recalled, tanned and virile with his beard, in an open-necked shirt and the local lederhosen, bare headed and smiling broadly, had appeared on the steps of the hotel.

She longed to run towards him, throw her arms about him, and feel once more that beloved body close to hers. She wanted to know the joy and comfort of being held by him, the pleasure of his lips caressing her, and his eyes, full of love and desire, telling her she was his.

She could not, dare not move. Deeply though she knew she still loved him, Richard might have changed. He might have a new love now. He might not relish the reminder of a younger, impetuous love which had separated him from his family; an obligation he would feel bound to obey. She had no right to demand that of him.

He greeted the pair in the cart. Marigold saw his lips move as he spoke, but he was too far away for her to hear the words. The girl in the cart thrust her basket into the driver's hands and without ceremony cast herself down into Richard's outstretched arms, flinging her arms round his neck and babbling happily up at him. Then she stretched up and kissed him full on the lips. Marigold's last faint hope collapsed.

The driver descended and hitched the reins to a post. He offered his hand to Richard who shook it heartily and then, his arm about the girl's waist and with the other man following, Richard led them into the hotel.

He looked so happy. Marigold sat on for some time, ignoring everyone, not knowing what to do. At last she rose, paid her bill, and walked slowly back to her hotel.

Quite calm now, she gave orders she wasn't to be disturbed. Then she removed her dress and lay down on her bed. The sight of her beloved after all these years when she had hoped and prayed he was still alive, refusing to admit his death, had given her both exquisite joy and unbearable pain.

He was alive, clearly fit and well. He had been told she was dead and he had recovered. He was happy with another girl who obviously adored him and they were to be married. What right had she to disturb that happiness? How could she claim him as her husband and perhaps destroy a hard-won peace of mind, ruin the new life he had carved for himself in this beautiful country?

Methodically she thought back over their courtship and marriage. It had been so unconventional. He had been young and might have regretted in later years marrying a servant. Would he relish having to resume that life and give up the one he had so clearly chosen here, with a new love to console him for the loss of Marigold? Inge, she thought without rancour, was very pretty, far lovelier than she was, and lively.

If he was happy, and her brief glimpse of his reception of Inge Schwarz convinced her he was, surely her greatest gift to him would be to keep silent, to retreat from his life, leave him in ignorance of her own existence?

What of Dick and his parents? her conscience asked.

He could have written to his parents at any time. And to know of Dick's existence would mean he knew of her own. That would destroy his present life. Dick had never known a father, and so many children had lost fathers during the war. It was nothing unusual.

What was of overriding importance was Richard's happiness, she concluded at the end of that long, agonizing day. No one else should know anything. She would return to England leaving Richard in peace.

*

It was time to go, Richard knew. Inge had come back from Helmut's wedding with Dieter, overflowing with excitement at the fact that Dieter had asked her to marry him. If Richard privately had a suspicion that Dieter saw an opportunity to acquire a flourishing business as well as a wife, should he be condemned for it? Inge would be happy and Dieter would, so far as Richard could judge, treat her well.

Richard, however, would be in the way. The newly married couple would not want him always around, and he had no desire to remain and simply find another similar job in a different hotel.

'Will you go back to England?' Dieter asked when Richard told them he would be leaving as soon as it was convenient for them.

'I may go back for a while, just to see old places again, but I think I would prefer to go to America.'

'You have enough money for the journey?' Inge asked anxiously.

'I have plenty saved. You've paid me well and there has been little to spend it on. I have enough to see me to America and to keep me for a few weeks while I look for a job.'

'Will you go and see your wife's grave?' Inge asked gently.

She had never referred to his wife and child since that dreadful day when he had received the letters from home. He had been grateful for her silent sympathy then and her reticence afterwards, and was rather surprised she should speak of such painful matters now.

'Inge told me,' Dieter said quietly. 'Forgive me, Richard, I know it is a private matter, but you have been such a good friend to Inge. We wish to help you now.'

'I don't understand,' Richard said abruptly. 'How can the fact you know about Marigold's death help me?'

'No, that is not what Dieter means, Richard. You must go and say goodbye to them,' Inge said seriously. 'You will soon start a new life in America. You must first be finished with the old.'

'I was finished with that long ago,' Richard replied. 'Once I hoped to go back. I spent years contriving my escape from Germany. After they died it was pointless.'

'If I had not had the accident you would have gone back instead of staying to help me,' Inge said. 'You have not finished with it;

you have not said farewell. I went to say goodbye to Uncle Friedrich and Aunt Gertrude while I was up in the valley. It was like closing a door. Now I can go forward and plan a new life with Dieter. You must do the same with your loved ones, Richard, or you will suffer regret always.'

Richard had not replied and soon Dieter spoke of something else. That night he forced himself to consider what they had said, and came to the conclusion Inge had once more shown a simple wisdom. It came, perhaps, from living so close to nature, isolated in her mountain valley.

It would be incredibly painful to see the grave where his darlings lay. He feared he would be unable to read the gravestone, his eyes would be so full of tears. Then he lifted his head. Would they have a gravestone? The Smiths were so poor he doubted whether they could have afforded one, and who else would have bothered?

For the first time he wondered what had happened to his own money, whether his parents had claimed it, or whether Marigold had left it to her sisters. What was the law when his death was not known for certain? That at least was something he could do. He would make sure a good, proper headstone with a few words of love from him was erected, and then he could see to it that Marigold's family was in receipt of the money and income that was rightly his.

To do this he would have to tell his parents he was alive. But he would deal with them through lawyers. He wondered if the man he had used in Birmingham was still there. It would be better to go himself rather than try to explain such a complicated matter by letter. Besides, there was nothing to keep him and the sooner he went the sooner it could all be arranged.

Inge begged him to remain for her wedding, and as it was fixed for the following month he agreed. A few more weeks would make little difference.

'And you can teach me how to run the hotel, my friend,' Dieter said cheerfully.

'I'll go the day after the wedding,' Richard said, and tried to curb his impatience as Inge talked excitedly and repetitively of nothing else.

He might have been going to his own wedding, to his own beloved bride, his eagerness to be back in England was so great. Never before had he faced the physical reality of Marigold's death. He was going to her but she was in a cold, comfortless grave.

He had known as an intellectual fact that she was no more. The aching loss, the void within him had remained as cuttingly painful as in the first moment of reading the letter. Now he would see her resting place; have final proof she had gone from him. It was something he had to do. Inge was right. He had to say goodbye before he could start a new life. He would never forget his love, never take another wife, but by saying farewell he would complete a necessary task.

There was time to make plans: decide which few possessions he would take; what sort of job he could do; and which part of America he would prefer to go to. Time to compose the explanation he would need to give the solicitor; the people he would have to contact. He supposed, thinking of it for the first time, the military authorities might also have an interest in his survival.

Almost he changed his mind and determined to sail for New York from Cherbourg without going back to England at all. He would encounter problems, delays, and such irritations that he knew would make his task there twice as difficult.

In the end he determined to go unannounced to Hednesford, and search alone for Marigold's grave. Depending on what he found and whether he could trace her family and discover how they fared, he would then decide on his future actions. Five weeks after Marigold had left St Moritz he followed in her footsteps back to England.

Marigold was away just over a week. During the journey home she felt numb, her anguish tempered by the knowledge that Richard was alive and happy.

She mourned her loss of him, the life that might have been hers. She never wavered in her determination to protect him from the distress he would suffer if she shattered his present contentment and his new marriage.

At one point on the long train journey across France it occurred to her that Richard's second marriage would be bigamous. Then she shrugged. Who would ever know? It was chance she had discovered he was still alive, or she might have married Bill, which would have been equally wrong.

That was the only moment when she doubted the rightness of her decision. She had more than once toyed with the idea of marrying Bill, more for the sake of his influence and control over Ivy than because of any love she bore him.

Now she knew she could never have gone through with it. Even if she had not discovered Richard was still alive, she could not have lain in Bill's arms, accepted his embraces, without feeling the revulsion of betrayal.

It never occurred to her to apply the same standards to Richard. She knew he had loved her, but still considered his wish to marry her an oddity, an aberration for which most of his own class would have condemned him, if they had lived together in normal circumstances. For which his parents had, indeed, originally rejected her, she reflected. Their change of heart had been largely because they wanted Dick, and Mr Endersby had approved her business venture.

Business would have to be her reason for living now. Poppy had gone and she might never see her again. She could never love Ivy again. Johnny had his own family, and although they were friendly they were not close to her as her sisters had been.

She still had Dick. One day she might tell him about his father, one day she might suggest they meet, when age had dulled desire and the revelation of Dick's existence would not ruin Richard's new life.

She arrived in Birmingham still in a numbed state. It was the quiet lull just before teatime and there was no one in the reception hall. She walked straight through into her office.

Bill was seated at her desk writing letters. He looked up with a frown as the door opened, then seeing who it was tossed down the pen and rose to greet her. 'Marigold, you look worn to a thread!' he exclaimed. 'Let me ring for some tea.'

She permitted him to help her off with her coat, then she removed her hat and cast it down on a side table.

She did not speak until tea had been brought, and Bill, seeing her total abstraction, had poured her a cup. 'Did you find him?' he asked anxiously.

'Yes. He is happy with this girl. I left them alone,' Marigold said tonelessly.

'You didn't tell him you were there?' Bill exclaimed. 'Why ever not?'

'How could I? They were happy; about to marry. I could not spoil that happiness.'

On the point of protesting, Bill suddenly realized the strain Marigold was under. She had made her decision and it would be wrong to try and argue with her. He did not know the full details of their marriage, no one could, so how dare anyone advise? He wished he didn't have yet more unpleasant news to impart.

He could not delay for long.

'How is Ivy?' Marigold asked with an effort.

There was no point in trying to soften the blow. 'She left the day after you did,' he said now. 'I'm sorry, I didn't think I needed to keep that close a watch on her.'

'Where is she?' Marigold asked in the same flat tone. Bill reflected wonderingly how, only a few days earlier, such news would have caused her great anxiety and stimulated a flurry of action as she sought to undo whatever harm Ivy had done to herself or others.

'She followed Poppy's example and fled to Scotland. She is waiting there to get married. I would have sent the police after them but I had no authority.'

'Married? Ivy? But to whom?'

'She left a letter. It was addressed to me. It seems she has persuaded some man to marry her – God help him. I wonder if she really did poison George?'

'Who can tell? I almost believe she is capable of it. Perhaps she only meant to cause him discomfort, embarrassment. I just don't know her any more. Poppy didn't love her as much as I did, and so she saw her faults more clearly, while I tried to excuse them. Ivy didn't like that.'

Bill regarded her with concern. She had let Richard go, now she had cast Ivy off. As if aware of his regard Marigold turned and smiled faintly up at him.

'Drink your tea,' he urged, and she sipped obediently. It seemed to revive her.

'Who is it?' she asked after a few moments. 'Who is Ivy to marry? Is it that student who runs her gallery? Will he be able to cope with her?'

'It isn't Herbie, it's a much older man. Algernon Frobisher.'

'I think she mentioned him once or twice. You say he's older? But a student?'

'He has money. Whether he's a serious painter, I don't know. Ivy boasts he is very wealthy, has his own house and studio. I made some enquiries. He's lived here for many years although he came originally from Wolverhampton, I understand. I'm afraid he doesn't have a very savoury reputation.'

Marigold shuddered slightly and held up her hand. 'He will marry her, though?'

'Yes, I believe so. Ivy boasted she would soon be back, after the three weeks they must spend there, and set up a salon for artists. I'm sorry, my dear. I feel I should have prevented her. Do you want to follow her to Scotland and try to persuade her to come back? I will come with you if you do.'

'Why? She has chosen her own way of life. It must be what she wants. I hope she will at last be happy.'

Bill's opinion was that Ivy had acted in a fit of pique and would soon be regretting it, but this was at least a chance for Marigold to be rid of her. He didn't want to risk that benefit despite his feeling of guilt, now that he saw Marigold accept the truth about her sister.

'You must have realized by now that whatever Ivy wants she manages to obtain somehow. You might have prevented this elopement if you'd locked her in her room, chained to an iron ring,' Marigold said wearily. 'I think I am grateful you didn't stop it. I need no longer feel guilty about her, no longer worry about her, no longer contrive ways of pleasing her. She has made her choice and rejected me. I can at last reject her with a clear conscience.'

Ivy stared at Algernon in utter astonishment. He gestured to her to leave the room.

'I said go up to your studio,' he repeated in a bored tone. 'I prepared it for you so that you wouldn't get in my way.'

'But – I don't understand, we have guests!' she protested, looking at the two girls who were seated, giggling together, on the sofa. 'Will you not introduce them? Don't you want me to order tea?'

'Rosa's the one with the big tits, Fifi has other – talents,' he drawled. 'Neither of them like tea. Now get out, unless you want to join in our little games. You could do with some lessons on how to please a man. You're a cold, lifeless little bitch.'

Ivy, shocked and humiliated, fled. So this was what Algernon meant when he'd said there were conditions before he'd marry her. She'd been desperate to escape from the hotel, for once in her life terrified of possible retribution if Richard came home knowing what she had done to him. She'd been eager to show Marigold she too could marry a rich man, and Algernon had been grateful to her for not claiming the child was his. He'd take her, he'd said then, but not a brat.

In her attic studio, the door locked, she was aware of faint noises, raucous laughter and sounds of unbridled revelry coming from the big bedroom she shared with her husband. When the sheer astonishment that he could treat her so subsided, Ivy fumed helplessly. She realized she was afraid of Algernon. He was often violent, and rough in his conjugal demands. He'd hurt her more than once since that hasty journey to Scotland, while they waited for the residence qualification.

They'd been home for little more than a week and for much of the time he ignored her. Even when he forced her to submit to him he now had no words of tenderness. He mocked at her scars, talked of the money she could earn by her paintings and what he would do with it. He wasn't, it seemed, as wealthy as he'd once told her. So far she hadn't decided on her best course of action, but she was determined to escape from this hasty marriage and his humiliation of her as soon as possible, as soon as she could devise some scheme.

It was late when he reached London, so Richard booked into an hotel near Euston for the night, after visiting a barber to have his hair cut and his beard removed. It didn't feel right in a big city, unlike the Swiss Alps.

He looked at this new London as he crossed the city by tube, and dined alone. He was intrigued by the new fashions, the short hair the girls now had, and the much greater freedom they displayed. It was far more widespread than he'd expected from seeing the fashionable visitors in St Moritz.

The motor cars on the streets, very different from those he had driven before the war, reminded him of the plan he had devised during the previous tedious weeks.

He would go by train to Stafford and then, since it would be difficult to travel about Hednesford in trains or the new motor buses, he would hire a motor car in order to look for Marigold's grave and, possibly, her family.

The letter from Mary Smith had said they were to go and live with her sister. Surely someone in the street would know where she could be found. Until he could be certain of their address he did not wish to announce himself to the solicitor, although it was possible Mr Thane could give him some help. Whether it was irrational or not, Richard wanted to do as much of the searching as possible for himself. It was the least he could do for Marigold.

He caught an early train the following day, and was in Stafford by mid-morning. It was an easy task to hire a motor car, and he drove slowly through the town.

It had altered little in the seven years since he had last driven through it. Some shops had changed hands, a few new houses could be seen, but so far as he could tell no great alterations had taken place.

As he began to drive up the long hill approaching Cannock Chase, a faint stirring of anticipation gripped him. At last, providing he could find the grave and it had been marked, he might discover whether he had fathered a son.

He cast his mind to the days he had spent with Marigold. They had been so happy walking and driving together in those hills. He wondered briefly whether his father still kept racehorses at Rawnsley.

Then he almost steered the motor car off the road.

Ahead of him, new and bright and clean, overlooking the town from this slight eminence, was a small, elegant-looking hotel set in pleasantly landscaped grounds. He braked sharply, and sat there, stunned. He must be dreaming. Why had his father opened an hotel?

He shook himself. Endersby was not an especially rare name. The proud scrolled title 'Endersby's' which surmounted the portico did not have to belong to his father. It had been a shock, startling in its suddenness.

Richard started the motor car again and drove on, looking towards the hotel and admiring its neat lines as he passed. It was obviously cared for, judging by its prosperous appearance and neatly tended gardens, in which groups of chairs were set invitingly.

A mile further on he halted again. He could not go on without investigating this mystery. At least he would ask to whom the hotel belonged. He might have lunch there.

There were several large motor cars outside, he noticed as he drew up in front of Endersby's. For a while he sat there, immobile, and almost started the engine and drove away again.

'Don't be a fool,' he chided himself and leapt down. Stripping off his leather gauntlets he strode in through the door into a spacious, quietly elegant reception hall.

A girl in a moss-green uniform was sitting behind a desk and she smiled at him welcomingly. 'Good morning, sir. Can I help you?'

'I wondered to whom the hotel belonged,' Richard said, and when the girl gave him a startled look he went on swiftly. 'I used to know some people of the same name, once.'

'I see. Mrs Endersby owns the hotel, sir, and several others.'

Mrs Endersby? His mother? With the greatest effort Richard could not imagine his mother condescending to run an hotel, or even own one. If by some bizarre chance she had acquired one it would certainly not have her name emblazoned across it. It would be something discreet, tasteful and anonymous.

'Is there anything else, sir?' the receptionist asked, and Richard realized he had been standing speechless for several minutes.

'Oh, I'm sorry. No. Yes,' he amended, suddenly making up his mind. 'Can I book a table for lunch? Just for me?'

'He beats me! He takes women to our bed! He – oh, Marigold, I can't even say what he does to me, it's too horrible! And when I wanted you you weren't there, I had to come chasing all the way to Stafford to find you!'

'There was a crisis, the manager was ill,' Marigold said, but Ivy ignored her and rushed impetuously on.

'Please help me, let me stay here, away from him! Or I could go to Coventry and manage the hotel there. I daren't come back to the Hagley Road for fear he finds me!'

Marigold hardened her heart. Her immediate instinct was to rush to protect her little sister, but when she recalled how that sister had wrecked her life and then Poppy's for no reason other than to prevent them from paying attention to anyone else, she could be firm.

'You chose to marry him and must put up with his actions,' she said levelly.

Ivy stared at her in consternation. Marigold had never before failed her. 'Why?' she whispered. 'Why have you suddenly turned against me?'

'Do I need to make a list? Can you *really* not know?' Marigold asked, rising from the chair behind her desk and beginning to stride about the office. 'Isn't it enough that you wrote to tell Richard I was dead, and his child? You let me go on mourning for him and caused him years of misery. Dick has never known his father or a proper family life!' She swung round to face Ivy who sat immobile on the chair facing the desk, staring at Marigold. 'I don't know if you poisoned Poppy's little dog, or even George, and I don't want to know – I'd rather try to retain some belief that you are not completely evil. Then you try to spoil what you think would be a marriage between Bill and myself by telling me at last Richard is alive. It was spite made you say that, nothing but spite. You would never have told me if you hadn't lost your temper that day. I cannot go on for the rest of my life making excuses for you, feeling sorry for you, for ever guilty because you burnt yourself –'

'Algernon used to be sorry for my scars but now – he mocks me over them!' Ivy interrupted, a catch in her voice.

Marigold regarded her coldly. 'I blamed myself for years for leaving you alone too long. But even then you were doing what you knew was wrong, because you were too selfish, too impatient to wait, too determined to have your own way just when and how you wanted it. We all gave way to you but it made you even more selfish, more determined to be the centre of our lives. You didn't offer a jot of real love in return. Real love makes sacrifices.'

At the thought of the supreme sacrifice she had made by giving up Richard, Marigold's voice broke.

'Go! Get out of here! You chose Algernon, so go back to him and make the best of your life on your own! I am no longer tied to you!'

Ivy was already at the door and had opened it. She turned to throw final words of defiance over her shoulder.

'I won't let you get away with this, Marigold! You'll regret not helping me!'

She turned, sobbing, and rushed across the entrance hall, ignoring the man just moving away from the desk as she brushed past him and almost stumbled. He glanced after her, startled, then turned and strode towards the door of the office which was closing quietly.

Unceremoniously he opened it and Marigold stepped back, shaken by the recent scene with Ivy. Was she dreaming? Was that really Richard standing in the doorway of her office, holding out his arms?

The receptionist, aghast at these unseemly happenings at the sedate hotel, ran out from behind her desk and across to the office. Was he a madman? He'd seemed so peculiar, so uncertain of what he wanted. Was he attacking her employer?

Fortunately she was a brave young woman and delayed screaming for help until she had ascertained the true facts. When she saw her normally calm employer clasped in the stranger's arms, laughing and crying but obviously perfectly willing to be so ardently embraced, she withdrew and gently closed the office door. There was no need to summon help after all. She returned to her desk, pondering on this odd but exciting development.

'Marigold! My beloved! They told me you were dead!' Richard gasped when he could speak coherently. 'All these years I couldn't bear it. I've felt so alone! Oh, but you're more beautiful than ever, my darling! It's like a dream!'

'It's no dream, Richard!' Marigold reassured him. 'But how did you find me? And the girl – Inge?'

'Inge is married now, she doesn't need me to manage her hotel. How did you know about that?'

'I went to Switzerland, and I thought – You seemed so happy with her – They said she was getting married.'

'To me?' He sounded both amazed and horrified.

'I must have misunderstood.'

'I will never, ever, want to hold another woman in my arms! How could I, after loving you, bear to be with anyone else?'

'That's how I felt,' she admitted shyly. 'I somehow always knew you were still alive.'

Richard sighed deeply. 'I thought I was coming to look for your grave. And – the child? Did it die?'

'No! Oh, Richard, we have a son! I called him Dick.'

'Where is he?'

'With your parents. We'll go there straight away.'

'Tomorrow,' Richard insisted gently. 'I can wait another day for my son, but I need you to myself for a while.'

Marigold was content. Suddenly her world was once more bright and shining. Richard loved her still.

Explanations could wait, they now had all the time in the world to rediscover one another. She cared for nothing else now she was once more safe in his arms. He was her love, her life, and she knew beyond all doubt they would never again be parted.